To my d~ ?
his fam

Ma's
Garden

With love

ELSIE JOHNSTONE

Mum

DEDICATION

For Graeme
Thank You

To the women who made the men who made
the country.

'The home is the real throne from which, for good or evil, the world is ruled.'

- From the Trafalgar & Yarragon Times, October 14, 1902.

.

CHAPTER 1

The train chugged through the foothills of the Strzeleckis, making its way deep into the green, luscious Gippsland countryside, passing through Warragul onto a stretch of grey flats, timbered mostly by white gum, but occasionally Blackwood. It did this twice daily, delivering passengers and supplies, and connecting the scattered settlements along its way. It was the carrier of news and newspapers, provisions and freight, horses, machinery and farm goods and most importantly, people.

This day, the train was full. In the carriage following the coal tender, just behind the engine, sat Miss Mavis Stewart, a prim, but handsome matron, not young but not, by any stretch of the imagination, old. She was attired for her journey in a navy blue slim fitting skirt, flounced at the hem, showing off her delicate red boots that buttoned with three gold buttons at the side. A lace blouse peeped from her navy blue tailored coat, which emphasised her tiny waist. Her mouth was full and sweet, her eyes round and as alert as a willie wagtail's, and her fair hair swept up and held in place with a straw sailor's type hat trimmed with red ribbon matching her boots. Definitely a stylish city lady! She sat upright in her allotted seat, with the pretty boots firmly on the floor and her gloved hands crossed in her lap.

Sharing her carriage was a woman of about the same age, tanned golden from exposure to the elements. Her travelling bonnet hid her hair but framed her open face with its thoughtful deep-set hazel eyes, straight nose and mouth. She removed her beige chamois gloves in order to settle the baby she carried in her arms and Miss Stewart immediately saw that these were the capable hands of a woman who was no stranger to work. The fingernails were cut short and there were calluses on some of the fingers. She was dressed in a sensible beige skirt, not as stylish and up-to-date as her own but of good quality fabric and of a cut that would have been modern at the end of the century. She wore a chocolate brown blouse and jacket, the blouse tied at the neck with a bow and a pretty jade jacket pin.

'That jacket must be a recent purchase,' Miss Stewart thought as she perused her travelling companion, 'it is the very latest fashion in Melbourne at this time.'

The woman began the task of settling the children, putting the baby down on the seat next to her and taking a pencil and notebook from her travelling bag.

'Do you mind if I take the window seats for the children?' she asked, turning to her fellow traveller. 'They can look out the window and it makes the journey go so much faster for them. I can have the guard set the table up so that little Jimmy can draw. He's a good boy but likes to tease his little sister if he has too much time doing nothing. I'm sure he will be very good,' she added hastily, seeing the look of horror that momentarily crossed Miss Stewart's face.

'By all means,' came the reply, 'please take the window seats for the children.'

She stood and moved further down the bench seat away from the window. 'Anything that makes the journey better for the children is in the interests of us all. And such bonny little ones they are too! Where are you travelling to on this beautiful autumn day? My name is Miss Stewart by the way, Miss Mavis Stewart.'

'Good day to you, Miss Stewart, and thank you for moving. I truly appreciate your kindness. We're taking the train to Trafalgar where we will alight. It is my hope that my husband Tom will be waiting with the jig at the station for us. I wrote last week telling him of our plans and as long as things don't go wrong on the farm he will be there. Sometimes there are tasks that just have to be attended to first. If that is the case then he will no doubt send my Jack, my oldest. He stayed to help his father while I took the younger two to visit their grandmother in Brunswick. And where are you going, Miss Stewart?'

'Trafalgar also, Mrs ..?'

'Donovan, Mrs Hannah Maria Donovan, but most people know me as Annie.'

'Pleased to make your acquaintance, Mrs Donovan! I have never done this journey before so you shall have to alert me when we are about to come to our station. Last time I visited Trafalgar I came by Cobb and Co. We stayed overnight at Pakenham, it was an irksome journey as it was done in the heat of summer, the coach was full and the air was still. I felt sorry for the poor horses. So this time I was smarter and decided to take the "iron horse". Much quicker and I think much more comfortable.'

'Do you have family or friends in Trafalgar, Miss Stewart? Do you have somebody to meet you?

'No family, and as yet no friends! But it won't be long before I make some. As to who will meet me, I believe that one of the staff from the Criterion Hotel will be there to take my bags and to direct me. Do you know that establishment Mrs Donovan?'

'I know of it my dear Miss Stewart, but I have never been inside. Mr Donovan sometimes takes a drink there on market days, catches up with the other farmers and talks prices and pastures, all those things that farmers talk about, but I have never found reason to go there.'

'I am taking over the lease to that establishment, so I shall be the new publican. I plan to make it a well-run public house where the ladies of the town can also come and feel safe while enjoying a good meal that somebody else has cooked for them. They have some such places in Melbourne and I believe that a hotel that welcomes ladies is a calmer, more refined place than one that precludes them. Ladies have a very civilising influence on men of all ages. They seem to behave much better when the opposite sex is present.'

'My, things have changed so quickly since the old queen died,' remarked Annie. 'Imagine, a woman running a public house! And a young pretty young thing like you, no less. Do you think that it will be difficult to keep the peace? How will you cope with the men's language? Have you had any experience in that field?'

'Fear not, Mrs Donovan. I was brought up in a public house. My dear father and mother operate a highly regarded establishment north-west of Melbourne, near the gold fields in Ballarat. I was weaned on service to the public and it is my experience that men go to a hostelry to sip ale and enjoy good conversation, and those who sup too much are much more mindful of a woman maitre d' than they are of a publican of their own sex. Most men respect women and will do as they are asked without fuss. I can honestly say, that I have never had any trouble keeping the peace.'

'So, why did you choose Trafalgar?'

'The lease for the Criterion came to my notice because the terms were good and I believe that the town has prospects because it is situated in the middle of the prosperous farming community along the Latrobe River. Besides, I am a woman in my thirties and I think the time has come for me to fly free from the family nest and do my own thing. As they say, nothing ventured, nothing gained. We shall see.'

'Good on you! I love to see a woman with spirit, and I hope you will be a tremendous success, although, to be perfectly honest, I think you will need your best diplomatic skills to convince some of the men of our town that you are capable of handling such an important project as the running of a public house.'

Hannah Maria Donovan was genuinely impressed that one of her own sex could be so modern and brave as to venture into this world of men. Secretly she thought it would end in tears.

'Good luck to you, Miss Stewart,' she added, 'it is women like you who will make it easier for little Dolly here. Perhaps somewhere down the track women will have more choices and you are carving the way.'

And so they settled into the journey, Annie attending to the children and Mavis taking out her copy of Mary Johnston's new novel, "Audrey", and holding it in reading position. But she was not reading. She was far too excited to keep her mind on the print. This was her life and she had taken it in her hands. It was her opportunity to fly free and embrace the future. Today she would embark on a terrifying but exciting journey. Like Annie she was aware that it would not be easy, but she was one who loved a challenge.

The train stopped at Dandenong to take on goods and passengers. A pert Scottish accent broke the harmony of the carriage.

'Ah, this seems to be my allotted seat. I've walked up and down the train looking for my number, but they seem to have landed me in First Class. Must be full down the other end with the poor people! This is my ticket. Seat Number 13. See it says it here. May I take my place here amongst ye, then? I promise to behave like the gentleman that I am.'

There, standing at the compartment door was a bushman, long and lean, with a bushy beard, wayward eyebrows and a battered hat which he raised to salute the ladies, putting his hessian sack with his meagre belongings in it on the luggage rack next to Miss Stewart's pretty, blue vanity case. He plonked himself down next to her, immediately beginning to wriggle, obviously uncomfortable with the situation of being upgraded to first class.

However, he discovered an ally in the young ones and not five minutes passed before he winked his eye at young Jimmy who took great delight in winking back at him. The bushman tugged at his ear and Jimmy mimicked him. This mirroring continued for a few minutes more, both participants obviously enjoying their little charade, whilst the women were oblivious to it. However, you can't play this game forever and soon the man engaged the boy in conversation.

'And what's your name then, wee laddie?' asked the man in his highland lilt.

'My name's James Donovan and I'm a big boy. I'm four.'

'Well, would ye read about that? My name is Jim too. Jim Robinson and I'm a big boy. I'm thirty-four. Pleased to meet ye, young Jimmy. You can call me Jock.'

He stood up, reached over and shook the young boy's hand solemnly.

'James is a great name. Ye must be very proud to have such a solid name, the name of kings and noble men. Have ye got a lady friend ye are going to marry then, wee Jimmy?'

'No, no I'm not that big yet but when I do get that big I'm going to marry my Mummy.'

'Have ye asked your mama yet, sonny? She might have other ideas and want to marry some other young laddie. Ye will have to sort it out with her before you go telling every Tom, Dick or Harry you meet on the train. And what do ye do for a living, James?'

And so the conversation went on in this good natured manner, young James protesting that he had some growing to do before he made the big decisions of life and the bushman asking questions he might ask of a fellow traveller around a campfire at the end of the day.

The two women exchanged glances and smiles. Both had lived long enough and were wise enough to know that a man can be a gentleman even though he may be down on his luck.

Before long young James divulged that they were on their way home from a holiday at Grandma's place where the tramcar rattled past the door and where there were lots and lots of shops, even a toy shop. They had left Jack at home, he was twelve, to help his father on the farm and Eileen, she was ten, had stayed behind to milk the cows and cook the meals. Only he and Dolly had been allowed to go with their mother. They talked about the cows and how there was one particular beast named Molly on the farm that James liked to milk, because when he sang "Sing a Song of Sixpence" to her, she let her milk down easily and seemed to have a smiley face. They discussed the chooks and how the young lad helped his mother clear and replace the old straw in the chook's house.

'This,' pronounced the lad, 'stops the chooks getting the smites that stops them laying eggs.'

The older fellow could not resist, 'Oh', he said, 'do you get smites when you get smitten?'

Of course this went over the lad's head, but the women smiled.

Jock was not unaware that he had an appreciative audience and played to it, telling James stories of the gold in the hills around Trafalgar which he would dig out so that he would become as rich and powerful as the new King of England. He had a stake up Tanjil way, and it was just a matter of finding it, because those hills were made of gold, especially around Walhalla and Tanjil .

'Where's Tanjil?' queried the lad, secretly determining to take his cart and pony and to get himself some of that gold.

'Tanjil is near where ye live, young laddie, in the hills beyond Trafalgar. Ye ask that hard working dad of yours and perhaps he might bring ye up for a camp out one day. It gets mighty lonely up there in those hills all by myself, so I could do with a bit of company. I have a little hut made of logs and kerosene tins and I could throw a swag on the floor for you and your pop. If ye do come, bring some eggs from those chooks of yours and some bacon and we will cook up a breakfast fit for a king. I'll even make ye some of my special damper which everyone says is the best this side of the black stump.'

'What's damper?' enquired the boy, thinking that perhaps it had something to do with water and cold. His mother had often said that everything on the swamp gets damp in winter.

'Damper is a special bread I make myself from flour and water. I mix it up and put it in the camp oven and it comes out hot and delicious. Add a slab of butter which melts into it and maybe some bush honey. With a billy of tea, ye can't do better. You'll see! Ye'll want to come up prospecting with me just for my world famous damper.'

'What's the black stump then?' queried young James, his imagination all fired up.

'The black stump, my wee laddie, is way out yonder where ye can't go any further and where the sky meets the earth. Beyond that there is just the black fellows and the kangaroos. Ah it's a long, long way, but I've never been there myself, so I can't give you an exact location.'

As the countryside rushed by, the atmosphere inside this first compartment from the front became cosier and cosier. When strangers are thrown together in a small space it is almost impossible to ignore each other and so gradually the women joined in the conversation and the time passed quickly.

They were interrupted abruptly when a kerfuffle erupted outside in the corridor and one small boy burst through the sliding door and collapsed in an untidy heap on the floor at their feet. Until that moment, three young boys had been having a great time in the long passageway that threaded its way along to the right of the compartments. There had been a fair amount of good-natured pushing and shoving, but the final push had landed the lad in the midst of strangers. The two other members of the mêlée absconded back to their own compartment, leaving the poor, embarrassed child to fend for himself. Sheepishly the lad immediately picked himself up, looked around in embarrassment and quickly disappeared.

Next minute he was back again, this time with a stern mother standing behind him. The entrance this time was much more refined, a knock on the door, followed by,

9

'Excuse me, please, I would like to apologise for my rough behaviour. I am sorry to have intruded on your journey and I hope you will forgive me.'

'Of course, we shall forgive ye, my wee laddie,' comforted Jimmy, ignoring the mother's presence, and focussing on the child.

'These things happen. I myself have fallen through many a doorway. Personally I blame it on those wobbly boots. Let's have a wee look and see if we can steady them up a wee bit.' The boy innocently proffered his foot for Jim to examine, which he did solemnly and carefully. 'Ah, I see the problem, here it is, it's this shoelace here. It's not tied tightly enough. Let's see if we can mend it.'

Taking the shoelace he untied and retied it, giving it a gentle nudge on the final bow.

'There ye go then. Done! No more falling through doorways now, wee laddie. Now was I right in hearing your brother say your name was Mervyn? A fine name indeed! Isn't that amazing then, we have two Jimmies and a Mervyn in this wee space. That's Jimmy Donovan over there, I'm Jimmy Robinson and you are Mervyn ..?'

'Johnstone, sir. Pleased to make you acquaintance, sir.'

'What's all this sir business? I'm really not sir material, I'm just an ordinary bloke, please call me Jock, if ye wish.'

'I'd prefer him to address you as sir, sir,' the mother spoke. 'Children should have respect for their elders. I beg your pardon for the disturbance my boys have caused you. It is difficult to keep them quiet on a journey like this. It would be good if the train could stop and let them have a run around a little to quell their youthful spirits.'

Annie, sensing the bushman's embarrassment at the reprimand, responded by standing up and introducing herself and her travelling companions. In return the woman gave her name as Ethel Johnstone, mother of three boys, who was on her way to Trafalgar to rejoin her husband who had been setting up business down there for the past eighteen months. 'In that case we shall certainly be seeing each other around,' ventured Annie. 'Trafalgar is such a small little place; it is difficult not to come across each other in some way or the other. Everybody knows everybody else, so do not hesitate to let me know if there is anything I can do. No doubt the boys will be going to the Trafalgar School. Young Jimmy here will be starting in July and our big boy Jack is studying for his Merit Certificate; he leaves at the end of the year to help Tom on the farm. Our Eily is in Grade 5.'

'I am in Grade 5,' Mervyn informed her, recovering from his embarrassment.

'Then you shall be in the same class as my Eileen. Mr Palmer is the Headmaster and you will find him a very pleasant man who treats the children well.'

Annie Donovan smiled at the little family clustered altogether in the doorway.

'We shall certainly meet up again. Of course, there is market day when we all come into town. Trafalgar may appear sleepy on the surface but there is always something or the other happening to keep us on our toes.'

'Thank you Mrs Donovan, I shall keep that in mind. In the mean time, I am sorry for the inconvenience Mervyn has caused and it's been a pleasure meeting you all. Good-day!' With that she went back to her own compartment.

'Mmmm! A little bit of this!' remarked Miss Stewart once she had exited, putting her index finger under her nose and moving it in an upward motion in order to indicate a member of the upper class.

Annie smiled but said nothing.

In the next carriage, also travelling First Class, sat important men of the Government. They had left their cosy gentlemen's clubs in Melbourne and were speaking of auspicious things in muted tones. Subjects such as the economic health of the city, the horse racing at Flemington, the cricket at Lords, the contests of the Victorian Football League and the Parliamentary Reform Bill that would mean, if passed, that women's suffrage would come to Victoria. 'That's definitely out of the question. Women are weak and emotional. Poor things are consumed with domestic and trivial matters and so are incapable of making important decisions,' a learned member pontificated as he leaned back in the plush green leather seat and stretched his legs in front of him to reveal expensive, well shined European shoes. 'Agreed old man, couldn't agree more.' Mr Nichols, who was the MLA for West Gippsland, may have represented the other side of politics, but in this matter, he was united. 'What next, for God's sake? They'd want to be joining us in Parliament? Can you imagine that? Where would we go for peace and quiet then?' The party also consisted of Mr Catani, the Government Engineer, Mr Thomas from the Lands Department, an "Argus" journalist named Darcy and a couple of Parliamentary Secretaries.

As the journey progressed, the conversation turned to the business of the day - the problems at the Moe Swamp where the settlers were unsettled. The Main Drain was not doing its job and the poor farmers had been contending with flood after flood. Already their crops for the current year had been destroyed by floodwater and it appeared highly likely that some of them would be forced to walk away from their land, as money and credit reserves had reached rock bottom. The Government of the day was in a bind, because they had sold the land with the assurances that the drainage was complete and that the land was ready for cultivation. It was in everyone's interest to have people living and working in the bush, away from the cities. Otherwise, it was feared, the wretched Aborigine tribes that inhabited those regions would continue to regard the land as their own. It was imperative that white people settle this area.

The men sat back smoking their pipes and settled into the journey.

'It's a damned tricky country this, damned tricky,' proclaimed Nichols, a small boned Englishman with round glasses and a natty little moustache. This was his patch, and although he spent most of his time in Melbourne, it was in his interest to make sure his constituents were happy. If he wished to be re-elected to parliament he should be seen to be doing things. 'On one hand,' he continued gesturing with elegant fingers, 'we have the Mallee farmers crying for help and threatening to walk because there has been no rain up that way for seven years or more and then, on the other, we have this Gippsland mob, whinging and carrying on because they have so much rain, the water won't go away. We simply can't be all things to all men! If you ask me, it's those damned Irish, they seem to think that they are our equals, and they're not!'

Thomas saw the opportunity to shift the blame from his Department and as the Irish were tolerated but treated with suspicion, he felt on safe ground. 'Those bog-dwelling blaggards have brought all their rancour with them from the old country,' he added. 'They'd pick a fight in an empty paddock. If I hear one more word about that damned potato famine I will shove a spud in the mouth of the fool that utters it. Leave past hurts behind and get on with it, I say.'

'Perhaps I shouldn't generalise,' replied Nichols. 'But I bet my last quid that the ones making all the noise are bloody

Irishmen. Can't have them crying foul though, makes us look bad. It's a damned tricky situation, damned tricky.' He held his pipe at arm's length because his glasses had fogged over, and poked and prodded his tobacco into the bowl with the end of a spent matchstick.

'Well, they're not all Irishmen out on the Swamp, there's Brits and Scots galore, there's an Italian family named Plozza, a German chap by the name of Schmirgal, even a couple of Danes,' retorted Catani, impatient with the local member's blatant bigotry, but happy for once that his lineage was Italian. 'Nationalities aside, the point is, the problem can be so easily fixed.'

'That so, that so?' Nichols replied, absentmindedly. 'How can it be fixed?'

'I have spent considerable time and effort on this matter,' Catani continued, 'and last month I submitted a plan to Treasury. You will see out on the swamp today that the bulk of the work is done. Solutions are simple and it will take very little capital injection. It just needs a little fine tuning.' Catani stood up to retrieve a hand written document from his briefcase that rested on the overhead brass luggage rack. 'Believe me when I tell you that they're good hard-working folk out there on the Swamp and they're doing their best under difficult circumstances.'

He handed the papers to Nichols, and in a conciliatory tone added, 'I am so pleased that you can make the journey to see for yourself, because I fear that unless we settle this matter, all the excellent work in getting people on the land will be undone, and the settlers will give up and go back to the city and the land will go back to bush. Look on it as Henry's bucket, we can take one tiny straw and fix it now. If we leave it to haemorrhage, eventually the hole will be so big that bucket is no good and will have to be thrown out.'

14

The learned men nodded knowingly. Important men making important decisions!

'So where do you suggest that we alight, Mr Catani? Is it best to get off at Trafalgar or Moe?' asked Nichols, changing the subject back to more immediate concerns.

'I suggest we go onto Moe first and make our way back to Trafalgar on the horses. That's the thing really. We can hire good horses and buggies at Moe whereas Trafalgar has nothing in the way of that kind of service. We would be relying on the goodness of the local men to provide mounts and that could prove a little difficult. My experience has shown that horses are like children. A master and his horse can be very in accord with each other and instinctively almost know what the other is thinking. However, lend that same horse to another man and the beast seems to know that this man is only transitory. If mischief is in his nature, he can easily make things difficult. Horses that are regularly put out to hire seem more resigned to changes in rider. So, the short answer to your question is that we should alight at Moe,' Catani replied.

Further down the train that day was a group of soldiers from the Mounted Horse Division that had been fighting for the Empire in the struggle against the Boers in Africa. They were in high spirits for they had been to a welcome home celebration at Parliament House. They talked in awe of their mate, Les Maygar from the Victorian Mounted Rifles, from Dean Station, near Kilmore, and who had been presented with the Victoria Cross.

'What exactly did he do?' asked Claude Lawrence, whose most defining feature was his lack of the bottom half of his left leg. It had been amputated to save his life after he had suffered a horrendous injury when his horse fell on him in a bloody battle. He had been lucky to survive; the horse did not. A wooden crutch lay on the seat beside him. It was going to be tough turning up at home, explaining this to his wife. She knew nothing of his war wound and was expecting him whole and intact, ready to take his place in the paddocks and in the milking shed.

'We all need a medal for surviving that hell. It was bloody tough over there for both the men and the horses, particularly in the early days. The camp was rife with typhoid and we were all exhausted and starving,' he added bitterly.

'I know that, but Les deserved the VC all right. He was a bloody hero that day,' replied Jack Ray, who had been a witness to the selfless act.

'None of us could believe it when we saw him ride out there in the middle of all the firing to rescue a bloke who had his horse shot out from underneath him and was in a pretty sticky situation. His number was well and truly up; he was a goner! Anyways, young Les rides out, dismounts, picks him up and puts him on his own horse, but the bloody horse bolts into boggy ground and they are in real strife. There was no bloody way the horse could carry both men, so the lieutenant dismounted, sent the horse and the wounded bloke for cover, while he made it out on foot. No doubt about it, he is a bloody hero; bloody lucky he made it out. It inspired all of us blokes. We ended up driving the Boer back and winning the battle that day. If you ask me, Les turned it around single-handedly. If anyone deserves a VC, he does.'

'Perhaps,' Claude reflected sadly, 'but he still has both legs. How am I going to be able to do the work on the farm with only one leg? We all did bloody amazing things. We were all bloody brave just being there. The bloody war was nothing to do with us. Getting on that boat was the worst bloody thing I have ever done. I wish I'd stayed home. It was hell on a stick and we were fools to go anywhere near it.'

'I know mate, I know,' comforted his best mate, Smithy.
'You had a rough ride all right, Hoppy. But you're here and
you're alive, and you're bloody determined to make a go of
it. You'll be right mate, you'll be right! Let's put all that
behind us and get on with it.'

Hoppy, as he had now become to his mates, bit his bottom
lip and put on a brave face. The truth was though, that in
their time away from home, fighting for the Empire, the men
had seen much bravery, but they had also seen things that
diminished them. Boer families shot in their beds, women
and children dragged from their homes, families starving and
thrown into concentration camps. They had witnessed man's
inhumanity to man at first hand. Unspoken horrors would
forever draw these men together, secrets locked in their
hearts, too terrible to talk about to anybody else. They had
marched to war optimistic and innocent, to fight for Queen
and Empire; they were returning, older and wiser and forever
changed. It would take time to fit in and adjust but, for now,
they were heading home to pick up the pieces of their lives.
Smithy produced a dog-eared pack of cards, limp from many
dealings, musty and thick from damp and moisture, and they
played, talked and bantered. Happy because they were
homeward bound.

At each station, there was much boisterous laughter and
good-natured teasing as one or another of a group of
Gippsland's best cricketers alighted at his stop. They were
returning from a very enjoyable assignment, playing Country
Week cricket down in the big smoke on the Melbourne
Cricket Ground. It had been a week of forming and firming
friendships and these Gippsland lads would always look back
and remember it as a most enjoyable time in their youth.
Young Billy Johnstone had been handpicked to join in the
training to play Test Cricket for his country. All he had to do

now was to convince his father to release him from the farm
so that he could live in the city and pursue his ambition. This
would prove more difficult than the act of being selected.
They needed him on the farm and his labour was cheap.
That train also brought first time settlers, Norma and
William Somerville, a young couple with dreams in their
hearts and resolve on their minds. Norma's grandmother in
England had died, leaving a small legacy, which they had
used to bid for, and win land in Government auctions
carried out by Jennings & McInnes at their city offices in
Bourke Street, Melbourne. They had bought property on the
Swamp, sight unseen. This was their one opportunity to
escape the poverty that had surrounded their families for
generations.

William had left England on a merchant ship bound for
Australia when he was a lad of fourteen and had absconded
in Geelong, excited by the rumours of the wealth to be made
on the goldfields. That's where he met and fell in love with
Norma who was working as a maid in one of the big houses.
Now perhaps, one day they would own a big house. They
were coming to toil in the fields and to make a good life for
themselves and their family. In the luggage van they carried a
tent for shelter while they built a hut and cleared the land by
grubbing and burning the tussocks. The dream was there,
waiting to be realised.

Patrick White and his two brothers, Joe and Tom, had also
bought packages of land at that auction, but they had come
alone, leaving their wives and children in the city while they
established homes for them on the land. The separation
would be difficult but, hopefully, not too much time would
pass before the White clan could be together again. In
Ireland, their home country, the oldest son invariably
inherited the land, the next one went into the Church and

younger ones had no place. For the White trio, they had to migrate just to survive. Things would be different here in Australia. They had bought their land sight unseen and, they would find, it was not as promised. Nevertheless, this was their golden opportunity.

CHAPTER 2

The Johnstone family was weary when Chris met them at the station that warm March day in 1902. They had left Mentone very early that morning, taking an electric train to Caulfield where they had waited on the platform for the train to Gippsland to huff and puff its way from Flinders Street Station, where it had begun its journey. The grandmother accompanied the young woman in order to help with the boys and stood, a lonely figure waving goodbye, as the train pulled out and disappeared into the distance. The mother held her breath as the boys hung out the window, gathering soot from the steam engine in their hair and eyes and calling and waving to their disappearing grandmother.

'The place will be so quiet without my three little men,' mused the grandmother as they waited at the station. 'Who is going to get the morning's wood for me, and who will walk with me to the Post Office when I post the mail. Who will take the carrot out to Bill the Baker's horse when he delivers the bread? '

She fussed over the boys and checked that the sandwiches she had so lovingly made for their journey were in the basket for their lunch,

'I will miss you all so much, but, my darling, I thank the Good Lord that you are married to a good and faithful man and that you have a beautiful family. Embrace and love them Etty, my darling, and never forget that I'll be praying for you every day.'

Ethel was sad to say goodbye to her mother, who was alone after Father had died three years previously, but she had her boarders to attend to, so it was impossible for her to accompany them. If the real truth be known, her mother loved Mentone and she her new-found independence. It was the first time in her life that she had enjoyed autonomy and she wasn't going to give it up easily. She would miss Ethel and the boys, but they were only a train journey away and she had other daughters who lived locally with their families. She kept her family in her heart and was pleased that her children lived interesting lives with decent men.

Chris had first broached the subject of opening a local newspaper in the little Gippsland town when he was a young reporter with the Melbourne "Argus". He became aware that an opportunity existed because his parents lived and farmed in the district.

'People in the Narracan Shire are starved of local news,' they informed him. 'There is a news-sheet, but it is published at irregular intervals and events are history by the time we read them. Trafalgar is the central town in our area and it is thriving; so if you must forego farming with us in order to write, then the business is there for the taking.'

Chris had considered their advice and only had to convince Ethel that it was a good idea. After a good deal of discussion and planning, it was decided that Ethel would stay with her mother while he went forward and did the groundwork to become established. He was going into the unknown, neither having a house nor a job. She could help her mother in the boarding house and the boys could attend Mentone State School. When things were ready he would call for her. Meanwhile, he travelled home once a fortnight to spend weekends with his family.

It was on one of these visits that he assured her, 'I think you and the boys will thrive. They will love the open spaces and the freedom and you will enjoy the townsfolk who are all good people like we try to be, not afraid to take a risk and who really want to make a go of things. Trafalgar is on the edge of a boom. I am sure there is gold in the hills and the town is growing every day. Our new house is just one of quite a few that is being built in the town and I was lucky to get the Cooks to build it for us, as they are excellent tradesmen. They really know what they are doing and it is coming together beautifully. It will be our home amongst the gumtrees Ethel and I can't wait to get my little family down there with me. I miss you all so much.'

That morning as the steam train carried Ethel and her sons to their new life, Gippsland was stunningly beautiful. The brisk, early morning air hung like gossamer over the foothills of the Great Australian Divide, the cows, sheep and horses supping on the green grass that had been freshened with the first rains of autumn.

One by one they passed through little towns – Pakenham, Nar Nar Goon, Officer, Warragul, Darnum. Settlement, until recently, had been confined to one spur of the Strzelecki Ranges, but weary from years of battling the heavy timber and dreadful roads many of the old pioneers had come down to the flatlands near the railway. Because the land was rich and the season long, they had resisted the urge to take up huge holdings. The farms were compact and sustainable and the settlements were close together.

'Look boys, a town called Bunyip,' the mother pointed out to her little tribe as they waited for the mail to be loaded aboard at the station, and watched a young man alight with his cricket bat tucked under his arm as his raucous mates called goodbye to him. 'Have I ever told you about the big Bunyip that lived in the swamp near my house in Mentone when I was a little girl?'

'Yes, Ma, you have, but please can you make another story about the Baldy Bunyip of Mentone, he is scary!' begged Aubrey. 'Yes please, Ma, yes please,' chanted the other two in unison. And so to pass the time and to take their minds off the journey she began a gruesome tale of the giant Bunyip that gurgled and snarled every night when the moon came out; it ate frogs and swans and would have eaten little boys and girls if they were silly enough to be out there and not at home tucked up in their cosy beds. But there was a black swan, who wouldn't be frightened ...

The story continued and Ethel had the boys spellbound and begging for more.

Somewhere between Warragul and Yarragon there had been a hullabaloo in the outside corridor where the boys were playing a game of sorts. Ethel had been settled back into her seat, eyes closed, glad that they seemed to be happy and out of her way.

'Ma, Mervyn has crashed through the next door and has disturbed the people in there,' informed Aubrey who always took pleasure in seeing his younger sibling in a spot of bother. Sighing, Ethel got up and firmly took young Mervyn by the arm. 'Mervyn, we are in a public space and that is no way to behave. You shall have to go and apologise to those people.'

'No Ma!' implored the culprit, 'don't make me, please don't make me.'

'Sorry Mervyn, but you have to do it. Here's what you can say. Just say, "Excuse me please, I would like to apologise for my rough behaviour. I am sorry to have intruded on your journey and I hope you will forgive me." Have you got that? I will come with you so that you feel safe.'

The unwilling repentant did as he was told, Ethel exchanged niceties with her fellow travellers and then retreated to take in the last part of the journey, all three boys in tow and sitting nicely in their seats. The party reached Yarragon, beginning the final leg towards the new life in this broad green valley of the Latrobe River that was flanked by loping hills that cradled the fertile, rich, abundant plains. They were almost there.

Even though they were tired, the reunion at the Trafalgar station was joyous. Ethel was every inch the modern woman, tall and slim. Her curly and normally unruly hair tucked inside her straw hat that was turned at the brim and worn with a little twist, as was the fashion in the city. After a year of mourning for the old Queen Victoria, colours were the order of the day and her pale green, full skirt flounced out a little at the hem, over her shiny, laced boots. She wore a smart black coat, much tucked and stitched, that was the ultimate in fashion. Her demeanour announced that here was a lady who knew her place in the world and, although she would play by the rules, she held her own opinions.

This is what Chris loved most about her; the fact that she was his intellectual equal, perhaps not as logical as he, but what she lacked in this aspect she made up for with intuition. She treated everyone with respect but did not suffer fools gladly, and was always forthright with her opinions if asked. She certainly turned heads at the Trafalgar station that day.

The town had won a lady and the admiring glances and nods as the couple walked arm in arm out of the station to a large, open, busy forecourt didn't go unnoticed by Chris. He was a proud man.

There was much hustle and bustle as many people milled around waiting for the highly prized mail because this kept them in touch with the outside world. The station master, Paddy O'Sullivan, emerged from the guard's van with a large postal sack, lock attached, which he opened with one of the many keys on the chain attached to his waistcoat. He upended the whole lot on a large table that was positioned just outside the waiting room door. There was a rush as people sorted through, searching for their own mail, but handing items onto their neighbours if they happened to come across something that belonged to them. It was a chaotic scramble.

'They're building a new Post Office across the road next to our new printing shop,' Chris explained. 'The plan is to have all the mail sorted, compiled and held over there so that anyone can pick it up at any time during the working day. At present it is all a bit hit and miss, and there is absolutely no respect for privacy. If you are expecting mail you have to come here to the station at the appointed time to collect it. It works for the moment, but we will all rejoice when the new building is complete,' he explained accepting a pile of mail from a frazzled woman who emerged from the crowd. 'Thank you, Myrtle. I'll do the same for you next time.'

He doffed his hat to the lady and went on, 'They also plan to move the telephone into the new Post Office when it is built. Right now it is in the waiting room at the station and everyone can listen into your conversation, and that is a bit off-putting, especially when you are talking business. No wonder that the news flies around Trafalgar. They call it the bush telegraph.'

Ethel laughed because the concept amused her and also because she was happy.

'Sometimes everyone else knows your news before you do yourself! We will have our own telephone in the Printing Office,' Chris continued. 'Ours will be Number 3. We have to wait until they bring the line across the road, but that won't be too long now.'

'Oh that is exciting. Our very own telephone! Mother will be impressed.' Ethel was excited.

CHAPTER 3

Chris left his family alone while he went to organise their luggage, crates and boxes. Ethel stood still and took in the scene around her. It was a hive of activity. Provisions, travellers, luggage and boxes that had been off-loaded from the train were being sorted and stacked aboard buggies, traps and carts, while horses waited patiently, nuzzling their bags of oats before the homeward journey.

She noticed the woman, Annie Donovan from the carriage that Mervyn had fallen into, in a family embrace with a broad shouldered, strong looking man with even features, a handlebar moustache and kind eyes. He was dressed in the working clothes of a farmer, polished hobnailed boots, dungarees and an old flannel shirt. He had taken his flat cap off to greet his wife revealing sandy coloured hair receding a little at the temple. Entwined in the embrace were two older children, while the younger ones who had been with her on the train scooted around the family circle. There was something solid and honest that she instinctively liked about the woman. It was evident that Tom Donovan was happy to have his Annie and the two younger children back into the fold after ten days away.

Three of the young cricketers were being heralded with a joyous round of applause. They had done well in the city and the town was proud of them and were there to tell them so. Men left their groups and came to shake their hands and offer their congratulations. They were pleased to be back home, but now in the narrow window before the football season began, there was work to do, fodder to be cut and stored for winter, and crops to be harvested.

Chris brought one of them forward, one arm on his shoulder in an embrace that heralded a comfortable familiarity. He was obviously happy to see him.

'Etty, my darling, guess what the train brought in? If I had known, you could have travelled together, but never mind. I found my little brother Billy. He's a big boy now and has been down in town playing cricket. The Gippsland boys did really well. Billy has been offered a training place with the Australian team. All he has to do now is to convince the old man to let him go. If it was up to me I'd be down there watching him play every weekend, but we will have to see what the old boy says.'

They exchanged pleasantries, Billy shadow boxing Aubrey and then Mervyn, pretending to box them around the ear holes and generally larking about. But there was not much time for chatter because Billy was whisked away to the farm on the back of one of his neighbour's carts. It was a long journey and they wanted to be home by nightfall. He bid his older brother's family farewell and disappeared in a cloud of dust up the Thorpdale Road.

A heated argument had developed between O'Sullivan, the stationmaster and the men of the Light Horse Brigade. After all the time away fighting for the King in a foreign country, the poor soldiers could not ride on home as their horses had been misplaced and were not on the train.

'You're trying to tell, me you don't know where our horses are!' Smithy was incredulous, as were the other soldiers.

'You can't lose four flaming horses. It's just not possible,' said Jack Ray, adding his feeling of amazement at the inefficiency of the system.

'When we got on the train at Flinders Street, the guardsman was loading them aboard the stock carriage,' Smithy explained. 'Either they have fallen out on the trip or they have been off loaded somewhere else. Sorry Paddy, but you are going to have to make enquiries for us. We can't go anywhere without the horses.'

'I haven't lost any of your horses,' Patrick O'Sullivan defended himself, 'I haven't seen any of your horses, but nevertheless I will do my best to locate them and get them back for you.'

Off he went off to use the telephone while the men waited. Hoppy leaned heavily on his crutch, weary at the turn of events, but secretly happy that the time to reveal his changed circumstances to his wife and family had been delayed.

A few minutes passed before the stationmaster returned triumphant.

'I have located the beasts. They are healthy and in good spirits but unfortunately they are still in the loading yard at Flinders Street Station. The good news is that they will put them on the next goods train and the bad news is that that won't be until tomorrow morning.'

'Well, can you credit that?' asked Hoppy. 'Those four horses have survived the guns and bullets of a thousand dogged Boers who didn't want us in their country and told us so, loudly and clearly. And we come home to Melbourne and the Royal Railways can't be relied upon to get them from A to B. You wouldn't read about it.'

'Come on,' coaxed Smithy, who had no ties and secretly knew he would miss the company of his mates when they went their separate ways. 'Let's make the most of a disappointing situation. We'll adjourn to the Criterion Hotel for the evening, get a bed, have a drink and play some more cards. We'll go on in the morning. No one is expecting us, so no harm done.'

What options did they have? They made off in a group across the road to kill the waiting hours.

'Miss Stewart will certainly have a baptism of fire on her first day as Lessee of that noble establishment,' thought Ethel when she overheard this. 'By eleven o'clock tonight she will have several drunken soldiers to keep calm.'

She noticed a tall lanky man with a swagger in his gait and a twinkle in his eye, who was collecting Miss Stewart's bags. He spoke to her Christie in a familiar manner, and made off across the road with the lady in question.

With the soldier's problems tended to, the stationmaster waved his flag, signalling the train to move off with the Government party still on board and bound for Moe.

Cr Frank Geach and Mr Alby Gibson, members of the Swamp Settlers Committee, were confused when their visitors were not amongst the passengers to alight.

'We're waiting for the Government Engineer, Mr Catani. Do you know what happened to him?' Gibson asked O'Sullivan. 'He was heading this way with a group of government men from Melbourne. We are supposed to meet them here with fresh horses.'

The stationmaster perused his running sheet and nodded sagely.

'It looks like they have gone through to Moe, Alby. They were on that train but they certainly didn't alight here. If I were you I'd head out to McKella's place. I saw Joe McKella yesterday and he told me Catani and his men were stopping to have lunch at his place. That's why they were in town. Mrs Mac was buying provisions.'

The waiting gentlemen were not amused!

'City slickers! Mucking us around like this! They're getting paid to sit on their bums on the train and here we are standing in the sun waiting for them like mugs.' Alby Gibson spat out his disgust.

'Yep, we could have done a morning's work. It's damned annoying!' Frank was in total agreement. 'But as you say, Pat, we will head out to McKella's and meet them there. Might even get one of Daisy's apple dumplings if we're lucky,' he added, cheering at the thought. 'I'm bloody annoyed though, all those blokes on the government pay roll and they and they can't get a simple thing like this right. You wouldn't bloody dream about it!' Collecting the horses they left.

A wiry little fellow with racing silks over his arm and two riding whips in his hand emerged from the thinning crowd, nodded to a few people, shook hands with a man Ethel presumed to be his father, jumped on a horse that was proffered and, without fuss expertly rode off.

'Take notice of that young bloke,' said Chris, as he came back to where she waited for him. 'His name is Willy Walker and he's been down in the city riding for the VRC races at Flemington and Caulfield. He's going to be a great jockey one day, in fact he is only sixteen years old and already he is winning first division races. Can't play football, but boy can he ride? He just becomes one with the horse.'

'Christie, you've not taken to the horses while you've been by yourself, have you? It's not the smartest way to spend your money.'

'Never, my darling wifey,' replied her husband taking her arm in his and squeezing it gently, 'I take an interest because Willy Walker is a local boy and as a local newspaperman it is my duty to know these things. But I do still say, there is absolutely nothing wrong with a small interest in a horse race as long as you can afford it. At the moment, my dear Etty, a punt is right out of the question because we are broke, but you wait until the newspaper is up and going and we are raking in the boodle, then I am going to Kevin Kelly, the local bookie and I am going to slap ten pounds in his hand and tell him to put it all on the nose of the horse that is under young Walker, and with the winnings you can go to Melbourne and buy a new hat with feathers and silk trimming. Now how do you like that?' he added with a twinkle in his eye.

'Oh Christie, you don't mean that. You are just teasing, just trying to get me going. But I won't bite. Whenever you have that much money from your endeavours you can do whatever you wish with it just so long as the boys and I don't go cold or hungry. Whatever am I going to do with you?' she laughed, happy to be with her man again.

'Never mind me, Etty, I'm just teasing. I'd forgotten how much fun it is to see you rise to my bait and snap it up, hook, line and sinker.'

'Gosh, this is a busy corner of the world,' Ethel added, changing the subject. 'I had no idea there was so much activity here.'

'It's not always bustling like this,' Chris answered. 'Trafalgar is mostly a quiet calm little place except for twice a day when the train whistles through. Then it is like Spencer Street in the city, but it all calms down after the rush, and you could fire a gun down the Main Street and not even hit a dog,' explained Chris as the family made their way through the horses and carts at the station court.

The boys scuttled around the feet of the adults, alternatively hopping on one foot and then the other, jumping and running, talking and laughing, like tightly sprung springs that had been let loose.

Chris guided his family out of the station yard and across the railway line. Ethel noticed that the little town seemed to be clustered around the station. The Cream & Butter Factory and a group of businesses stood on the north side with a few houses dotted in and out amongst them, and across the line was the commercial centre of town that consisted of some small shops situated along the Main Road and houses here and there of various designs and condition. The wattle log and bark huts of early settlement sat next to Victorian cottages and more substantial modern homes. What would all become so familiar to Ethel in the future was at that moment just a mix of unrelated buildings and shelters, quite unlike the swanky homes she had left behind in the new avant-garde beachside playground of Melbourne's Mentone.

The group stepped across the street; Chris led them past Gordon's Hotel, patting Dondi, the hotel pony and introducing him to the boys. 'Dondi is the most famous resident of the town. If you want to live happily in Trafalgar then you must bring Dondi a carrot or an apple at least once a week. That is the rule. Everyone knows and loves Dondi, so give him a pat boys and let him take in your smell.'

They then went next door to The Federal Coffee Palace where Mrs Lawless took in boarders and provided meals at all hours.

'I have booked us in here for two nights,' explained Chris, 'I know you will be tired after your journey, Etty, and I want you to have a good rest, no meals to cook and no beds to make up until tomorrow, when we will go to the new house. I have asked Mrs Brown, the blacksmith's wife, to come and give you a hand at getting things in order. They have only recently arrived in town so if you get along well I shall employ her to help you in the house, Ethel. I think you will like her and she is young and fit. Jimmy Kenny and I will take the boys out of your way, out into the bush to camp for the night, where we will teach them how to shoot a gun and catch a fish.'

Seeing the expression of alarm on Ethel's face, he quickly justified himself. 'It's something that country boys need to know, Etty, and they may as well learn it now. Besides, it's a great sport and we will only be shooting at targets, not kangaroos or anything like that.'

Aubrey, Mervyn and little Vernon could barely contain their joy and excitement – camping with their father, shooting, fishing. What more could little boys want? And so it was arranged that Mrs Brown and Ethel would have two days to unpack the boxes that were still on the station but would be delivered next day to the new home on the Main Street.

CHAPTER 4

That evening over a delicious meal of kangaroo tail soup, steak and kidney pie and golden syrup dumplings, cooked in Mrs Lawless' kitchen, and eaten in the front dining room of her establishment, they were all together at last after many months of separation.

The only other guests at Lawson's that night were a couple of travelling salesmen, Bill and Norma Somerville, and the Government party, tired and worn out from their adventures on the Swamp. Conditions were every bit as bad as had been reported and it had proved not to be a good day for the visiting dignitaries.

It was the talk of the town with everyone enjoying a laugh at the city slickers' expense. Ned Nix had witnessed the whole debacle and happily held the stage down the road at Gordon's pub that night, spinning out the story and making the most of his eye-witness knowledge.

'There they were then, all three big knobs from town, plus their entourage, on their horses sitting up there like the lords of the manor, looking as if they knew what they were doing.

But they hadn't accounted for our Moe mud after a bit of rain, had they?

There was this young city bloke who was reporting for "The Argus", green as a young sprig, hands on him as white and soft as clouds, never seen a day's work in his short life. By golly, he was lucky he wasn't killed. I reckon that the sum total of his horse riding is probably a light canter by the river on a warm day with a fair lady by his side. Anyway, his horse's hoofs got bogged in the Swamp, and the poor blighter bit the dust. I swear the horse rolled on him, but fortunately his feet were free of the stirrups and he managed to escape with nothing injured, only his pride. But he looked like a gollywog when he got up, covered in black mud and as sheepish as can be, I felt a bit sorry for the poor bugger.'

Ned took a quick sip of his beer and then continued before anyone else could step in.

'And then, to top it all off, Mr Grant's horse came a cropper down the bank on the Main Channel. It fell heavily and then it reared right up. Spooked it was! Grant was thrown off and had one foot caught in the stirrup and was being dragged around like a rag doll. Pandemonium broke loose. Everyone was trying to help – grabbing the reins and catching hold of the bridle. Now that was pretty scary, but he came out of it with just one hell of a fright. I bet he will be a bit sore when he lies the body down tonight. Lucky to be alive, he is! If they're not convinced that something needs to be done about the old swamp after today then nothing will ever convince them.'

'Thank the good lord for Daisy McKella and her two lovely lasses,' put in Alby Gibson, who had missed all the excitement of the morning, but had managed to join the party for lunch. 'The dinner she served was splendid and went a long way to making the city fellows mellow. Mr

Nichols told me that he would do all that he could to have the matter resolved. He even remarked that he didn't know how the decent, hardworking folk of the swamp survived under such trying conditions.'

The White brothers, who were in the bar that evening enjoying a stout and relishing their new found freedom away from wives and children, listened and took notice, for tomorrow they would head out to the Swamp to take possession of their land, sight unseen.

'My good gracious God, Tom, do you reckon we've been sold a lemon?' Joe was beginning to panic. 'They told us that the land out there is ready to plough and plant our spuds. It sounds like that is not the case.'

'She'll be fine, Joe. Calm down! The good lord will look out for us. We're all young and fit and healthy and we know farming inside out. It may be tough going for a bit but we will prevail,' consoled Tom, afraid that his brother was allowing the gossip to cloud his judgement.

Patrick patted his twin brother affectionately on the shoulder. 'Joseph, take it easy lad. It's as Tom says. We are good farmers. We know that. Anyone who can grow a spud in the bog that sits on the piles of stone they call the hills of County Mayo, with the freezing cold west wind blowing right through your bones, can turn the soil in this God blessed country and grow a crop that will make him a fortune. Let's not give up before we start. Tomorrow we will go out there and see what we have to deal with, but tonight let's enjoy ourselves, because it may be a long time between drinks.'

They were interrupted when Alby Gibson came over, hand extended, unashamedly staring at the twins. 'Have I had so much to drink that I am seeing double, or are you two blokes out of the same mould?'

Indeed Paddy and Joe White were like two peas in a pod, carbon copies of each other, stocky with black, unruly hair, thick dark eyelashes hovering like clouds over deep-set dark eyes. Their mouths were straight and resolute. They were saved the fate of appearing sinister by the dimples that danced around their top lips and cheeks, giving them both an almost comical, asymmetrical aspect. Tom was red headed, with the pale complexion of a man from the Emerald Isle, where the sun was reluctant to shine. He was tall and wiry, his skinny frame belying his strength. Nobody would pick him for the twins' brother.

The three men laughed, introduced themselves and were brought into the group, easily accepted for they would become one of them, living at this time and in this place. Their accents were broad and they talked fast but everyone there that night warmed to the good-natured banter, even though they could hardly be understood. Patrick and Joseph would soon become known locally as 'Irish' for no one could tell them apart.

At the Lawson's establishment, the Johnstone family acknowledged their fellow diners and sat down to eat.

'Isn't it funny that they would call a town in Australia after a battle that took place on the other side of the world, in Spain?' Ethel mused, cutting Vernon's meal into small, manageable pieces.

'You're right, Etty. Must have been some old army fellow with a penchant for battles and glories past. He probably had a hook for an arm, an eye patch, loved a double whisky and walked with a limp.'

Chris put down his fork, stood upright at attention and saluted, and then in his best Brigadier's voice announced to Ethel and his boys, "Chaps, gather round. At ease! You may smoke if you wish. Chaps, I have been thinking hard and I have decided that we shall name this town Trafalgar in honour of the great Napoleonic War sea battle when the French and Spanish fleets were destroyed at the hands of Britain's great, victorious Lord Nelson."

Adopting the whine of a lowly private, he continued: "But Sir, we are a million miles away, on the other side of the earth. You must have a good reason for this?"

The Brigadier had his measure: "No reason, son, I just think it's a good idea, that's all. We shall march on the Boers tomorrow at noon, be prepared. Dismissed!"

Chris energetically saluted and sat down and the family all laughed. So too did the Somervilles who were seated at the next table. They were a young couple, barely twenty years old, full of optimism for the future and excited about this chance to forge a decent life for themselves. They were eager to be up early in the morning to journey out to their holding, pitch the tent and to begin the task of making a working farm that would provide for a family.

Chris had a way with words and he could always turn them to suit his wishes, in this case to entertain his young family. Ethel could never resist his humour, he could always see the joke in any situation and he could be so funny. Now he had an audience and was playing to it.

'Yarragon is the next town as you head towards Melbourne,' he went on, 'apparently it used to be called Waterloo. Must have been the same fellow that named them both.'

"Chaps, gather round, gather round," he said, reverting to his Brigadier and private scenario. "At ease, smoke if you wish, I've been thinking and I have decided that we shall name this here place, Waterloo."

"Sir, please can you tell me, is there any reason for this?"
"No reason, son, I just think it's a good idea, that's all. Dismissed!"

Everyone laughed again.

'The locals tell me,' he resumed in his normal voice, 'that it wasn't long before it was changed back to Yarragon, its aboriginal name meaning fruit bearing gum trees. But they still call the road that connects the two towns Waterloo Road. Believe me, Etty, there's no place on this earth that is less likely to remind you of a battle. It is as green as the rolling hills of England; it has four distinct seasons and on a sunny day you might think you are in heaven itself. In fact, Sunny Creek is just up the road. Now that's a better name.'

'Are there other settlements?' the mother enquired anxiously, picturing her and her three sons isolated in the middle of nowhere, never seeing anybody and talking to the kookaburras and pet kangaroos that were their only company.

'Of course there is, my sweet darling, our house that you will see tomorrow is on the main road and is directly opposite the railway line where the train steams away to the east to a place called Orbost which is almost into New South Wales. Close by, if you head east, past our house, you pass through Moe and then there is a bigger town called Morwell and then Traralgon that has dentists, doctors and just about every service that you can find in the city. It even has a department store.'

Etty began to feel a little more comforted.

'Further east is the Port of Sale,' continued Chris, 'where boats carry passengers and cargo through a system of lakes that finally run into the sea. After that there is apparently a pretty little town on the Mitchell River called Bairnsdale, but I have never been there. The story goes that Macmillan, a Scot, who was one of the first white men through there, was enthralled by the number of aboriginal children playing by the river and the billabongs and that is why he named it after the Scottish word for child. Now, he had more imagination than our old friend, the Brigadier!'

This time adopting the broad accent of his parents' native Scotland, he went on, "Laddie, would you take a peek at all the wee bairns playing in the sunshine, and none of them with a stitch of clothing on their wee bodies."

The boys loved that bit.

"Aye, but they are all so happy; we'll name this pretty valley Bairnsdale, a place where the bairns play."

With barely a second's breather, Chris continued with a reply, this time in a posh English accent. "I say, steady on old chap. You said that the next place we came to would be named after me! I've been here with you since we left Sydney and headed south. I've carried your compass, written up your manual, lit your fires, fed your horse and now you tell me that you are going to name this place after a bunch of children. I'm absolutely appalled and I have a good mind to tell you to shine your own boots tonight!"

"Aye, I understand how ye feel, laddie, but bear with me on this one, Munro, I promise ye the next place will be named after ye."

As the boys considered this, Ethel took the bait. 'And is there a place called Munro?'

'I think there is. I think there is!' replied Chris quickly, although he was not sure and keen to get back to the task at hand, which was to alert his young family to their position on the continent.

'Go west from our house and eventually you will come to Warragul, which is aboriginal for wild dog. There's a creek there called Brandy Creek and rumour has it that the water there tastes better than a wee drop, but I've yet to taste it. Anyway, Warragul is a thriving place where all the local farmers gather to sell their stock and produce. You came through there on the way down. It will be fun to go there for a day out on cattle sale day or for the agricultural show. We shall buy you a new hat, my lovely, and I will show my girl off to the whole world and you boys can all have as much fairy floss as you can eat.'

Wanting to take a grown up part in the conversation, Aubrey recounted to his father the tale about the Mad Mentone Bunyip.

Chris added to the intrigue by telling them in a spooky voice, 'The town of Bunyip is called after a monstrous, swamp-dwelling creature with the harsh call that the aborigine people have seen and remembered. But there is something even spookier that I can tell you about. Near to Moe is the Haunted Hills. Do you know why they call them that? It is because strange things happen in those hills at night when the moon is full and the dingos howl. Just ask any drover who has ever passed that way and he will tell you that some wild, mysterious, cattle eating monster lives there. The cows get spooked and don't want to be near the place; they moo and tremble and try to turn around, wanting to go back the other way. The cattlemen can never rest their cows on those hills at night; no matter how late it is they always have to keep going until they reach the other side. Ghosts walk in the moonlight in the Haunted Hills.' Seeing the terror on the three little faces, Chris figured he'd told enough tall stories for the evening and attempted to lighten the mood by adding, 'Why, once a cow even jumped over the moon!' Relieved at last, the boys gave a nervous laugh.

'I shall tell you one thing that is worth remembering, though,' continued Chris, going into teacher mode. 'Trafalgar is the only town in the world called Trafalgar. The place where Nelson's great battle was fought is a headland in south-west Spain, known as Cape Trafalgar.'

The parents shot each other a proprietorial, parental smile. How she loved her man – his stock of black curly hair framing his square honest face and showcasing the kind blue eyes with the long lashes. The solid Scottish frame would weather any highland wind. He was handsome, sturdy, dependable and so much fun to be with. They looked at the boys' earnest faces as they considered the hauntings. How they both loved their boys; they were so proud of them; healthy good-looking boys with endless energy and so much zest for life. This was their family and they were together now, a new life had begun. Tomorrow Ethel would go to the brand new house, unpack the chests and see what awaited them.

CHAPTER 5

Mrs Maggie Brown, the new blacksmith's wife, was a female replica of her husband, George. She was young, not yet thirty, strong, capable, no-nonsense and efficient, an open face with blue eyes, blonde hair and a sunny disposition. She came to the Lawless establishment early the next morning wearing a sensible gown and carrying an apron to protect her clothing while she worked. She was armed with a wicker basket containing cleaning rags, a bottle of Vinegar, and a bar of soap in a calico bag. After Chris had completed the introductions and the small talk had dried up, she suggested that she would head on over to the new Johnstone house and begin the task by opening up and dusting the place.

'The road kicks up lots of dirt and dust and with all the traffic passing your front door it will be a source of annoyance for you, Mrs Johnstone,' Maggie said. 'I know, because we live at the back of our shop and suffer from it constantly. It's a never-ending battle to keep things clean. We can't keep the door shut because it is a business and people are coming and going, so the dust blows right in all the time. Right up the passageway as bold as you like looking for a place to settle, and settle it does.

'However, Mrs Johnstone, you should try to remember to keep the front door closed and the windows down in the daytime because it will cut down on the dust and save you a lot of work, you mark my words. Of course it gets worse in the summer. Then everything is so dry and that north wind is intent on causing havoc.'

Ethel listened but was preoccupied, for she was preparing the boys for their adventure in the bush, but she assured Maggie that she would be down to the house presently, just as soon as the camping party was ready to depart. Chris handed Maggie the house keys and the helper departed with a wave and a cheery, 'I'll be seeing you shortly then.'

Aubrey and Mervyn dressed themselves each morning but Vern was only four and needed the assistance of his mother. She took three clean white starched shirts from the luggage and laid them on the beds along with sturdy grey trousers for each boy. She also added clean underclothes and long socks that she had knitted on the long nights last winter. She did not want her boys being judged by the townspeople as shoddily dressed. She made sure that they had sturdy boots and warm coats because the nights could get very cold, even in March.

Chris assured her that he had plenty of sausages to cook on the campfire and that he had gallon bottles filled with water. Mrs Lawless had especially baked and iced a butter cake and they had a billy for the tea. As well, they had fresh apples plucked from the tree in the backyard that morning and some bread, baked fresh by Mr McCrory, the baker at the end of Main Street. The party was taking a packhorse with bedding, provisions, the guns and fishing gear aboard, but they weren't going far, just up into the hills a bit.

It was difficult for her to release the children into their father's keeping to go out into the wild, unknown bush, but a mother must learn to stand back and allow her sons to be educated in the ways of men. There could be snakes and spiders and God only knows what out there, and she wouldn't be there to protect them. However, Ethel had a job to do and that was to make a house a home. It would be easier without children under her feet. The boys were almost dressed when a deep voice called from down the stairwell.

'Is there anyone home?' Up the dark mahogany stairs came the same tall, lanky man she had seen picking up Miss Stewart's bags at the station yesterday. He was aged in his late twenties and dressed in dungarees and a checked flannel shirt. He wore an old felt hat that had corks that hung from its brim and danced around his laconic smile.

'They're to keep those pesky flies away from my face,' he replied when Mervyn questioned him, 'those flies would drive a man to drink, they would. They are as big as Christmas beetles and there are thousands of them. We might even catch some and put them on the campfire for dinner tonight! You just watch and mark my words! Before you've been here two months you will be coming to me and begging me to hang corks off your hat, just like mine. I bet they don't have corks on their hats in Melbourne, but them city blokes know nothing. They wouldn't know whether they're coming or going, whether they're Arthur or Martha or whether it is a fly or a bumblebee and they certainly don't know how to catch a fish for breakfast. You stick with me, son, and I'll show you how to be a real countryman. You'll never go back near that city, mark my words.'

'Meet my mate, Jimmy Kenny, Ethel,' laughed Chris. 'This is the man who has kept me sane in the eighteen months since I have been down here. Jimmy's family have been on a farm out on the Seven Mile Road for over ten years, but he is the second son and there is no room for him anymore, so he is going to be my right hand man in the Printing Office. He's moved into the town to live and he has helped me with the machinery and with setting it all up, and when we put the first paper to bed in May, Jimmy is going to be working the presses. Jim is a jack-of-all-trades and can turn his hand to anything. I might even let him loose with a few words or three. He can be my farming expert. Jimmy, this is my lovely wife Ethel, you'll be seeing a lot of each other, in one way or the other. Boys, I would like you to meet Mr Kenny. Jim this is Aubrey, Mervyn and Vernon, our new recruits.'

Jimmy offered his hand to the boys, 'Stick with us lads, and we'll show you the ropes,' he said. 'Pleased to meet you boys. Now let's see, you must be Aub, Chris told me you are ten, and you have to be eight year old Mervyn, great name you have there, mate, and you,' he said, shaking Vern's hand, 'you must be Albert, and you are thirty six and have hairs growing in your ears.

'No, no, you're wrong!' they all cried in unison.

'I'm Vernon, and I'm a big boy because I'm four,' declared Vern, 'and I haven't got hairy ears.' He stuck out his tongue at which point his mother reached over and gave him a gentle slap across the cheek.

'Poke out that tongue of yours again, Vernon, and you will have very sore ears,' warned Ethel. 'Now say sorry at once to Mr Kenny for being such a cheeky boy.'

'Sorry Mr Kenny, but you shouldn't say I have hairy ears.'

'You will have to take Vernon in hand, Christie.' She gestured helplessly to her husband. 'That comes from spending too much time with adults at Mother's place. He has become very cheeky and needs a father's firm guidance.' Turning to the man at the centre of all of this she continued. 'Very pleased to meet you Mr Kenny. I always seem to be apologising for my boys. They will give me grey hairs. I appreciate all you have done for Christie. You make a good team. He has told me all about you.'

'Christie, eh! You didn't tell me about that!' he said, turning to his boss. 'I thought you were just plain Chris, good old Chris, solid everyday Chris and now I find out that you are really high-falutin' Christie,' he teased, his eyes crinkling into laughter, his wide smile revealing a missing front tooth. 'Wait till I tell the boys at the pub. Christie indeed! I don't think I can go camping with a bloke called Christie. Sorry boys, I'll have to call it off!'

Shouts of protest all round.

'No, no, just kidding; just pulling your leg.'

Ethel was more than a little taken aback as she hadn't met a man who spoke in that manner in her previous life in the city.

'Please Mr Kenny, I call Christopher, Christie. I am the only person in the world other than his mother who uses that name. Please continue calling him Chris. I would hate him to be embarrassed.'

Both men laughed. 'Don't fret, Ethel,' soothed Chris, putting his arm on her shoulder affectionately. 'You'll get used to it. Everyone here takes the mickey out of everyone else; it's a country way of communication and you are not supposed to take it seriously. It just means they like you.'

CHAPTER 6

By the time the campers had left it was getting on towards ten o'clock in the morning, so Ethel tidied herself, gathering her curly hair, piling it into a knot and firmly pinning it down. She was in constant battle with her hair. It was determined to fly free and do its own thing when all she wanted from it was sit neatly and behave. She secured it tightly in a headscarf to keep off the dastardly dust that Mrs Brown had warned her about.

'Mrs Lawless, would you please be so kind as to accompany me to the house, as I am unsure of its location. It has not occurred to Christie to take me there. So much like a man!' she called to her hostess who was in the kitchen.

'I'll be right with you, Mrs Johnstone, just as soon as I put this egg custard in the oven for lunch.' She busied herself, preparing a water bath in which she placed the dish containing the whipped milk, eggs, sugar and vanilla essence, and slid them both into the oven.

Ethel went to the drawing room to wait. The young couple that had shared the dining room with them the previous evening sat shyly on a sofa. They were excited about their adventure, but were uncomfortable in their surroundings for they had never before stayed in an establishment such as this. The young man stood up as she entered, waited until she sat down and then made his introductions.

'My name is William Somerville and this is my wife, Norma. We are just waiting for the horse and cart we have hired to take our goods and chattels to our new block. Today we start our new life as farmers.'

'How wonderful,' smiled Ethel. 'So young and with the whole world in front of you, but do you know what? I am doing exactly the same thing. Today brings new beginnings for me also. My name is Mrs Johnstone, by the way.'

And so they chatted and told each other their stories until Mrs Lawson had finished what she needed to do in the kitchen. She came into the room, interrupting their conversation. 'I'll just take off this pinny and we'll be on our way,' she said divesting herself of her floral apron and hanging it on the coat rack in the hall.

Ethel wished her young companions good luck and the two women closed the front door and stepped out into the street. 'That business belongs to Nicholas, my husband,' Mrs Lawless explained pointing out the Hairdresser and Tobacconist next to her establishment. 'He's the hairdresser, and a very good one he is too, so if you need your hair done for some occasion or another he will do a good job for you. We've only been in the town for three years but before that Nick had an establishment on Swanston Street in Melbourne city. The rents got too much for us to manage. There was just no money in it once we'd paid the landlord, so we decided to head to the bush. We rent the whole premises here for half of what we paid in town. It used to be Nelson's Hotel but I run it as a boarding house while Nick does his cutting and perming next door. It works out well and we love this town and the people. Mind what you say though, news travels fast in a place like this. Of course Nick hears all the local gossip while he'd fiddling with the ladies' hair, but he keeps his lips sealed. Can't afford to offend anybody in a small town you know, and you just have to learn to bite your tongue and say nothing. You have to be so careful of what you say and to whom you say it.'

They crossed Contingent Street. To the left Ethel could see that the town had two banks, solid wooden structures housing the Colonial Bank of Australasia and the State Bank of Victoria. They walked past the general store, under the verandas of two or three smaller shops, past one of the banks and its comfortable house, past the almost completed Post Office and onto her new house that sat in a large paddock on the edge of the settlement. It looked north over the railway tracks and open paddocks. The main road to Moe snaked its way past the house to the east. To the south, pretty wooded hills cradled the valley in which the little town rested. The Printing Office was on the west and town side of the block. It was a simple, rectangular building with five windows down each side, and a chimney at the back. It had a high-pitched, and newly painted dazzling white roof that basked in the sunshine with signage that proudly announced, 'Established AD 1902, THE TIMES PRINTING OFFICE, Founder and Prop. C. Johnstone'. Ethel felt a surge of pride that this was her Christie's business.

Sitting comfortably next to the office was their new home. It was beautiful; a largish house for the times, set back from the road behind a white washed picket fence, a veranda across the front shading two windows and a wide middle door. From the front you could see two chimneys on the western aspect. After the gaudiness of the Victorian era where houses were adorned with gargoyles and ornaments she was pleased to note that this modern home presented its face to the world with clean lines and measured elegance, simple and functional. It was painted a smart shade of cream and trimmed with a deep green. Her heart jumped. This was to be her home; she loved it from the start and was anxious to get inside.

'Can this really be for me and my family?' she exclaimed in her excitement, 'It is almost too good to be true. It is simply beautiful. I can't wait until Christie and the boys get back tomorrow and we can begin our life together here in Trafalgar.'

'You are indeed a lucky woman, Mrs Johnstone,' Mrs Lawless remarked. 'A brand new house and such a lovely design. You will be the envy of many ladies in the town. I would love to stop and chat but I have to get back and see to lunch. All hell will break loose if I'm not there. It will be absolute bedlam, so I shall see you later Mrs Johnstone. Dinner is at six.'

With that she took her leave.

Mrs Brown met Ethel at the front door with feather duster in hand. She had been busy for the past hour sweeping through the main rooms to ensure that it was ready for household items to be distributed when the lady of the house arrived to make those decisions.

'It's a lovely home you've got here, Mrs Johnstone. Mr Johnstone has seen to almost everything, the furniture arrived last week and he got George to help him place it where he thought it should go. All we have to do now is to unpack your boxes and set things in place. Just tell me what you want and I will do it. But first of all, shall we have a cup of tea and talk about how we will go about it? I have the kettle boiling.'

Pausing at the door, Ethel stroked its stained wooden mass and glanced back towards the front gate as a goods train laden with wood steamed noisily past on the opposite side of the road. 'Thank you, I am so excited. I can't wait to make it ours.' Ethel moved to step inside the wide passageway, but her eye was caught by a green crop brandishing a white flower. It was obviously thriving in the ploughed ground on either side of the pebbled path, stretching the whole width of the block and down the side towards the back.

'What are all those plantings in the soil, Mrs Brown?' she asked.

'Please, don't stand on ceremony, please call me Maggie,' came the reply. 'We shall see a lot of each other and I know we shall be friends, so enough of the Mrs!' Maggie laughed the easy laugh that would soon become a familiar sound to the Johnstone family, for she was an unsophisticated woman who had a happy disposition. 'About that planting, that's exactly the same question I asked George when we walked past the place last Sunday on our constitutional. He said that they are potatoes and that Mr Johnstone had put them in on the advice of one of the farmers who suggested that a potato crop was the best way to break up the ground to get it ready for a house garden. Apparently it will also keep the dust down while you are settling in, as you won't have much time for the garden for a while.'

'Now, isn't that interesting?' Ethel replied. 'That dear Christie of mine gets up to the funniest things. I had no idea that he is interested in gardening and here he is preparing the soil for me. Isn't he just the sweetest person? He knows that I love to fiddle in the garden and that it's my dream to have a beautiful one. What a dear soul he is to think of getting it all started? He knows how much it means to me.'

Maggie was visibly taken aback about such a public expression of love and devotion. She knew that her George loved her but he rarely told her so, and he would never in a thousand years allude to his affection outside of their own four walls. The Johnstones were going to be interesting people.

They went inside. The house had a bedroom on either side of the centre passageway; the one on the right had an open fireplace that backed onto another in the sitting room. The windows on this side of the house looked over to the Printing Office. A door to the left opened from the sitting room to another bedroom. The kitchen spanned the back of the house and had a wood burning stove and large wooden table that would become in the future, the central point of family life. It opened to a deep back veranda. Against the wall nearest the kitchen there was a large Coolgardie safe. At the far end of the veranda was a bathroom with a bath, an absolute luxury for that time. An out building that was the washhouse with the copper in it was a few feet away from the back of the house. Against the back fence, was the lavatory, accessed via a gravel path that looked as if it had been hastily laid down in the previous couple of days. Over the back fence was a lane that the night man used to access the cans on his bi-weekly sewage collection.

The fire in the kitchen stove was alight and the kettle was boiling on the hob. From the pocket in her pinnie Maggie took a small brown paper bag that held tea leaves. To Ethel's absolute horror, she emptied them straight into the kettle and let the tea brew from there. Taking on board the advice given to her this morning by her landlady, Ethel bit her tongue and didn't say a word. Perhaps this is the way they did things in the bush. Besides none of her things had been unpacked, so if they wanted a cup of tea it had to be this or nothing.

'Sorry, there is no milk. Can you take it black?' enquired Maggie, 'I did bring some sugar to sweeten it up. I could go outside and pick a couple of gum leaves if you want the real taste.'

'Anyway will be perfect,' replied Ethel, and she sat down at the long, scrubbed wooden table to a hot, sweet cup of strong brew unlike any of the teas she had tasted in the city. In the conversation that followed she learned quite a bit about Maggie and George Brown.

'I woke up this morning to find three burly Irishmen lined up for breakfast at my place,' laughed Maggie. 'They came in on the same train as you did, Mrs Johnstone, two of them swarthy fellows who look exactly alike. Two peas in a pod, two eggs in a nest, two ducks on a pond, if you know what I mean. Plus a redhead, all brothers. They have bought land hereabouts and had nowhere to sleep the night, so George, being the soft touch he is, brought them home with him from Gordon's to sleep in the back shed.'

'Is Gordon your friend?' Ethel asked innocently.

'Not my friend, but certainly George's friend,' Maggie replied, laughing. 'No, Mrs Johnstone, Gordon's is a watering hole, one of two public houses on the Main Street.'

'Oh, does your husband frequent public houses?' asked Ethel, almost immediately realising how priggish she sounded.

'Him and almost every other man in Trafalgar!' Maggie retorted. 'There's not too many taken the pledge around here. In fact, that's where your Christie met my George and found out about me doing this kind of work,' she added a little indignantly, thinking to herself, 'There, that should put Mrs Lah De Dah City Lady back in her box.'

Holding the thought, she continued, 'If it weren't for his nightly trip to the pub George would not have got to know anyone around here. That's where he gets a lot of his business. Besides, as far as the three Irishmen go, it's not so long since we were new here ourselves, so he empathised with them, knows what it's like. George and I are green skins really, only been in the town for about three months.'

Maggie was not one to hold onto things and once she had said her piece, she let it go and good naturedly chatted away while Ethel listened.

'We came down from Mallacoota, a fishing hamlet on this side of the New South Wales border. George knew we had to get away from the isolation up there when I miscarried my last baby. We'd only been married three years and I'd lost three babies, all in the fifth month. It was awful; one after another and so far away from anything, it was frightening. We hope that this move might change things and that one day soon we might be blessed with a healthy baby.'

'A healthy baby is the greatest blessing God can bestow,' Ethel added. 'I shall pray that happens for you Mrs Brown. Has your husband always worked as a blacksmith?'

'Yes, Mallacoota is where he learnt his trade. His father was a fisherman but George never really liked the sea, he found it too wet and scary, so he plied his trade for the horses of the old bushies up there who go out into the bush gathering wattle bark for tanning, as well as harvesting the tall timbers of the native forests. Now that's dangerous work. He also made pulleys and winches for the inlet and sea fishermen. They were very sorry to see him go. He is a wonderful tradesman.'

'So, did you want to leave?' asked Ethel.

'It almost broke my heart leaving Mallacoota,' confided Maggie, over the warm, sweet tea. 'I'd been born there and it was all I knew. I couldn't imagine living anywhere else; it was such a tight knit little community and we all knew each other. I met my George at Mrs Allan's boarding house on the hill where most of the fun happened. I was working for Mrs Allan and he was boarding there, making equipment for the bullockies. Now, they are amazing people. You have to be good with animals to work a team, they have to trust you and you have to sort of kid to them and call them all by name. Funny creatures. A bullocky can never hurry; he just has to be patient and co-operate with his animals. I could hear them coming in the evening from miles away. The chains would rattle. It was all lovely, but …'

'But ..?'

'After we got married and I had suffered my third miscarriage, George put his foot down and said, "We're getting out of here, Maggie, and we are going to Melbourne. We can't go on like this because if we stay you will surely die. Mallacoota is too remote and removed from anywhere else, you have to go to Orbost to get a doctor, anything could happen. We have to go and that is that."

'Well, I cried and I cried until in the end, Mama said to me, "It's no good, Margaret, you have to go with your husband. He is boss and you have to obey him. Dad and I will be fine; we left our parents in County Cork to come to Australia. That's just the way it is. We are old and our work is done but you have everything to look forward to and your whole life before you. George is a hard worker and a good man, so go with him and take our blessings with you."

'So, hard and all as it was, we packed a dray, attached our two horses, and set out before dawn one day in the middle of last summer. It was so hot that the bush crackled with the heat and the stillness. It took us fifteen hours just to get to Orbost, the little mill town on the great Snowy River, and both we and the horses were exhausted. We stayed two nights at Marshall's Hotel and then took the track to Bruthen, which was a little better than the previous one. We stopped off at Mrs Macs on the hill overlooking the Tambo River. It's all very beautiful. Then, on we went through Bairnsdale to Stratford and from Stratford to Sale and from Sale to Trafalgar. And here we are.'

'But you were heading for Melbourne. What made you stop here?'

'We had no plans to settle, but the landscape reminded George of his County Meath in Ireland. We saw it, we liked it and we stayed. He said that he felt right at home. So we made a few enquiries, and opened up shop as a wheelwright and blacksmith's business. Even though there are others in the town who do that sort of thing, the prospects are still good. The railway will require much ironwork and the farmer's co-operative will probably build a brand new butter factory. George is also interested in specialising in farm machinery. He reckons there is going to be a big push towards changing from the old wooden ways to iron and steel. Says it's got to come, that steel is just so much stronger and more pliable than wood. So far, so good! We have rented premises across the road near the station, backing onto the railway, and we are working hard to make a go of it. The business is slowly building, and we reckon that it won't be long before we earn a good living because George's work is good and his prices are fair. So it looks like we're not going anywhere for the minute. We like it here!'

Maggie smiled, took another sip of her tea, and with Ethel remaining silent, finished her story. 'In the meantime, I'm taking on domestic jobs like this one to tide us over until the business is up and running. Your husband engaged my services to help him organise things and I have enjoyed doing it. It's like playing house when I was a little girl. You have such a lovely new home to work in.'

When it was revealed that her helper was married to an Irishman, had Irish parents, and, on top of that, had three burly Irishmen sleeping in her shed, it was as much as Ethel could do to apply the 'bite your tongue' rule. She'd never been in a room by herself with a person of that nationality before, and she had to admit that she was more than a little nervous. She herself was of English descent and the English had absolutely no time at all for those uncouth Irishmen who were clearly inferior and, to make matters worse, most of them were Roman Catholic. She couldn't understand how Christie would have put her into this awkward position. 'Hmmm! Well, good luck to you Mrs Brown. I hope all goes well,' she said, clearing her throat and standing up to take her cup to the scullery. 'But this is not getting the house sorted, is it? Best we get on with it. You know what they say – well begun is half done. What if we unpack this box with the kitchen things in it first and then, next time, we can have a cup of tea made in a teapot?'

Sensing disapproval in Ethel's tone, Maggie's lips tightened. 'Whatever you say, Mrs J. You're the boss. Let's see if we can hit this on the head by lunch time.'

So the two women began working side by side in Ethel's new kitchen, unwrapping crockery, cutlery, glassware and kitchen utensils and finding a spot for them. Maggie, quickly recovering her cheery disposition, chatted away, exclaiming on this or that or the other as it was revealed once unwrapped from its newspaper, blissfully unaware of how ill at ease her companion felt about her Irishness.

CHAPTER 7

As they worked it became obvious to Ethel that Maggie was
a country girl with an open and honest soul and who
harboured no agendas. She was completely unaware of
wickedness in the world and just spoke as she thought and
worked as she spoke. When they had all but finished in the
kitchen it was gone midday.

'Let's take a break and grab something to eat,' Maggie
suggested. 'I have to go and prepare Mr Brown's midday
meal. He works hard you know, all that lifting and pounding,
so he will be starving and looking out for me. Would you like
to come with me, Mrs J? You could meet George and share
our meal. He'd love to meet you and I have already prepared
the stew. I put it to slow cook on the hob before I left this
morning. It won't be anything flash, mind you, but it will put
a lining on your stomach and take you through until you get
finer fare at the boarding house this evening.'

Ethel hesitated, dreading the proposition of actually sitting
down to dine with a real live Irishman. It didn't bear thinking

about, but she didn't want to offend the good-natured Maggie.

'By all means, you go and see to your husband, Maggie. I won't impose on your kind hospitality at this time, but thank you all the same. I will stay and fiddle about here a bit, there's plenty to do, and I am not really hungry. Perhaps I will walk with you to the General Store to buy a few provisions, and I shall come back here and make myself a cup of tea.'

The two women took off their aprons, adjusted their hair and clothing and stepped out together into the autumn day, Maggie to go home to feed her hungry husband, and Ethel to run the gauntlet of the inevitable excitement her appearance in town would undoubtedly bring. Their ways parted on the corner of Contingent Street and Main Street at the General Store. It was a double fronted affair with the grocery department on one side and the haberdashery on the other with a passageway running down the centre. There was a storeroom out the back that separated the shop from the house where the grocer and his family lived.

The bell sounded when Ethel opened the door and entered and all eyes turned to examine the new lady in town. Ethel was a little taken aback as she hadn't really expected to be the centre of interest. However, her impending arrival had been the subject of gossip for the past week or so as the townspeople had observed the completion of the new house and its adjoining Printer's Office with interest. People were very curious indeed about this family who was coming to live amongst them.

Ethel removed one glove, holding it lightly across the palm of the other hand and quietly waited. While the customers in front of her bought their provisions she took a seat and looked around. The typical grocery smell of spices and honey was evident; the walls were well stocked with bottles and tins containing an array of products, all with labels, neatly written in capital letters describing the contents. On the wooden counter was a large basket containing straw, amongst which lay dozens of hen and duck eggs with a sign saying one shilling a dozen. A tightly strung wire whisked the money from the counter to the cashier who occupied prime position, high in the middle of the two departments, over looking proceedings on the floor beneath. A very prim looking lady took it out, tallied it and placed the change and a docket into the capsule, whizzing it back to the grocer who was waiting patiently to hand it to his customer and complete the sale.

Two pretty young girls hustled about, packing bags of flour and sugar, fetching honey or treacle from the vats out the back and helping to fill out orders. Anthony Albert Bernicke, an imposing figure, presided over the front wooden counter, arms stretched wide in welcome as each customer came in, always having a personal word for the one he was attending at the time, his deep baritone voice singing out the gossip as he cheerfully filled orders.

'How did young Alby get on with the bruised knee that those Bunyip blokes gave him in the practice match last week, Mrs Gilbert?' He was addressing a tall, well-dressed lady who had come in for vanilla essence to add to the custard in her trifle.

'Arthur has got a fine mare in that new animal he bought at the sales, Mrs Tullo. I would have bought it myself if I had the money,' he said to another.

'And how is the old man getting on?' he enquired of a third. 'Is he still suffering badly from the kicking that young bull gave him when he was branding last month? He should leave that kind of work for the young blokes.'

Occasionally he would make a statement to everyone in the shop. 'I hear our good neighbour, old Harry Foley, is about to meet his maker. He'd have nothing to worry about before the supreme judge though; he is a jolly good bloke. Nevertheless, we will miss him. He has been in Trafalgar since the beginning; knows all the ins and outs, a walking historian.'

And so it went on. There was no sense of urgency. It took as long as it took and the customers were happy to wait. Anthony seemed to know everybody and they were quite at ease with him. He was the font of local knowledge. When all before her had taken their leave and left the shop with a nod, a cheerio and a ring of the bell, it was Ethel's turn. She stood up and went to the counter

'Ah, my lucky last customer before we shut for lunch. A good afternoon to you, Madam, and what can I do for you today?' enquired the grocer, good naturedly, wiping his hands on the front of his white apron which had been tied around the waist and at the front. 'You're new in town aren't you?' This was a purely rhetorical question as the whole town knew all about the arrival of the Johnstone family, but he asked it anyway. He leaned forward and rested both hands on the counter, determined to elicit information from the hapless Ethel.

'Yes, I am. I only arrived yesterday.' Ethel was a little nervous, as she wasn't used to such direct questioning.

'And what brings a city lady like you here to our lovely little nook of the woods?' he asked, even though he well knew the answer.

'My husband, Mr Christopher Johnstone, is launching a new local newspaper; we will be occupying the residence next door to the new Printing Office. '

'Yes, we have watched the house being built; Cooky is doing it, isn't he? One of the best builders going around, he is. It's a beautiful house, one of the finest homes in our town. Welcome Mrs Johnstone. Let me introduce myself. My name is Anthony Bernicke, and I'm the man you come to for all your provisions. I'm here to serve you. I know your husband well. I was only having a drink with him last week and he mentioned his family were on their way from town. He was very excited about it, said he'd got the house ready and he wanted it singing with the sounds of children's voices.'

'I'm very pleased to meet you, Mr Bernicke. Mr Johnstone has taken the boys out to the bush for the day while I organise the house and I have just come by to pick up a few staples, but I shall be putting in a bigger order later in the week. Do you deliver?'

'Do we deliver? We'll even unpack it and put it all away in your pantry if you want us to. Of course we deliver. Anthony is my name and service is my game!'

'Wonderful, I shall keep that in mind, but in the meantime can I please have half a pound of tea, a pound of butter, some milk, a loaf, a jar of honey and a pound of sugar.'

'Can do all but the milk. You will have to go over the dairy on the other side of the railway line for that, I'm afraid. But if you hang on a minute, I shall see if Mabel, my wife, can give you a cup to save you the walk.'

And with that he went to the outside door and called in a loud voice, 'Mabel, can you spare a jug of milk for Mrs Johnstone here? She's up at the new house and wants to make a cup of tea.'

'I'll be there in a minute,' called back a voice from outside, 'I'm down at the clothesline but I'll come up and get it for you.'

'In the meantime, let's get you sorted with the things you need, Mrs Johnstone,' he said coming back to the counter. 'Now where were we? Butter, honey, bread, tea, sugar! I'll pack it up and get my boy to drop it down to you. It will save you carrying it. And here's a few boiled lollies for those young lads of yours,' he said, as an afterthought, going to the lolly jar, putting a few sweets into a paper bag and adding them to the items on the counter.

'Here's that milk then, Anthony,' said a cheery, middle aged lady who emerged from the residence at the back of the store, 'and a few slices of homemade fruitcake to go with it. Welcome to Trafalgar, Mrs Johnstone, it's a pleasure to meet you.'

Mabel was round and pink as a strawberry. She had an easy familiarity about her, which made even the newest acquaintance feel comfortable in her company.

Ethel smiled.

'You may call me Mae, I prefer that to Mabel, but call me whatever you like as long as you don't call me late for dinner!' she chuckled.

'I believe you have Maggie Brown helping you with the unpacking,' she continued hardly drawing breath. 'She's a lovely lady. Only been in the town a few months but she fits in like a glove. She's a beautiful singer; she got up at the community singing last week and sang 'Two Little Boys', the first time I'd heard it. She had us weeping in the aisles, she did. It's about two soldiers in the Boer War, the one who got the VC, you know, anyway his mate had his horse shot from under him and this hero got off his own horse, picked him up from the gravel and dirt and rode him to safety through all the shooting,' she hesitated realising from Ethel's expression that she may have been going on for too long, and added, 'I believe you're musical too, Mrs Johnstone. Mr

Johnstone has been asking around about a piano. He thought it might be a comfort to you if you miss life in the city.'

Ethel was taken aback by Mabel's shameless audacity, but, at the same time, couldn't help thinking that it was sweet of her Christie to think of that. For the second time that day Ethel cleared her throat.

'Hmmm, yes, well, I'd best be back to the house. Thank you for the milk, Mae. I shall return it next week when I am organised. And the cake is very much appreciated. So nice to meet you both!'

With that she picked up the jug by the handle, adjusted the doily that was trimmed with little shells to keep the sides anchored and which sat on top to protect it from the flies, and hurried out the door and towards home.

'Oh my, she's a bit 'lah de dah', isn't she?' Mae commented to her husband when she had gone. 'She may have to come down a peg or two if she is going to fit in around here.'

'Don't be so quick to judge, Mae.' Anthony intervened on behalf of his newest customer. 'She's been brought up a lady, that's all. She'll fit in; just you wait and see. Chris Johnstone is a really good bloke. In any case, her money is as good as anybody else's!'

The delivery boy was waiting on the veranda when she got home, so Ethel went inside, cleaned the tea dregs from the kettle, walked outside to fill it with water from the tank, brought it in and put it back on the stove top to boil. She wandered around looking into the rooms of her new house, imagining how it would be when it was alive with the sounds of their busy family of small boys. This was the first time she had a chance to take it all in and she breathed deeply and enjoyed the solitude. It seemed that Chris had incorporated all the things she had asked for, the wide front veranda for sitting on sunny days and warm nights, the generously proportioned rooms, three bedrooms, all set back from the road so that she could enjoy her roses and exotic plants in the front garden, while still having enough room at the back for a vegetable and herb garden and for the boys to play. The house was lovely, all any woman could wish for. She had lived in both a grand house with many rooms and a small, three-roomed cottage, but this house was the ideal compromise, not too big and not too small, just perfect. She made the tea, buttered a piece of bread, spread some honey on top and sat at her kitchen table savouring the peace. Outside, she could hear the click clack of horses' hoofs as they carried their burdens down the dirt road in and out of town, and the occasional sound of a train passing through or shunting at the station. The birds sang and the trees rustled. She was daydreaming about the garden that she would one day make when Maggie returned from dinner, calling from the veranda, 'Yoo, hoo! Are you there, Mrs Johnstone? I'm back.'

'I'm out here in the kitchen, Maggie, just having a bite to eat. Come on in,' she replied, brushing the crumbs off the table into her hand, walking to the back veranda and releasing them onto the potato crop.

'My, that didn't take long. How was your husband? Did you have a nice dinner?'

'George was fine, M'am. He's been busy all morning. One of the farmers on the Mirboo Road came in and commissioned him to make two brand new drays, so he has that to do, plus all the small jobs that come in regularly. This morning there was a couple of horses that needed to be shod and he mended a pot for Tim McLaughlin. He's a butcher, you know, and the pot he uses to boil up the lard sprung a leak. He needed it fixed pronto. George was very pleased with

himself, and said if he makes a good job of the drays he is
sure that word will travel and more work will follow. He can
see light at the end of the tunnel and that pleases him. The
Irishmen have gone out to their holding but they will be
back tonight. They'd like to stay in the shed until they build a
shelter out there, so George has said they can stay for six
weeks. That will give them a start.'

This was all said in one breath as she took the pinny from
the back of the chair and laced it around her tiny waist. 'As
for the stew, that was delicious, just what the doctor ordered.
You would have loved it, Mrs J, a good old Irish stew made
from mutton and all the root vegetables and eaten with
bread and butter. George said it was the best one I have
made since we left Mallacoota, almost as good as my
mother's. So that's mighty recommendation. What about
you, did you get what you want from Anthony? And did you
have something to eat?'

'Yes thank you, Maggie, they were very kind at the store.
Mae, she told me to call her Mae, lent me some milk to save
me going across the line to the dairy and Anthony had his
boy deliver my few things. It was here before I got back. I
made myself some bread and butter and a cup of tea,
followed by a piece of Mae's cake which she kindly cut for
me. Now it's time to get back to work, we'll see if we can hit
the bulk of the unpacking on the head by four o'clock. I was
thinking that perhaps the next job on the list might be to
make up the beds so that they'll be ready for us all tomorrow
night. The sheets and blankets are in that crate there, the one
marked "Linen". The children's clothes will be in that other
one.'

At the end of that afternoon their hard work had
transformed the house into a home and they walked down
the street together tired, but pleased with their efforts. They

parted, agreeing that tomorrow they would come back and do the final touches.

Maggie went home to heat up the-left-over stew and to add enough vegetables so that it could be shared between George and the three new boarders.

Ethel returned to the Federal Palace, dined at six and went to bed after saying her prayers and asking the Good Lord to look after her husband and her three sons who were out in the bush somewhere, bedding down on the ground after a day of fishing and shooting. How life flings up small challenges!

CHAPTER 8

The next day, a carriage arrived early at the boarding house to take away the family's trunks that held their personal possessions, the Bible, clothes and keepsakes. The two women met at the house, lit the kitchen fire, cleaned the windows and oiled the wooden floorboards.

As she stood on the back veranda shaking the dust from the cleaning rags, Ethel looked past the ghost gums that stood sentinel at the far end of the block and observed the township that stretched back to the foothills. Houses of the other settlers were scattered along tracks and lanes, some standing alone and others in small clusters of three or four together. Most were small modest affairs made of timber of one kind or another from the surrounding forest. Almost all had a verge of lawn surrounding the house, an orchard of sorts and a garden carved out of the native vegetation. These gardens were the way women of the bush tamed the often-hostile environment and made a home from a shack.

'My garden is a blank canvas, waiting for me to wave my magic brush and bring this barren block to life,' she mused to herself. 'I think I will have a scented creeper climbing up the back veranda posts to keep us cool on hot summers days and fruit trees for blossoms in spring, shade in summer, fruit in autumn and sunlight in winter. I want roses and plants with fragrant perfumes to lift my spirits and a lush lawn for the boys to roll on. I don't want rows, but I want plants that self seed so that they are free to grow in any way and in any place.' In her mind's eye, Ethel could see all of this.

Directly behind her home, a few hundred yards away, Ethel noticed another house that mirrored her house almost exactly, obviously designed and built by Mr Cook, the same builder. It was almost complete.

'Who owns that house there?' Ethel asked Maggie, 'will they be good neighbours?'

'Well, it's the Lawrence's place, so they tell me. I don't know them personally,' Maggie replied, 'but the word is that the old man made some money in Ballarat with the gold while his wife was up in the bush near Tanjil, milking the cows and keeping the farm going. Not that he is saying anything about his newly found riches, but he's moving the family into town and has bought a property on the Moe Road to run some beef cattle. Apparently, his oldest son and his wife will continue to run the dairy farm. I don't know how that will go though as he has just returned from war in Africa and he has lost a leg. He was on the same train as you came in on yesterday. Poor man might find it very difficult.'

As they talked, they distributed the contents of the trunks throughout the house. Photos of the boys as babies and one of her and Christie on their wedding day were placed lovingly on the wide mantelpiece over the sitting room fireplace, while precious vases and ornaments given to her with love by her mother and grandmother took pride of place in the big kitchen cabinet along with the good crockery. The one rug that the family owned was placed strategically in front of the open fireplace in the sitting room and the brown leather sofa and comfortable chairs were arranged so that the family could enjoy the fire and talk to each other. A sturdy oak sideboard stood at one end of the room next to a matching round extension table. Because the window was quite large and it faced west, the afternoon sun streamed in. The walls were papered in a lemon print wallpaper that had a pattern not unlike small bunches of white forget-me-nots. It was a very inviting room.

'I am determined that this room is going to be used every day,' Ethel told Maggie, 'I am not going to make the mistake that I have seen other women making of never using the best room in the house. It becomes so musty and unloved and the only time anyone sits in it is at stressful times like funerals or when the headmaster calls to complain about something that your son has done. I want the walls to be marked with little boys' fingerprints and the furniture to have the odd rough patch from overuse. We are going to enjoy using this room. Just as soon as I see a clearing sale I will buy some more rugs for the floor and some other bits of furniture.'

Maggie had brought with her a huge bunch of white and purple Easter daisies from her back yard and they arranged and placed them in two vases, one each on the kitchen and dining tables. The end result was very pleasing and Ethel and Maggie stood back and admired their work, well satisfied.

'All we need to do now is to await the returning troops. Let's make a cup of tea and move our chairs to the veranda to sit in the sunshine and watch the world go by, Maggie. Isn't it good that we are facing north? This veranda is a little suntrap.'

'I will only do that if allow me to call you Ethel, Mrs
Johnstone, it feels awkward calling you Mrs all the time, like
I am a servant and you are the mistress. I'm just not used to
such poshness.'

'Oh, you do speak your mind, don't you Maggie? My
goodness, I never thought you would think like that, it's just
that everybody, except my family, has called me Mrs
Johnstone since the day we married and I haven't really
thought about it. I'm sorry if I made you feel uncomfortable.
It certainly wasn't my intention, but don't call me Ethel, call
me Etty, I reserve that name for my friends,' placated Ethel,
somewhat taken aback, but, at the same time thinking,
'These Irish are a bit presumptuous, aren't they!'

'Oh, I'm afraid I do! Speak my mind, that is. Comes from
living up there in the bush, I suppose. We're all equal up
there, all relying on one another to keep alive and if we were
to go putting on airs and graces then I shouldn't think it
would last long. Somebody would surely tell you. Sorry if I
offended you, but that's just me, Etty. Now that sounds
better than Mrs J, doesn't it? Besides you were Etty long
before you became a Johnstone, so that's your real name.'
And so it was agreed; they would call each other by their
Christian names and as a result, the relationship became
easier and the seeds of friendship were sown.

'Now tell me about the businesses in town, Maggie, tell me
who gives the best goods and services and where I can go to
buy good meat?'

'The thing about all of that is,' Maggie explained, 'in a small
town the businessmen cannot afford to offend a customer or
give poor quality or service. They would be out of business
in a moment because word travels, so they are all pretty
good. George and I try to spread our custom around and to
give everyone a turn. It keeps the wheels of commerce

moving. George says all the people in town are prospective customers so it's in our interest to make sure that they all prosper. What goes around, comes around, so to speak. We need to look after each other.'

'Good advice indeed,' replied Etty. 'But my main problem at the moment is where shall I buy the meat for tea when the boys get back?'

'Let me think, now,' Maggie applied herself to thought. 'Magnuson's make beautiful sausages and cure delicious bacon. I got all my Christmas meats from them and it was perfect. We could walk down there now and you can pick up something for tea. Then I will take you to Perriman's. He's the green grocer and I'll show you where to find George McCrory the baker. He's on the Thorpdale Road at the end of the shops, opposite the doctor's place, so you can order your bread to be delivered tomorrow morning. If you like, I will dash across to the dairy and order the milk cart to call in the morning. You just put out the billy each day and they fill it up with milk. At the end of the week the milkman picks up the money you owe him. His name is Stan Golding. You'll find that he sometimes has potatoes as well. He'll let you know when.'

And so the ladies finished their cuppa and set out to shop, at the end of which time they parted ways, Maggie home to feed her George and the Irishmen, and Ethel returning to the new house to prepare a meal and wait for her husband and children to come home from the bush. She stoked the fire and added more wood, prepared the joint for roasting and put it in the oven. She peeled an onion and placed that in beside it, a trick her mother had taught her.

'An onion cooking in the oven makes the house smell good,' advised Mother, 'stirs up the digestive juices and gets everyone excited about the meal you are cooking.

Sometimes, if I am running late for some reason, I put the onion in the oven and everyone thinks that dinner is on the way – and it is, but it will just take a little longer than anticipated. There are tricks to every trade!'

Ethel prepared the potatoes and placed them in a saucepan of water so that they wouldn't turn black, peeled and cut up the root vegetables and set about making tomato bake, an old recipe passed to her by her mother.

Tomatoes were in season so she sliced them thinly, added sliced onion, pepper and salt and a sprinkling of sugar. On top of this she spread the previous day's bread - buttered and cubed - and set the whole thing aside to put in the oven later. She peeled and quartered four cooking apples, added sugar and made a crumble out of flour, sugar, butter and honey to go on the top. Just some peas to be shelled and then she would be ready for the onslaught. All done!

She wiped her hands on her apron and was about to hang it up when the patter of little feet on the wooden floorboards quickened her heart. They were back and they were so excited to see her and to tell her all their news. It had been wonderful. They had learnt to pull a gun apart and put it back together again although they hadn't done any actual shooting. That was for another day. They had caught three fish which they had gutted and cooked on the campfire and had played bushrangers. They all wanted to talk at once, telling her all about their exciting adventure in the bush. And they were hungry! Little Vern curled up on her knee to have a cuddle and soon his eyes became heavy and the warmth and comfort of having his mother close by again sent him off into a gentle slumber. It was hard work keeping up with the big boys! Gently she extricated herself, laid him on the sofa and covered him with a rug, tiptoeing away so as not to disturb him.

'You two can have some quiet time in your room to organise your things. There are some bits and pieces in that box there, your books and toys, put them away where you want them and have an explore. Do you like your new house?' she asked, opening the door to their new room and showing them their freshly made up beds.

'Oh Ma, it is truly splendificus and luxurious!' Merv waxed lyrical, always one to try out big words when he got the chance, even if he made them up. 'I think we are simply going to love living in Trafalgar.'

'Don't be such a ponce, there is no such word as splendificus!' said Aub, grabbing his younger brother in a headlock and dropping him onto the nearest bed. 'That's your bed, mine is the one by the window.'

'Calm down boys and be nice to one another. Dinner will be in an hour. Amuse yourselves and I will call you when it is ready.'

Ethel busied herself by bringing water for the boys to wash up and get ready for tea,

She went into the kitchen and put the vegetables in with the meat and the tomatoes and apples in the oven with them, thinking to herself that this dinner would not be perfect, as she was not used to this stove. It would take time to learn its moods.

'Where's your father?' she asked the boys.

'He and Jimmy are next door at the office. Father said to call him when tea is ready as they have things to do. We had so much fun, Ma. Father really knows a lot of things about the bush and Jimmy says he was born and bred in the hills and we went to sleep in our clothes and didn't have to clean our teeth, and I caught the first fish and Jimmy made damper, and Dad said he would take us panning for gold next time.'

Merv and Aub sat on their new beds and told their mother about their first excursion into the great unknown, keeping some things that only the men should know to themselves. They didn't want her worrying and banning future adventures.

With the dinner in the oven and everything was under control, Ethel took off her apron, pinned her curls into place and went next door to say hello to her husband, and to have a guided tour of the newspaper office.

CHAPTER 9

'May I come in?' Ethel called, at the same time tapping on the door of the office.

'Of course, my darling,' came the reply, 'I'll be with you in one minute.'

As she patiently waited at the bottom of the wide step, Ethel was aware of a scuffle of feet and hasty tidy-up noises coming from inside. The door eventually opened and there stood Christie, looking rather sheepish, with his breath smelling of beer. Behind him sat a ruddy-faced Jimmy Kenny sporting a rather guilty lopsided grin while awkwardly trying to conceal a half empty beer bottle with a sheet of newsprint on the floor at his feet.

'Christie, you have been drinking alcohol!' she accused him. 'I wondered why you didn't come into the house. I didn't know that you partook of that poison. What have you to say for yourself?'

Christopher took a deep breath, retrieved his watch from his waistcoat pocket and stared at the time while he considered whether he was guilty as charged or not. He knew from experience that Ethel could never stay cross with him for long when he laid on the charm, so he simply ignored her comments about the alcohol. That could be dealt with later.

'First of all, welcome to the engine room of the "Trafalgar & Yarragon Times", Ethel.' He bowed and bent forward, taking her hand in his, bringing it to his lips and lightly kissing it.

'This is where it will all be happening come May 2nd, in this year of Our Lord, 1902, when we plan to have the first edition out on the streets. Please allow me to show you around, my smart and beautiful wife.'

Perhaps he was lathering it on just a little too much! Taking her hand, he led her to a wooden chest containing many thin drawers. He opened the top one to reveal it was divided into small compartments, each filled with tiny pieces of grey metal.

Christie picked up one of the pieces from a compartment and held it up for her to observe.

'See,' Christie said, 'that's the letter "e" for Etty.'

Etty peered at it. It didn't look like an 'e' to her.

'This is the type – letters, numbers, punctuation- that we use to write stories and advertisements. So tell our valued clients that we are composing the type and it will make them think we are artists, like we are composing a song. We will become hometown legends!'

He chuckled at his own joke. Ethel remained silent as he picked up a small wooden tray. 'What we do is to take the type, letter by letter, and place it into this stick to build the words into lines of type. 'Then,' he said, moving towards a large table-like object with a wheel attached at one side, not unlike a steering wheel on a ship, 'we transfer it to here.'

He waited a moment as she took it all in.

Ethel stared at the machine as if it was from another planet.

'That is called the chase,' he said pointing to a flat bed at one end of the machine. 'We lay all the typesetting down in it and it becomes a forme, containing two pages of the paper.'

He paused and then continued. 'Now, here is the nifty bit,' he said, picking up a piece of rectangular wood. 'Any spaces on the page are filled with these chunks called furniture. They hold the print in place and are slightly lower than the surface of the type, so as not to pick up any ink. They make white space in the paper - very important because it makes the print easy to read.'

'Amazing,' said Etty, her eyes flitting from one piece of equipment to another.

'Ah, but we are not finished yet!' said Christie. 'We keep it tight and secure with these expandable quoins.'

'Coins?' repeated Ethel. 'Money?'

'No, It's quoins, with a 'q', not coins with a 'c'. We lock it securely together and then coat it in ink, put paper on top, turn the wheel, run it through the press, and voila, the page is printed, and hopefully we have a paper.'

'Gosh, Christie!' exclaimed Etty. 'However do you remember all of that? Let me get this right – the letters are made into words that are made into lines. They are then all laid together to make columns, which are laid together to make stories that are laid together to make pages that are put together to make a newspaper. Amazing. It's not unlike James Weldon Johnson's new song about bones - the leg bone is connected to the knee bone, the knee bone is connected to the thigh bone, the thigh bone is connected to the hip bone … is connected to the back bone … is connected to the neck bone!'

She was impressed and happy, so spontaneously burst into the chorus. 'Ezekiel cried dem dry bones, I hear the word of the Lord!'

Jimmy was more than relieved to note that Ethel seemed to have put the alcohol thing to one side. Eager to keep things sweet, he stood up from the chair where he had been keeping a low profile and joined in the singing, urging Chris to contribute. They danced around the new Printing Office, putting their hands in the air and spreading their fingers in the popular minstrel show tradition of the time until the song had run its course.

'All right, that's enough!' puffed Chris, a little out of breath from his exertion. 'This machinery will determine the future of the "Times". If it and we are working well, then you will find, Ethel dear, that I am a happy man. We are planning a trial run next week, so you'll see it all in operation then.'

'So, this is what you have been doing in the past eighteen months, Christie?' she asked. 'It must have cost a fortune to set up. Did you rob a bank? Where on earth did you get all the money for this?'

'First you call me a drunkard, and now you say I'm an outlaw,' Chris declared in mock horror. 'Tell me what you really think of me, my little wifey. Am I really that bad?'

'Of course not, it was just a manner of speaking, but I am curious, where did you get the money?'

'Well, for a start, this here printing apparatus is hardly state of the art. It's really quite outmoded, but will have to do for the time being. They have this machine called a Linotype now that takes a lot of the hard work out of composing, but it will be a while before we can afford one. All the modern printers in the big cities are using them.'

Ethel nodded, not daring to ask what a Linotype was exactly, as she was sure the answer would be very involved.

Chris continued. 'There's a wealthy fellow here in Trafalgar; goes by the name of Mr Alexander Matheson and he's one of your mob, Ethel, a Christadelphian. He runs the services and Bible readings from his home over there by the football ground. It's the one with the iron lacework on the verandas that go all the way around. Anyway, he is well off and lends money at very low interest rates to local businesses to help them get off the ground. It's his Christian way of sharing his wealth. They tell me he was lucky on the gold fields and then invested wisely, but I don't know the exact story. Anyway, I told him about my plans and he liked the idea because he dislikes the other paper in town, says they are bigots because they called him a communist for speaking against British imperialism and the way the Brits go to war at the drop of a hat. Also he has ideas about religion that are distinctively different to most other people's thoughts.'

'And what would they be?' asked Ethel, interested.

'Well he reckons that we all inherit the religion that we practice from our parents, so we all take a very narrow view of scripture, simply taking for granted what our preacher tells us. So, if he is wrong, then we are wrong as well.'

'Absolutely,' returned Ethel, 'that's why I don't follow any organised religion. I go straight to the source and simply study the scripture and form my own opinions. That's what we Christadelphians do.'

'Mmm!' said Chris, a little taken aback. He was always learning something new about his wife.

Bringing the subject back to the business, he continued. 'So, getting back to the story, Matheson agreed to finance me and got a bloke called Frank Veach, who is a barrister from Warragul, to draw up an agreement and it's all signed and sealed. I was able to order the machinery and, the best part is, I don't have to begin payments until this time next year. He said he'd give me time to get on my feet.'

'I am so impressed and proud of you, Christie dear. It is all so professional. You have done amazing things while the boys and I have been spirited away in Mentone with Mother. I am absolutely flabbergasted by all this. In the meantime I have a standing rib roast on for our tea, followed by an apple crumble. Would you like to join us, Mr Kenny? There is plenty to go around and you can all relate your bush adventures for me.'

'Thank you, Ethel,' said Jimmy. 'I may call you Ethel, mayn't I? It is gracious of you to ask but I'm afraid, being a bachelor, I am not used to young boys and they have worn me out. Perhaps another time, but for tonight I just want to go back to the boarding house, soak in a bath if there is enough water, and slink off to sleep the sleep of the just. Thank you just the same.'

'Goodness me,' thought Ethel, 'that's two people today who have taken the liberty of asking to use my Christian name. Should I just run with it and not take offence? Perhaps that is the way they do things in the bush.'

'The truth is, Etty, young Jimbo here wants to go and check out his new landlady,' Chris teased. 'He's boarding at the Criterion Hotel and a lovely young thing by the name of Miss Mavis Stewart has taking over the business. Jimmy is a bit toey, he was sent over to help her with her bags the other day and methinks the lad likes what he sees. Seems to have taken a shine to her!'

'She'd be the young woman I met on the train on the way down here when young Merv fell through her carriage door,' Ethel informed them and told them the story. 'She's a very smart looking lady, and extremely well dressed. I was introduced and she kindly invited me to dinner at her establishment when she gets settled.'

She glanced at Jim and noted that he was blushing. Perhaps he was interested in Miss Stewart in a grown up sort of way.

'There you go Jimmy,' said Chris. 'Ethel just gave you a conversation starter, so off you go to your Miss Stewart. I'll just do a few things here, and I will be over to the house in ten minutes, and you can show me what you and Maggie have done while we have been out of town.'

With those dismissive remarks, Ethel took her leave, returning to the kitchen where she opened "The Sweet Girl Graduate" by Sarah Ann Curzon, a feminist play she was reading, and became absorbed in that while waiting for her husband to return.

'You have done a magnificent job, beautiful Ethel,' called Christie later as he came through the front door, happy to be home. He walked down the central passage with the two younger boys clinging to his arms as they excitedly showed him the furnished rooms and then led him into the kitchen where the roast was emitting the reassuring aroma of family. 'It looks and smells like a home already,' he added. 'You have done a great job pulling it all together. You must be weary, Etty.'

He kissed her and from behind his back he brought forward a damp hessian bag.

'The boys and I have brought you a little house warming present from the bush. They're to start your new garden.'

'Oh Christie, what is it?' asked Ethel a little apprehensively. 'Please tell me it's not a snake.'

'No, not a snake, silly woman,' Chris laughed as he gently unfolded the bag to reveal several varieties of ferns, roots and all, including half a dozen very small tree-ferns. That morning, before they had left the camp they had dug them up from the gully.

'We can make a fernery on the south side of the house where the sun doesn't shine, perhaps by the washhouse there,' he said. 'First thing in the morning I will add some more soil and put them out under the tank-stand to take root. Then, when they look strong enough we'll plant them out.'

'Thank you, Christie and thank you boys! That is very thoughtful of you and I love them. Ferns! We will be able to sit in amongst them on a hot day. And Christie, thank you for planting the potatoes to prepare the soil. Our garden will be beautiful. I didn't realise that you liked to garden.'

'I was brought up on a farm, Etty,' Chris replied. 'If we didn't grow things, the family starved. I don't like it much, but I know how to do it. The garden is your domain, Etty. I will help with the heavy work.'

Ethel imagined the cool fernery, perhaps by a little pond where goldfish swam and water lilies grew. They would sit there on a summer's evening and listen to the frogs sing. She turned to attend to the roast in the oven. 'Christie, the house you had built for me is just wonderful and I thank you. It is such a beautiful home and I want us to use it and enjoy it.'

If Chris was thinking that his gift had distracted her thoughts regarding the alcohol, he was wrong. She was not going to let him off so easily. After dinner when the boys had said goodnight, she broached the subject.

'And tell me, Christopher McCallum Johnstone, when did you begin drinking alcohol?' She asked the question with a steely look in her eye.

'Ethel, I was only having a beer with Jimmy as a way of a thank you for his coming away with me and the boys. He was wonderful out there in the bush. I couldn't have done it without him. He is a real bushman and has a lot to teach the lads. The man has a heart of gold and I count him as a true friend. I consider that I could not have a more reliable or more able business associate. He is true blue. The boys had so much fun.' He paused, considering what he was going to say next.

'And as to when did I begin drinking alcohol? Well, to tell the truth Ethel, I have always enjoyed a drink, ever since my dear old Dad took me to the local pub and bought me a cooling ale on my twenty-first birthday. There is nothing better after a hard day at work than a pint of the amber liquid. The old man did warn me though.'

Chris applied his father's Scottish brogue and went on, "Sonny, the drink can be thy friend or it can be thy enemy. Consider it a privilege, laddie, to be able to take a drink in moderation and use it to enjoy thy life and thy friends. Aye, lad, I've seen it be the ruin of many a good man who never knew when to stop and who drank on until damnation. Ye can become a slave to it, lad, so be mindful."

Reverting to his own voice, Chris continued, 'I have taken his counsel. Ethel, I love to imbibe, but I do know when to stop, you have to trust me on that point. Besides, I have been down here in Trafalgar for eighteen months all by myself and I would have gone insane if I had been deprived of the company of the boys in the pub. Would you have preferred me to pine away in a lonely room? In any case, going to the hostelry is good for business; you meet other businessmen and make contacts there. That's where I met Jimmy.'

'That's all very well, Christie, I'm surprised to see you partaking, that's all. And I certainly don't like you sneaking around drinking behind my back. You didn't think I would know about it, did you?' she admonished him. 'We are married Christie and I disapprove of secrets; we must be honest with each other. It is entirely your decision as to whether you wish to drink or not and although I firmly advise against it, I will not stop you. But if you do wish to take a drink at the end of the day then please, bring your friend home and drink it in the comfort of our lovely new sitting room with your family around you. Please, don't go hiding around corners.'

'All right Ethel. I have heard you. You never cease to surprise me. Other women would throw me out on my backside for bringing drink into the house and here you are, telling me to do just that, and to bring my inebriated friends, as well. That's what I love about you! You are so unpredictable; you keep me interested. So from now on I shall do what you ask. You speak and I shall obey!'

He bowed over at the waist as if in homage. She came to him and straightened him up with a laugh, twirled him around and then did a little curtsy.

'If I don't tell you, you can't know, and at least I speak my mind,' she said. 'But please, promise me one thing. Don't ever get one of those giant red proboscises that gentlemen who drink too much whisky seem to acquire by the time they are fifty. I don't want to be waking up next to that each morning.'

'You won't my dear. I never touch spirits. I am purely a beer drinker in summer and a stout man in winter. You don't get red noses from that, just a nice comfortable stomach to drape my fob watch across. I shall look positively affluent when I am fifty, you wait and see.'

He put his arms out and she relaxed into them enjoying the feeling of warmth and protection of his solid Highland frame and taking comfort in the knowledge that he loved her and she adored him.

'You are a wonderful man, Christie Johnstone, and I am proud to be your wife.'

Things would be fine once everything was settled. They cuddled and made up, ready to begin their family life in their new home in the little town of Trafalgar.

CHAPTER 10

The days that followed were busy. Ethel made lists and, in stocking the pantry, she learnt some of the names around town that would in the future become so familiar to her. Settling Aubrey and Mervyn into school was easy. They were eager to be amongst other children and to take their places on the rough hand-hewn benches of the classroom to make new friends, as children so easily do. It was a functional building, sitting in the middle of an unfenced paddock. To get to it they could either cross a couple of pastures on the outskirts of their side of town or they could go the long way, down Main Street and up Contingent Street over Kitchener Street to School Road. Of course they took the short cut, but they weren't alone. To the side of their house was an empty paddock and along the fence there was a well-worn path that most of the children from the eastern side took to and from school.

Ethel was keen to impress upon her boys the importance of learning, so there was no doubt as to what was expected of them. They were to listen and to ask questions, do their work to a high standard and not make any trouble for the teacher. For two happy, spirited boys, that was a tall order! Trouble was, Vernon, just four years old, was left hanging around the house with no playmates, pining for his big brothers. Ethel made an appointment with the headmaster, Mr Palmer, to discuss the matter. 'I know he is not at full school age, yet, Mr Palmer,' said Etty. 'But he is a bright little boy and takes things on board very quickly. And he is so missing his older brothers. He's at a loose end at home and school will be good for him.'

After consideration, it was decided that Vern could join the classes in the Infant Room, and so he started school at an early age. Because he was so used to keeping up with his older brothers, he settled in very well.

On all but the darkest winter days, when the boys arrived home after school, they had a bite to eat and disappeared out into the back paddock to join the Lawrence's and other neighbourhood children, playing games of cricket, chasey, hoppy, skippy and assorted ball games, the relatively new code of Australian Rules football amongst them.

Many of the farm children had already done a day's work by the time they arrived at school, having been up early to milk the cows and do the farm chores before riding a pony or walking several miles for their lessons. For these children school was a welcome rest as, at the end of the day they arrived home to more milking and more chores. On some days when she had the time, Ethel would bake biscuits and stand at her gate offering the farm children sustenance as they walked or rode their ponies past on their way home from school. Sometimes she made toffee. She began to get to know the children's names and was taken by their country honesty and rustic charm. They told it exactly how it was and that appealed to Ethel who had been in trouble all her life for doing just that.

The country children were earthy and hard working but a little mischief was always high on the agenda - birds dropped out of the sky when a well aimed slingshot hit its target, many a time the pounding of hoofs in the lane next door heralded a race for the Main Road, and the side paddock was often the designated venue for fisticuffs. The cry would go up, "Fight on! Fight on!" and children would emerge from seemingly nowhere, form a circle around the feuding pair, and barrack.

It was not always boys who did the daring things. One day, Ethel had to rescue little Eileen Donovan, who fell from her horse when the Bourke girls, Therese and Margie, put a thistle under the saddle of her pony, causing the animal to buck and throw her off. They thought it was a jolly gag and enjoyed the whole scenario, but the pony was upset and so was the little girl.

Ethel picked her up, brought her inside and attended her tears and her bloodied knees.

'Let me take you home, Eileen, where do you live?' She applied Mercurochrome and a bandage and handed her a sweet from the lolly jar that had been hidden at the back of the food cupboard, away from hungry little boys.

'Out on the Seven Mile Road, but it's a good way, about a mile and a half.'

'Never mind, I shall accompany you and if we see those naughty girls on the way, I shall give them a good talking to,' replied Ethel.

Calling to the older boys that she would be gone an hour or so, she took young Vern's hand and with Eileen leading Ned the pony, they headed off. They had only gone about half way when dust stirred up on the road ahead indicated a cart was moving towards them at a good speed. As it drew near and slowed down, Eileen remarked that it was her Mammy. 'Whoa! Steady!' the woman cried as the horse came to a stop. 'Eileen, where have you been? I was worried about you. I'm cross with Jack because he came home without you, so I had to leave everything and come looking. Where have you been?'

Ethel realised that this was Annie Donovan, the same woman with whom she had shared the train carriage on her first journey to Trafalgar, and so remarked that the pair had met before. She relayed the sad tale of the thistle under the pony's saddle and her part in the rescue. Of course Annie was extremely grateful and told her so, but she had to get back to the baby who was in Jack's care, and to milk the cows that wouldn't milk themselves. Next time she was in town she would bring Ethel some fresh eggs.

'But please,' she begged, 'don't be too hard in your judgement about the Bourke girls. Dick, their father is very sick and in awful pain with gangrene in his leg after a horse kicked him. He's been ill for over a year now and I think it's touch and go with him. Their mother already has an awful lot of worry just keeping things at the farm going and making ends meet. Therese and Margie work like men in the milking shed, they must fall into bed exhausted each night. No wonder they need to play a bit, even if it is at my Eileen's expense. They are good kids whose family has hit bad times. I only hope that they don't lose the farm.'

Ethel agreed to keep her counsel. 'If that's what you think is best, Mrs Donovan, then I shan't do any more about the matter. I shall let it rest.'

Bidding them goodbye, she turned to head for home, happy that she had done her good deed for the day. When she returned, the boys were in the back paddock kicking a ball back and forth and tussling each other for possession. She had once seen the men playing a game of football on swampy ground near the Mentone Coffee Palace. It seemed to go on for an eternity with players from both sides milling around the funny shaped ball that wasn't round but elongated. Every now and then someone would pick it up and boot it with his foot; there would follow more pushing and shoving until the same thing happened again. Sometimes the man in white blew his whistle and tried to bounce the wretched thing. Barrackers on the sidelines seemed to hate this man and loudly told him so. At the time, it seemed to her that it was a lot of argy-bargy, and she would have continued through life quite happily if she never saw another match.

It was therefore a surprise to learn that this code of football was of immense importance in Trafalgar and, even in the off-season, was often the main topic of conversation amongst both men and women. There was great goodwill towards the town's team. Over the years that followed she would be seeing a lot of football and sometimes even she felt compelled to abuse the poor man in white.

'It's a grand game. I love it,' said Christie, when asked why there was so much excitement about the opening of the forthcoming season. 'We play every second game here at our oval at Waterloo Road, on the other side of the tracks, and every other game, we play away. Our strip is red and white and the boys wear black sporting trousers for a home game and white ones for an away game. It helps to distinguish the teams. We call ourselves "The Bloods."

'My, what a rough and tumble name,' said Etty.

'Well, it's a man's game, Etty. Jimmy is what they call a ruckman because he is fast and can jump high. He plays a good game but reckons he only has one or two seasons left in him. He is getting too old and it is starting to catch up with him.'

'Ah,' said Etty, her hand automatically going to her mouth, 'is that how ..?'

'Yes, that is how he lost that front tooth of his. An elbow in the mouth from the opposition.'

Ethel groaned in horror. 'Can't he do anything about it?'

'To replace a tooth like that would be very expensive, my dear, and besides, I think sometimes Jimmy wears it as a badge of honour.'

Chris warmed to the task of informing Ethel about his favourite topic.

'We play teams up and down the railway line like Moe, Yarragon, Warragul, Bunyip and Morwell. So on an away day the team and all the supporters travel to the game on the train. It will be a great day out for you and the boys. Everyone goes. You won't find many people left in dear old Traf on an away game day. I'm too old to play now, but I am on the committee down at the club and last year when you were in Mentone, I had to pull on the boots a couple of times and play for the seconds because they were a player short. That only proved to me that it's a young man's game. I pulled up sore as can be and took a couple of weeks to get over it. It can be pretty rough and things can get heated. Last year Bunyip cheated us out of four points.'

'Cheated?'

'Yes, they had their Secretary write to our bloke and tell him that they couldn't field a team, so not to make the trip. Then, when we didn't turn up, we lost the points. Everyone was outraged because we missed out on the finals by those four points. It'll be a grudge match when we meet them this season, mark my words. We have a bit of angst with Warragul as well; they don't like us and we don't like them.'

Listening to Christie's excitement about the football, Ethel realised that her Wednesdays in winter would be well accounted for. They were living in this town and may as well embrace its ethos. She must set to and knit red and white jumpers in team strip for the each of the boys.

'And what about the girls?' Ethel asked. 'Is there anything in the town that the women can do for recreation?'

'Well, let's see,' said Chris, stroking his chin and giving the matter consideration. 'There are stacks of things you can do once the season gets into full swing, Ethel. The ladies make afternoon teas to sell at the home games to make money for the club, and there is always a raffle each week outside Bernicke's General Store; the ladies organise that and sit there all day Friday selling tickets. Plus there are the jumpers to wash and take care of; sometimes they need darning, also the ladies scrub out the dressing rooms. You'll find that there is some function or another almost every week. The ladies prepare the local hall and make the suppers for those, and then clean up after it's over. The funds raised all go to the club. At the moment we are trying to get enough money together to put in some decent drainage so that the ground doesn't become a quagmire. Ernie Nurse, he's one of the butchers in town, donates saveloys from his butcher shop that his wife cooks up in a big copper behind the footy shed. She puts them in a long bun, sloshes tomato sauce on them and sells each one for a penny; they call them 'hot dogs'. Apparently they have done that for years. So don't worry, my dear, you will have plenty to keep yourself occupied. There's always something for the ladies to do at the footy club.'

That wasn't exactly what Ethel had in mind! Nevertheless, she took it on board and later made some discreet enquiries about recreation for herself. She was delighted to find out that the nearby town of Yarragon boasted a Literary and

Debating Society that debated issues of the day in a friendly manner. She joined, and was given her debate for the next meeting to be held in the dining room of Gordon's Hotel in three weeks time. The team she was on would take the negative of the proposal that 'dancing is a sin.' She was fine with that because she and her Christie loved to dance but she had never been on the premises of a hotel before so that was going to be a steep learning curve.

Miss Stewart, from the other establishment, had also put her name forward to join the debating. She was on the opposing team and was wryly amused at Ethel's timidity in the matter of stepping into a place that sold alcohol.

'Don't be put off by the soothsaying of the do-gooders,' she counselled. 'It is just a room like any other, except that we are on licensed premises. I have taken on a lot just convincing people in the town that a hotel is not necessarily a house of iniquity. Nobody is going to take you and force alcohol down your throat if you don't wish to partake, but you will find that the room is comfortably furnished and warmer and more convivial than in a public hall.'

'Of course,' Ethel agreed. 'But I can't help my reservations. I was brought up to be wary of alcoholic beverages and public houses. I know the Victorian era has passed and I must free myself from those shackles. And I am trying!'

'Of course you are. And I understand. But for myself, I am finding it an uphill battle to change people's opinions. I am refurnishing my hotel in an elegant and modern manner, where townspeople can eat in the most auspicious conditions. It will take time to build up a loyal group of regulars but, you will see, one day the crowds will come and patronise me.'

'You should consider an advertisement in Christie's paper telling people what you are doing, and inviting them to come and see for themselves.' advised Ethel.

'I shall certainly consider that, Mrs Johnstone. I know that if the glories of my establishment remain a well-kept secret then my future in this town looks bleak. I am really very proud of the ambience I am creating and I know my hotel premises make the best venue in town for smoke nights or musical recitations. Come and see for yourself. Please be my guest and come for luncheon with your husband, perhaps we can achieve a barter arrangement until things get better for us both.'

'That seems an excellent idea. I shall talk to Christie,' Ethel promised, 'but give me a couple of weeks as I am not ready just yet. There is so much to do just getting the family settled.'

CHAPTER 11

The day of the dummy run dawned. The big litmus test!
Could they do it? Could they do it to a deadline?

They were working on a four-page broadsheet, comprising
local news and notices, national news, international news,
things of topical interest and informative articles to help
farmers keep up with the latest techniques in land
management. It was an ambitious notion and this dummy
run would give them an indication of what was, and was not,
possible.

When Ethel got to the office that morning, after she had
seen the boys off to school and tidied the house, Chris and
Jimmy were in great shape and everything was going to plan.
Chris was bent over a tray selecting type, composing
sentences and passing them to Jimmy who would carefully
gather the lines of type and take them to the wooden cradle
where he was making up a page of print. They were not
entirely sure of what they were doing, but the page was
gradually building up. They were getting there.

'Christie, you are so clever! Jimmy is quite right. Practice does make perfect. But how ever do you know what you have written there?' asked Ethel, scanning the print with her eyes. 'It's all inside out and back to front, probably upside down as well.'

'Well, now my little one, that's another thing that you didn't know about me,' teased Chris, 'I can mirror read, in fact, in this profession you have to be able to mirror read. Jimmy here is learning fast because that is what we do all day. I'll pull off a proof and you can see what we are writing.' He used a roller to run ink over the top of the metal, took a piece of newsprint, placed it on top, and then rubbed it down with block of wood to gather the image. As he peeled the paper back, he declared, 'There you go, only a rough proof, but what do you reckon about that?'

Ethel glanced over it. 'That's pretty jolly good. Did you make up the stories? Where did you get these advertisements, are they real?'

'No, at this stage nothing is real,' Chris said, pausing at what he was doing. 'We have mocked up the advertisements for some of the businesses in town and we shall show them a printed copy of the dummy run to persuade them to buy the real thing. For the first couple of issues we may have to carry some free ads until people get the feel of the product. But not to worry, Trafalgar is a thriving town and once they see how business improves after a month of advertising on these pages they will be lining up at the door to give us their money. Businesses will be begging us for a front page spot.'

'I have no doubt of that! You, Christopher Johnstone, could sell sand to the Arabs and have them ordering more. You have the gift of the gab,' she laughed, pushing her wayward hair out of her eyes. Soon she was busying herself picking up papers from the floor, sweeping, dusting shelves, tidying the front desk and cleaning the windows. By the time they went home to eat their midday meal, things were well under way and the place was beginning to look like a business. That afternoon they would lock the dummy up, put it to bed and print a newspaper.

Chris had worked in enough newspaper offices to know that hand setting print was a time consuming and arduous job. 'I've watched the compositors and printers do this job when I worked in the city, but I didn't really realise how involved it is. Compared to those blokes I am like a tired old draft horse who is required to face up to a field of thoroughbred race horses and just knows that he is never going to be able to run as fast as they do. Printing is indeed a noble craft,' Chris lamented as he endeavoured to master his new trade.

'Keep at it laddie,' counselled Jimmy, 'Practice makes perfect, y'know. In twelve months time those fingers will be dancing across the type. The way I see it is to take your time and try to be accurate; get it right first time. The last thing we want is to have to pull all the letters out to rearrange them.'

Once the printing press was inked and ready to go each sheet of paper had to be individually laid over the cylindrical cover and carefully lowered onto the print. Each time it was rolled through, it responded with a thump. The peace in that corner of Trafalgar was shattered as the printed pages spewed out.

Chris gathered the first copy as it emerged from the press and with great anticipation, took it and laid it out over a table. He and Jimmy eagerly leaned forward and read each word, exclaiming at the clarity of print and the delicacy of layout.

For Chris it was the culmination of eighteen months planning and work, for Jimmy it was the beginning of a new job and a new era, and for Trafalgar a new newspaper was born that would tell their stories and keep the community informed.

The two men shook hands heartily with joy, congratulating each other, 'It's going to be good.'

Chris put his arm around Ethel's shoulder, gave her an affectionate squeeze, and said, 'It's going to be all right Ethel. I think it's going to work. Jimmy and I have a newspaper.'

All afternoon local people were popping their heads in the door enquiring, 'Heh, Chris, Jimmy, what's going on here?' They looked, they wondered and they went away and told others who, in their turn dropped by to investigate. The boys came home from school and, instead of heading for the back paddock as usual, they also came to see. Before they could escape, Chris had them lined up, folding the pages. He even found a little hassock for Vernon to stand on so that he could be at eye level with the top of the folding table.

'This is Daddy's new newspaper,' Ethel explained, ' today is just a practice but next week we are going to print the very first copy of the "Trafalgar & Yarragon Times" and it will tell everyone what is happening in our district. It will have all the news and sport and all the Hatches, Matches and Dispatches.'

Three sets of eyes looked at her in bemusement.

'What does that mean, Ma?' asked Aubrey.

'It means, Aub,' Ethel explained, 'that we will announce all the important things that happen in people's lives – births are hatches, marriages are matches and deaths are dispatches, so everyone in town will know exactly what is going on. You just wait!'

Chris was relieved and elated. He took Ethel in his arms and waltzed her around the confined space of the front office, singing with gusto, "Rule Trafalgar, Trafalgar rules the news," to the tune of the patriotic British anthem, "Rule Britannia."

Jimmy picked up the broom and joined them and the boys left their folding and formed a conga line. Everyone was happy.

That late April evening, as Ethel and the boys made their way across the potato patch to their home, they felt the first chills of winter, with the dew beginning to settle on the ground. The nights were beginning to draw in. Ethel lit the lamp and began to get the boys something to eat.

Chris and Jimmy took a bundle of newspapers and headed down to Gordon's Hotel where they were showed off their handiwork and regaled the other drinkers with the benefits of advertising with their brand new publication. They indulged in a few celebratory drinks, as well.

After Ethel organised the boys' tea and hurried them off to bed so that they would be bright and fresh for school the next morning, she pondered on the significance of the afternoon's events.

'This new venture will be good for Christie, good for the family, good for the town of Trafalgar and good for the surrounding district,' she wrote to her mother as she sat in her usual place by the kitchen fire and reflected on the day's happenings, waiting for her husband to come home. 'It will help process and document public thought and it will give the people of this little town a voice. If we do it right it can be a real source of good in the community. I am so excited by the whole thing and I wonder what I can do to help Christie make sure that it is not just a good newspaper, but a great newspaper.'

She heard Chris before she saw him, the black stillness of the night broken by his rendition of the old Scottish folk favourite, "The Skye Boat Song." As "speed, bonnie boat, like a bird on the wing" echoed through the darkness, Ethel busied herself in her new kitchen, putting the frypan back on the hob and the bacon in the pan. It always seemed a happier world with her Christie by her side; she would never be lonely while he shared his life with her.

'Come in, Mr Newspaperman,' she said, 'come and eat with me the feast I have prepared for you.'

Taking the sides of her apron she made a little curtsy as he entered the room and with a flourish directed her husband to the table where his place had been set.

'Tonight the cook has prepared for you – bacon and eggs - a meal that is pure in its simplicity but one which any king would be pleased to eat. And how, Sir Galahad would you like your eggs? Sunnyside up or head over easy?'

'Aha, thank cook for her consideration and tell her that, of all the meals that I have eaten in my time, bacon and eggs is by far and away my very favourite dish. I love it! And I love you! I will have my eggs sunny side up, because tonight I am feeling just that way.'

He took off his coat and hung it on the nail at the back of the door and went to sit down. Ethel put out her arms and brought him into an embrace, looking up into his hazel eyes.

'I'm so proud of you, Christie, and I want you to know you have my complete support. I will do anything you ask to help you make the paper. It is going to be good.'

'Thank you, Ethel, my dear. I am doing this for you and our boys first, and for the community second. I think it is a worthwhile venture that we have set out upon. May the good Lord bless our endeavours. And yes, I will appreciate your help, particularly on Mondays and Tuesdays as we will be very busy meeting deadlines. It will all evolve in time. Let us eat and we can talk about it.'

And so, at the dawn of their new life Ethel and Chris talked and planned and then they went to their bed, eager to wake fresh in the morning for what awaited them.

This was the first of many Tuesday evenings when their domestic lives would be disturbed by the publishing deadline.

Tuesdays would never be the same again.

CHAPTER 12

A few days out before first publication day, Christopher Johnstone was a worried man. For this all-important first edition, he had bought in national news from an agency in the city, had purchased international reports from a source with world links, and had written a stirring editorial that told his story.

"Trafalgar" he wrote, "is a prosperous place surrounded by a large district containing hundreds of well to do farmers and it deserves to have its own newspaper. The 'Times' will be a mouthpiece for the community and will publish without fear or favour, discussing and debating the issues of interest to, and affecting, the Trafalgar public."

He had even gone so far as to buy a serialized novel called "A Blade of Ribbon" by A. A. Brown, to be run over many weeks and which, he hoped, would keep the readers coming back to discover what would happen next.

All he lacked was local news and gossip!

He and Jimmy discussed the situation at length, for without local news, no-one would want to pay a penny for the paper and, without readers, no businessman in his right mind would pay good money to advertise on its pages. It was a conundrum that they needed to resolve fast. In their planning they had factored in running at a loss for the first two months, but after that the paper must pay its way or they would all go broke. There was little or no slack.

Like the true newspapermen that they thought they were, they had kept their ears and eyes open for topics to write about, but with the deadline looming, they didn't have much that would stir local interest. In desperation, they managed to persuade their mate Arthur Tullo to write a letter stating that the local Mechanics Institute was dilapidated and uncared for; that it suffered from neglect, was an eyesore in the middle of town and an example of lack of civic pride. Perhaps a committee should be set up to oversee renovations, concluded the author.

The general talk about town was that, on the first Saturday of each month, McInnis & Jennings, Stock and Station Agents, would conduct livestock sales at the new Trafalgar Sale Yard. This would be good, as it would bring the farmers in from outlying districts and make the town buzz with activity, so they wrote it up.

Mr Frank Geach, the barrister and solicitor from Warragul, added that he would be in attendance on that same day so the townspeople could seek legal advice. That was news, too, so they wrote that.

Their financial backer, Alex Matheson, was upset about the footballers that were taking a short cut to the football ground across his paddocks, disturbing his cattle. That could almost be considered news!

The paper commented on the relocation of the Post Office. When opened the mail would be sorted and awaiting them to pick it up at their convenience. Now that was good news!

The local member for East Gippsland, Mr Harry Foster, had died and would be buried in Melbourne, but seeing as he came from down Bairnsdale way the locals would not be too interested in that. Still it would take up space and they had plenty of that. For their purposes, it was news!

Young McCrory had executed an amazing run right down the wing to score a goal against Lardner last Wednesday in a football game that Trafalgar had won. That was very good news!

All these items could be considered worthy stories, but Chris knew deep in his being that they would not completely capture the imagination of prospective readers. For the newspaper to be successful, the people of Trafalgar must want to take ownership, but how were these two men to achieve that?

'I don't know what we are going to do, Ethel,' he complained the Sunday before publication, as he sat with her on the front veranda, the smell of the soil of the newly dug potato crop in the paddock opposite filling the air. 'Nothing ever happens in this town, and if it does, no one wants us to know about it.'

'Christie, there are many, many things happening, you just don't know hear about them because you are locked up in that office of yours, up to your ears in newspapers and you never get out and about to know what is going on. Apart from the football, the only other place you go to is Gordon's hotel.'

Ethel pushed her hair back behind her ears as she finished shelling the last of the peas for dinner the following day, draping the tea towel over the bowl to protect them from the insects. For a rare moment, Chris was speechless.

'You need only to stand in Bernicke's Store waiting to be served to find out many of the ins and outs of the town!' continued Etty.

'Do say, do say,' commented Chris. 'Tell me more!'

'Just take a look across the railway line at those potatoes lying on the ground, waiting to be collected and bagged tomorrow. They belong to Mrs Alice Burbill and she has developed a new breed of pink potato that will be more resistant to disease. I even think she has put a patent on them. I bet all the other potato farmers in the district would be interested in that little bit of news. By the way, do you know what makes a good potato? I bet you don't.'

'I do know that you know and that you are going to tell me, whether I want to know or not,' Chris teased. 'Tell me, what does a good potato look like?'

'Maggie let me in on the secret the other day when she was over here to mind the children the day we went to Miss Stewart's for tea. She was going to mash some of Alice's new pink potatoes for the boys and she gave it the 'good potato test'. She cut it and pronounced it splendid.

'She was so funny with her witty repartee and she declared that those pink spuds were good enough to feed to the Pope,' Ethel laughed. 'That girl can make fun out of anything; she has such a happy disposition. The boys adore her. She told them, "Mrs Burbill's pink potatoes are indeed a new and wonderful thing to behold. They are the perfect colour, look at them boys - yellowish white, you can't get better than that. And take a gander at this. My Irish mother always told me that potatoes must have perfect consistency, just moist enough, but not too moist because that makes them gluggy and no Irishman in his right mind would eat a gluggy spud. Now see this, my wonderful young men," she added, rubbing the two pieces and producing froth at the edges. "Froth is good. Don't ask me why but I imagine that a frothy spud makes a better kind of the old poteen that the men liked to drink on a cold winter's day. And the final test is the test for starch and you do this by holding two pieces and allowing them to cling to each other. Clinging is grand." Ethel stood up, took the peas inside and then came back, again wiping her hands on her pinny.

'The other night while we were out to tea and you were talking to Ted Duckett, Miss Stewart told me that Mary O'Connell who lives out on the Moe Swamp came in for luncheon to meet up her neighbour.'

'They were talking about a poor child named Alice Nelson, who was about Mervyn's age and who had been starved to death by her family. Just left to die, the poor little mite and none of the neighbours knew about it until it was too late. Her little body was covered in sores, and she was skin and bone. It is criminal. Mary lived three farms up from the family and can't believe that something like this could happen without anyone knowing. If you ask me the Society for Prevention of Cruelty to Children should be brought into it. In any case that's a story that should be printed if only to make good people aware that there are bad people in their midst and, if good people say nothing then these things can happen again. If you like I can get the full facts from Maggie Brown. She knows Mary O'Connell well as they go to the same church.'

'That's awful, the poor little girl,' said Chris. 'But, yes, that's the sort of story I was thinking about – human interest – we all like to know the ins and outs of things, don't we? That would be good if you can verify what you have just told me Ethel. Have you anything else up the sleeve of yours, clever girl?'

'Well, another man out on the swamp had a stroke and died during the week. I think his name was Mr Hamilton but I can check that from the notice board outside the new Post Office.'

'Good girl, that's the kind of thing people like to know so that they can pay their respects to his family.'

Encouraged, Ethel went on, 'Then, there was the really sad death of Mr and Mrs Price's little one who died of croup in the night. The oldest child ran for the doctor but by the time he got there it was too late. The poor things; the whole family is heartbroken and there are quite a few of them. The little bloke was their youngest and they all loved him to bits, so different from the poor little Nelson girl. They say bad things come in threes and they do.'

'Yes, yes, that's the kind of thing we should be reporting,' replied Chris, 'it's what we call a story of the heart and we all relate and empathise with the family. We know how dreadful we would feel if the same thing happened in our own family.'

'Well,' continued Ethel, 'the saddest story of all is the one I personally witnessed myself. I was down in the doctor's surgery waiting to have Vernon checked out because he had been coughing badly in the night. After what happened to the Price's baby I didn't want to take any chances, so I made an appointment to have him looked over.'

Chris nodded. 'Rightly so, rightly so Etty, better to be sure than sorry.'

'Anyway, this farmer named Claude Lawrence, you probably know him, he has part of one leg missing below his knee and I think the other chaps call him 'Hoppy'. He came in weeping uncontrollably and carrying a baby wrapped up in a blanket. He has some sort of prosthesis now and has thrown away the crutch, but still limps horribly.

'The poor man was in total despair; it was heartbreaking to be a witness. Anyone could see the poor child was dead, he was limp and a blue-grey colour and didn't move at all, but Claude still hoped the doctor could fix it. He'd carried his son on horseback from their farm out on the Thorpdale Road.'

Chris was silent while his wife took a deep breath and continued.

'Apparently the little boy had drowned in the well and he was supposed to be looking out for him because his wife was out in the paddock doing the heavy work. She had to, because he had come back from the war and was still adjusting to life without his leg. He became aware that little Joseph wasn't near him, but swore he could only have been missing for a few minutes when they started the search. They called and looked for him everywhere but could not find him. They found him at the bottom of a well.'

'Oh my god, that is terrible,' said Chris.

'The little fellow fell in head first and his unfortunate father found him with his head stuck in the clay at the bottom,' Ethel continued. 'He was only three years old. It was so very upsetting. That poor man has had to suffer so much already! It broke my heart. This can be such a cruel country. The Lawrence family over the back are devastated because that was their grandson. I made them a cake, but that doesn't help.'

Ethel had tears in her eyes as she related the story. The couple sat there together both deep in their own thoughts, feeling melancholy about the sadness that was around them in this little town at the frontier of this large, foreign, newly settled land. But they were young and optimistic and so couldn't stay depressed for long. Ethel was the first to break from her reflective mood.

'Something else that might interest people, Christie, is the appeal they are having in the town to supply the school with two hundred more library books. You should see the motley collection they have at the moment. The copies of Dickens smell like old dog and have had the print read off their pages. Besides, the library has nothing in the way of the works of modern Australian writers like Henry Lawson or Banjo Paterson. Various people have donated books. Mr Gilbert got up in the pulpit last Sunday and offered to give one pound for every four pounds that the congregation managed to raise. Perhaps you could relay that to people and ask that donations be made.'

'Etty, you are not just a pretty face! You have only been in the town a few months and already you know more about all its comings and goings than Jimmy, who has lived here all his life. You certainly know more than I do.'

'I do know one thing, and that is that your Jimmy is in love. Did you notice how he hung on every word that Mavis Stewart said the other night when we were out to tea? He positively sparks up when she is in the room. Mark my words Christie, they will be announcing the bans before the year is out.'

Chris filled his pipe, tapped it a few times on the base of his hand and contemplated, clearing his throat in a husky way.

'You are such a romantic, Ethel. I very much doubt it, Jimmy is a confirmed bachelor, he told me so himself.'

He lit his pipe.

'Come to think of it, though, I do notice he takes every opportunity to speak her name.'

Another pause, as he reflected and pondered.

'No, you must be wrong! I hadn't considered Jimmy being in love. He told me that he had been let off the hook once and he was not going back there. He is a confirmed bachelor.'

He sucked on his pipe, thought some more, and broke the compatible silence of the black night.

'Women never cease to amaze me,' he reflected, 'how is it that people tell you these things? No one tells me anything like the sad story of the little boy in the well; in fact I saw Hoppy in Gordon's the other day. He was standing by himself at the end of the bar, spoke to no one, just came in, had one beer and hobbled out. I had no idea that he had lost his little boy. Nobody told me. He is a bit of a loner, seems to be finding it a hard to fit in after his time away at war, and his leg makes him different from all the others. He no longer uses the crutch, but has an Army issue artificial leg, which apparently causes him the devil of pain. He just can't do some things the other blokes do. Smithy, his army mate has gone out there to share-farm with him until he gets on his feet, to coin a phrase,' chuckled Chris, acknowledging the pun he had unconsciously made. 'I was talking to him just after the mob of them arrived back and he said that it was the least he could do for a mate, that he had no ties, no family, so he would settle Hoppy and make sure he was all right before he moved on. This will break all their hearts.' Silence again.

'You know,' said Chris, 'the other blokes talk to me about the football and the cricket and the racing. Sometimes they talk about the price of cattle or the lack of rain but they never tell me anything about their families.'

He took a burnt match, dug around at the bottom of the bowl of the pipe, tapped the spent tobacco out and began the process of refilling it again. He then relit it, put it to his lips, inhaled and sat there with the pipe in his mouth, making the 'pppp, pppp, pp, ppp' sound that signalled he was thinking.

113

'Etty, you asked me to let you know what you could do to help me with the paper,' he finally said. 'Well, I'm going to make you my Local News Editor. You, my darling wife, can be responsible for gathering of the local human interest stories. How does that appeal to you?'

'But Christie, I can't write. You are the writer in the family. I am just a wife and mother. I read a lot but I certainly don't write. I am just Ethel Johnstone, housewife of Trafalgar. I don't know whether I can do what you ask of me.'

'Of course you can, Ethel. Of course you can. Trust me, I know that you have a wonderful ability to think and reason. I have seen you take on the best of men in that debating society of yours and you have had them begging for mercy when you applied your scissor sharp mind to the argument at hand. I have no doubt as to your ability. You and I will be a team and you will be great. I will help you but I guarantee you that before this year is out, you will have mastered the craft of writing a news story. Please tell me you will do it Ethel, if only until I can afford to get somebody else.'

That is how Ethel got roped into the family business.

CHAPTER 13

Although it was a weekday, Annie had dressed in her Sunday best outfit for this trip into town and appeared a little unsure and nervous as she approached the reception counter where Ethel was working.

'Mrs Johnstone, my name is Annie Donovan. You may not remember me, but I met you on the train that day you travelled to Trafalgar, and it was my little girl who dropped off the eggs to you on her way to school after you had rescued her from the incident with the pony.

'Why of course I do, Mrs Donovan! And now it is my turn to be embarrassed. I meant to call on you and thank you for the eggs. They were fresh and lovely. You really needn't have done it. It was my pleasure to help young Eily, I would like to think that somebody would do the same for one of my boys. But you know how it gets? I am up to my ears with household chores every morning and now most afternoons I am tied to this office. The men are so busy and are out and about a lot of the time, but Mr Johnstone assures me that it is just temporary and he will hire a girl soon. You don't want to hear my grouches, so I shouldn't complain. Now what brings you to the office, Mrs Donovan?'

'First and foremost, I would like to congratulate you and your husband on the wonderful job you are doing with the newspaper. My Tom and I read every word of the first edition from cover to cover and loved it. I look forward to reading it every week and a lot of other people in the district have told me they will, too. I believe that it will be a very valuable asset for our little town.'

'Why, thank you so much for the compliment,' replied Ethel cheerily, feeling warm inside. 'I shall pass your comments on to Mr Johnstone and Mr Kenny. It's good to hear we are having some impact. And what else can I do for you, Mrs Donovan?'

'Well, forgive me for being bold, but it was Mr Kenny who suggested I talk to you. Jim's parents, Moira and Brendan, are my neighbours and that is how I know Jim. He said you might be able to write something in the paper for me. I suppose you have heard the sad news about John Shaw who was found dead out on the Moe Swamp last Thursday?'

'No, but do tell me,' encouraged Ethel.

Annie relaxed a little. 'John was a decent, hard working man who left behind a wife and eight children in very poor circumstances,' she explained. 'And the community would like to do something to help his poor widow who is bravely coping on the farm, trying to keep things together. The children are wonderful but the eldest is only twelve and there is a limit to what he can do. He helps with the milking and chops the wood. The next one down is a girl. She is a second mother to those children but the family is really struggling. We think the least we neighbours can do is to get some money together to tide Mrs Shaw over, as we would hate to lose a good family like that from the district. So I'm asking you, Mrs Johnstone, would you be so kind as to publicise a meeting at Gordon's Hotel to see if we can consider a concert or something of the kind in order to raise funds that may help to alleviate some of their suffering?'

'What exactly happened to Mr Shaw?' enquired Ethel, 'we don't always hear the news from the farms.'

'Nobody exactly knows really. He was out there working on the drainage works but was found dead, apparently from heart failure. We've had a couple of bad seasons and he was doing the extra work to make ends meet, but in the end, it killed him, poor chap. By the time Doctor Phelps arrived it was too late.'

'That is very sad,' sympathised Ethel. 'My husband is happy to give space to anything that is of local interest. If you write down the date and time I shall get Mr Johnstone to put a notice in next week. No charge for a good cause. I shall even try to get to the meeting myself to lend some support. If I can't go, I'll get Jimmy Kenny to attend. In fact he is here now, would you like to speak to him?'

She called Jimmy and he came from behind the presses. The two neighbours stood at the counter chatting and laughing, obviously familiar and happy in each other's company. Ethel observed them. There was something about this woman that she liked – her frank approach, her honesty, her matter of fact attitude.

'Mrs Donovan, would you care to come over to my house and have a cup of tea before you head home? You have a long walk home in front of you and I would enjoy a break from the counter,' she asked, surprising herself, as she was usually very reserved. Perhaps now that the family was settled and the business was up and running, it was time to make some friends? This lady looked like she was busy enough with her own life not to be interfering with others, but sociable and intelligent enough to be good company.

'Thank you,' said Annie, 'I would enjoy that if you are sure you can take the time.'

Ethel went out the back, told the men she would be gone for an hour, gathered her coat and left the office with Annie.

'You know,' said Annie as they walked through the wilting potato crop in the front yard, 'I'd be getting those spuds out of the ground before they rot and you lose them all. What say I come over with the pick and fork and give you a hand one day next week in return for the notice in the paper? I'd be happy to do it.'

'You don't have to repay anything, but nevertheless I'd really appreciate your help. I have been at my wits end to know what to do about them. Christie put them in before the boys and I arrived, apparently to prepare the soil for planting, but he is so distracted with the paper these days that he has forgotten all about them. I am anxious to get my garden going so it would be good to gather the potatoes and have everything ready to go in the springtime. Thank you for the kind offer, it is accepted with pleasure. Which day do you propose?"

'Wednesday's good for me. Tom, Jack and Jimmy go off to watch the football and so it's just me and the girls at home. I'll bring them and they can help gather the spuds. If you like, I'll also bring some cuttings from my garden and we can put them in and see if they will take root. You know, out here we rely pretty much on all our neighbours for cuttings to get our gardens going. It's difficult to buy plants. There's a man who comes down from up around the Murray River with bare-rooted fruit trees and roses, usually a little later in the winter. Keep an eye out for him. And you can order seed from the catalogues at Bernicke's, but otherwise it's cuttings.

Most people are happy to give them to you, but the odd one is like a dog in the manger and wants to keep something just for herself, a sort of one-upmanship. I can't understand it myself. I always say a little prayer for the donor when a plant in my garden comes into flower.'

'Wednesday is perfect,' returned Ethel, as she busied herself taking the kettle from the hob, pouring water into the teapot and swishing it around to warm it, adding three spoons of leaf tea and then setting it aside waiting for the kettle to boil. 'Our Aub will probably go to the football with Christie, but the other two are really not that interested. They will enjoy gathering potatoes. Now, how do you like your tea?'

She took the tray and they moved to the sunny veranda where the two women chatted away, the first of many conversations that they would ultimately enjoy. They were as different as cheese and chalk. Annie was a farmer's wife, Ethel was the wife of a businessman; Annie came from very working class Irish background, Ethel from privileged Anglo-Saxon circumstances; but their beliefs and politics were similar. They both believed in a fair go for everyone and each had a healthy distrust of the ruling classes. They both enjoyed gardening.

'And what sort of a garden do you propose to create, Mrs Johnstone? Have you a plan?' asked Annie.

'Oh, do you need a plan?' enquired Ethel, rather surprised at the concept, for she was used to established gardens and had never considered that they may have been planned. She assumed that they just grew.

'I'd have to give it some thought, but now that you ask me I suppose that I would like a shady garden where the trees keep the summer heat off the ground. I think they would have to be deciduous because I like the winter sun. And I will plant plants that let me know which season is which –

bulbs and blossoms for spring, water plants beside a pond and special shady spots for summer, fruit trees and roses for autumn and camellias, violets and daphne for winter. How does that sound?'

'Sounds wonderful! Would you plant them in straight rows, in clusters or just anywhere?' asked Annie again.

'A bit of everything, I suppose,' answered Ethel. 'I'd like roses either side of the path to the front door so that I could enjoy their fragrance every time I come or go, and I'd have a carpet of violets underneath. I'd like bulbs that just pop up everywhere and anywhere surprising me. I must have Lily of the Valley because that is my very favourite plant. The fruit trees could be spread around so that they don't catch disease from each other and the exotic camellias and the like will look good in clumps. One thing I must have is a big tree where I can hang a swing for the grandchildren. I don't suppose it will be big enough before the boys grow up. Of course I will have a vegetable garden to make sure my boys grow fit and healthy and I will just put the cuttings in willy-nilly so, like you Mrs Donovan, when they flower, I can say a prayer for the person who gave them to me. I like that concept. So how is that for a plan?'

'It sounds good. You know, I have a little theory about people's gardens,' ventured Annie, 'I believe that a garden reflects the kind of person who makes it.'

'Well, what does my plan tell you about me then? Be kind because I can be sensitive,' joked Ethel.

'I'd say that you are an interesting mixture of conservative and radical, new and the old, modern and old fashioned. The line of roses up to the front door tells me that you like things to be ordered and calm. You like the perfume of roses and violets so you are quite creative and use your senses to feel the world. The fruit trees and vegetable patch tells me you are practical and focussed on your family's well being and the clumps of exotic plants tell me that there is room in your life for new ideas and people, but only after you have looked after your own people. The swing in the tree tells me you are aware of history and what it teaches us, and the cuttings gathered from friends and then left to their own devices to grow says something about not interfering too much in other people's affairs. However, the fact that you pray for the donors tells me that you value friendship. Am I close?'

'Well, I never,' exclaimed Ethel, 'I'm not going to tell you. You will just have to find out for yourself because I hope we will be friends. And, just to seal that friendship, don't forget your promise to bring me some cuttings from your garden so that I can say a little prayer for you when they come into flower.'

'I will certainly do that. I need all the prayers I can muster,' laughed Annie. 'Until next Wednesday, I must be off. I can hear the children coming from school so I shall walk home with Eileen and Jack.'

'I'll walk to the gate with you, and in the meantime you can tell me what other things your studies of gardeners have uncovered? I'm fascinated.'

'Don't take it too seriously,' remarked Annie as they stood up and made their way to wait for the children, 'but I reckon that those people who hide their house behind a hedge, often hide their lights behind a bushel. Or could it be that they just don't want anybody sticky nosing into their business?'

They both laughed.

'And I have noticed that it is almost exclusively male gardeners who have very structured gardens with straight rows of plants and the topiary that makes the bushes look like roosters and cows. My theory is that they are frustrated with their lives and they would like to have more control over what's happening around them.'

'Hmmm, interesting,' remarked Ethel recalling the structured Italianate gardens of Mentone and the people who owned them.

'Then there are the people who start out with wild enthusiasm and make a garden in a couple of weeks and then don't go near it for months so that the weeds take over and all their good work is lost. They are the impulsive kind who never finish anything.'

'Fascinating, tell me more,' Ethel urged.

'Let's see. I can't leave out the kind person, who unwittingly cultivates her garden and is surprised when someone disillusions her by pointing out that the flower she has so lovingly nurtured is, in fact a weed. Perhaps she is the nicest of all because she takes things on face value and is non judgemental. She knows that the difference between a flower and a weed is only a judgement.'

'I like that. Young children often pick a dandelion and give it to their mother with love and they are the most trusting little creatures in the world. To them a dandelion is beautiful. But tell me about the gardener who specialises in growing just one thing?'

'A gardener who perfects one plant, say roses or chrysanthemums, is a little obsessive and likes to excel and get things just right. However, his world view may be blinkered. Whereas, the person who only grows vegetables and fruit trees is extremely practical, and might do well to take the time to enjoy some of life's pleasures. Equally, the gardener who only grows flowers is a bit of a flibberty-jibbet and is probably not at all practical. A well balanced soul grows both and has life's priorities well worked out.'

Ethel was impressed. This was all new thinking to her but she suspected the ideas may have some merit.

'You have thought all of this through,' she commented .

'Yes, it's a little hobby of mine. I have taken note over the years and like to test my hypothesis. There's more! The cottage gardener is a purely emotional soul who finds it difficult to be decisive and likes to hang onto the past. She loves her plants like children and mixes them all in together so that the strongest survive.'

'And somebody who doesn't have a garden at all?' asked Ethel.

'That person has no soul!' Annie concluded bluntly.

They laughed again.

But then Ethel frowned. 'Oh dear, that can't be,' Ethel could not help herself correcting, 'everyone has a soul. Perhaps it is just that he or she is more interested in dogs and horses!'

Before they could get into further discussion, the noise of happy voices could be heard from down the track.

'Ah, here come the children,' said Annie. She opened the gate and stepped out.

'Thank you for the cup of tea, I have had a lovely afternoon. It's not often that I take time off but I had to see to that notice and my sister Kate is down from Melbourne, so she is minding the little ones for me. She'll need a lie down when I get back. Good day to you Mrs Johnstone. Thanks for the cuppa.'

'I guarantee it won't be long before the two of us are on a first name basis,' reflected Ethel as she gathered the tea things and took them inside. 'I really like that lady, she was here for an hour and didn't gossip once. I look forward to next Wednesday.'

CHAPTER 14

Autumn changed to winter and the days drew in. The firewood was gathered and stacked along the back fence. It was Aubrey's job each Saturday to transfer four wheelbarrow loads to the shelter of the tank-stand to keep it dry for the fire.

Backyard fruit was picked from the trees and made into jam and preserves. Home-grown tomatoes were harvested and made into sauce, with the final green ones that still clung to the vines being cut up and made into green tomato pickle. Ethel had none of these duties this year, as her garden was still in embryonic form and she did not know her neighbours well enough to receive their offerings.

The winter rains began and the Moe Swamp once again became a quagmire, dangerous for the horses and wagons alike. It became difficult to get stock and produce to Trafalgar for transportation via train to market, causing great concern for the settlers. The children walking or riding a pony to school slipped and slopped through the mud.

'Your family are out on the Moe Swamp,' Chris quizzed Jimmy one evening after work, as they were enjoying a beer in front of a roaring fire in the lounge across at the house.

'Alby Gibson keeps coming in with notices of this meeting and that, trying to get things done out there. Why do the settlers feel so aggrieved?'

'Well, that puts it mildly,' stated Jimmy, 'they are more than aggrieved. They are mightily disillusioned by the powers that be. The whole thing has been a giant catastrophe from the very start. And most of it is the Government's fault!'

'Why is that?' asked Chris as he settled back in his chair to listen to the answer.

'The blokes in the city released this land for settlement before the drainage was completed. By that time, settlers had come from all over Victoria and had paid their deposits in good faith. It wasn't easy for them because although the swamp is free from timber, it is overgrown with coarse tussocks that have to be burned in summer and then rooted out and turned over by plough and incorporated back into the soil. It is jolly hard work, but they were happy to do it. However,' he said lighting up a cigarette and drawing in deeply, 'the Main Drain is a huge stuff up. Those city blokes have underestimated the tremendous volume of water that it carries when it rains. The important thing is, work on it should have been completed before the settlers were placed on their lands. It's an absolute botch-up. There have been three major floods in as many years and the poor folk out there have had to stand by and watch as their potato, corn and fodder crops get washed away. Sometimes the water has come up so quickly that people have had to run for their lives.'

'Is that so?' Chris queried.

'Yep. Things are bad. Our neighbour, Mrs Donovan, was lucky to escape. She had to hold the two little ones up high over her head. Otherwise they would have drowned. Ask her about it. She says that the water came up so quickly that she took her babies and ran, heading for the highest ground she could see. She said it was terrifying; there were snakes and wildlife swimming for their lives beside her. Like Noah's ark without the boat! The water went right through her house – above the window ledge. She came back to mud and sludge that all had to be cleaned out. But that wasn't the worst of it – they lost almost half their stock. Set them back five years.'

'Was that a few years ago?' asked Chris. 'Have things improved since then?'

'No. It's still happening all the time.' Jimmy was getting his ire up. 'Only recently, McDonalds lost twelve good milking cows that were hemmed in a corner of a paddock and drowned. It's heart breaking. Father was telling me about a new couple who took up a holding a couple of months back. Spent every last penny on buying the land and were told that it would be productive almost immediately. They have this arrangement where they pay instalments every three years. Bill Somerville is his name. The land is so water logged they can't put a plough to it, so they have had to move in to town and wait for summer to do any work out there. He has taken a job working on the roads to tide them over and his wife is doing the laundry at Mavis's place. They can do that because they haven't got children, but it wasn't what they expected.'

'Yes, I know them. They came down on the same train as Ethel and the boys did.' Chris attempted to steer the conversation away from the Swamp as he was beginning to regret having asked the question. It seemed that once started, Jimmy could go on all night about the subject.

'There are good family people who are down to their last penny of savings and all the Minister for Lands can say is "if the present settlers can't pay their instalments then they had better clear out as there are plenty of others waiting for the land." It's a diabolical attitude. They are not asking for compensation, but merely for a concession in time with regard to the next lot of instalments.'

'What is the Moe Swamp?' interrupted young Aubrey who had been copying cartoons out of comics as he lay on his stomach on the floor in front of the fire, 'does it have its own Bunyip like the Mentone Swamp?'

'It probably has,' Jimmy laughed at the thought, distracted from his rampage. 'A great, hairy flood bunyip who pours water from the sky and doesn't mop it up properly! We should capture it and send it down in a cage to those blokes in Parliament. That would put the wind up them!'

They all chuckled at the imagery.

'But to answer your question, Aub, the Moe Swamp is the land lying north of the railway line between Yarragon, Trafalgar and Moe and is about three miles long and one to three miles wide, about thirteen thousand acres in all. Things can get pretty bad on the Swamp in winter.'

CHAPTER 15

The chilly morning mist often hung low over the valley until after ten, ice forming a toffee coating on the puddles created when the rain settled in the carriage ruts that seemed to be a permanent feature of the main and side streets. Sometimes the sun shone through, heralding a glorious day, but there were other dull, dreary days when the wind and rain kept temperatures low and the townsfolk shivered.

By early evening the town was dark and still, save for the area around the station which had street lights and which intermittently burst into activity with the coming and going of a train. In the houses scattered around the settlement that was spreading into the surrounding hills, the curtains were drawn and the fires glowing in the grates. Mothers knitted woolly jumpers to keep their families warm, children played board games and Jacks indoors, and stews and puddings bubbled away on the hob.

Before the boys' bedtime, Ethel warmed bricks by the fire, wrapped them in bath towels and placed them in the children's beds to keep them warm. On a really cold night she would take the overcoats from the wardrobe and pile them onto the bed ends to keep cold feet snug. In spite of this, some nights it got so cold that the boys slept together just to keep each other warm.

The children minded none of this. If it rained they jumped and played in puddles and if the sun shone they kicked the football back and forth, back and forth until their shoes needed mending.

On wet days and evenings the Johnstone boys drove their mother crazy playing a form of hallway football with the cushion that used to be on the crib and which Ethel had kept because she couldn't bear to throw it away. She could put it to her nose and still smell her precious babies. In this game the door to the kitchen and the front door became goals and the aim was to get the cushion through the gap by using only feet. One of the boys would be in the middle and it was his job to wrest it from the others. He could score at either end. Things often got very intense and usually ended in tears but boys would be boys and so Ethel stayed in her kitchen leaving them to sort out their problems.

She went about her family duties as she had done before, but now that Christie had burdened her with the task of finding and reporting the local news, she was always conscious of the newsworthiness of the information she gleaned as she moved about the town doing her messages, transacting with local business people and attending to the well being of her family. She hoped that this did not impinge upon the strength and quality of her daily interactions and friendships, but suspected that the very nature of her new capacity made her an outsider looking in.

Chris was always first one up each morning, no matter how late he had been working on the paper or attending a meeting the night before. He used the kindling that the boys had gathered and stacked on the hearth after school, and he prodded and poked until the fire was going in the grate. He would then put the kettle on the hob, wait until it boiled and take his Etty a cup of sweet white tea.

This all took about forty minutes and it was his thinking time. He used the solitude of the morning before the family roused to consider his editorial for the week, to think about what he had to do that day and to problem solve.

After Etty had sipped her tea she would dress, tie her hair in a scarf and come to the kitchen to cook Christie his breakfast which varied, but always consisted of something and eggs. He needed a full cooked breakfast to tide him through the day for he often did not have time for lunch.

The house on Main Street would slowly yawn and come alive. One by one, the boys would amble sleepily into the kitchen, kiss their mother, greet their father and take the warmest place by the stove to awaken, gently embracing the day. Young Vernon needed the sleep eased from him by means of a long, gentle cuddle from his mother. She would sit in her chair by the stove with him snuggled up on her knee, stroking his curls and talking quietly to him about his dream of the night before, or his plans for the day ahead. A few minutes of this and he would be up and off, engine fired and ready for anything. This morning ritual soothed Ethel and she cherished it because the others were big boys now and were moving beyond cuddling. Occasionally, when the world seemed beyond his control, young Mervyn would take his place on his mother's knee, but these moments were less common these days. How she mourned their passing.

Breakfast for the boys was usually porridge with butter and sugar on top and bread toasted on a long fork in front of the fire. Sometimes they would have a little of what their father was enjoying.

They dressed, gathered their things together and when they heard the first of the country kids making their way to school, they would join the procession and head off. Ethel would be left with dishes to be washed, beds to make and clothes to tidy. With three young boys in the house there was always plenty of clothes washing to do. Muddy items that needed to be scrubbed were left for Maggie on a Monday when she was engaged to help with this task. Getting the washing dry at this time of the year was very difficult even on the days when a brisk wind blew across the valley from the snow covered mountains of the Baw Baws. There always seemed to be clothes drying in the house, draped over chairs in front of the kitchen or sitting room fires.

When the house was spruce, Ethel headed off down the street to buy provisions. She then prepared the midday meal because it was the main one of the day. The boys came home to a cooked dinner, nearly always meat and three vegetables – a white one, a green one and a yellow one. This, her mother had told Ethel, was the secret of a balanced diet. If Christie was out of the office for the day, she put his meal aside to be reheated on a pot of boiling water later that evening when he came home. This was to become one of the rituals of their married life; because it was the only way she could accommodate her husband's inclination to eat at irregular hours.

Her afternoons were mainly spent looking after the office while the men got on with their work, out and about in Trafalgar and district. When the boys came home from school she liked to be there for them. She was able to sneak some after-school time for her gardening, preparing the soil and making small inroads into the task of making a garden from scratch. It was a busy schedule but she was happy.

Every other Wednesday afternoon, the whole town gathered at the oval on the Waterloo Road to cheer the young men as they played football against neighbouring towns. This year the side was boosted by the presence of the three White brothers who were fast and tough. They brought with them the skills of their native Irish code that was not unlike the Australian one.

After attending a game against Yarragon at Yarragon, Chris arrived home visibly upset. 'A terrible thing happened in the last few minutes of the game,' he told Ethel. 'The captain of the other team, a young bloke named Tommy Higgins took a boot in the stomach, but played on and seemed to be all right. Then he collapsed. Poor kid, he was bent over with pain and moaning. My heart went out to him, just a boy, only seventeen years old. They had to carry him home and the rush was on to find Doctor Trumphy to get him to come and have a look at him. We are all concerned because he didn't look too flash, poor fellow.

'The worst thing about it is, that it was one of our players who kicked him, the young Irish bloke who is new to town. There are three of them out on the Swamp on a farm and they have been having a wonderful time at Gordon's pub every night because their wives are still in Melbourne with the children. Nice enough blokes and great barbershop singers. They team up with Patty Linane and they're very good. Anyway, one of the twins had been playing rough all day, real nasty behind the play stuff. The trainers had to come out to another couple of their blokes that he had hurt. It's not the way we want the game played. He should be rubbed out.'

Tommy Higgins died from his wounds and the funeral was scheduled for the following Thursday. Everyone was shocked.

'It was a very sad service,' Chris reported to Ethel over tea that night. 'I can't believe that the young boy can die as a result of playing a game of football. The Yarragon people are very angry and refuse to accept that the unfortunate incident was an accident. They reckon that the White twins had been involved in three previous incidents on that same day and it seemed that they'd been sent out specifically to target the Yarragon players. They're threatening not to field a team against us unless the responsible twin is identified and never allowed to play for Trafalgar again. The trouble is that it is virtually impossible to tell them apart, and they're closing ranks, not telling us which one is responsible, and no one else has a clue. I reckon we'll have to suspend the two of them.'

Ethel listened and nodded. 'I agree. Are they the young men who are boarding with Maggie and George? Perhaps they don't know the rules.'

'It's Rafferty's rules to them.' Chris was angry. 'Quite frankly, those two are running amok. The red headed brother is a good bloke and he does his best to rein them in. But it's an impossible task. They come into the pub and drink too much and get into brawls. They're a nightmare, those two. Tom told me that the sooner their families join them down here, the better. He reckons the wives will calm them down.'

'Christie, I heard down at Bernicke's that Mr and Mrs Higgins have lost their three other sons through misadventure and illness these past two years. Is that right?'

'Yes, Tommy was all they had and now he has died playing football. It is an absolute tragedy and really sad.' Clearly her husband was badly affected by this and Ethel's eyes welled with tears of sympathy. Chris put his hand across the table, took it in his and they sat together in silence for several minutes, contemplating the utter misery that Tommy Higgins' parents must be enduring at that moment.

'I just hope this is a wake up call to those two mad Irishmen. Those pair of them should never be allowed to pull on a boot again. They bring disgrace to Trafalgar.'

Pat and Joe White were banned from the football competition, much to brother Tom's embarrassment. It would take a long time to live this incident down and he was angry. 'Those two eejits would do better to spend their energy on clearing the land and getting the farm up and running so that Bridget and Edna can come down here and keep them under control,' he declared. 'To be perfectly honest with you, I have no hope; they are just out of control and it's a great pity because they are good lads. But put them on a footy field and the very devil himself gets into them.'

The three Irishmen had enough sense to keep a low profile around the town for the next few months. They moved out of Maggie's shed onto their land and only came in every other week for provisions and the mail, knuckling down and clearing the land in preparation for spring plantings.

The Higgins parents grieved and life went on. Nothing would bring their boy home.

CHAPTER 16

The friendship between the Ethel and Annie firmed and, although both were busy with their lives and didn't have a lot of time for socialising, they were drawn to each other. The children were about the same age and got along remarkably well. Young Mervyn who was a poetic kind of child, more interested in books and learning than in football and cricket, formed a quiet bond with Eileen Donovan and the two were content to play make believe and draw while their mothers shared a cup of tea. Jack took Aubrey under his wing, introducing him to the older boys while the two four year olds played together happily.

These budding relationships were cemented about the same time of the social event of the year, the Weller-Dangleish wedding to which Ethel and Chris were invited. It would be their first big outing as a couple since the family had settled in the town.

Initially it seemed that there was no one to mind the children. Ethel was loath to leave them by themselves, even though it was common practice in the bush where the children were resilient and capable. Jimmy Kenny and Maggie Brown, the only people with whom she would have trusted her mites, were also on the guest list. Annie Donovan came to the rescue by suggesting that the boys should be sent out to the farm to stay overnight and she would return them on the Sunday morning on her way to Mass.

'Mass?' thought Ethel. It hadn't occurred to her that Annie Donovan might also be a Catholic. She hadn't mentioned it and she certainly didn't act like one. In fact she was a perfectly normal and likable lady. 'It seems that I am destined to be surrounded by Catholics,' she mused. 'I wonder whether she has all those burning heart icons on the wall and whether she knows I'm a Protestant. It's a bit scary really. But the one thing I am not, is a bigot, so I shall take her on face value and see what happens.'

Giving Annie a way out if she had made the offer too hastily, Ethel inquired, 'Are you sure you have room for all three boys?'

'It's fine. We have plenty of room,' Annie confided. 'When we had to rebuild after the fire, Tom declared that he would make the house big enough so that we never needed to be crowded together again, and so he made a bedroom for each child and one for us. We have a big veranda that spans the whole house so there is always somewhere dry for the kiddies to play. As it is, the girls like to sleep in the one room and we still have Dolly in with us so we have a spare room for when family visits, as well as a music room. We Donovans love a good sing-a-long around the piano. I suppose it's the Irish in us.'

'Oh, I didn't realise that you were Irish,' stated the naive Ethel, a little taken aback. 'It never occurred to me.'

'What? With a name like Annie Donovan? My Tom was born in County Westmeath in Ireland. His mother died when he was only two and his father remarried, to an old crow of a woman, and they went on to have other children of their own. She treated poor Tom dreadfully, favouring the others and locking him out of the house and making him do the work of a grown man when he was only a child. I blame the father. He was as weak as a jellyfish and never stood up to her. He just let it happen and never demanded that Tom be treated equally. My Tom says that the old man didn't know the half of what went on. The old bag was always as nice as pie when he was close by.'

Ethel moved to ask a question, but kept her silence. Annie was in full flight, relating a story she knew extremely well.

'In the end,' she continued, 'it got so bad that the neighbours couldn't bear to see the poor lad suffer any more. So one of them wrote a letter to his aunt, who wrote to her brother who had done well out of the gold rush in Western Australia. He sent the money for Tom's passage. He was only fourteen years old when he arrived in Australia, so he stayed with his aunt who lived next door to my family in Brunswick and went to work on the Sydney Road tramline. So that is how I met him. After that job finished, he came down here to work on the Main Drain and was lucky enough to be around when the first release of land on the Swamp happened. He selected land and came back to town to ask Father if he could marry me. I was only seventeen but we were already in love. Young and silly! If I'd have known what was in front of us I probably would have insisted that we stay in the city, but you don't know these things.

'We got married at the cathedral and he brought me back here to live. Me, a girl who had never stepped foot in the country in her life! I had never seen a cow. I soon learned! Anyway, we knuckled down, cleared the land and got the farm up and running, and here we are!'

She stretched her arms out wide and smiled.

'So that's the story on Tom's side,' Annie continued. 'My mob came out from Ireland, too, to escape starvation in the potato famine, so you could say we're as Irish as Paddy's pigs. My maiden name was Shortis. It doesn't sound Irish, but it is. There is nothing but Irish blood flowing through our children's veins. Do you have a problem with that, Ethel?' Annie asked defensively as she was well aware of the disdain some people held for the Irish.

'Not at all!' Ethel replied almost too hastily. 'It's just that I hadn't come across many Irishmen until I came here. In Mentone, we seem to mix more with the English and the Scots.'

'Don't worry Ethel. I will look after the boys. They will come home in one piece. God willing,' she hastily added, blessing herself. That last gesture did little to reassure Ethel, but nevertheless, she braced herself and put her trust in her new friend.

'Thank you Annie, the boys would love to spend the night on a farm. It will be a new experience for them and it would allow me to enjoy myself without the worry that they may be getting up to mischief. I shall come out and fetch them on Sunday morning; it will save you the bother. What time shall I bring them out to you?'

And so it was arranged that Annie would care for the boys while Ethel and Chris attended the wedding.

The cream of society was invited to the Trafalgar Mechanics Institute to witness the vows and take part in the celebrations. For the first time since she had arrived in the town, Ethel worried about fashion, as on this occasion she wanted to look stylish. She settled on a natural silk, slim fitting skirt and teamed it with a matching, heavily embroidered and laced silk jacket borrowed from her sister

Ella, who was two years younger than she was and almost exactly the same size. She had it sent it down from Mentone on the train and nobody knew any different. Anthony Lawless put her hair up in a giant circle that formed a halo like surround to her face. It was a common do amongst the ladies of Mentone but the first hairdo of its kind ever seen in Trafalgar.

When she was ready to go out Christie looked her up and down, kissed the tops of her fingertips and declared, 'Etty darling, you make me very proud to be stepping out with the best looking girl in the whole of Narracan Shire. Let's go and have some fun.'

She and Christie enjoyed the celebrations. Already they felt part of this community and the townspeople seemed to accept them. They were optimistic and happy.

The morning after, Ethel was up early, dressed and set out to walk out to the farm to collect the boys. The air was brisk; the grass by the road was painted delicately with misty dew that sparkled in the weak sun. She could easily imagine her life unfolding before her, always with these hills as a backdrop. Later that day it would rain, but at this early hour it was grand to be alive.

She neared Annie's house on the hill, with the smoke curling from the chimney, signalling that the kettle may be whistling on the hob and that a cup of tea was not far away. As she drew closer, she was surprised to see washing flapping merrily on the long clothesline out the back.

'Not a very Christian thing to do!' she secretly thought. 'Fancy washing on the Lord's Day? My dear mother would run a mile from a woman who did that, and here I am leaving my children with her family.'

The boys spotted her as she approached, stopped their playing on a flying fox that began its journey from a gum tree on the top of the slope and ran downhill one hundred yards to the bottom of the incline, and ran to greet her. 'Ma, we have had the best time,' they puffed in excited voices. 'Ma, can we come back again?'

Annie came from the house, undoing her apron as she approached. 'The boys have had a wonderful time,' she told their mother, 'they rode Barton the pony, helped with the chooks and gathered the fire wood, ate well and then last night we had a bit of a hooley and a sing-a-long. Eileen plays piano, Jack the mouth organ and Tom is a great fiddler. The Irish lads from up the road dropped in on us. It was grand. They were showing the kiddies how to do the Irish jig. Feet banging out the rhythm on the floor, but hands perfectly still. It's hard to do! Young Mervyn is a comedian. He caught on quickly and had us all laughing. He loves a party. 'And my word, young Aubrey has a wonderful soprano voice. It's beautiful. I could have listened to him all night, but he only knows a couple of songs. We'll have to expand his repertoire. Now tell me about the wedding?'

'It was wonderful,' replied Ethel. 'Young Grace is so beautiful she would look good in a hessian sack; she has a languid beauty and so much grace and charm. Of course, James Weller was like the cat that got the cream; he could barely keep the smile from his face. He is indeed a lucky man. The talk of the evening was about the gold brooch shaped like a magpie in diamonds and black opal. Would have cost James a fortune. The story goes that it was a magpie that brought them together. Apparently he went to Grace's rescue when a very angry mother maggie swooped her. He was the hero, diverting it so Grace was able to escape. Funny how these things happen! Everyone sees it as a match made in heaven. Down the track those two farms could be joined to make one big, wealthy farm, no doubt.'

'Money attracts money, I suppose. Those two families are certainly the aristocracy around here.' Annie was dismissive and ever practical. 'I suppose if you have money you have time to think about romantic ways to spend it. Tom is too busy putting bread and butter on the table to be buying me brooches. He says that one day when we are rich he will buy me a tiara if I want it. Can you imagine, me milking the cows in a tiara,' laughed Annie.

'I suppose they received some lovely gifts?' she then inquired.

'The wedding presents were all very nice,' said Ethel. 'Christie was asked to make a list of the givers and the gifts to publish in the "Times", so you will be able to peruse it when the paper comes out. I find it funny that they would publish a list of gifts.'

'No doubt it keeps everyone on their toes so they won't be seen to be giving less than the next Joe,' Annie replied.

'I don't think they do it in the city,' reflected Ethel. 'In any case, I know we didn't! Anyway, the young couple went off together on the last train, but we all went back to the hall and the dancing continued until well after midnight. Christie and I had fun. It was a great night. And I have you to thank you for having the boys, Annie. It was a lovely thing for you to do.'

She leaned forward and kissed her on the cheek. 'You are such a precious friend. I am glad I found you.'

'Come on, let's have that cuppa.' Annie led her friend into the house and began the ritual of making a cup of tea. She laid out a tray and placed it on a battered wooden table on the veranda, and went back into the house to bring out two kitchen chairs. Ethel stood watching the children whirl past to the bottom of the hill, pick themselves up and run up to fly down again and again.

When they sat down together, Ethel needed to get one thing clear. 'Tell me Annie, do you always wash your clothes on the Sabbath Day?'

Annie was taken aback by the question and its implications, but nevertheless she was not going to be judged by other people's standards and came out all guns blazing.

'Now you tell me Ethel, what am I to do? We're out here in the middle of nowhere, the children's clothes need cleaning for school tomorrow, I have been out in the paddocks helping Tom grub tussocks all week and next week we have to get the stock ready for market. With four children, washing is a big job. I need help, and Sunday is the only day that Tom can give it to me. Besides Tom, me, and the baby were up and into the six o'clock Mass this morning, so I've done my bit for the Lord today. If you want my opinion, and I'll give it to you anyway, these Protestant rules have got very little to do with religion and were made for the English upper classes who have never done a day's work in their life. They had servants to do it for them. I do my washing when I have time to do it, and I don't care what the neighbours think.'

'Please forgive me, Annie dear, I'm such a prig. Of course you're right. I must go home and see if I can find a verse in the Bible that says nobody is to do washing on a Sunday. I'll ask Mr Matheson at Bible Class this afternoon, he'll know. I'm sorry Annie; the washing looks clean and bright and is almost dry. You are well ahead of me. I do mine tomorrow and I do have help. Maggie Brown comes in to help me, so I quite understand that bit. Please forget I asked and I will consider that I have obtained some wisdom today.'

'Cleanliness is next to Godliness,' Annie quoted. 'Now who was it that said that?'

'I have no idea,' Ethel replied, 'but whoever it was certainly wasn't washing his own linen. He obviously had some poor slave doing it for him.'

The two women shared shy smiles and all was forgiven.

'I do tend to get on my high horse a bit,' admitted Annie. 'It's the Irish in me. But I do get sick of the bigotry that goes on just because we all do things differently. In the end we're all the same, all doing the best we can for our families, getting on with life, praying to the same God and trying to be fair to the people around us. Now let me pour the tea and cut you a slice of my passionfruit sponge. I made it this morning. What a naughty girl I am?'

She smacked herself playfully on the wrist and they both laughed.

CHAPTER 17

On the Friday morning, the Donovans enlisted the children's help to walk the cattle into town where they were to be sold. Annie piled the two youngest into the old perambulator and joined the procession, every now and then reaching out to switch a wayward beast on the flank with a twig in order to keep it with the group.

After the sale was over, Tom was a happy man.

'It has all been worthwhile, Annie,' he mused in his broad Irish accent, as they waited in the queue to finalise the paperwork. 'All that hard work has been rewarded with the prices we got today. It will keep us going for a while. Did you see that mountain of a wether that Arthur Arnott and Norman Bryant produced? It must have weighed in at one hundred and fifty pounds. It was the size of a baby elephant.'

'Are you sure it wasn't an elephant with his trunk whittled down?' joked Annie. 'In my book it was too big for a wether.'

'To be honest with you, and considering that the average weight of a wether is somewhere between sixty and seventy pounds, you are probably on the money there, Annie. It was twice that size.'

'It must be something they put in the grass out at Bloomfield. We shall have to find out what it is. But we'll keep it away from the children!' laughed Annie.

'We've been lucky with the weather, too. That is, w-e-a-t-h-e-r,' said Tom. 'All the farmers were happy chappies today. Everyone is doing well at last. We're getting record prices for our cattle, fat sheep and potatoes. It's grand news for everybody because when the farming is good, we all prosper and share the bounty.'

'So far, so good,' Annie replied, 'I love the frosty mornings and mild, sunny days. That's why we've been able to get so much tussock grubbing done in the bottom paddocks. But for me, Tom, if I had my choice, I'd rather it be cold and wet and miserable so that I can stay indoors and get some knitting done.'

'That's grand, Annie, and it will get cold soon enough to give us both a bit of a rest from the paddocks. Then you'll be complaining about me being around your feet inside the house.'

'If that happens you can go into town for a stout,' suggested Annie. This reminded her to ask, 'Are you going to call in at Miss Stewart's for a drink today? And if so, do you reckon Jim will be there, making eyes at her? Ethel tells me that the boy is in love again. And she thinks that Miss Stewart is the lucky lady.'

'Hush, Annie, it's gossip you're after!' Tom chose to ignore that last question. He was not going to be drawn into Jimmy's affairs of the heart. Besides, he had others things on his mind.

'I would love to go and have a pint at the Criterion, but I have to drop by the Creamery to organize a payment. That last cheque they sent was wrong.'

'Will you be long? Will I wait?'

'No, no, you go on home with the children and I will catch up with you later.'

Annie, well used to the mile and a half walk, strolled on home, singing to the little ones as she went.

When next she saw Tom, he was not a pretty sight. He staggered into the farmhouse kitchen looking like the walking wounded. His clothes were awry and there were buttons missing from his shirt. Over his right temple was an angry gash that was not bleeding now, but obviously had been. Congealed blood had formed a stalactite that hung precariously over his eye. 'Whatever happened to you, Thomas Patrick Donovan?' said Annie, alarmed. 'Have you been in an accident? You look like the banshees have got you!'

She anxiously wiped her hands on her apron, went over and took her husband by the hand, gently sat him on a wooden chair, and began to examine his wounds. He was not a pretty sight.

'No, not an accident, Annie,' said Tom, slowly. 'Don't worry. I got into a bit of a blue down at the Creamery, that's all. I may be looking crook, but Peter Wilson is looking crooker! And he will be smelling pretty sour by now.' Things were not so bad now he was home and he began to cheer up.

'What do you mean, smelling sour? Tom, it's not like you to be out looking for a barney.' Annie had never known her man to be in a fight before. It was not in his nature.

'It's funny, if you stop to think about it,' he said, jumping straight into the story. 'There we were, going at each other. I was holding up my end, but neither of us were actually winning. Everyone was standing around enjoying watching us two silly buggers going hammer and tong and getting nowhere and then out steps Joe White to come to my aid. Well, I think it was Joe. It could have been Patrick! Anyway, it was one of them. He laid on one punch and sent Peter flying straight up in the air, over the edge, and straight into the milk vat! Poor bugger can't swim, either! He started thrashing around, screaming for help, and eventually someone pulled him out, spluttering and spitting. You have to laugh, really!'

Tom – starting to recover from his wounds and enjoying the attention of his beloved Annie – was just beginning to see the funny side. He began to laugh uncontrollably at the thought of his combatant drowning in the milk vat. Annie joined in. The children watched helplessly as their father and mother held each other with tears of mirth rolling down their cheeks. Had they lost their minds?

Each time the mirth subsided, one would start the other off and away they would go again until their sides ached. Eventually they could laugh no more. They were spent.

'Oh Tom, you're hopeless, and you'll probably go to hell for this, but what in heaven's name were you arguing about? I thought you liked Peter Wilson?'

'That, I do. But when the bigoted bugger had a go at me about being Irish, I couldn't take it lying down. He said all us Paddies, as he called us, wouldn't be welcome at the King's Coronation celebrations on the 27th; that we should all be locked up in our Papist church for the day, so the English could celebrate in style.

'I told him that after all the pain and suffering that the bloody British had inflicted on us Irish, it would be over my dead body that I'd be bending my knee to any English monarch. I said that I didn't care if his poncy prince was going to get coronated or cremated!

'So he hit me. And I hit him back. And he hit me again and I saw red. Joe, or it may have been Patrick, stepped up and landed him a beauty. You should have seen his feet go straight up in the air as he went over into the milk. It was worth it, even though the whole lot had to be drained out and fed to the poddies.'

'And what happened to the twin?' laughed Annie.

'Nothing. Nobody was going to argue with a bloke who had killed another bloke on the football field. The fight was over. Everyone backed off and Peter and I limped off home. Peter will probably need three baths to get the smell off him and they will probably take the price of the milk off our next month's cheque.'

Annie busied herself cleaning up his wound and making a soothing pot of tea. 'That may be,' she chuckled, 'but it was worth it for the laugh. I won't be able to look Peter Wilson in the eye again when I see him.'

While Annie generally agreed with her husband's views on the British Empire's treatment of the Irish, she had been born in Australia so was not quite as rigid in her opinions as him.

'We're a long way from Ireland, and from England for that matter, and the children will enjoy the fireworks, so I think we should go and enjoy the hooley,' she told Tom later in the week after she read about the proposed celebrations in the "Times".

'You do what you like,' Tom retorted, 'but I'll be working on the farm that day, so you'll have to go alone.' He had publicly made his point and there was no going back on it now.

'Come to the celebrations with me and the boys,' Ethel offered when Annie told her of Tom's stance. 'We can make a great day out of it. Everyone will be there. It would be a shame for you to miss the fun.' So that was what she planned to do.

Like everyone else, Maggie Brown was also caught up in the excitement of the event. It entirely captured the imagination of the girl from Mallacoota.

'I hear that Queen Alexandra has so much money and time that she collects miniature animals made out of precious stones,' commented Maggie to Ethel as they changed the bed linen together. 'You know, it would be grand to be rich and never have to do a day's work ever again. That's my idea of heaven. Imagine it, Etty, you could just lie on the chaise lounge and click your fingers and all the servants in the place would come running to ask if there was anything they could do. "Oh, bring me a little bit of fish," I'd order. And then I'd say, "And make sure that it was raised in the mighty Snowy River, the purest water on all the earth." The girl would bow and scrape and leave the room reverently backwards, bowing and nodding all the way. Then the little vixen would get out into the kitchen and say to the cook, "The old bag wants a fish from the mighty Snowy, how are we going to manage that?" And the head chef would ponder on the problem for a bit, scratching his head and stroking his chin and say, "Give her majesty that fish that Arnold the footman caught yesterday in the Latrobe. The old girl will never know the difference."

She laughed heartily at her own joke and went on.

'Do you think the new Queen will get a new crown for the coronation? She keeps hundreds of them in the Tower of London so no doubt she'll just get one of the servants to go over there and choose one to match her dress. Do you think

I would look good in a crown, Etty? Do you think that they could dress me up to look like a princess?'

'A crown would surely look becoming on you, Maggie,' Etty said, gently. 'I have no doubt that you would make a lovely princess. You have beautiful soft blue eyes and pretty fair hair with just enough curl to make it a charming frame for a bejewelled headpiece. And you have a sweet little figure that would make any gown look good.'

Etty stood still as she further appraised her friend.

'But, Maggie, on the negative side, perhaps your smile is just a bit too wide for a princess. Your nose would need to be larger and more aquiline, so that you could peer down it at people of little consequence. And you are definitely a bit too boisterous to belong to the royal family. No, I think that you would definitely have to do some work on that hearty laugh, and stop jumping over puddles with the boys. You would need to train yourself to be demure. No doubt that could be done. Miracles do happen!'

They both laughed while Ethel considered the proposition again.

'Then again, perhaps not! Maggie, my dear,' she teased. 'I think you are almost beyond redemption. In any case, if you were a princess, then who would help me with the boys? No, you can just stay plain Maggie Brown, we all love you that way.'

Later, when they having morning tea, Ethel continued with the theme. 'If the truth be known, Maggie, I think you might be too smart to be a princess. I don't believe that Alexandra is the brightest candle on the palace chandelier. I read somewhere that her old governess, back in Denmark, I think her name was Miss Knudsen, said that the princess only ever read one book in her entire life.'

'And what was that? Was it the same book that I read once?' asked Maggie humorously. 'Did it have a green cover?'

'That's funny, Maggie,' chuckled Ethel. 'No, I believe it was "The Heir of Radclyffe" by Miss Yonge, a bit of an old pot-boiler, so no great intellect there! However, you mark my words, it's a difficult job to be a King or a Queen, and it can't be easy always having somebody checking up on you all of the time, and having to go and make speeches and open bridges and do all of that.

'Besides, I read in one of those magazines that Christie buys in, that the old Queen Victoria never liked our new king, even though he is her oldest son. She always thought that he was not as smart or likable as his big sister, Vicky. That would be hard on the poor fellow. Victoria didn't think him capable enough to sit in on meetings of state until after his fiftieth birthday. Can you believe that?'

'Imagine not liking your own child?' Maggie wondered aloud as she took another biscuit. 'Why do you think she was like that?'

'Rumour has it that she blamed him for Prince Albert's death. Apparently, Albert caught pneumonia after he made a rushed trip up to Scotland where the young prince was having an untoward dalliance with one of the ladies of the court. The old boy took him by the ear and brought him back to London, but the excitement was too much for him. He took to his bed and never got up again and Victoria held it against her son until the day she died.'

'Heavens, she could hold a good grudge.' Maggie was intrigued.

'But the dislike was mutual,' Etty added. 'Apparently, the prince thought she was an old battle-axe, even saying at one stage, when it looked like she would never die, "I don't mind praying to the Eternal Father, but I must be the only man in the country afflicted with an eternal mother." And the other thing was that he made a promise to his mother on her deathbed, that he would call himself King Albert Edward I. And now that she has gone, he has broken that promise and has chosen to use the name Edward VII. So revenge comes to those who wait patiently.'

'It's very sad, really,' said Maggie. 'You know, I would be very upset if my child grew up disliking me.' She began to think of the child she might have one day. 'Even though she was queen, she was still his mother.' How her arms ached to hold a baby, but she kept this to herself.

'As far as I am concerned,' Etty concluded, 'I don't care how many crowns they have on their heads and palaces they live in. Give me my little home with Christie and the boys in it any day. I don't envy the royals one thing.'

'Well, hard and all as it may be,' Maggie retorted, 'I'd be willing to take the risk and give it a go. Just a few short months of complete and utter indulgence would do me fine. And if I got bored, I could always ride off to one country or the other and shoot a few foreigners, or throw a few struggling tenants off their land, or hurl some petty thieves into a dungeon never to see daylight again. And if things got really dull, I could send a few troops off to Africa to shoot and pillage a few Boers. Yes, it would be very hard to belong to the royal family. I believe not!' Maggie huffed, forgetting her longing for children and warming to a favourite subject of hers, the ills of the Empire. 'They didn't mind letting a few hundred thousand Irishmen starve while they were living it up in their flash palaces, did they? I have no sympathy for them at all.'

'Mmm!' thought Ethel, 'I didn't know that the Irish felt that way. Annie's Tom is not alone. We come at these things from entirely differing angles.'

Biting her tongue, she kept her counsel and allowed Maggie to continue.

'But you know, all of those things aside, it's a good excuse to party and I reckon most of us Catholics will join in the celebrations. Besides, the Pope has said we can eat meat on that Friday the King is being crowned, so you know what I'm going to do? I am going to have bacon and eggs for breakfast, a huge steak for dinner, and lamb chops and chips for tea. So how do you like that?'

'Well, good for you,' retorted Ethel, a little huffy on account of her English ancestors, 'that will be good for the butchers. Besides it would be a shame if your community missed out simply because of the politics. We're a long way from England, you know, and things should be different here.'

Maggie reported to George at tea that evening, 'I think I tried dear Ethel's patience a bit today. I got on my high horse about the way the English treat the Irish, and she didn't like it much. I will really have to watch what I say.'

'That you will, my love. Everyone in this town is a prospective customer,' George replied as he sawed through the loaf so that he could soak up the gravy from the stew with a thick piece of bread. 'What you say is probably right, but it is no good making enemies.'

CHAPTER 18

As it turned out, the Coronation had to be rescheduled because the King contacted appendicitis in the week beforehand and had to undergo life-saving surgery, enduring two operations within a few days of each other.

His subjects were afraid for his life and this cast a gloom over the colony, making everyone realise that they were isolated and alone on a far-flung continent at the southern end of the world. But word soon came from London that the King wished that all festivities proceed as planned, if only to celebrate the end of the African War.

Chris wrote an editorial stating that "not since Nelson lost his life in the Battle of Trafalgar have the people celebrated with such mixed feelings, truly bitter sweet."

The Latrobe Valley decked itself out in red, white and blue, stopped work for the day and donned their Sunday best. Yarragon was a focal point, with a couple of thousand happy souls in celebration mode, including Etty and Annie and the children.

'And who is this lad that looks like he has run through hell with his hat off?' Annie asked Jack, who had brought his companions to sit with them on their picnic rug.
'Mother, this is Tommy Clarke and he is an excellent football player, got a bit of a temper though haven't you Tommy? And these lads are Leslie Watkins, Alfred Jolly, and Herbert Green.' He gestured to three other youths who were covering their eager faces with sticky threads of fairy floss. They stopped dutifully echoed, 'Hello, Mrs Donovan,' and went back to the task at hand.
'Redheads are allowed to have a temper, aren't they Tommy?' Annie kidded, sensing the lad's embarrassment and trying to make it better. 'The others will have to learn to learn to read your moods and to keep out of your way when you are out of sorts. Very happy to meet you boys,' she added indicating to the happy faces that confronted her, 'are you having a good time?'
'Just the best time ever!' Tommy replied, punching his sticky hands in the air. 'Aub knocked down all the ducks in the shooting gallery and Les won a stuffed golliwog by knocking over six bottles with a hard ball.'
'I gave it to my little brother,' Les added in case they may think he was going to snuggle up with it in bed that night.
'Yes, and we all went on the swing out horses; they are so much fun,' piped in little Mervyn who was trying his best to keep up with his big brother and his mates. 'But I think I might stay here with you for a bit and play with Dolly,' he added, afraid to state his real purpose. That was to have some quiet time with his friend Eileen. The big boys would tease him if they knew that.
'By all means,' his mother replied and she and Annie shifted over to make way for him to sit down. 'Off you go then boys, have fun!'

They disappeared quickly, grateful that they didn't have to look out for Aub's younger brother any more.

Ethel took in the scene around her. She was quietly surprised at the number of people she actually recognised after only three short months in the district, and Annie informed her about the ones she didn't know.

Sam and Emily Cook paraded by with all of their five children dressed in red, white and blue. Old Mary and John Igoe were sharing a party within a party with their three grown up children Dan, Bill and Elinor. Lucy and Henry Walker were out in force with all nine children in tow, as proud as punch with their tribe of healthy, happy children. It was a great gathering.

'Who are those two?' asked Ethel as two middle aged women, dressed in apparel fit for a royal garden party, promenaded before them with hats sitting elegantly at a jaunty angle and parasols shading their fair complexions from the weak winter sunshine.

'That my dear friend, is society as we know it in these parts,' informed Annie who had lived in the district long enough to be well acquainted with all of its residents.

'That is Phoebe and Wilhelmina Murray from Springbank Estate. They are here today to represent the empire, and they do it as well as the queen herself, would you not agree?'

'I do indeed,' smiled Ethel. 'It must be very frustrating for women of such class to have to wander amongst us plebeians. Sit up straight now, Annie and hold your shoulders back. Mind your p's and q's.'

They both laughed as they did so often in each other's company.

Although every woman present had done her best for the King's celebrations, for many of them, money was scarce and last year's fashions simply had to make do. The Murray

girls would be much more at home in the elegant crowd at the Melbourne Town Hall, not in a paddock at Yarragon. When it came to preparing the feast, the women had not held back either. 'All the ladies have their specialities,' Annie informed her friend as they perused the luscious luncheon, everything from a variety of delicious sandwiches, to scones of all descriptions, sausage rolls, cakes, sponges, meringues, toffees and marshmallows. She herself had brought a basket of sausage rolls, enough to feed a dozen people and Ethel had donated two large hams in the name of the paper. 'You will never go home hungry when the ladies of the district put on a feast,' Annie remarked to her friend. 'Anastasia Byrne makes fantastic pastries, probably because her husband Pierre is French and knows about these things. They say the French eat well. Mary Harkins is famous for her fruitcakes and Elizabeth Duff makes the best ginger fluff in the country. She has won prizes in the Melbourne Agricultural Show. Mrs Morrison always makes the most mouth watering passionfruit sponges and her sister Mrs Appleby does a wonderful cheesecake.'
'I didn't know those two were sisters,' replied Ethel, 'they always seem to be together at the football games, and now you say it, they do look alike.'
'They are more than sisters; they are twins. I think they were Kathleen and Joan Allen, and I believe they have five more sisters, seven girls in the one family, and two or three boys as well, I believe. Can you imagine that? They're a noisy bunch but they all seem to be happy people, must be in their makeup, I suppose. The family is spread from here to Lakes Entrance, a little fishing settlement on the Gippsland Lakes.'
'Christie has mentioned Lakes Entrance. Always with the promise that when we have some money we will hire a boat and go fishing there. He says that an old fisherman told him

that the fish are so plentiful they fight to get your bait. The boys love that idea.'

'It's a fair way to travel, but lots of people go there and stay at one of the guesthouses. You get there by boat; just take the train to Sale and then a paddle steamer on from there. One day when the cows come good, we might even go ourselves. Jack loves to fish.'

The food was lavish and plentiful. There were fizzy drinks for the children and tea for the adults while some of the fathers satisfied their thirsts in the bar of Martin Kier's Commercial Hotel.

After lunch was over all the children were hustled together in their school groups by their zealous teachers and set off marching to stirring music in the direction of the train station. The adults followed in a more relaxed manner, groups of two, three and four, talking and laughing because everyone was enjoying the day and there is nothing like the sound of a brass band to lighten the mood. Eventually everyone gathered around the flagpole waiting for the flag to be hoisted. The National Anthem was played and special medals presented. Unfortunately, about halfway through the presentation they ran out. Embarrassment all around! No one had predicted that the celebration would be so well attended. What could they do? The organising committee apologised, saying that all they could do was to order more to be distributed at a later date. The children who missed out were bitterly disappointed, some even shedding tears.

'That was the one hiccup in an otherwise fantastic day,' Ethel commented to Christie that night when the children were in bed, dreaming of kings and queens and soldiers and fairy floss.

'Apart from that, they had such a good time. Aubrey and Merv loved the sports and games. And, isn't Jack Donovan quick on his feet? I declare that he will be able to run faster than anyone in Trafalgar in a couple of years when he grows; he is very athletic. There was certainly no lack of prizes; all the boys got more than one each.'

'Mack McColl donated all the toys,' Chris informed her.

'Isn't that very sweet of him?' Ethel commented, untying her hair and allowing it to fall free. 'You know, Christie, I had tears in my eyes when I was listening to old Miss Spence. Wasn't she wonderful? She took me right back to her girlhood in London when she recalled the coronation of Queen Victoria, all the bunting and street parties. I could just picture her, a little girl of eleven with pigtails and a short frock, with her dear mother and father. How sweet is life, that almost sixty five years on, she was able to stand up in Yarragon on the other side of the world, in a place that was then known as New Holland, and tell us all about it. It was so emotional! To me that was the highlight of the day.'

'Etty, you are such a romantic, do you reckon we'll be around to tell the tale in sixty five years time?'

'I doubt it.' Ethel murmured, climbing into the bed. 'Granted, it was a moving speech but you know what I enjoyed most about the day?'

'No, tell me.'

'I loved the concert before the ball. Gosh, I laughed when Tom White rendered his Irish jig. I have never seen legs move so fast, or arms move so little and the impish look on his face was priceless. Once he got into it, he was back in old Ireland, a-dancing and a-jigging with his kin. I loved it. As well as that, the parodies they managed to get together were priceless. Max Hodgson doing "I Couldn't, Could I?" was hilarious. I don't think I have laughed so much since we began putting this paper together. It did me the world of good. Not that there wasn't pure talent there as well. Who was it that sang "Jessie's Dream"? I love that song. And Peter Calvert singing "Killarney" was moving. He sang it right from the heart. What is it about these Irishmen? They love to lament all they left behind. Mrs Sandy certainly has a beautiful voice. What was it she sang?'

'It was "Rohin Adair",' replied Etty, yawning. 'Time for bed now Christie. You'll have lots to write about in the next issue. Best we get some sleep. It all goes to show, doesn't it, that any party is a good party, and even though we had a coronation and the king wasn't crowned it didn't matter one hoot. It was great just to go out and spend a day having fun with our family and neighbours. After all,' she continued, snuggling down and pulling the eiderdown up around her neck, 'we're all a long time dead.'

'Indeed, indeed!'

Chris's mind was already a million miles away, planning for the next week.

CHAPTER 19

Because winter was the dancing season, the Mechanics Hall was rarely in darkness on a Saturday. This year, on a glorious moonlit night, the eagerly awaited Trafalgar Football Club Ball was first for the season and Ethel was nervous because it was her unenviable job to choose the Belle of the Ball. When she arrived, the hall vibrated with music provided by Miss Rice and her string quartet as handsome young men, resplendent in their evening suits, and pretty girls, dazzling with youth, excitement and beauty tripped the light fantastic. She was surprised to note that their very own Maggie Brown was singing with the band.

'Maggie, I didn't know that you sing so well,' Ethel commented between brackets. 'You certainly hide your light under a bushel.'

'It has never really come up,' Maggie replied as she sipped a glass of water. 'I love to sing, always have. At the first sound of music I can't help myself. I just have to sing along to it. You can't stop me. They tell me you are judging the Belle tonight, Etty,' she added steering the conversation away from herself.

'Not my choice at all! All young girls are beautiful and they all look lovely in their Sunday best. Far be it for me to single one out to be proclaimed better than the rest. I told that to Mr Mulvennia when he asked me, but he said they had no one else and because I have recently come from Melbourne, I am acquainted with the fashions of the moment. What could I do? Besides, I can kill two birds with the one stone by reporting this for the newspaper.'

The band struck up and both Maggie and Ethel set to work as the prospective Belles and their partners shimmied around the dance floor to the "Blue Danube Waltz". After much thoughtful deliberation, Ethel finally chose a girl in an elaborate fairy costume that had obviously been constructed over many hours of painstaking work. She realised she had made a faux pas as soon as the announcement was made.

'We don't usually need to go outside of the town to find a Belle,' the Master of Ceremonies announced to one and all. 'But this year we are crowning a Moe girl, Susannah Bennett. Will you please come forward.' The applause was embarrassingly restrained as he draped the sash over her shoulders. He then went on to add, 'Let's hope that this is not an omen of things to come, and that at the end of the season, it will be a Trafalgar lad, not a Moe one, accepting the Premiership trophy.'

'I had no idea that there would be hometown politics involved in selecting the Belle,' Ethel lamented to Christie that night as they walked home, arm in arm with the full moon lighting their way. 'Somebody should have warned me that the title was reserved for a local lass instead of pretending otherwise. All the girls looked beautiful; there was so little difference between them. But perhaps some good may come from it. Now they won't ask me to do that odious task ever again.'

'Oh I don't think it was the girls that bothered about the result. It was their mothers.' Chris was astute enough to know that they all wanted their own daughter to win.

'That much I realise now,' replied his wife. 'Perhaps subconsciously that was another reason why I chose an out-of-towner. I didn't want to make a choice between the Trafalgar girls and turn all the other mothers against me. Oh dear, I've done the wrong thing. Now I will be the butt of gossip.'

'You judged as fairly as you were able, Ethel. It's all subjective, anyway. I thought you were the Belle of the Ball tonight. You look beautiful. Don't fret, my love, it will all be forgotten before the sun comes up tomorrow. The main thing was that everyone who was there tonight had a marvellous time.'

They opened the gate and walked up the path to the front door and an empty house. The boys were staying the night with the Donovan family and would be home in the morning, but until then it was just the two of them, home alone.

CHAPTER 20

Ethel popped her head into the office on the way down to the butcher's shop the following Monday morning. 'We missed you on Saturday night. Where were you Jim? I didn't see you at the Football Club Ball? But your sisters looked magnificent,' she told him, 'I loved their costumes. They were both made out of the same delicate cream satin, but Anne-Marie's was elegantly plain and Norah's was trimmed with pale green. Who makes their dresses? Is your mother the needlewoman or are they?' she asked.

'For a start Mrs J, Anne-Marie and Norah are not my sisters. I only have one sister and she is married to a bloke on a farm out behind Mirboo North. We don't see much of her anymore; she's busy with a young family. Mother makes the journey to mind the kiddies when another one pops his head up, and she goes over there every couple of months for a day or two. No, those two pretty girls are my cousins and, I agree, they are gorgeous. I really couldn't say for sure, but I think they do their own sewing although I have seen Aunty Kate with needlework in her hands. And as for the dancing; I don't dance; I've got two left feet and the girls don't

164

appreciate having their pretty little shoes trodden on. Besides, you know what women do when they get hold of you. They'd have me into the church and up the aisle before I knew whether I am coming or going. Best stay away.'

'What about Mary Walsh? Now there's a lovely girl there for you, Jimmy. She was Miss Elegance herself in black and white satin. Black and white always go well together,' said Ethel warming to the task of convincing Jimmy that he should consider marriage. Because she was happily married herself, she could not countenance that Jimmy may not think that way.

'And what about the two Davis girls?' she continued. 'Caroline was dressed as Red Riding Hood and Alison came as the Maid of Erin. They are smart, gorgeous girls. You should go to these things Jimmy.'

'Once bitten, twice shy! I give girls a wide berth,' retorted Jimmy, at the same time giving the page of print an unnecessarily heavy thud with his rubber mallet. 'Besides, I was out at the farm on Saturday night. Mother cooked one of her roasts and we played Euchre.'

Ethel could see that there was no good in pursuing the topic so bid adieu and continued on her way. Later in the week she learnt the underlying truth. She and Annie had been weeding and planting in the garden together and now they sat on the veranda sipping tea and discussing the Victor Prince Musical Company that had recently come through Trafalgar with their new show, "Couple of Ducks". It was an American comedy that had a fair quota of acrobatics and dancing in it and little Mervyn had laughed so much at the antics of the cast that he had chewed a hole in his new jumper.

'The boys have become overnight mini thespians,' Ethel commented. 'After seeing the travelling show they have the sitting room set up as a theatre and have spent every waking moment constructing little plays and doing sight gags, singing and dancing and learning acrobatic and magic tricks. I'm always being summoned to take my place in the audience. When Maggie is here she can be a scream; she adds funny touches, singing a song or saying a verse to make everyone laugh. I must say it was the best four and sixpence I have spent all year. It has kept the boys happy and busy for days.'

'Jimmy's little girlfriend was rather gifted in the gymnastics area. She could turn herself inside out. She had this act that she put to music for the concerts and musical evenings, a real talent,' commented Annie.

'What's this about Jimmy's girl?' asked Ethel surprised that the two words had been uttered in the one sentence. 'Jimmy told me he wasn't interested in girls.'

'That's because the poor lad had his heart broken,' Annie replied. 'He was head over heels in love once, to a girl named Daisy Featherstone, whose parents conducted a book-keeping and wordsmith's business on the Main Street, near Walls' shop. Apparently, you could walk in there and get your figures done and your tax matters attended to and even business and personal letters written. Daisy was a sweet and graceful little thing who could do wonderful things with her body, almost what you would call double jointed. Jimmy met her through the athletics at one of the sports days. She had a cute birthmark in the shape of a heart on her cheek near her eye.'

'Tell me more,' encouraged Ethel. She did like to know the ins and outs of things of the heart, particularly when it involved their Jimmy.

'They met the year she made a clean scoop of all the ladies events, the running as well as the jumping. Jimmy was the men's champion and apparently love blossomed on the dance floor at the celebration ball and after that, the two of them became inseparable. They went everywhere together and we all thought that it was only time before they got married. She was a bit younger than he was, so we assumed that they had to wait. But it turned out that both sets of parents neither approved nor liked the relationship. It all boiled down to the fact that Jimmy was a Catholic and Daisy was Church of England and marriage between them just could not be countenanced. The poor young things were torn but seemed determined to have their way and had their own tryst, meeting secretly and both wearing the other's rings. Then suddenly, the Featherstones packed up and left Trafalgar overnight, taking Daisy with them. They just disappeared off the face of the earth.'

'Did he go after her? Did he try to get her back?' asked Ethel.

'No, not immediately! Poor Jimmy was heartbroken; he lost weight and went into a deep melancholy. He just took to his bed and didn't move for months on end. His parents weren't any support because they were pleased that the romance was over, and they told him so. They said he had to get over it and get on with his life and find a nice Catholic girl, one of his own kind. It was about that time his sister Emily married and moved to Mirboo North so he lost the support of the one person who understood him.'

'Poor Jimmy,' Ethel sympathised. 'Go on!'

'Poor lad, he was in a pretty bad way. He made a few trips to the city thinking that Daisy was in Melbourne and trying to search the family out, but it's a big place and he couldn't locate her. Eventually, he realised the fruitlessness of his endeavours and gave up. Moira, that's Jim's mother, told me later that he discovered the family had gone to Geelong and that after only ten months, they had found little Daisy lying face down in the river at Werribee, dead, with Jim's ring still on her finger. It was awful! She had jumped from a bridge. The poor pet, I can only imagine how unhappy she must have been. She was an only child, so now, nobody could have her, neither Jim nor the parents.'

'That is so, so sad.'

'It really is,' mused Annie. 'Jimmy never got over that sorry episode and vowed never to marry and he was never any good working with his parents on the farm again. There was a wedge. When your Chris came along with his grand plans for the newspaper, Jim emerged from his melancholy and started to smile again. I suppose it gave him some vision for the future and he seems to have adopted you and your family and let the past settle and stay where it belongs. It was an awful thing and to think that everything could have easily been so different. He still wears the ring she gave him.'

'I have noticed that and have often wondered about it. I thought it must have been a family heirloom,' Ethel commented.

'No, little Daisy gave it to him. It's all he has left of her,' lamented Annie.

'But,' she added, cheering up, ' the good thing is, he was out at the farm last Saturday evening and he brought his Miss Stewart from the public house out to meet the folks. As happy as Larry, Moira told me, and she said they made a lovely couple. Mavis accompanied him on the piano while he sang with gusto. So there you go, love is in the air. Moira feels dreadful about the Daisy thing, so she's praying to the good lord that Jimmy has found love again.'

'Well the old fox! Imagine that, Miss Stewart! He has kept that under his hat; not a word to anyone, ' exclaimed Ethel. 'But nevertheless, that's fantastic; I do hope it works out for them. She seems a very nice woman. She was on the same train down here as we were that day, and she is on my debating team. She's smart and witty. I can see why Jim likes her and, I believe she was very brave coming into the unknown. And so capable as well, she has certainly turned that business around. We were there for tea a couple of weeks ago, and now that you mention it, Jimmy was hovering. I thought he was happy to see us, but perhaps it was that he was happy just to be in the same room as our dear Miss Stewart. Well, I never, will you fancy that?'

'It's no wonder Moira feels guilty after all the fuss she made,' concluded Annie. 'Nobody should meddle in affairs of the heart. We all have our own preferences, somebody for everyone so they say. I would go to my child's wedding even if it was down the back yard in a dunny. But you can't bring back the dead, that's for sure. Poor Jimmy!'

Armed with this knowledge, Ethel vowed never to quiz Jimmy about prospective brides again and scrupulously avoided that topic in future. She did however, notice just how many times Jimmy incidentally mentioned Miss Stewart in his conversation. It seemed that they spent a lot of time together.

CHAPTER 21

'Christie, I'm glad you've given a column over to the woman named Sylvia to cover some of the things that we ladies might be interested in,' Ethel congratulated her husband, after a column for women's news suddenly appeared alongside the usual fare.

'Well, I'm glad you approve,' Chris answered. 'Our fair ladies deserve some space of their own, and while we are mentioning it, I was going to ask you something, my dear.'

'And what would that be?' Ethel asked.

'Would it be possible for you fill in for the lovely Sylvia on those occasions when she fails to make the deadline? Hopefully that won't happen too often.'

'I don't know how you think I am going to fit it in, Christie. In case you haven't noticed, I'm a busy lady.'

'You know what they say, Ethel; if you want something done well, give it to a busy person. You will cope, my lovely wifey, because you are strong and resilient. It is as simple as that. It may never come to pass, but just in case.'

Ethel reluctantly agreed.

Over time, it seemed that Sylvia was often away from her desk and, on those occasions, Ethel gathered items of interest to women from every source she could muster. She'd write down tips passed to her by her mother and sisters, embellish titbits she heard from the other ladies in the town and scan the magazines for news that women might like. At every opportunity she called on past real life experiences to fill the column. But secretly, she and her friends were concerned that when the real Sylvia appeared, she was sending the wrong messages to young women.

'I don't know who this Sylvia is,' Annie remarked to Tom after she had scanned one of her columns. 'Sometimes her advice is good and at other times it is all over the place. She doesn't live in the real world. The place she talks about is a man's nirvana, all the things that men would love and the ordinary woman is far too busy to give. She lives in lah-lah land.'

'Don't go letting other people get into your head, Annie. This man's nirvana is happy children, a meal on the table every dinnertime and a hooley on a Saturday night. We're doing all right, you and me, so don't go reading that nonsense,' Tom counselled. He was right. Best mind her own business and look after her family in the way she saw fit. But it annoyed Annie to think that some women would act upon Sylvia's advice.

Ethel voiced her doubts, too. 'I haven't met this Sylvia woman yet,' she remarked to Maggie as she rubbed the boys sports trousers against the scrubbing board, releasing the thick Trafalgar mud into the steamy water. 'But she makes it hard for mere mortals like me. Christie would think he has died and gone to Heaven if I did all the things that she thinks women should do.'

Maggie laughingly agreed with her friend. 'If we even took half of the good Miss Sylvia's advice, we'd be canonised saints, you and me. I reckon that to live up to her high standards one would need to have the disposition of the Blessed Mother of God, the work ethic of Saint Theresa of the Little Flower and the alluring qualities of Mary Magdalene. Now that would be some woman!'

She was so busy prodding the clothes in the copper into submission with her stick that she didn't notice Ethel stop what she was doing and wipe the suds from her hands.

'Hush Maggie, that is sacrilegious talk. You'll get no luck from speaking that way and you make me feel uncomfortable.'

'Ooh! I've done it now,' thought Maggie, deciding to pull her head in and get on with the washing. They continued in silence until Ethel went inside to put the sausages on for the boys' dinner, leaving Maggie to peg the final items on the clothesline.

That night, at dinner Maggie related to George what she had said. 'I'm always opening my mouth and putting my big foot in it,' she told him. 'I stepped over the mark with Ethel today, again!' He listened and laughed because he was used to Maggie's grand statements. That was what he loved about her.

'You can take the girl out of Mallacoota, but you can't take Mallacoota out of the girl,' he teased her. 'I want to meet this Sylvia, too. She sounds like the perfect woman to me. You make sure that you read up on every word she writes, Maggie. And then put it all into practice. I think I would enjoy it.'

'Now that would be the day, Georgie Porgie, puddin' and pie! I'd have to be losing my mind first! You just be content with the Maggie you have and don't go trying to make me better than I am. I'm just Maggie from Mallacoota. What you see is what you get.'

'And I love what I see,' said George, meticulously spreading the "Times" on the kitchen table before setting to work, shining his boots. Maggie tidied the dinner dishes and sat on the window seat to crochet the white shawl she was working on.

The truth finally dawned upon Ethel one day, not long after, when she walked in to the office to find Jimmy sitting at the big, oak desk with a worried look on his face and a pencil in his hand.

'What's up Jimmy, you look like you've just lost sixpence and found a penny?'

'It's this column I'm writing, Mrs J. I reckon I've just about scraped the bottom of my barrel as far as women's news is concerned. I know nothing about the sweet creatures. In fact, they puzzle the life out of me.'

'Oh,' she exclaimed, pointing and laughing, 'you're not telling me that you are the famous Miss Sylvia! You? Jimmy Kenny? You have been writing all that stuff about how a woman should behave and look after her man? It is all starting to make sense now. All of us women in the town were thinking, "Who is this woman who makes herself a door mat for her family?" And all the time it's you, Jimmy, feeding the women of Trafalgar propaganda. That's the funniest thing I have ever heard in my life, I'll have to sit down, you have made my day.'

She just couldn't quell the laughing and was still chuckling when Chris returned from a train derailment just outside Moe that he was covering for the paper.

'Well, we all seem to be having a splendid time while us workers are out gathering news. And what exactly is so funny?' Chris asked, employing the royal plural.

'Oh, we were just talking about the staff,' Ethel replied, evasively.

'Staff? What staff?' Chris asked distractedly as he took off his coat and sat down to write while it was fresh in his mind. 'That is something we sadly lack, especially as I have just made a commitment to provide a reporter for every meeting of the Council.'

'And just who have you in mind to do that job? Sylvia?' Ethel couldn't resist asking.

'Very funny, Etty!' replied Christie. 'No, it will probably be me. We really can't afford to pay somebody else at this stage. Jim has said he will fill in if the football club meetings clash with the council meetings, and maybe you can fill in for the fill-in if he can't make it. '

'So when do you imagine, am I going to get time to do my gardening?' she asked, a little annoyed at the presumptions that were made as regards to the use of her time.

Chris walked over and put his arm around her. 'Please, don't be cross with me Etty. I'm doing my best. I promise you that one day I will hire you a muscled up gardener and all you will have to do is point to a place on the ground and say to him, "Plant that rose there and remove that weed from here." It will be all worth it in the end, Etty, you'll see.'

Ethel knew he was right. 'My, you are a little overwrought, aren't you? Let me make you a cup of tea,' she offered in a conciliatory manner, sorry that she had made fun of him. 'Of course I will help where ever or whenever I can. When are these council meetings?'

'They hold them on Wednesday, and the first one is tonight.'

When Chris announced some weeks later that a staff member would now regularly visit the towns of Thorpdale, Narracan, Coalville and Willowgrove to gather news, Ethel couldn't help herself and was moved to pose the question.

'And who do you have in mind to be your special roving correspondent? Sylvia?'

Chris ignored the barb and winked at Jim. 'Well, Jimmy and I have been interviewing this wonderful bush poet, who is intelligent, witty, good looking, and just the man for the job. We have almost got him on board but there is the question of appropriate recompense. However, we are sure that we can reach agreement on that by the time the day is out.'

'That sounds almost too good to be true, Christie,' said Etty. 'Is he from Trafalgar or are you getting him from town? Please stop and consider whether you can really afford to pay somebody a big wage, Christie? Who is he?' Ethel's curiosity was stirred.

'So many questions, my lovely lady, so many questions! And to answer them, yes, he is from Traf, and yes, I can afford to pay him, because he will work for the love of the job. And his identity? Well you know him well, fair maiden. I know you consider him to be strong and handsome; as good a man as ever walked the earth, a fine cut of a fellow is exactly how I have heard you describe him.'

Ethel looked perplexed, not understanding. She certainly did not remember describing any man of her acquaintance in that manner.

'Ethel, my darling wife, you are looking straight at him. It is I, fair maiden, your devoted husband. Me, Christopher McCallum Johnstone! I shall be the special correspondent. '

'Christie, where ever are you ever going to find the time?' Ethel shook her head in disbelief because she could not imagine how he would fit everything into the day.

She was soon to learn that while Chris was out and about, it was she who was confined to the office, attending to all the bits and pieces that had to be done – taking the advertisements, recording the births, deaths and marriages, and talking to the townspeople about all things local that make a country paper so interesting to the readers. It was also she who dealt with any complaints or mishaps. People were coming and going to the office all the time and she was chief trouble-shooter.

Each Tuesday night the boys came in after school and it was all hands to the wheel, folding, counting, bundling newspapers and taking them to the train station to be delivered up and down the line. Sometimes they had finished by six o'clock, sometimes by seven and at other times, because of some hold-up or other, they worked on late into the night by lamplight until the job was done. One small hitch in the system could put them back an hour.

On late nights Ethel would take the boys home, give them tea and stay with them until bedtime, only to return and help the men. No matter what hour it was, when everything was done the men would go back to the family home to debrief and to enjoy a beer. Ethel began taking a small glass of sweet sherry to keep them company.

'If my dear mother could see me now,' she remarked, 'sitting around taking liquor with two disreputable gents. She'd be disgusted.'

'Best we not tell her then!' Chris replied happily, topping up her glass.

Perhaps that is why when an excited Isabella Brown came to the front desk one day and said, 'Mrs Johnstone, I am marrying George Webb in a fortnight and have come in to ask you to put an announcement in your newspaper; I am giving up work at the Sunny Creek Creamery, and I am going to get married,' Ethel looked up, pushed her wayward hair out of her eyes, shook her head and counselled the excited bride-to-be.

'My dear Isabella, when you get married, you don't give up work. The reality is that you are only just starting it!'

CHAPTER 22

'The man who finds a way to make the dust stay on the road
and not come into the house will make a fortune, and I
personally, will make him a roast dinner every Sunday for the
rest of his life,' Ethel stated, as she wiped over the wooden
furniture with a damp cloth sprinkled with linseed oil.
'That's interesting, Etty, because I read that in Sydney they
are using crude oil to spray on the streets in order to lay the
dust,' Christie told her. 'Apparently two applications a year is
enough and has a hardening effect on the road, smoothing
the surface.'
'What about the bottoms of ladies gowns, does it mark them
and make them stink?' Ethel queried.
'No, apparently it doesn't damage the clothes at all. It
exudes a bit of a kerosene smell at first, but the wind and the
sun dry it and soon take the odour out of it. I tell you what?
I shall get myself voted onto council and suggest we use it
on the road out here. That should solve your dust problem
and I then you could cook me roast dinners until I am an
old, old man. How's that?'

'I will always cook for you, silly man, and I don't need to share you with any more civic groups,' laughed Ethel, coming around to the other side of the kitchen table and giving him a hug. 'The boys and I don't see enough of you as it is.'

Nevertheless their discussion got Chris thinking and so he sat down to pen his editorial on that subject. '

'Victoria does not have the ability to supply herself with enough coal for her needs, and the important thing about this new liquid oil is that there is no waste.' That was as far as Chris had written when his brother Billy burst through the office door, greeting him with a handshake and a hearty pat on the back.

'Heh, big brud! Whatcha up to?'

'Just writing an editorial,' answered Chris. 'It's good to see you, young fella. How are the folks? And to what do I owe the pleasure of this visit? We hardly ever see you in town.'

'That's because I'm too busy on the damn farm working my arse off for the old man. Have you got time to come and have a beer with me and to give me a few hints on how to deal with him?'

'I know nothing. You are asking the wrong man. I haven't had to negotiate with Robert the Bruce for years. Why, what's the problem?'

'He won't let me go to town to follow my career as a cricketer. Says he can't spare me from the farm and that all play and no work will make Billy a sad, bad boy.'

'I don't like your chances much if he's made up his mind,' Chris replied. 'He's all doughty Scot, digs those heels of his in and won't move an inch once he has formed an opinion.'

'How did you get away from the farm then?' begged Billy. 'How did you talk him around? It's my big chance, and the old bugger won't let me take it.'

'Spare the swearing, Bill. That won't help anything. Just give me a couple of minutes and we'll talk it over.'

'What are you doing? Can you come now?' Billy asked, for his time was limited and he was impatient.

'I'm writing about this wonderful new stuff they call crude oil,' Chris told him, putting his pen down and blotting the copy. 'Come on, let's go, tell me all your worries.'

As they walked down the street together, Billy filled Chris in on the details of the offer he had received from the cricket authorities. He could play district cricket for South Melbourne, but there would be no guarantees about a place in either the Victorian or the Australian sides. If he measured up, they would help him find a job, but that wouldn't come until a few months down the track.

'But,' Billy reasoned, 'you can't be picked to play cricket for Australia if you are feeding cows down in the bush. I need to be in amongst it.'

It was a leap of faith and he was happy to make it, but he was restrained by lack of money. 'I could just do what I want, and to hell with the old man. But I've got absolutely sweet bugger all. I have been working on that farm since I left school and I've never had a penny to call my own. I wouldn't even have the fare to Melbourne, let alone setting up expenses. I need Father to give me his blessing, and a bit of that stash he keeps inside the lining of his feather bed in the new house I have just finished helping him build!'

Chris heard Billy out but realised that his was probably a lost cause. He himself wasn't yet in a position to lend the money to tide him over. Perhaps a little further down the track he may be, but not right at that moment. These chances come your way only once and by then it would probably be too late.

'I'm hearing what you say Bill, and I sense your frustration. But the way I see it is that you can't go if you have no money. My business has only just started and I have a wife and children to keep so I can't help you out either, mate. I'm sorry, but at the moment money is in very short supply.'

'I wasn't expecting you to give me money,' Billy was quick to state. 'I would like you to have a word with father. See if you can make him see it my way. He respects your opinion and he might come around.'

'I can certainly do that for you Bill. I have to take the Surveyor General up that way to visit Fawkner's mine in the next month or so. What say I spend the night with Mother and Father and have a heart to heart with the old man then? You just never know. What I would say to you, though, is to pay him some respect and quit the swearing. You know what he's like. He digs in and puts his prickles up like an anteater. He's old. Just go easy on him.' Chris reprimanded his younger brother, but added what he thought might be a solution. 'See if you can enlist Mother on your side, Billy. She's the only person who can turn the old man's thinking around. She may be able to get him to see your side of it.' Chris bought his brother another beer, discussed the farm and the family, and then the two men shook hands and departed - Billy, home to the farm with his dream still unresolved in his heart, and Chris to wrestle with the delicate matter of who to support in the forthcoming Council elections.

Neville Murray was a young man who was challenging the cosy position of Dr Frederick Lloyd who had been a member of the local council for more years than anyone cared to remember. It would be a tussle between an old experienced councillor and an able and popular younger person.

"East Riding is not as well represented as it should be and change is urgently required," Chris wrote. "Mr Neville Murray is completely in touch with our district and knows its many requirements. I believe he will serve our interests in no half hearted manner."

'There, I've voiced my opinion and made at least one enemy,' he remarked to Ethel, showing her the proof. 'The old doc will never come near my paper after this. I certainly hope I don't find myself in his rooms with acute appendicitis. He'll probably tell me to go home and suffer in my boots.'

'Oh, you do talk nonsense,' retorted Ethel. 'The good doctor is a man of the world enough to know that everyone is entitled to an opinion.'

'Ah yes, but my opinion is not just mine any more,' Chris added. 'People actually read what I write and it may sway their final choice.'

'Then the onus is on you to be fair and considered, Christie, and to not say anything that you will regret once you see it in print. That is quite a responsibility.'

Ethel hoped that all of this newfound power would not go to her husband's head.

CHAPTER 23

Mrs Lawless and Mavis Stewart were waiting patiently for attention at Nurse's Butcher's shop. 'I don't know how the government expects us to make money from our business,' Mavis commented pointing to a sign across the road at the Post Office that had been erected by the Health Department the previous day.

"Public eating places can spread disease," large red letters cautioned as a warning to the population regarding the highly infectious diseases of Tuberculosis and Consumption. 'They will succeed in frightening the life out of the entire town,' Mrs Lawless agreed. 'Nobody will come out to eat soon. As if we would have the same diseases in our establishments as they do in the slums of Melbourne. I know that I dish up good, fresh country food every day and I make sure my hands are clean. No one gets diseases at my establishment.' She was indignant as it seemed to her that the people who ran the government in Melbourne took great pleasure in bleeding hard-working people in the country dry.

'Exactly,' Mavis replied. 'I couldn't agree more. They may as well close us down and be done with it. I seem to be fighting a losing battle on quicksand. People have this straight-laced idea about going into a public house and seem to think that the devil himself will strike them dead if they set foot in my place. I am having enough trouble convincing the locals to come and try what I offer, so I really don't need government in Melbourne telling them my food spreads disease. They really have no idea of the negative impact they create.'

Mavis Stewart was feeling despondent, as she had spent much time and energy trying to ensure her establishment presented the same as the high-class city teahouses that were so popular with ladies of society in town. The furniture was made of solid Australian wood from the local mill and crafted by Chris Whitaker, a craftsman of high repute. She kept it scrupulously clean and polished. The patterned rugs and red velvet drapes imparted an air of restful opulence and the ornate lighting provided agreeable ambience and warmth for diners. Those locals who had actually tried her fare agreed that it was indeed a salubrious place to enjoy a meal, but word was spreading more slowly than she would have hoped. There was a core group of women who would never countenance entering any licensed premises, even with a man by their side. Mavis was beginning to think that perhaps Trafalgar might be the wrong location for such a business.

'If I can only get them to step inside and to see how elegant it is,' she told Maggie who enjoyed a meal and a sing-a-long every Friday night with her husband. They had been used to socialising at Allandale in Mallacoota and were delighted when Mavis opened her doors to provide them with food and entertainment. They became her first regular clients and as time progressed, she always joined them around the piano when the kitchen closed for the night. Not surprisingly, more often than not, Jimmy Kenny was there as well.

'It will build. Be patient, because it all takes time. Once people learn what a wonderful night can be had in Trafalgar, they won't be travelling to Warragul for their celebrations,' Maggie consoled her, knowing that not everyone was as open minded as she was. 'We just have to get the word out to them. Perhaps you could put an advertisement in Mr Johnstone's newspaper. Jim is the man to help you with that.'

'It sounds good, but what do I write?' Mavis asked. 'I don't think people realise that we have a snug all set up for unaccompanied ladies. They don't need to go anywhere near the public bar and they can chose whatever sort of drink they want – tea, soft drink or a beverage. And I am about to introduce the ladies of Trafalgar to Australian grown coffee.'

'Coffee? I didn't know we grew coffee in Australia?' Jim queried.

'Indeed we do. There is a group of farms up in the far north that specialises in the bean and even exports it. But getting back to the advertisement, what I am asking you, Jim is how do I tell them that my place is a great place? I need to let them know that I run a reputable house, not an occasion of sin.'

'Let me ponder a little. I will ask Chris and get back to you,' Jim replied. 'You have to remember that I am new to this newspaper caper. This time last year I was out on the farm squirting milk from the cow's udders. You know, though, sometimes an occasion of sin can be great fun.'

Mavis blushed, Maggie and George laughed and Miss Smallacombe began playing the notes for Banjo Paterson's new popular song, "Waltzing Matilda." Everyone joined in with gusto and sang well into the night.

CHAPTER 24

'I've got some spare space in this week's edition, so do you think we should pen an advertisement spelling out exactly what we do and what we stand for?' Chris suggested to Jimmy as they started work for the day. 'Set the record straight so to speak, just so no one takes offence when I report something truthfully.'

Chris stroked his chin as he considered the options. 'I could write something like "independent in tone, impartial in Council matters and other topics", adding that our columns are open for discussion on topics of public interest and stating that information on all subjects of interest is thankfully received. How does that sound?'

'How about cheapest newspaper in Gippsland at just one penny a copy?' the ever-practical Jimmy ventured. 'And don't forget to tell them how good our job printing is and how our circulation is increasing in leaps and bounds. We may as well let everyone know that we are doing well!' He smiled. 'Any publicity is good publicity, so they say.'

'I reckon, Jimmy, that we are in the right place at the right time and that Trafalgar is the place to be. It's all happening.

George McCrory at the bakery reckons he's going real well and that young Nick Lawless has taken up the agency for Colonial Mutual Life.'

'Yes, the bloke's a magician! As well as the life insurance, he has managed to squeeze into that small shop a collection point for rents and debts, a newsagency, stationer and bookseller, a selection of pipes, tobaccos and cigarettes, and a display of the latest comics and magazines,' answered Jim. 'Tell me about it,' Chris added. 'Every week, my kids wait at his store for the latest comic to come in on the train. He'll send me broke. Good on him, though.'

'Good luck to him,' answered Jim out of the corner of his mouth as he hammered some print into place.

'You know, with all this happening, I am thinking of becoming the agent for Alfa Laval Milk Separators myself,' Chris ventured.

'Take it easy Chris; we're flat out like lizards drinking as it is. I don't reckon we could fit any more into the day.' Jimmy was a hard man to convince because the way he saw it, they already had too much on their plates. 'We barely have time to scratch ourselves, mate. Let's not take our minds off the job. Best we just stick to the thing we are good at, and that's the newspaper. We are up to our ears in it already, Chris. If you want to get bigger we'll just have to put some more people on to help us.'

'Well, you may be interested to know, Jim, that I have that in hand. My brother George has come home from the West and is at a bit of a loose end, and I'm thinking of taking him on. He has a good brain and I reckon he could be an asset around the place. You'll like him. He loves a pint of the frothy stuff. Let's not hold back, Jimmy, we are on the forward thrust and I reckon we will do great things together, you and I, so stick with me, mate. We're becoming legends in our own life times, even getting ads in from Morwell.'

'Maggie told me that her George is taking on staff to do all sorts of things. They are even making bicycles and windmills,' added Ethel, who had been busily sorting bills and receipts.

'It's all in quality control,' Chris commented. 'People are learning that George would never do slipshod work.'

'Yes,' Ethel chatted on, 'Maggie says that his chimneys are becoming famous because they not only look good, but they work perfectly. Brown's chimneys never smoke! Well, that's what she says.'

'Good luck to them! They are a great couple,' Jimmy added.

'Do you know them well, Jim?' Ethel enquired, a little surprised that Jim had an opinion about Maggie and George. 'Oh yes. They almost always come over to Mavis' to eat at least once a week. They love a good sing-a-long and are excellent company. We have had some good times around the piano. You and Chris should come. You'd enjoy it.'

'We'll keep that in mind,' replied Ethel, a little perplexed because Maggie had never mentioned Jim and Mavis to her. Perhaps it had never occurred to her to do so. 'I am becoming very fond of Maggie. She's not only a good worker, but she's great company as well. The boys love her sense of fun. She's always making them laugh.'

'That's just Maggie. She makes everyone happy, and she has the singing voice of an angel. The room stops still when Maggie sings. George is a good bloke, too.' Jim seemed to know the young couple well.

Encouraged, Ethel chatted on. 'Maggie's pining for a baby and I just so want that to happen for her.'

Ethel suddenly observed that she had lost the attention of both the men with that last remark. Jimmy was embarrassed to hear such things discussed and Chris was not much interested in personal or domestic topics. That was frivolous women's business and he had a newspaper to run.

'Yes, yes, best get to and do some work,' said Chris, changing the subject. 'There's a council meeting tonight, and then tomorrow I thought I might take a trip out to see how the family are getting on up in the scrub. The Government Surveyor wants me to take him out to Alex Fawkner's reef and we could stay over night at the old farm before we head back. I haven't seen the folks since we started putting this paper together. It would be good to take Aubrey out of school for a couple of days, teach him a bit of bush craft and take him to visit his grandparents. He hasn't seen them for a while. So, when you go home, Ethel, could you please make me up swag of provisions, as we will need to take the early train to join the party at Morwell? I'll hire a horse from there.'

Ethel bit her lip. She really didn't want her eldest son going off into the bush and missing school, but had learnt that when Chris put his mind to things it was better to run with him. He would make sure Aubrey was all right and, and she knew deep down, that it was good for the boy to be with his father and to be comfortable amongst the men. Besides, Mary-Jane and Robert would be thrilled to see their grandson.

'I'll finish this and then I'll duck down to the butcher to pick up some corned beef to cook up to make sandwiches,' she replied. 'I'll go home and bake a fruitcake. Is there anything else that you want, Christie?'

'What would I ever do without you, Etty?' Chris came to her and gave her a hug. 'We will be stopping off for meals with settlers along the way but a few things will be good so we don't get hungry. When you are down the street, some

189

bananas won't go astray and if you wouldn't mind picking up an extra loaf and a slab of chewy cheese, I could take that to the old man, thanks Etty.'

She fixed her hair, opened the door, blew him a kiss and called a farewell to Jimmy, who was by this time, was down the back melting lead.

'By the way, one more thing Jimmy old man,' said Chris after she had gone. 'You can tell your "Uncle" Chris. Is the rumour about your impending nuptials true? Are you stepping out with one Miss Mavis Stewart?'

Jimmy blushed uncomfortably. 'Absolutely not! Who told you that? I can't believe the gossip in this town. Mavis is far too an independent young woman for that. She has the business to run and she does a wonderful job of it. She has all but turned it around! I must admit though that I do like her company, and I do get plenty of it, seeing as I board at her establishment. Nothing romantic though, we just hit it off right from the start and I help her out by chopping the wood and things like that. She makes it up to me by giving me an extra chop at dinnertime. It's a good arrangement.'

'So you are not wooing the lady in question then?'

'No, a free man is a happy man, Chris. I believe Mavis is of the same mind. I started my way down the bridal path once before and got kicked off it by a bucking horse.'

'That so, that so,' said Chris as he returned to the task at hand, humming the popular "Glow Worm Song" as he worked, "Lead us lest too far we wander, love's sweet voice is calling yonder."

CHAPTER 25

Next morning, after their usual breakfast of bacon, egg and sausage, Chris and Aubrey caught the first train of the day to go through to Morwell where they joined the Government Surveyor's party that was heading for Scanlon's place, about ten miles on from Yinnar.

Whitelaw's Track was a good road in the scheme of things but after travelling about six miles along it, they began their ascent into the hills.

'I certainly hope all the hills aren't as steep as this one is,' commented Chris as they tackled the first, all of them bar the driver having to get out and walk alongside the wagon to make the load lighter for the horses.

'This is Kaye's Hill and it is pretty steep,' the Government Surveyor commented. 'If I remember rightly, the gradient is something like one in eight.'

They were glad to finally puff their way to the top, stopping every now and then to regain their breath and to gaze at the valley below that revealed itself through the tall timbers.

That evening they made it to the Scanlons, where they were

to stay overnight. Aub, the youngest, was the freshest of them all but even he was happy to take a rest.

The family were very pleased to see them as they rarely had visitors. Joe helped them feed, stable and bed the horses down for the night. Kathleen Scanlon, a tiny redheaded woman whose fragile beauty belied her strength, both physical and mental, came to the stables and spoke to them. 'Lads, I have put soap and water outside the kitchen door for you all to wash up after your journey. It can get pretty dusty out on that track and it's hard work getting up that incline, believe me. It gives me night terrors just thinking of it. It's grand having you here with us and tonight we are going to party. Now lads, I have had a fatted calf killed and we are going to have a feast with a bit of singing, dancing and maybe some card playing, so don't waste a minute, come inside and we'll eat.'

After a sumptuous meal, Chris pushed back from the table and gave his tummy a pat. They had just enjoyed a standing rib roast with all the accompaniments, including home made sausages and fried liver on the side. There were peas, beans, potatoes, pumpkin and spinach done in a creamy sauce. And to top it all off they had a large, fluffy Yorkshire pudding, which puffed steam when it was sliced. 'Well, that was a meal fit for the king, ' he commented. 'You must surely be the best cook in the country, Mrs Kathleen Scanlon. That is the most succulent steak I have ever eaten and the gravy was the best I have tasted. You ladies of the bush never cease to amaze me the way you can cook and serve a meal like that and still look beautiful at the end of it.'

'That's very kind of you to say so,' blushed the lady of the house, 'but it wasn't all my doing, you know. Young Nellie here did the gravy and Bridget has made the apple and rhubarb pie for dessert. Young Patrick chopped all the wood for the fire, so it was a joint effort. We are so pleased to have visitors and you are very welcome.'

After the pudding had been eaten and commented upon, the ladies left the room to clean up and the men talked about the next day's journey. It was abundantly clear that wheel traffic would be impossible from that point on, so they would have to leave the wagons. They would collect them on the return journey.

As they talked, Joe scanned the newspaper they had brought with them, his eye catching the story about the dreadful explosion at the Mount Kembla Mines in far away New South Wales.

'I had heard about it,' said Joe Scanlon, 'because Father Coyne came up to say his monthly Mass last Sunday and had us praying for the souls of the one hundred and thirty men who lost their lives. It is indeed a dreadful thing.'

'I feel so sorry for the ones they left behind,' commented Kathleen, reading over his shoulder, 'can you imagine how that Egan family must be suffering, losing five sons like that, and the poor woman is already a widow. Apparently her husband died when the boys were young and she has had to struggle to bring them up. She has only one son left. That poor dear soul, I will keep her in my prayers.'

'It says here that her daughter's husband was in the pit that day as well, and her three sons,' added Chris. 'It's just awful. Can you imagine that poor girl? She lost five brothers, a husband and three sons in a matter of minutes. She'll never recover from that. It's terrible.'

'The eye witness report says it all,' said Joe, reading to them: "The valley could well be termed the valley of death for along its lovely slopes were carried at painfully frequent intervals, coffins containing the mortal remains of men who a few hours before had lived and moved and had their being, but who had now been called on in the midst of life to meet death in the darkness of a living tomb."

'So poignant and so sad!' added Joe. 'It could happen to anyone underground, even the blokes we are going to see tomorrow on the reef. It's not easy getting the gold out of the ground.'

The group contemplated in silence, but their spirits didn't stay dampened for long. The Scanlons had visitors and were going to make the most of them. The remainder of the evening passed happily with a jolly sing-a-long, some Irish jigs and a few hands of cards.

Next morning the party was up bright and early and after a hearty breakfast they headed off towards Duggan's, about seven miles away. The route led off Whitelaw's Track and was used by the Shannon, McWhae and Duggan families. But first they had to pass Don Campbell's place.

'Don has been a very busy boy. He must have been hard at it, working day and night. By gosh, the farm is looking very good,' Chris commented on the many improvements that were evident to the passer-by.

'Yes, Don is a good farmer,' Joe told them. 'He has proven that it is possible to harvest two crops a year on only thirty acres by having ten acres of apple trees and ten acres of pear trees, while planting root and vegetable crops in between the rows. He runs cattle on the other ten acres and harvests their manure for fertiliser. Good farmers and good farming go hand in hand.'

'This looks like a dairy herd up here, so where are the fruit trees?' the surveyor asked, looking around.

'Yes, you're right. This is a dairy run by young Donald. Old Don does his bit down in the valley by the river. It's the young one who does the work up here.'

By now they were traversing the top of the ridge overlooking the picturesque Morwell River Valley, which spread before them like a page out of an English picture book. Shannon's place was three miles further on and it was there they began their descent into the valley, via a winding track. Two miles down the hill, they passed McWhae's holding. Macca, his wife and three little ones came to the letterbox to say "Hello" and offer them freshly made lemonade. It was here they heard the sad news about Jack Ray, who had returned from the horrors of the Boer War only to be killed out hunting ducks, when his gun accidentally went off, shooting him in the heart as he climbed under a fallen branch.

'I know the man you are talking about,' Chris responded when told. 'He was a good mate of Hoppy's. Didn't his mob own the next farm? He was out with Hoppy when his little boy was drowned, too. Poor Hoppy. Ethel was at the doctor's when he came in with his little son, all lifeless. He is struggling on one leg to keep the farm going and cannot take a trick.'

Saddened, they moved on and finally made it to Duggan's. 'We can't take the horses where we are headed,' Mick Duggan informed them as he secured the animals. 'We'll have to hoof it; it's too rugged for the nags. They'll be all right if we leave them here and travel the rest of the way on foot.' Brightening up, he added, 'Not too many people come our way. We've been looking forward to your visit, so come inside and sit down with us. Louise has been cooking all morning, so you won't be going hungry!'

They enjoyed a wonderful midday meal with the Duggan family, accompanied by some lively conversation but, as pleasant as it was, they had to move on.

'Well, it's me who should be thanking you,' Mrs Duggan replied in response to their gratitude. 'You brightened me up a whole lot. Mick will tell you truthfully that I have been so sad about poor old Yankee Bob. It broke my heart to think of that poor man down there on his claim, badly burned and with a broken arm, and all on his own in the cold. I cried and cried when I heard of it. He was rough and ready character but I liked him. Poor man was some mother's son. No one should die all alone like that.'

'So was it an accident then?' queried Chris. 'I heard that he committed suicide, poor bloke. What was his real name? Did he have one? I always knew him as Yankee Bob when he came into town.'

'His name was Robert Fordyce; his mail got delivered here and sometimes I would take it down to him, sometimes he would come up here and collect it. We found him three days after the explosion and he was in agony, poor fellow. We got him to hospital, but it was too late. He didn't last long after that. Yankee Bob will never find gold in these hills now. There I'm becoming melancholy again,' she said, wiping a tear from her eye.

On that sad note they set off, to complete the remaining couple of miles down the track to Turton's Creek, where the mine was located. Mick was their guide and the path was steep so they chopped off sturdy branches to use as walking sticks and carefully navigate the steps that miners had cut out of the rock to permit footholds.

'It's amazing,' remarked Chris who had been pondering on these things of late, 'the settlers have had to lay this track down for themselves with no help whatsoever from our indolent local council. We are well overdue for a change.'

'You know what they say? If you want something done, then do it yourself,' replied Mick, stating the obvious in a flat, matter-of-fact way.

They rounded a bend and descended to the bottom of the hill where they saw two huts made of wattle logs, which had been cleared from the surrounding forest, sawn in half and then laid end on end and tied together with rope. The huts had no windows and just one entrance covered with a hessian bag nailed to the doorjamb. Timber beams had been slung across to form a roof and native ferns had been lashed on top.

'Good-day to you all,' Mick called to the miners who were seated around the fire, eating dinner at their camp. 'We've come to see this here gold that is scattered around these hills. I reckon we'll go away rich men.'

'So this is the best address in town, where all the likely lads hang out and where dreams come true,' Chris added in jest. There were laughs all round, and in the little clearing in front of the huts with the tall timbers whispering above, the party was welcomed with typical bushmen's hospitality.

'This is indeed, the flashest joint around,' laughed the tall, lean, weathered bloke that introduced himself as Alex Fawkner, the man leading the dig.

'Come and join us, we've been expecting you, the billy's on, would you like a cuppa?' Alex then addressed young Aubrey who was shyly keeping a low profile next to his father.

'Pleased to meet you, son. There's gold to be had up this way. Stick with me and you will be a rich man.'

Aubrey smiled but secretly resolved that there was no way he was leaving home to come and work for these men. It looked far too primitive for his liking.

'No one ever drops by,' continued Fawkner, 'so it will be good to hear something different from the normal jabbering that goes on around here.' He nodded towards a long, lean man with a bushy beard and battered hat. 'Half the time we can't understand a word of what Jock here goes on with. If you don't understand laddie, just nod your head and smile.'

Aubrey quickly recognised that the man named Jock was the Scottish bushy that they had met on the train and who had offered to fix Mervyn's wobbly boots.

The big man smiled at the boy. 'How are those boots of your brother's?' he grinned. 'Still not wobbly I hope? Come on, laddie, I'll take ye and show ye around while the men talk. Have ye seen my little pet wallaby?'

He took Aubrey to the side of one hut, where he unpegged a hessian bag from the branch of a tree and there, snuggled up and keeping warm, was a joey. 'We had a big storm up this way and a huge branch fell on the wee lad's mother,' explained Jock. 'Poor thing died and we would have just thrown her down the gully and out of the way, but we saw a wee head peeking out of the pouch.'

'Oh, he's so cute! And so tame!' exclaimed Aubrey as the joey licked his fingers.

'He's looking for honey on those fingers. I've been feeding the poor mite with honey and powdered milk. I made this here to drip it into his wee mouth,' he said pointing out a hollow twig. 'He's just started eating a wee bit of grass. Pull some off and see if he'll take it.'

Aubrey plucked some grass that was growing nearby and proffered it. 'What his name?' he asked as the joey sniffed at the grass.

'I christened him Robert the Bruce after the great Scottish warrior. It's a grand name but most of the time I just call him Wally. He likes that better.'

'Here you go, Wally, have some sweet, juicy grass,' Aubrey coaxed. 'How long will he stay in the sack, Jock?'

'A few weeks, maybe months yet, he still a young one. He'll start to move around soon I suppose, but until then I have wrapped him up in my old woollen jumper and now he thinks the wee sack is his mother. He's as snug as a bug in a rug! Let's hope it doesn't get so cold that I'll be wanting my pullover back.'

He gently pegged the bag back on the branch, looked around and pointed out a large rock about fifty yards up the path. 'Listen, laddie, can ye hit that rock on the ledge with a stone?' Jock challenged him. 'I'll give ye three tries.' He bent over and picked up half a dozen stones, handing three to Aubrey and keeping three for himself. At first the boy's stone fell short, but noting how Jock threw himself into his throw, he imitated him and by the third throw he came within cooee. Jock, of course, hit his target every time. They spent the next half hour in this manner while back at the camp the men talked business.

'I hear that Ford and Stewart had their alluvial sent to Bairnsdale for testing, do ye know anything about that?' queried Fawkner.

'I do know this much,' returned Duggan, 'that they are pretty tight lipped about it all. They must think they have something there, as I believe it cost a small fortune to have the testing done – that is, by the time they transported it all there, and that. If you ask me, I will tell you that I reckon that all this tip toeing around is bulldust, it's in the interest of the public to know the state of play with these things.'

They nodded sagely as they shared the tea. The miners took chunks of the fruit cake that Ethel had baked for the journey and devoured it hungrily with their sweet black brew. It was quite a while since they had eaten home baking.

Jock and Aubrey rejoined the group and Alex then led them all through one hundred yards or so of dense forest to another clearing where it was evident that a tremendous amount of hard work had been done.

'As you can see, it has not been easy to clear the land before we could start,' ventured Andy Douglas. 'Jock, Alex and me spent a good three months felling and grubbing huge trees to make way for the digging. You can't see the gold, but we know it's there. Even though it's not visible to the naked eye, we all have no doubt that the rock contains it. It's only a matter of time before we are wealthy men, living it up in the city.'

'We have grand plans for the mine and intend to cut into the hill further and to open it out even more,' Alex commented. 'However, our problem is that we are fast running out of cash so we're hoping that we will get some outside assistance, and that's where you gentlemen come in. There's enough gold in these hills to go around and if you can convince the gentlemen with money in the towns to put their hands in their pockets, then we are willing to do the work. Here, take a spade and have a bit of a dig for yourself. See what you think.'

They each selected a pick or shovel and proceeded to dig out a sample. Aub took a piece of rock, cleaned it of dirt and held it to the sun examining it as if he knew what he was doing.

Chris put his in his pocket; he would fracture it with a hammer when he got home to see if gold was inside. On the surface, it seemed a good mine and if, as they said there was gold to be had, he wanted to be in on it. They were all made to promise that they would not breathe a word to anyone about its location.

Being mindful of time restraints as they wanted to reach Johnstone's that evening, they left the miners with the remainder of the fruitcake and boiled beef, said their goodbyes, wished them luck and began their homeward journey back to Duggan's where after another quick cup of tea, they retrieved their horses and started out to Robert Johnstone's holding, about six or seven miles off on a different track.

CHAPTER 26

Darkness descended gently, the lantern moon hanging low over the hills and lighting their way so that the native trees and scrub became a glorious moonlit wonderland that captivated both the horses and their riders.

'Dad, is it always like this at night when we are in bed?' the son asked his father. 'If this is how it is, I never want to sleep, ever. It is so beautiful.'

'Son, this is how it can be, but tomorrow night may be dark and cold, so let the horse have her head and enjoy the moment. Remember this night when you are an old man and say a prayer for your dear old Pa who will long have gone to his grave.'

With that sobering thought they rode on through lonely bushland until they came to a recently constructed modern house where they were greeted by old Robert, one of the earliest settlers in those parts.

Chris hadn't seen the finished building and was pleased to note that his mother now enjoyed wooden floors instead of the earthen type, that the walls were solid and wind-proof and that the kitchen was under the same walls as the remainder of the house. A wide veranda encircled the entire structure. He felt that she had struggled to keep house in a settler's hut for more than two decades so she deserved some modern comforts.

His brothers, Billy and James, took the horses from the men and led them away to be rubbed down, fed and bedded for the night. Aubrey squirmed under the affectionate hugs of his grandmother and his two aunts who were thrilled to see him and who fed him hearty shepherd's pie before showing him his bed. His head was no sooner on the pillow than he was sound asleep, dreaming of gold.

Billy and James joined the party that had assembled in the dining room to eat and then adjourned to the sitting room to sample Robert's home brew.

'Now, remember that you promised to have a word with the old man regarding the cricket,' Billy whispered and Chris acknowledged that he would, but that he was biding his time for the right moment. The room was soon bubbling with laughter and good cheer as everyone kicked back to while away a few hours listening to Robert relate his pioneering experiences.

'You know when I came up here from the city, it was a real rude awakening. We had no idea of the hardship and privation. Baw Baw country was a veritable wilderness, black man's land and the Gippsland to Melbourne road was just a cattle track. The mail had to be carried on horseback and passengers and goods taken by steamboat to Port Albert. It was drovers that kept the pot boiling between Ararat and Rosedale.'

Robert stopped and cleared his throat as the others waited, enthralled.

'I built a bit of a hut which I reckoned would do us for the first six months, until I cleared some forest. I really thought that all a settler had to do was clear some land, stock it and then manage it. How wrong I was? It is so remote and I went through my capital. You know how long it was before we got to build a better house? Six years! And then it was another fifteen until we got this here new place. Mum's happy now, aren't you love?'

He referred to his wife who was sitting beside Chris, and who nodded her head in agreement, happy to have her boy home by her side.

'Of course, we weren't the only ones crying in the wilderness. There was the O'Connors at Old Bunyip, the Jones at Cannibal Creek, Jacksons at Tarwin, Browns at Shady Creek, Millers at Moe and Campbells at Traralgon. They're just the ones I knew. There might have been some others, of course.'

He raised his glass and winked.

'The best thing about it all was that nobody cared if you made your own ale, and we all did. There was plenty of places a brew could be produced without attracting the excise man.' He sipped from his glass and warmed to the story. 'It was a very splendid location for secret stills, too. Chris, do you remember the one we had down the hill a bit in the bunyip's cave?' He smiled as he thought of the hardships they had endured and of the help they had received from the strong bootleg whisky to survive.

'You know, there may not have been a farm or a settlement from Bunyip to Morwell but there were possums, kangaroos and wombats galore. Ducks, geese, swans, that's what we lived on, and the rivers and streams were chock-a-block with fish, absolutely swarming with them. Never went hungry, did we, Mary Jane?' he asked addressing his wife who had heard all of this before, and who was sewing beads on her daughter's wedding gown.

'I reckoned it was in the Government's interest to support farmers. After all, we are Australia's principal industry. How wrong can a man be? They never lifted a hand to help; we were too far away from the city, out of sight, out of mind. Anyway, we love it here now, don't we lovie?'

His wife nodded her head in affirmation.

'But the government has to be more accountable, it can't just do as it pleases. Those city blokes sometimes call the Gippsland farmer a perpetual grumbler, but we have every cause for complaint. Life is hard up here.'

And so it went on until late when, tired after their long day, they all hit the sack, Billy included. Chris stayed on with his father to put Billy's case regarding going to the city to play cricket, but to no avail.

'I hear what you are asking, Christopher,' the old man explained, 'and your mother and I have discussed it, but we're old and we rely on Billy. He's the youngest and he's the only one here to help me. James' health is no good since he had that bout of consumption, so he really can't do much. Can you believe that I had eleven children and now it's just down to me and Billy to run the farm? Elizabeth will be marrying Moser soon, so she will be moving away. We need Billy here, not playing games in the city. He has to stand up and take his responsibilities like a man.'

Chris could see he would not change his mind, but he had done as he had been asked. 'Billy will just have to grin and bear it,' he thought as he pulled off his riding boots and fell into bed. The party rose early next morning and began their homeward journey. Billy would be staying on the farm.

It was good to visit to the old people,' Chris told Ethel on his return. 'I really must make more of an effort to get up there more often. Poor Billy is trapped on the farm and probably will never get away. If he does escape it will be too late for a career in cricket. But that's his problem; there's not much I can do about it. Just be thankful, Etty, that I got out when I did.'

'Poor Billy! I feel for him but, as you say, the old people need care and he is the only one who can help them. You have a family and a business, and that comes first.'

What could Chris say? Billy was needed to look after his parents and the farm, and that was all there was to it. Chris did not want that responsibility put onto his own shoulders.

Later that night, over his bowl of tripe, he continued discussion about life up at Yinnar. 'It's a wonder they don't all go crazy up there in those hills,' he said. 'They never see another living person from one end of the week to the other, and yet they still love company. You should have seen the old man last night holding court and telling yarns, and mother just listening as if she hadn't heard them all before. God knows how many times I had heard them, so she must know them off by heart. We had to tell him to go to bed in the end. He loves company, but equally he seems to love the solitude.'

Chris put down his knife and settled into yarn-telling mode, not unlike his father.

'He did tell me a couple of funny yarns though,' he continued. 'The best one was about old Buff Duggan, I think he's a cousin of Mick's. Anyway he lives right up Ensay way, tracks dingoes for the bounty. They tell me he's pretty smart, but he wasn't smart the way Dad tells it.'

'Tell me then,' encouraged Ethel as she began to set the table for breakfast the following morning.

'It goes this way,' said Chris, needing little encouragement. 'Apparently, Buff and a bloke called George Baker were having a night on the town at the Ensay hotel. George has a big family to support so he doesn't go to the pub much but Buffy was in town and he was allowed off the leash for the night.

'The upshot was that they both had way too much to drink and when it came to home time it was pitch black outside, not a star in the sky. "Never mind," Old Buff said, "we'll be all right. We'll just follow the fence line by feel and we will get to the track." What they didn't know was that the hotel owners had just built a brand new tennis court behind the pub and they had stepped out into it. So they followed the fence all right - around and around and around and around.'

'That's funny!' laughed Ethel, 'did they finally find the way home?'

'No,' chuckled Chris, 'in the end they had to sit down and wait for dawn. I can't imagine what they thought when they found out they were inside a tennis court!'

'That's one of the funniest things I have ever heard,' said Ethel, holding her sides from the mirth. 'Let's celebrate our differences, your father is a bushy, you're a townie and yet you both think you will find gold in those hills. Remarkable isn't it?

'I'm thinking of investing some money in the mine we saw yesterday,' he continued. 'I'm sure there is gold in the hills.'

'Promise me one thing Christie,' she asked.

'And what is that pretty wifey?' Chris responded.

'Promise me that if you must put money into Fawkner's mine, you will wait until we have some more staff helping us, and we are more on our feet. You can have too many fingers in too many pies, my darling.'

CHAPTER 27

Max Gordon vigorously applied his cloth to the bar bench with the wide, circular motion that he had honed over the years, rounding up the wayward spills, collecting them in one place and then with an extra glide of the hand, swooshing them into the bucket that lay in waiting on the floor underneath.

'I've sold the joint,' he declared to his band of regulars around the bar. 'I'm done with the long hours and blokes who don't know how to hold their booze, so I'm out of here.'

'That's sad to hear Max, we are used to you, in fact we like you,' commented Chris from what had become his corner of the bar. 'You run a good place here, Maxie. I know you have had a bit of trouble with drunks lately, but I didn't realise that they had tried your patience so much. Are you sure we can't talk you into staying on? Problems always come with progress, things will settle, you'll see,'

'The missus has had enough, says it's bad for the young ones to be living on licensed premises. Besides, I am getting sick and tired of having to break up all the fights and trouble outside this place of late. I throw the buggers out and they continue their scrapping in the street.'

'What Trafalgar needs is its own Police Station. It will never get better until that happens,' put in Dan Baillee, who had been standing idly by, one hand in his pocket and the fingers of the other drumming unconsciously on the bar top.

'Exactly! By the time I call the constabulary and they finally arrive from Moe or Warragul, all the scoundrels have fled the scene. There's only so much a man can take.'

'Well, it's a sad day indeed,' Tom McGrath was moved to comment. 'Are you off to the big smoke then, Max? Heading back to the city with a stack of coin in your back pocket?'

'Nope! You blokes don't get rid of me that easily. We have put in a tender to buy some of the land they are opening up and on the other side of Yarragon. So, instead of pulling beers, I'll be pulling cows' tits. And you know what? I reckon that cows have it all over drunks. They may be up early in the morning but they go to sleep early at night and that is it. They are always in the paddock where they should be; they don't fight, they feed themselves and they certainly don't swear.'

'Yes, but they leave shite all over the place!' Dan quipped. They all laughed.

'What about Miss Stewart over at her place then? Does she have trouble with drunks?'

'She doesn't seem to!' Chris put in his oar. 'The way Jimmy Kenny tells it is that she may present a pretty face, but she can pack a mean punch. She only allows a bloke one mistake. If anybody plays up on her, he is catapulted out of the Criterion's door on the end of her pretty boot, and she never ever relents and takes him back in.'

'That's the trouble,' moaned Max. 'We are getting all her rejects. I think all the blasted roughies have come over here to me at Gordon's.'

'Jimmy tells me she's lost a fair bit of business over the few months she has been in charge, but on the upside, she only has quality patrons,' Chris added. 'I have absolutely no hesitation in taking Mrs Johnstone to Miss Stewart's establishment for dinner but, with all due respect Max, I wouldn't bring her here.'

'Come on Chris,' bantered Dan Bailee. 'We all know why that is. You don't want the missus hanging around the place that you have made your patch. I reckon you own that corner of the bar by now. It has your name written on it.' They all laughed again. It was a Wednesday evening after the football match and they were there for the company and collective wisdom.

'Tell everyone you see to roll up, roll up, I'm having a clearing sale - all the fixtures and fittings,' Max announced. 'What are you doing with the animals?' enquired George McCrory.

'Hard as it will be, I am going to have to part with Dondi. He is a Trafalgar local and needs company, and we just won't have the time to give it to the dear old nag at the new place. We'll be too busy clearing land and setting up a herd. But, I'm not selling him. You would never sell your best friend. I am giving him away to a good home. I'm selling Betty the cow, though. Is anybody interested? Anybody want a cow?'

'We are looking into getting ourselves a house cow,' suggested Chris, taking the opportunity on offer. 'We would always have fresh milk and the boys could take responsibility for milking her. How about I will give you your price for Betty and you can throw in your old mate Dondi for free. We'll take care of him.'

That is how the empty paddock next door to the Johnstone's became home for Betty and Dondi.

'I think I will need to make Dondi a coat for winter,' suggested Ethel while she, Chris and the boys were in the side paddock inspecting the new additions to the family. 'It's more exposed here in the paddock than it was in the middle of town and there's not a lot of shelter. Dondi is used to spend the nights in the shed at Gordon's, so we can't have him getting sick. What would the townsfolk say?'

'Yes, best not kill their dear Dondi!' Chris added sagely. 'That would certainly have tongues wagging!'

CHAPTER 28

The day Mr Ah Woo from Mildura set up his bare-rooted plant store in the station courtyard, Ethel was amongst the earliest customers to arrive because she was anxious to have first choice of his roses and fruit trees.

After her purchases were made, she almost skipped home, so happy was she that at last she could get some serious planting done. As she passed the Printing Office she stuck her head and called to Chris. 'I got my roses! And they all match. They will be beautiful, double whites on either side of the path and ruby reds to climb the veranda posts.'

'Good girl! Good girl!' Chris returned in his distracted manner. 'How much did that set me back?'

'They are worth every penny, Christie. The garden will be beautiful as well as fragrant, and I have enough fruit trees to keep us in jam and preserves for the rest of our lives. Can either you or Jimmy take the wheelbarrow over and pick them up when you have time? I have already paid for them.'

'I'll go now while I think of it,' volunteered Jimmy. 'Show me where the wheelbarrow is and I'll get them for you.' He walked back to the house with her, collected the barrow which was leaning against the washhouse and set off. There were so many plants that it took three trips to collect them and line them all up beside the front veranda ready for planting.

'Yell out if you want some manpower to dig the holes for you, Mrs J,' Jimmy said. He put the barrow down, reached into his top pocket, pulled out his tobacco pouch and proceeded to roll a cigarette. It had been frosty that morning but the cold had lifted and the day was sunny and brisk, an ideal day for gardening. 'I love nothing better than a day of digging,' he continued. 'At the moment I am organising a kitchen garden for the hotel. Mavis says that if we can get one up and going in the springtime it will ensure that she always has fresh produce. I've dug it all over and covered it with straw from the old man's dairy, so I'm just waiting until it gets warmer to begin the plantings.'

'Gosh,' said Etty, 'whatever will Mavis do if you get a house of your own, Jim? It sounds like you are her right-hand man.'

'Yep, I am that all right!' Jim smiled at the thought. 'But I like doing it. The place feels like home to me so I don't think I will be moving out any time soon. I'd best get back to Chris. Let me know if there is anything else I can do.'

Ethel thanked Jim and went inside where she changed into her old clothes, putting a straw hat on her head and gumboots on her feet. There was absolutely no way that she was going to the office today. The men could do without her. She had been previously busy preparing the soil by composting her kitchen scraps and incorporating the animals' manure, as well as adding the urine from the boy's night-time potties. Now, she purposefully prepared to plant her roses, soaking the roots of each one in a bucket of water. Taking the spade from where it had been resting with the wheelbarrow, she dug wide holes, set the plants down and spread their roots, and back filled with soil and water. Suddenly the garden was beginning to take shape.

When the roses had been planted out, she stood at the gate and took in what she had done that morning. Spring would soon be here and, with its coming, these dormant roses would burst into life. It was a waiting game. How she would have loved to work all day in the garden, but there was dinner to be put on the table for her hungry boys, so the fruit trees were put aside in the shade of the tank stand to be planted another day. Perhaps Aubrey might help her after school.

She was rostered to help prepare the hall for a football club card night at the Mechanics Institute that afternoon, so immediately after the boys went back to school and the dinner things were cleaned up, she headed over there.

'We had another tragedy out our way last weekend,' Marie Nix told the other ladies. 'A little fellow got out of his bed in the middle of the night and wandered away and drowned.'

'How on earth can a thing like that happen?' Ethel was flummoxed as to the why and wherefores.

'No one knows exactly,' replied Marie, 'the parents say they checked the children before they retired and everything was fine. The child was safely asleep in his own bed. But, during the night, somehow, he got out of the house and wandered off.'

'There is a condition called sleepwalking that I have read about. People have been known to do all sorts of things in their sleep and have no recollection next day.' Ethel was busy trying to rationalise the situation in her mind.

'Nobody has mentioned that, but it is possible,' Marie answered continuing her tale. 'The family dog barked non-stop all night and Albie, that's the lad's father, tried to call it in a couple of times, but it would not budge and continued barking and howling. In the end, he gave up, put the disturbance down to wombats or possums, and went back to bed. When poor Albie and Jane woke up they discovered their lad was missing. Of course they went into a panic and immediately began the search. The dear souls didn't have to go far because they found little Bertie's body, with the dog next to him. That faithful old fellow wouldn't leave the boy's side even after the little fellow had been laid out ready for burial.'

'That dog is a hero, so faithful and true,' Ethel said. 'And those poor, poor parents! That is an absolute tragedy. I can't imagine losing one of my boys. They must be heartbroken.'

'Yes, it's horrible. We are doing our best to rally around Albie and Jane, and we all have shed tears for the little one, but nothing can take that pain away from them. The grief will follow them 'til the day they die. It's an awful, awful thing to happen. They will never, ever get over this, but I agree, that dog is a hero.'

Life could be very hard and cruel in a small isolated community where bad things happened regularly. The talk was also about Emma Mitchell, a widow who had only recently married her dead husband's brother, William. The courts had intervened and dissolved the marriage because it was deemed illegal. Emma was declared guilty of committing the crime of bigamy. Although a man was allowed to marry his dead wife's sister, the reverse was not the case.

'Tut, tut, tut, tut, tut,' was the general consensus. 'Wicked, wayward, disgusting bigamist.'

'The poor dear, how was she to know?' retorted Ethel, boldly coming to the widow's defence. 'In my opinion, it was up to the brother to find out these things before he came courting, so that he didn't put her in this awful predicament.

In any case, what harm were they doing? William was happy to take on the responsibilities of his dead brother's family and to make sure that they were all right and I think that is the honourable stance to take. And who made these laws, anyway? Why is there one rule for the men and another for the women? We're all in this together, you know! Emma can come to my kitchen table for a cup of tea any time she likes; I will be honoured to pour it for her.'

The silence that followed this remark was telling, most of the ladies shocked that Ethel should come to the defence of a wayward woman. Eva Lawrence, sensing the awkwardness, commented on the Methodist Church anniversary celebrations the previous weekend.

'Little Ivy McMahon recited the saddest poem called "Little Jim, the Collier's Child",' she said. 'There was not a dry eye in the hall. I shall have to ask her for a copy of the words so I can learn it. It makes a wonderful party piece.'

'What? Learn the words just so you can make us all cry?' queried Mildred Willie, lightening the mood further.

'Give me a good laugh any day,' Lillian Charles added. 'I was there and I must say I loved the piece that Barry Ludwig recited called "The Lifeboat". It was the funniest thing. All about the wheeling and dealing that went on after everyone had escaped a sinking ship but were still far from help. I could just imagine it happening. There are always those who want to be King Pin and those who will follow, those who are optimistic and those who are pessimistic, the capable and the bumblers, the bossy and the meek, the gentlemen and the scoundrels. It was exactly like life, really. We are all in the same boat together, being taken along by the current. Do we paddle or do we go with the flow? Barry summed it all up in verse. So funny!'

An argument had been averted.

'I made a bad impression on some of the women today,' Ethel told Chris over dinner that night, and related the story. 'They all think I have low morals now, but somebody had to put Emma's side. Poor dear was being castigated for something that was definitely not her fault.'

'Best be careful of the impression you make Ethel,' advised Chris, sipping his tea. 'In a small town like this, nobody likes anyone else to stand out from the crowd in their opinions. People can be judgmental and self-righteous. I'm not saying don't stand up for the underdog. Just choose your battles and remember that our family has to live in this town.'

'Are you telling me to let the gossip fly past me and to bite my tongue, Christie?' Ethel asked, somewhat annoyed. 'Who was to stick up for the widow if I didn't?'

'All I'm saying,' Chris added patiently, 'is that it is better to say nothing at all than it is to open your mouth and let it all loose. The widow's plight is not your business, so don't make it so.'

'Well, that's exactly where you and I differ, Christopher McCallum Johnstone. You are the diplomat who talks in circles and I speak the truth as I see it. You may be right, you may be wrong, but I have to do what's right for me and my conscience, so put that in your pipe and smoke it,' Ethel huffed.

The silence lay heavy between them.

'Did you know that Murray, Matthews, Sullivan and Bernicke have resigned en masse from the Hall Committee?' Ethel asked in a conciliatory manner after five minutes had elapsed. She immediately had Chris' attention. For a man who purported not to gossip he was mightily interested in the affairs of his fellow townsmen.

'Why is that? Has there been some sort of argument?' he queried.

'Don't ask me why, because I don't know, but they must be unhappy about something. We ladies are soldiering on with the Bazaar because we think a brand new hall gives the town something to be proud of. Also we have employed a librarian.'

'Oh yes. Who would that be?

'He's a man called John Dusting. He comes from Moe, I think. We will have him organising and cataloguing the books and planning a few talks and things. He's already managed to get Mr Frank Geach to agree to talk about Pioneering in South Gippsland. That should be entertaining. The hall really is a valuable asset in the town. It is used every day.'

'My father could give a pretty good talk on pioneering,' chided Chris.

'Well, he's not here; he's miles out in the bush. So, Mr Geach it is, until you can get old Robert to come into town. Now that might be a long time coming! He's such an old bushie!'

The distance between them had closed and everything was back to normal. They chatted on until Chris stood up, put on his coat, checked his fob watch and said, 'I'm off down to Lawless' for a meeting.'

'Another meeting? What is this one for?'

'We reckon it's about time the town had a public tennis court.' '

'Tennis? Who would have thought?' Ethel had to be convinced.

'We need something that the men and women can play together socially. Council has already granted us land that we can use. Tonight we just need to organise a working bee so that next summer our young people can enjoy a game. Whole families can play tennis together. The boys will love it!'

'Yes, there are good civic minded people in this town who are always making things better, and you Christie Johnstone, are one of them.'

He kissed the top of her head and left. She picked up the socks that lay in the sewing basket, threaded her needle and sat at the table to darn, awaiting her husband's return.

CHAPTER 29

'The new tennis courts are going ahead. There is a working bee this coming Saturday,' Ethel informed Maggie as they worked together on Monday washday.

'Well, I shall send George down to help,' said Maggie. 'We would love a tennis court in town. We used to play on a Sunday afternoon in Mallacoota. It's great fun. We had some grand matches and we always had a delicious afternoon tea afterwards.'

'You and George are the most sociable couple I know,' Ethel observed. 'As for us, we seem to spend our weekends at home. Christie is always so distracted about the paper. He thinks about it continually and I seem to be either outside digging in the garden or inside playing board games with the boys.'

'Yes, we are always out and about, I suppose. George needs a break from the hard physical work and I'd go mad if I didn't see people. If we had a child it would probably be different,' she added, her voice drifting off as she contemplated the possibility.

Sensing her melancholy, Ethel quickly brought the subject around to something she had been pondering of late.

'Maggie, what is it about you Catholics?' she asked, prodding the boys' muddy football pants with a stick in the boiling hot water of the copper. 'How come that all the other balls in town are struggling to get a half decent crowd, and yet, when your mob has a ball the place is packed to the rafters. I went down there to report on the dresses the other night and I could hardly move around in the crowd. There was the Coglans, the Walshes, the Days, the Conleys, the Paynes, the Kennedys, the Lawlesses, the Kennys, the Donovans and the Lynches and that was just the beginning. There was even an Italian family, Plozza, I think was their name. Mrs Plozza had made this wonderful dessert, like a trifle, but where she had used cold coffee to soak the cake instead of sherry. She did something wonderful with the custard too. I've never tasted anything as exotic. It was delicious. Anyway, what I mean to say is, everyone was out in force and they were all dancing and having a great time. It went all night. Annie tells me that they were still dancing at dawn.'

'Well, I must admit it was a grand night,' said Maggie as she pegged the socks on the line to dry. 'George and I had a great old time and Mary McCrory told me that they could have sold twice as many tickets if the hall had been big enough. We partied on till the wee hours, but we all got up and went to Mass on Sunday morning, mind.

'There was quite a lot of yawning when Father Coyne was going on with his sermon. I saw a few heads nod off in front of me. I suppose the Catholic balls are best because most of us are Irish and we all enjoy a good hooley. Dancing has never been a sin for us and we all love to sing. Besides, I'll let you into a little secret if you promise not to tell. Our men dance because they always have a little supply of the poteen out under the hessian bags in their buggies. It makes them jolly, but that's just between you and me. Don't let it go any further.'

They both laughed.

'Well, you know what?' said Ethel. 'When I die and go to heaven, I think I want to go in the Catholic section, it appears to be more fun!'

Ethel turned away. 'Oh, I can't believe I just said that,' she thought, putting her hand to her lips. 'Imagine saying that I'd like to be amongst the Catholics? I must be letting Maggie corrupt me. I'd never met a Catholic before I came to this town.'

Maggie continued, 'There was also a bit of fun that had us all laughing after the ten o'clock Mass last Sunday. Do you know old Paddy McCormack from out Thorpdale way?'

'Yes, I have seen him in town on market day,' said Ethel, turning back.

'Well, he rides his white horse to church every week and tethers her under the big peppercorn tree. While he was a praying away inside, head down and bottom up, some of the young lads took the horse and gave her a coat of black shoe polish. Old Paddy comes out, blinks in the sunlight, looks around and can't for the life of him see his horse. In the end his mare was the only horse left in the paddock and he knew he was the butt of a prank. "God help me," he says in his broad Irish accent, "I began the day with a white 'arse and the good lord has changed it to a black 'arse." We all laughed. It was so funny!'

The women chuckled about this story as they continued their task. Eventually Ethel broke the silence.

'We'll be able to have a few at home evenings ourselves soon,' she commented, as she emptied the dirty water to make way for a clean lot for the bed linen. 'You know it was my birthday the other day? Well, darling Christie has gone out and bought me a brand new piano that will be delivered any day now. There's a fellow named Nicholson in Morwell who makes them especially for Australian conditions and we are able to pay it off for five shillings a week. Christie says that we can manage that now that the paper is up and running and doing well.'

'Ooh! I love a good sing-a-long. It would be wonderful to own my very own piano. Lucky, lucky you, Etty.'

'I was thinking perhaps we may have our first musical evening when Sir John Madden comes to stay. He and Chris and a few others are going on a shooting expedition out into the bush.'

'Oh la de dah! Sir John, heh? You'll have to be on your best behaviour then, Ethel, you'll have to mind your p's and q's, ' teased Maggie, not realising that she had just stepped over the line.

Although Ethel was egalitarian in her views and friends, not far beneath the surface she was still very British and she liked the way that society was structured so that one instantly knew a person's worth by his title. She may now mix with Catholics, may even like some of them, but it was wonderful to have men and women of substance amongst her friends. Of course, a girl like Maggie who was raised in a remote fishing village and now lived in a country town would know nothing about high society, and so Ethel strove to put her right.

'He's a very nice man, Maggie. I have known him since I was a little girl. He did business with my father, so I'll thank you not to make fun at his expense. Sir John is a man of letters, has a Law degree from the university and has been honoured by the old queen herself for his work in the colonies. Now he is Chief Justice of Victoria. That is the only problem with

223

a little town like Trafalgar. We are removed from the niceties
of life and sometimes we can become cynical. You will
probably meet him when he is here, so please pay him the
respect that is his due.'

'I'm sure he's a wonderful human being, Ethel. But since you
move in those lofty circles, perhaps you can tell me all about
our new Governor-General, Lord La De Da Tennyson. How
come when he is being sworn in he won't be accompanied
by his wife but by another man, a bloke called Lord La De
Da Neville? Now that could take some explaining.'

'Maggie! Where did you get that information?'

'I read it in your paper, Ethel.'

'Oh, I see! Well, I shall leave you here with this while I go
across and take the men some lunch at the office. Monday is
such a crazy day; they barely have time to turn around.'

'Mmmm, certainly, I'll finish up here and make my way
home to get George's dinner,' replied the chastened Maggie.
She liked Ethel very much, but there was still something of a
gulf between them; they had been brought up in two entirely
different worlds.

CHAPTER 30

Chris was scribbling away at the front desk when Ethel walked into the office with a plate of mutton and pickle sandwiches made from the previous night's roast.

'Could you hear our stomachs gurgling from the house, Etty? We are absolutely starving, aren't we Jimmy?' said Chris.

'Certainly are. Pleased to see you Mrs J,' replied Jimmy waving at her with a welcoming grin.

'Is it me, or the sandwiches that you are pleased to see, Jimmy?' she asked responding to his goodwill.

'Etty, your Mr Matheson has just been in. He is a strange character, isn't he?' said Chris.

'What do you mean, my Mr Matheson? He's more, your Mr Matheson! Was he not the man who was good enough to loan you the money to start up the paper?' Ethel retorted, already a bit out of sorts because of Maggie's remarks about the Chief Justice. 'But why, what has he done?'

'Well, have a look at this,' said Chris, putting a piece of paper in front of her. She quickly scanned it and saw that it was a paid advertisement offering a challenge to all readers of the

"Times". It read: "I will gladly pay one hundred pounds to any person who can prove to me via scripture that man has an immortal soul".

Showing that he had obviously done his research, Matheson went on to point that in the Bible, "the word soul is used five hundred and thirty times, one hundred and ninety of these in reference to life and living, thirty one to people and twenty eight to beasts, but never once is there a reference to immortal soul."

'Well, you have to give the man credit for going through the Good Book with a fine-tooth comb and getting those statistics,' said Chris as he moved towards the table to prepare the advertisement for the next edition. 'My Godfather, he must live an exciting life! It must have taken him years to do that. Mind you, I'm not complaining. His money is as good, or better, than anyone else's, and he has paid upfront for a series of advertisements urging us heathens to discard the theology of the pulpit and to accept the Bible as the Word of God. He has even provided a reading list that people might use to find the information they need to win the money from him. I might get onto that as I could do with a hundred quid.'

'Leave him be, Christie,' warned Ethel. 'He's a good man and he's probably right, you know. He always opens up his home for Bible readings and prayer services and you can be sure that what you see is what you get with Alex. We Christadelphians read and take the Bible literally. We don't swing it around to suit our purposes like the established religions do. Our beliefs have as much validity as yours or anyone else's, so put that in your pipe and smoke it!'

Christie was interrupted by Jimmy from out the back, where he was melting lead, sandwich in one hand. 'You've been told, mate!' Jimmy called out. 'Put the advertisement in and stop teasing Etty about it. Matheson's beliefs are his own business, let's just be grateful that he is supporting us. And eat these delicious sandwiches that your lovely wife has made for us.'

'Mmm, that's interesting,' thought Ethel to herself. 'Good on you Jimmy for sticking up for me.'

'Thanks Jimmy,' she called back, 'Christie loves being a Scotsbyterian, but scratch the surface and we are all basically the same underneath.'

Chastened, Chris came home that night with the suggestion that Ethel should take a break. 'My brother George is doing a great job for us, so it is a good time to leave the office work to the men and make a trip to Mentone to spend some time with your mother,' he suggested. 'Leave the two older boys with me, if you like, and we shall be bachelors together. Best you take Vern though. He'd fret for you otherwise.'

It only took all of five seconds for Ethel to decide. 'Yes, Christie, that will be wonderful. I so miss mother and my sisters and so do the boys. It will soon be the September school holidays so I shall take all three boys and then you just have yourself to care for. I am so excited! I will write to Mother straight away.'

She flung her arms around her husband, planted a loud kiss on his cheek and took him dancing around the kitchen. She then went to the sideboard, took her leather stationery set and sat at the kitchen table. She opened the inkbottle and began to pen a letter, telling her mother of her approaching visit. It would be wonderful to spend time with her family.

When the letter arrived at Mentone, her folks were delighted. Mrs Gilbee immediately began to make preparations to ensure that the visit was a happy one. 'I have so missed my little men - and you too, of course, darling Ethel,' she wrote. 'The cousins cannot wait to play with your boys and, as well as that, I have planned a treat. I managed to obtain tickets to the theatre to see the new musical sensation, "Cyrano de Bergerac" with Miss Janet Waldorf as Roxanne, and Henry Lees as Cyrano. I think you will all love it. The reviews are certainly very favourable and I think it is an ideal way to introduce Aubrey and perhaps Mervyn to the theatre. Hopefully, the boys will learn not to judge a book by its cover. You may be able to obtain a copy of the book from the library to read to the lads before you see the show.'

Ethel was very much looking forward to the outing to the Melbourne theatre. Trafalgar had its own hardy collection of thespians who put on many entertaining shows, but Ethel always came away thinking that it was amateurish. 'That's a problem for me,' she'd explain to Christie who always defended the local shows. 'I grew up going to professional theatre with mother and father, so it's difficult not to compare the two.'

The day for the journey arrived and the family, dressed in their Sunday best and with bags packed, headed across the road to the station to wait for the train.

'You look lovely, Etty,' Chris said shyly as he appraised his wife in the simple but elegant travelling outfit. The well-cut navy blue jacket had been made exceedingly chic by the addition of tiny, dull gold buttons. She teamed it with a creamy lace blouse and a straw hat trimmed with shaded red roses.

'Is that the outfit you have been working on of late?'

'Yes it is, do you like it?' replied his wife. 'It took me absolutely forever to do it. If I had a sewing machine I could make something like this in less than a week.'

'Really, is that so? When you are in the city, why don't you explore the possibility of buying one, then?'

'They are quite expensive, but perhaps we can buy one second hand,' Ethel suggested, taking the opportunity to put her case. 'I was talking to Mrs Griffith's down at Bernicke's the other day and she told me they are having a clearing sale at their place. All the farming machinery and the herd are going under the hammer, as well as a lot of household furniture, including her perfectly good Singer sewing machine. She doesn't use it so much now that Margaret has married and moved away and they can't take it all the way to the west with them. 'So,' she added applying a certain turn of the head she knew that Chris couldn't resist, 'if you go to the sale, Christie darling, would you put in a bid for me, as I would find so many uses for it? It would come in very handy with the boys' clothes; they are growing so fast now that I can't keep up with them and they are so rough and ready that there is always mending to be done. You'd see, it would pay for itself within the year.'

'Yes, I can see what you mean; it would certainly save you time. You go and enjoy yourself, Etty. I will go to the sale and see what I can do, and maybe when you come back you will have your sewing machine. But we may not be the only ones interested, so don't be disappointed if I fail to make the final bid.'

Prompted by the mention of a clearing sale, Chris added some information about his brother as an afterthought. 'I saw David at the Yarragon sales yesterday and he is selling up and leaving.'

'Why? He has a wonderful farm there at Yinnar, only two miles out of town and he's been dairying for years. He must have a couple of hundred head of cattle, as well as his pigs and chooks. Why would he want to leave all that?'

'Don't ask me, because I can't tell you. But leaving us he is, and he's having a sale on the seventeenth of September.

You'll be back by then so we will go along and lend some moral support and help eat the luncheon that they are providing on the day. Sarah is such a good cook that it alone will be worth going for. They might have a sewing machine. I'll keep it in mind to ask.'

The boys came running to them, interrupting their conversation.

'Ma, I can see the smoke!'

'Ma, the train is coming!'

'Come on Ma, hurry, let's not miss it.'

The train drew in and amid the hustle and bustle they said their goodbyes, promised to keep safe and waved as the train chugged its way towards Melbourne. Chris went back to work and Ethel settled down with the boys for the journey ahead. It would be good to see her mother and sisters again and to go into Bourke Street to look at the shops and do some shopping.

CHAPTER 31

After watching the train head down the track and disappear around the corner, Chris rubbed his hands together, turned on his heel and headed back to the office to do some work. At precisely five o'clock he, his brother George and Jimmy shut shop and headed for Gordon's. Ethel was away, so it was time for play!

The new publican, Peter Fallon, had recently arrived from Queensland where the crocodiles were big and the men were thirsty. His grandfather had been an Afghan camel driver and he had a considerable amount of Bedouin in him to attest to this fact. His black eyes twinkled from under his luxuriant eyelashes and wayward eyebrows. His dark hair was slicked back off his forehead and his beardless, rugged skin was dark from the northern sun.

The locals had already dubbed him the 'Eagle' combining a play on his name by converting "fallon" to "talon", with the fact that he had a large beak of a nose. He was a wiry fellow and the word around town was that he was good on a horse and packed a mean punch.

'Well, here comes trouble; triple trouble, in fact,' the Eagle greeted them with a smile in his voice as they arranged themselves around the bar, Chris in his usual corner. 'And what can I do for the good men of the press? I'll get you all a beer while you tell me the most interesting piece of news you have heard all day.'

'Sounds good,' George joined in good-naturedly. 'How about the story of the bloke in America who woke up from his sleep and swore black and blue that he had swallowed his false teeth. He was in a bit of a panic so he went to the doc and told him the story and they operated on him. Slit his oesophagus from go to whoa. The operation killed him and the poor beggar died. After the funeral when the women were cleaning up his bedroom, guess what they found under the bed? His false teeth!'

Laughs all round. 'That teaches you to check your facts,' said Chris, always the sage.

'Has your wife finally left you then, Chris? I saw you down the station this morning, bidding her adieu,' teased the Eagle, as he drew the final beer and handed it over the counter.

'Leave me? Never! Not a handsome chap like I am, not on your life,' Chris replied. 'No, she has taken advantage of the Government's kind offer of free train travel for us poor blighted country folk and has gone to spend ten days with her mother in Mentone. The boys can experience some of the city lights and she can have a break from the newspaper. 'And,' continued Chris taking a sip of the amber liquid, 'with my lovely wife away, we have ten days ahead of us when we can take a drink every night. I shall miss the dear girl but every cloud has a silver lining, so I shouldn't complain.'

'When the cats away, the rats will play, so to speak,' laughed the Eagle.

'Have you met my brother, George?' Chris asked gesturing to the thickset fellow with the greying hair and handlebar moustache on his left. 'I have him on board now. He is back from the West with no gold in his pockets and no hope, so I talked him into coming with me. He's single and fancy free so he can do what he likes. I've brought him down for a pint. George, meet Peter. Peter, meet George.'

'Good to meet you, George! I hope you can put away as much beer as your brother. Now that would be good for business.'

'Not if I drink up the road with Mavis at the Criterion,' laughed George, shaking Eagle's hand firmly, as his father had instructed he should when he was a boy.

'That woman is taking all my best customers,' the Eagle lamented. 'I'll be left with all the riff raff like you blokes if she keeps doing that. We can't have women meddling in men's affairs.' The Eagle warmed to the subject and jumped his argument to the matter of suffrage at state level. 'Look at them agitating for the vote. If you ask me, they haven't the wit for politics and, love them as I do, I really believe that we would be placing our colony in jeopardy if we let the dear girls loose with the vote.'

'I don't think my Ethel would agree with that,' thought Chris, but kept his counsel, choosing to say nothing. Why create friction when his ideas were clearly in the minority?

'I reckon there's enough business to go around,' said Jimmy, coming to his landlady's defence. 'By the way, George, have you met Declan?' He gestured to an older man who had been leaning on the bar, not doing much.

'Pleased to meet you, George.' Declan Shanahan came forward proffering his right hand, then turning to Chris asked, 'Exactly how many bloody brothers do you have, Chris? I know of young Bob out in the hills there, and David from Yinnar, and Bill who was in here with you a while back. Are there any others, the place seems to be alive with Johnstones?'

'I reckon that all the Johnstones around here would be related,' said Chris. 'Now, let's see. We had two Johns, one who died when he was just one year old and the other we call Jack, and then there is Mary Ann who everyone calls Polly who married Jack McKendry and is up at Mollongghip. The young ones, Jimmy and Bill, are out on the land with the oldies and the two girls; Jane and Elizabeth and then we have David, and George here.

'You've forgotten Robert, Bob we call him,' George put in, 'he's up the back of beyond on a holding in the hills. You might know him, he comes into town occasionally, an old bushie.'

'Big family, and where do you come in all of this, Chris?' asked the keeper of the house, wiping the bottom of a glass.

'I am number 9 of 11. George is number seven. I have seven brothers and three sisters at the last count. We're all jolly good folk. That I know, for sure. And I'm the only townie, but I have George with me now so that will make two. I started out on the land with Pa until I was about twenty, but James and William were behind me and I had the urge to write, so I went to Melbourne, became a journalist on "The Argus", met Etty and then came back here to get the paper up and running.'

'Well, there you go! I thought I was always coming across Johnstones, but now I know why. Your lot breed like bloody blowflies mate,' laughed Declan.

'That'd be the Scot in us. We're a pretty hearty mob. Brought up to be stoic and strong. Old Bob, my father, came out from Dumphries to Ballarat on the goldfields about half way through the last century. Mum was Mary Jane McCullens from County Clare in Ireland, and they say that it's pretty rugged on the west coast of Ireland. Have to be tough to survive. I was born in a place called Dean near Ballarat, but we came to Yinnar when I was fourteen.'

'With ancestry like that, the Irish and the Scots, there's one thing I can be sure about you,' Declan smiled.

'And what's that, pray tell,' enquired Chris taking the bait.

'You love to take a drink and you hate the bloody English.' They all laughed.

'Could be right! But whatever you do, don't tell Ethel. She doesn't like me to imbibe too much and she's British through and through. Her blood runs red, white and blue. She thinks the Celts are savages, not up to the standards of the English at all.'

They chuckled again and sipped on their beers.

Over the course of the next ten days, while Ethel was out of town, there were unlimited topics to be discussed and debated at what was once known as Gordon's hotel, but was now the Eagle's eyrie. Around the bar, beers were sipped, pipes filled and cigarettes smoked. No need to rush home, best stay and enjoy the conviviality.

CHAPTER 32

"The boys and I are having a marvellous holiday in Mentone," said the letter. "And I love spending time with mother. However, we all miss you terribly and are looking forward to seeing you in a couple of days. And, by the way, I have managed to purchase the most beautiful sequinned gown just like Princess Alexandra wore for the Coronation. I will get plenty of wear out of it during the Ball season."

Chris put the note down and turned to George. 'Better get back to work and leave the pub alone for the next few days!' he said. 'That gown sounds like it has cost a fortune. Besides, Ethel won't be happy if she knows that I have spent so much time in the public house.

'But,' he added, 'I did manage to buy her that sewing machine that she so badly wanted, so that should put me in the good books. And it will be good to wake up every morning with a clear head and to the sound of my boys welcoming the day.'

Chris was wise enough to engage Maggie to come in to clean and air the house, light the fires and put one of her famous

Irish stews on the hob for the returning family. At the appointed time, he was down at the station looking for the telltale spiral of smoke that heralded the arrival of the train, secretly excited that his family would soon be home. Ethel was thrilled with her sewing machine and the couple were pleased to see each other. The boys regaled their father with tales of their adventures and the house came alive once more with the family sounds.

Aubrey was so pleased to be home again that he was up early the next morning with a smile on his face, cheerfully running down to pick up the newspaper from Lawson's, bringing it back and presenting it to his father. He tousled Vern's hair as he went past. 'How's it going, young Vernon?' he asked. 'Come on, put up your dukes,' he said to Merv as he danced around him, shadow boxing.

Before he sat down to his toast and honey he gave the fire a poke to get the flames roaring in the air. He was a happy boy because he was home with his father whom he hero-worshipped. Chris noticed and smiled lovingly at him, sharing his joy.

'While you were away, my wee lad,' he said, 'we men have been talking about making a rifle range for you boys up the other end of town there in Murray's paddock. We decided that there have been a few mishaps with guns lately and before something really serious happens we are going to make a place where you and your mates can go and practice your gunmanship in safety. So how does that sound to you? As soon as this wretched rain stops we are going to make a weekend to have a working bee and set things up. We just have to clear it with Council first.'

'Christie, you are a good father,' Ethel commented, pouring the tea. 'That's a wonderful idea. Guns and small boys always worry me; it's a tragedy waiting to happen. What a sweet man you are to be thinking of the boys when I know that you wouldn't have had time to turn around. How did you get all that going?'

She came over and kissed the top of his head.

'Where there's a will there's a way, Ethel dear. Having George in the shop left me free to move around town a bit and see a few people. You know my philosophy – listen well, answer cautiously, decide promptly and always know more than you are expected to know! Difficulties are only there to be overcome and failures should be treated as stepping stones to success.'

'You are full of it!' laughed Ethel. 'Is there any more platitudes that you would like to throw my way?'

'Platitudes, my dear? Let's see. Preserve by every means possible a sound mind in a sound body and, if it is somehow lacking, then make good use of other men's brains. And the other thing I do know is, that when a few good men get together good things can be made to happen!'

He did have the grace to blush just a little as he sipped his morning cup of tea.

CHAPTER 33

The yellow blossoms of the wattle trees blew about in the warm north wind as busy, bush bees buzzed their pollen collecting tunes. The sun soaked up the water from the seemingly permanent puddles along Main Street and in every garden spring bulbs bubbled and bloomed, reminding everyone of countries far away in the northern hemisphere where the glorious coming of spring was celebrated after cold, long and dark winters. Hay fever was rife because northern noses had not yet acclimatised to the pollens and grasses of this alien southern land.

Gardeners eagerly looked forward to the Trafalgar Horticultural Society's Annual Daffodil Show where they could examine and compare the blooms and discover the secrets from fellow gardeners who knew how best to judiciously prune and pamper plants so that they peaked exactly on the 11th of September to win a prize. But the Daffodil Show was about more than that. Awards were given for the best roses, carnations, violets, camellias and stocks, as well as for domestic arts and crafts.

On the previous day, kitchen ovens in Trafalgar and district had been stoked with good, slow-burning red gum to produce an even heat, and women had slaved over hot stoves to bake the best scones, cakes and biscuits possible so that they could to be judged at the show.

The women eagerly awaited the awarding of medals for the fancy work, cross stitch, sewing and knitting they had been busy working on all winter as these were considered badges of honour in a community where such skills were highly prized. This year everyone admired the glorious quilting of Gwendolyn Fisher, which was hanging on the wall for all to see, with a large blue "Best in Show" sticker attached to the corner. The reds, browns and the various pallets of colour in between, depicted life in the country; every square delicately appliquéd or embroidered, then joined together, hemmed and quilted. Ethel and Annie stood admiring it.

'That is a truly beautiful piece of work. I am truly flabbergasted by it,' said Ethel. 'Oh, how I wish that I had the talent to combine such intricate needlework, colour combinations and artistic quality. It is a wonderful work of art.'

'I agree. I have never seen a quilt I liked so much. It would look good on any bed, but it is almost too good to use. Gwen is indeed a craftswoman. Ah, here she is now! I'll ask her about it.'

Practical Gwendolyn came towards them, competent and business like. She was a woman who projected a strictly no-nonsense approach to everyday living. Her brain was sharp and Trafalgar didn't offer her sufficient challenges. She was discontented and told people so.

'We're admiring your work, Mrs Fisher,' said Annie. 'It is so labour intensive, just beautiful. When do you get the time? '

'Thank you for the compliment, Mrs Donovan. I have the time because I am bored out of my mind with nothing to do. I would go crazy if I didn't have my quilting and knitting because it makes the day go quicker for me. I would much rather be busy like I was when I was young and the children kept me active, believe me.'

'That's sad to hear, Mrs Fisher. Where are your family? Have they left the district?'

'My Harold died ten years ago, and now the children have grown and gone to the city for work. I do miss them. I came here with Harold when he found work at the creamery, but we don't own farmland so there is nothing here for the children now. Perhaps I will move to the city when they have grandchildren, but I own my freehold, so perhaps not. That's why I have time on my hands, there is absolutely nothing to do.'

Annie was taken aback with the lady's honesty, but Ethel seized the opportunity to further a plan she had been hatching.

'Then you may be just the woman I need, Mrs Fisher,' she said. 'I have been thinking that it would be wonderful to pass on the skills and knowledge of older women in our community. Would you be interested in helping me form a group where women can come to learn and practise some of these crafts that you do so well? We could meet and learn. What do you think?'

'I'd have to think about that,' Gwendolyn Fisher said cautiously. 'I can see that it would be a good thing. There are lots of other ladies I know who do wonderful craft work, and perhaps they could be persuaded to take part as well. It would certainly get me out of the house and give my days a sense of purpose.'

Ethel sensed that she warming to the idea. 'Well, you consider it and I shall make some enquiries and find out if there is somewhere we can meet and we shall have a chat about it in a week or two. You live over near the school there, is that right?'

'Yes, my little cottage is on the Thorpdale Road just before School Road. Drop in and have a cup of tea next Monday morning and I can show you some of my other pieces and we can have a chat and see where we go from here. I'm not promising anything, though, but right now I consider it an excellent idea and I am interested,' she concluded. She bade the two women goodbye and continued on her way.

'You always surprise me Ethel,' Annie commented. 'How long have you been thinking about that?'

'Almost since I arrived in the town,' answered Ethel. 'I thought then that it would have been nice to have a place to go to meet with other women and make friends. Until you came into the office that day, the only other women I had spoken to were Maggie Brown and Sophia Matheson. I was very lonely.'

'So that's why you had me over on the veranda drinking tea as quick as a shot. That explains it. You were lonely. It had nought to do with my sparkling personality,' laughed Annie.

'Well, I will admit, I did miss my mother and my sisters. I think there are a lot of women locked up in their houses who would love the company of other females. But, on the other hand, my asking you to tea had everything to do with your personality. I instinctively liked you from the day we met on the train, do you remember?'

'I do indeed. I thought you were a bit stuck up, but,' Annie added quickly, 'I admired the way you looked and how you insisted little Merv displayed good manners. I liked that, but I never thought we would be friends – a farmer's wife and a newspaperman's wife. I missed you when you were in Mentone. Who would have thought?'

She chuckled again, slipping her arm into Ethel's in easy friendship, and walking on to look at the displays of country cooking.

'It takes time to get to know and understand an oven,' Ethel commented as they gazed at perfectly made fruitcakes and light-as-air sponges. 'It will be years before I can produce anything nearly as good as any of these, if ever.'

'Yes. Making a cake rise is quite like raising a child, really. A good oven is essential, just like a happy home. You must be able to heat it to the proper temperature, read its moods so that you know when it is ready, make sure that you give it time to be cooked through, and watch over it carefully so it doesn't spoil.'

Annie realised that her thoughts were not quite clear to her friend so added, 'If you know what I mean. Oh! Here comes Tess Wilson. She has won first prize again,' she continued, changing the subject and pointing to a beautifully presented plate containing the lady's famous lamingtons.

'Well done, Theresa,' Annie said, greeted the smiling young woman. 'I see you retain the title of Tess the Lamington Lady. Good for you!'

'It was touch and go this year,' said Theresa. 'Last night I thought it was all over for me and that somebody else would pinch my glory. I managed to snatch victory from the jaws of defeat, but only just.' She laughed and went on to tell the tale. 'As you know, I have been secretary this year and it is quite a lot of work, so it was only late last night when I got around to doing the lamingtons. The mixture was all right and the cake came out light but substantial enough to take the icing. That was when I got into trouble. It was awful! My first lot of icing was all lumpy and not chocolaty enough and

I didn't have any more in the cupboard. In desperation I put the whole thing into a double boiler on the stove and reheated it, stirring and praying at the same time. Fortunately it worked and they turned out well, so I'm happy with the result. But next year I won't be waiting until after tea the night before the show to do the job.'

'Congratulations, Tess, you won and that is the main thing,' said Annie. 'Never mind how you did it. A win is a win.' Annie was happy for Theresa as she had been secretary herself one year and knew that it took a large amount of time and effort to bring the show to fruition. 'Come and join us for a cup of tea and one of Betty Windsor's fluffy scones topped with Kate Hobbs' delicious strawberry jam.'

'Let's not leave out the lashings of cream,' laughed Ethel. They sat down and ordered Devonshire Tea, sitting together amongst the flowering bulbs, and savouring the delightful scones.

'Next year,' Ethel confided, 'I am going to leave planting my bulbs until a bit later in the autumn. They were planted too early this year and have finished flowering ages ago.'

'You'll be up against some pretty stiff competition, Etty,' Annie warned. 'People like Evelyn Rankin and Albert Rees have been taking the top prize for years. They won't like it if you steal it from them.'

'They will have very little to worry about. I most probably shan't win, but I shall enjoy trying,' Ethel concluded. The bulbs that she had planted out in clusters in autumn had been the first things to flower in her new garden and she welcomed them like newborn children that held untold promise. When their flowers were spent she resisted the temptation to trim and tidy the foliage and instead, made loose knots of each clump, leaving them and the sun to do their work. Ethel understood that it took thirty years to make a garden. In order to achieve the lush, green, perfumed one of her dreams she would have to wait.

For now she tendered her embryonic garden daily, plucking weeds, bending to investigate newly shooting plants, rejoicing in small changes, planting tomatoes, beans, carrots, radishes and beets in her vegetable beds down the back and watching and waiting as her roses came into flower. She made a border of asylum each side of the path and planted the violet tubers that Annie gave her. Next year she hoped it would be a display of white, green and purple and the perfume would enrich the senses. She intuitively knew she would one day think back fondly to these times when the family, the house and the business were young.

'Time goes so quickly!' she thought. 'Next week, Christie and I have been married for fourteen years. We were young and now we are practically middle aged.'

Christie came home on the evening of their wedding anniversary with a palm tree in a pot that he had bartered from Mr Ah Woo, the bare-rooted rose and fruit tree man, in return for an advertisement in the paper.

'When I get old,' he told her, 'I want to sit on the veranda and listen to the birds in this tree. It will take at least fifty years to reach maturity, but I am prepared to wait, as long as you are by my side.'

'Oh Christie, you do plan to live to be an old, old man,' Ethel exclaimed clapping her hands together and giving him butterfly kisses on his cheek. 'This tree must have cost you a fortune. I saw that Mr Ah Woo had a couple of palm trees that he brought down that day, but the cost was exorbitant, so I didn't buy one. It is exactly the feature I need to give some structure to the garden. Thank you, thank you, thank you!'

He enjoyed the accolade, avoiding explanation about its cost. Together they planted the tree in the middle of the lawn on the right hand side, out of the way of stray footballs and cricket games, warning the boys that this was precious and it was to be protected with their lives.

CHAPTER 34

Trouble was brewing. Swords were crossed. Ripples of discontent wavered just below the surface and social and business life was dividing. And it was all over a minor point of issue. An argument that began about a double booking of the Mechanics Hall was rapidly becoming a Catholic versus Protestant assault, splitting opinion in the town. Through no fault of his own, Chris had been inadvertently caught in the middle when the books of the warring committees were brought to the "Times" office so that "Mr Johnstone could examine them and support our case."

'Keep me out of it, please,' Chris begged, 'I want nothing to do with it. You sort it out between yourselves.' Nevertheless, the books were presented and Chris had no option but to inspect them.

'I can't be seen to be taking sides,' he confided in Ethel. 'I wish they would leave me out of their squabbles. It gets me down. I can't be seen to be favouring one religion or the other, one political party over another or refusing to publish

247

a wide variety of opinion. If I did that, then this business is doomed. We need to have the goodwill of the whole district.' 'I understand, Christie,' Ethel comforted her husband. 'It's not easy reporting the news week after week with balance and without offence, particularly in a place where everyone knows everyone else. They all think they can produce a newspaper, but none of them ever do. You are doing a wonderful job, Christie, and the paper is an asset to our town, so just keep doing what you are doing so well.'

'I don't know what I would do without you, Etty. Sometimes I begin to doubt myself, but you always put me straight, tell me to back my better judgment and not to give in to the nattering crowds. You are wonderful.' He put his arm around her and gave her an affectionate hug. She held his embrace for a minute, pushed back and held him at arm's length.

'Well, you're not too bad yourself, Christie Johnstone. And you know what? You make very good decisions, so measured and well thought out. Sometimes your methodical way can drives me crazy, but that is because we are so different.'

'Enough of that, you two!' George came from the back to get Chris' attention. 'Chris, I need you here for a second to sort something out. We seem to have a stray sentence in the middle of this forme. Doesn't make sense.'

'Sense? What's the panic about sense all of a sudden? We've been writing nonsense for nearly six months and getting away with it! Come on, let me have a look at it.'

Chris retreated to the back of the shop with George and hearing the sounds of children's voices in the side paddock, alerting her that the boys would be home soon, Ethel gathered her jacket, bid her fellow workers goodbye and stepped outside to be confronted by an altogether weird phenomenon. The headlights of the Sale train on its eastward journey burst eerily through a weird, red glow that had displaced the spring sunshine. Looking back towards the town she could barely see the buildings through the haze. The hills were outlined in red so that it was difficult to see the giant ghost gums as they retreated into the background. Was hell descending upon Trafalgar?

She called to the men, who came to stare and wonder, the pragmatic amongst them declaring that it was a natural phenomenon. Nevertheless, it stirred up great excitement in the passing throngs of children making their way back from school. White horses blushed as they underwent an amazing transformation and the day remained surreal until early evening when eight points of rain fell – six points of water and two points of Mallee dust.

It was the main discussion point at the dinner table that night as the boys pondered the actual cause of the event. Could it be the end of the world? Perhaps it was an alien invasion? Or maybe dried blood in the air? They were disappointed when Chris curtailed their speculation by telling them the actual metrological reason. The wind had picked up the Mallee topsoil hundreds of miles to the northwest and sprinkled it like fairy dust, far and wide. At the same time, he couldn't resist teasing Ethel just a little. 'Your Mr Matheson is sure that God is trying to tell us something.'

'Don't joke about it, Christie Johnstone. Perhaps Alex is right. Perhaps we are being given a message. And, I've told you before, Christie, Alexander is a good man. And just so you know, he's more your Mr Matheson than he is mine. I simply worship with him, you owe him money!'

'No. We owe him money, Etty,' Christie corrected, as Ethel cleared away the dishes with a huff and a puff.

CHAPTER 35

On the first Saturday in November, after he had finished business for the day, Chris waited for the some of the town lads to assemble at the "Times" office. They had planned to meet at midday and go to the cricket ground as a group to play their first game of the season as the newly reconstituted Trafalgar side.

'But Christie,' Ethel said in dismay when she heard of his plans to manage the team, 'you have three sons of your own and you promised you would come home and take them on a practice run for the sports day cross-country race. They'll be so disappointed. It's all very well organising cricket for other people's children, but you never have time to see your own.'

'It won't be long, Etty, before Aubrey is old enough to get a game in the Seniors,' Chris defended himself, 'and the other two boys are coming along. I am doing all this for our family as well as for other families in the town. I do have to admit that I love the game, but it is important that we put structures in place that make Trafalgar a good place for kids to grow up. Sport keeps them out of trouble and helps them enjoy their lives. The boys loved being part of the footy this year and I could tell that even you enjoyed being in the kitchen with the other ladies at the games. I heard you all laughing and chatting as you made the sandwiches.'

'I must admit I did meet some nice ladies and I did manage to keep up with everything that was going on. But I was, nevertheless, in the kitchen making sandwiches, and that, Christopher Johnstone does not constitute a day out.'

Chris reached out and touched her hand. 'Etty, my dear wife, we men rely on the support we have from our spouses. The clubs would not operate, perhaps not even exist, without all the work you women put in. But, come on, confess, you do love getting amongst the ladies in the kitchen. I know you do!'

Ethel knew she would not win this battle so simply put her nose in the air haughtily and went to throw the dishwater onto the ferns by the back door, giving Chris time to think about what he had said.

'These things need to be done for the good of the town and everyone in it,' he repeated, as she returned to the kitchen to wipe the empty bowl clean. 'We're well on the way to getting a horse race meeting up and going as well. You have to remember that Trafalgar is not like the city. Out here in these little settlements we have to do things for ourselves. I'm not the only one; most of the blokes in the town pull their weight and help. It's for the kids that I'm doing it, Ethel, our boys and their children. What we do now will continue through the generations. We're building a community here, Etty.'

'Of course Christie, I understand that, but I do miss the comforts of Mentone where all those things are in place and it is just a matter of enjoying them. It can be hard work having a good time in this place.'

'Even in Mentone, my dear, men have to put their hands up to volunteer, someone has to take responsibility for civic duties.'

Thus quietened, Ethel withdrew. However, her scolding had the effect of spurring Chris into action so that next day he took time out to spend with the two older boys.

'Grasshoppers are beginning to be a problem for the farmers, and because we had good winter rains there are lots more snakes about this year,' Chris remarked to the boys as they set out with their guns to spend some time shooting targets at Murray's paddock.

'That should fix it then,' piped in Aubrey.

'What do you mean?' asked Chris.

'Well, the long grass encourages the snakes, right?

'Yes, that correct,' replied Chris.

'And the grasshoppers will eat all the grass, right?

'Yes,' answered Chris, wondering where this was all going.

'So one cancels out the other, right?'

'Where do you get all of that from?' laughed his father. 'You have an answer for everything, you young sprat! But seriously though, be careful where you walk in the long grass and keep an eye out for snakes and, whatever you do, don't stand on one. It's a good idea to make a bit of a noise as you move around because snakes are timid and will slink away if you leave them alone. The other day a young fellow from Yinnar was feeding the calves down at the cowshed when he was bitten on the finger by a snake. He kept his cool and applied a tourniquet to stop the poison going into his system and cut the wound with his knife. The amazing thing is that he had the presence of mind to poke his finger into a poddies' mouth for him to suck it out. They have a pretty powerful suck those young cows.'

'Wow! That's amazing Dad, is that true?' exclaimed young Merv. 'If my cow saved my life like that I would pamper her until the day she died. I would pet her and call her Sweetie and give her the first pickings at the best grass in the paddock and I would never sell her. I would just let her die of old age or over eating.'

They all laughed. Chris loved these moments with the boys but, with the pressure of work and all the civic duties he had taken on, they were getting to be few and far between. He seemed to see more of them on a Tuesday evening after school when they came over to the office to help fold the papers than he did for the rest of the week.

Ethel confirmed this when she spoke to him later. 'I know you are busy and distracted much of the time, Christie, but if you would just say a word of encouragement once a week to each of your sons it would such a difference to how they think of themselves. It strengthens the family if you share time to encourage them and listen to their opinions.'

He listened and took note.

CHAPTER 36

While Chris and the boys were out of the house, Ethel and
Annie sat on the veranda, enjoying the perfume of the spring
roses that lined the path to the door and leafing through
copies of the new women's magazine, "New Idea". Ethel
had ordered it every week since it had first came out in
August, trying some of the recipes and knitting a garment
from one of the patterns they published. After she had read
each edition, she would hand it onto her friends who would,
in turn, hand it on again. One "New Idea" certainly went a
long way in Trafalgar!

Little Dolly played with the white stones of the path while
Vernon and James used sticks to play pretend bushrangers.
The two women began planning future plantings in the
north facing front garden. Although it was not exposed to
the road on all sides, passers-by could still see in and survey
the scene quite readily. Ethel thought they needed to plant
some privacy.

'I could make a cosy corner on the secluded part of the
garden by planting a screen between us and the street,'

suggested Ethel as she sipped her tea, 'but I can't wait for a hedge to grow. Perhaps there is a quicker way to screen the area.'

'You could probably achieve that in a few months by making a trellis of wire netting supported by stakes,' proposed Annie. 'And we could plant something like nasturtiums, beans and hops to climb over it. I can give you plenty of seeds from last year and they don't take long to grow. Perhaps some convolvulus would be good as well.'

'Excellent, and just to layer it a bit I could have forget-me-nots. I do love them and they make a fine display very quickly. Mother gave me some seeds from her garden when I was home and I have seedlings all ready to plant out, as well as candytuft and some lobelia. They make a pretty border.' Ethel visualised her special place. 'I can just see myself sitting here on the veranda sewing, or in my cosy corner, reading in the summer air. I could even sit and shell the peas for dinner. And the best thing will be that no one can see me from the street, so I won't be interrupted.'

Considering the practicalities, she thought aloud. 'Maggie's George is good with things like that so he won't mind moulding the trellis for me. I shall order the wire netting and the stakes and get Aubrey to dig it over for me. That will be good for his leg muscles if he wants to ride a bike. I'll have it ready for planting next time you come by, Annie. I love new gardens. It will be fun to see it grow.'

'You are such an optimist, Ethel,' observed Annie, 'you just assume that everything will go well and you will have your cosy corner by Christmas. How is it that there are some people who constantly live under cloudy skies while others are good weather folks?'

'I wasn't always that way, Annie. In fact when I was young I was always waiting for something better to happen. I was always planning for the future and imagining how good things would be for me down the track. But as I grew older, found Christie and had children, I realised that it is best to live in the moment and to enjoy things as they come along. Good times don't last but then neither do bad times, so it's best just to make the most of each day and deal with hiccups as they arise. Always expect the best and it most probably will happen.'

'I have a cousin, who says exactly the opposite,' Annie lamented. 'He says, "Always expect the worst and then if nothing good happens you won't be disappointed." It's a dreary way to live your life. But you are so right, Ethel, one must always adapt to the changing ways of the world because it certainly doesn't stand still for us. You know it took me to be thirty years old before I learnt to be patient and sympathetic. It's the young ones who teach us these things. They may try your patience but they keep you in touch with the world, don't you my little Dolly?' She fingered Dolly's curls and gave her a hug.

'So what you're saying is move with the times and avoid becoming a carping and disagreeable old sod,' summarised Ethel for her.

'Exactly! Do you think we can both do that?'

'Well, we have to try. Chris's mantra is to be polite and obliging and treat everyone the same. It's good for business! I believe that you should treat people that way because it is good for everybody.'

'Whether we achieve that or not is another matter,' Annie added.

'You know, the Mechanics Committee is doing a really good job but you wouldn't know it because some of the older ladies are angry with the world and are always whinging about who does what and who doesn't do anything. I see that they're arguing about the Euchre now. They tell me that Jas Finlay has been appointed caretaker at the hall and he is also going to act as booking clerk.'

'That's closing the gate after the horse has bolted, if you ask me?' Annie chuckled thinking of the recent uproar about the bookings. 'About the sports day,' she continued, 'we have the program at home. If you like, I will drop it over to you and the boys can chose an event or two they'd like to enter. It's a great day and it will be in the middle of the school holidays so you will want something to keep them busy.'

'The sports committee will have a huge job cleaning up that pig's paddock of a recreation ground for the day. I asked Christie who was supposed to be looking after it and he said that the bloke who had been doing it had left the district and no one had told the new one that he had been elected to the post!'

They laughed and, hearing voices, the two women stood up and went to the front fence, watching as Chris and the boys headed back up Main Street.

'Ah, here come the warriors returning from the shoot,' said Annie, waving at them.

'Be careful of the magpies swooping!' Ethel called, as a warning for the boys to put their hands up over their heads. 'They are quite aggressive, aren't they?' she continued, turning to Annie. 'Young Roy Wayne had his eye pecked out last week. He's in the hospital but they can't save his sight. The bird was a pet of Mr Devine's and was supposed to be tame. Apparently Roy poked a stick through the fence at it and it went crazy. Such a tragedy!'

'I'll be taking my chances with the maggies, and love you and leave you then, Ethel,' said Annie taking her leave. 'Come on Dolly, come on James! Tell my Jack to come as soon as they have cleaned their guns. We have a big night tonight, there's a function out at Willowgrove to say goodbye to the Dunbars. They will be missed. We took up a collection and bought them a solid silver tea service and we've had it engraved. They can't possibly forget us now.'

She left and with both Dolly and Jimmy sitting in the perambulator, she headed down the Seven Mile Road towards home and milking.

Ethel greeted the boys and took them inside for afternoon tea and to hear all the news of the day's happenings.

CHAPTER 37

November turned to December, and the people of Trafalgar began to prepare their acts for Miss Townsend's Musical Evening. Miss Smallacombe was torn, as her repertoire was so extensive that she had difficulty in choosing one item that would display her talents in their best light. Not so for Mrs Metzeler! She only had one party piece, and most of Trafalgar had heard it already because if you happened to be passing by her house you could hear her practising it on the piano.

Mr Trood, the town's dentist and celebrated illusionist, had some new tricks up his sleeve, but was keeping them well under wraps, even to his own family. Down along Waterloo Road, in Mrs Gregory's cowshed, the words of the popular song, "Whisper And You Shall Hear" could be heard as she milked her cows. Dan Bailee and his merry bandsmen were busy practicing their suite of popular marching tunes, because if they were good on the night, it was likely that they would recruit interested brass players to swell their numbers in the new year. The Johnstone boys practised their acts as well. Aubrey was playing the banjo and singing an old Scottish song "Loch Lomond", Mervyn was playing "Für Elise" on the piano and Vernon was doing an interesting rendition of some popular nursery rhymes. Ethel, who also took lessons, was to play Mozart's Concerto Number 2. It was high pressure all around.

The Bazaar ladies, having won the battle for the use of the hall, were working diligently to make Christmas gifts for sale and that is the reason they had assembled in the supper room with their craftwork set out on the big table where Gwendolyn Fisher was teaching them how to make rose petal cushions. This was the first of many sewing circles she would preside over. Already she was enjoying herself. Previously the ladies had been busy collecting and curing rose petals. Today they would begin stitching the fine muslin covers and embroidering them with roses before inserting them. The final touch for each cushion was a lavish satin bow.

'I think these are absolutely lovely,' purred Ivy Hill, sitting back and admiring the cover she had just completed. 'They would make a beautiful ornament for any room. I may even buy one myself.'

'Why would you do that when you can simply make one?' asked the ever-practical Marge Cooper as she cut muslin squares. 'You could make two or three on one winter's evening at home in front of the fire. I am always looking for things to keep me busy; I don't like to just sit there. I'd go stark raving mad!'

'Talking of which, did you hear there was a lunatic loose in Moe the other day,' enquired Martha Crabtree. She suddenly had everybody's attention.

'No, what happened?' they chorused, waiting for her to continue.

'Apparently, last Saturday morning, poor Sergeant Bretherson was sound asleep. He'd been down at a shooting contest in Williamstown the day before and was having a bit of a lie in. He reckons he was dreaming happily when he was woken by loud banging at the door and opens it to find Macca, you know him, Dick McAllister. He'd been out exercising one of his horses, Domino, I think they said, and he saw this man, naked, not a stitch on, no hat, no boots, no trousers.'

'Yes, yes, we get the picture, go on!' Ivy encouraged her.

'Anyway, Macca approached the man thinking he might need help. Poor fellow was brandishing a stick, shouting and waving it around madly. Macca just he couldn't get anywhere near him. So he went to get the Sarg.'

'Poor Sergeant Bretherson, I wouldn't have had my Harold doing that job. Having to deal with madmen!' Gwen sympathised.

'Exactly!' Not to be side tracked, Martha continued her story. 'So when they got down there, the Sarg tried talking to him to calm him down. He did his best to leave him some dignity, but the poor tortured soul ranted and raved and went on like a lunatic. He was well and truly out of his head. Sad really! By that time my Fred had heard the ruckus and had arrived on the scene. Just as well really, because it took the three men to subdue him. Fortunately he wasn't wearing boots so all the kicking didn't hurt them. When they got him to the Police Station he kicked and howled and tried to bite anyone who came near him and when the Sarg gave him a bucket to wash up, he fair chucked it back at him. It turns out the poor fellow is an escaped resident from the Kew Cottages down in Melbourne. Once the episode was over, he apologised and begged the Sarg's forgiveness; said he couldn't help himself; it's really very sad.'

'It must be a full moon because that wasn't the only madman that Sarg had to deal with last week,' continued Sarah Bretherson, the sister-in-law of the sergeant in question. 'This fellow came to the Police Station and begged Brian to lock him up. Said that if he was on the loose he would kill somebody and he would be happy to be safely in jail where he could do no harm. Brian did as he was asked, but he made sure the poor man was given a roast dinner and had extra blankets. It is pretty hard for a fellow in his fifties to be in gaol, even for one night. But that is what he did and the bloke was fine in the morning. He got up and went home, sane as you or me!'

'If you ask me, this country is abundant with stark raving lunatics!' Betty Duff said through her teeth with which she held two pins and while tying a bow and trimming the ends. 'I was at Box Hill station a few weeks back waiting for a train and there was this young man, with not a stitch of clothing on. I didn't know which way to look. I just kept on knitting, averted my eyes and pretended I hadn't noticed. When the train came along he shouted out to everyone, "All aboard for the express train to heaven." I was a bit of two minds, because although I hope to be going there someday, I don't want to go just yet. Besides, I thought the train I was getting on was going to Lilydale. By that time the cops had arrived and they took the poor disillusioned fellow away. You expect these things in the city but I would never have imagined it happening on our doorstep.'

'What on earth were you doing at Box Hill, going to Lilydale?' asked the curious Dotty Garrett.

'I was staying with my cousin and we heard that Madame Melba was going to visit her childhood home so, as it was quite close by, we thought we'd go and see the lady. She has just come home to Australia after sixteen years abroad, singing in Europe and America. Anyway, we were glad we did. It was marvellous. Her hometown people were so proud of her that all the businesses closed for the half-day and along the route the houses were decked out in flowers and greenery. Lilydale had gone to no end of trouble; they are so proud of their most famous daughter. She gave a splendid concert, backed by a choir of school children all looking like little angels in white. And she was wonderful, so gracious and so beautiful and with a voice made in heaven. I wouldn't have missed it for the world, just a wonderful, wonderful day.'

'I'm so happy that Nellie Melba is receiving all the accolades she deserves. It's about time we paid tribute to women and artistic pursuits in this country,' ventured Mavis Stewart who had brought in a plate of scones, hot from her oven, to keep the working bee ladies at their task. 'In my next life I want to be an Ashanti woman.'

'Why? Pray tell?' Ethel asked on cue.

'I want to be treated equal to men,' answered Mavis, obviously more than a little frustrated with the unfairness of society. 'The Ashanti lady goes out and keeps the money coming in while the men do the weaving and sewing.'

'Can you imagine that?' Ethel chuckled out loud at the thought. 'Our men would certainly find that idea a little revolutionary. '

'They certainly would,' laughed Olive Furnell. 'This morning, when I complained about the amount of housework I do without help from a houseful of men, my husband had the cheek to tell me that it keeps me beautiful. If you please, he said that sweeping made the arms graceful, washing up is good for the fingers and hands and making beds is good for the eyes and my sense of symmetry. He was lucky I only had the feather duster in my hand and not the broom or he would have never made it out the door.'

'Are you having problems at your establishment, being a woman and all, Mavis?' asked Dotty sympathetically, 'Do the men give you grief? I think you are doing a marvellous job with that hotel. Trafalgar now has a place where we ladies can go and feel safe and the men can enjoy a drink in our company.'

'It would be good if everyone thought like you do, Dot. Not all the women in this town are as enlightened as the company in this room. I think perhaps some of them have drunkards for husbands, and so they are firmly prohibitionists. If they would only give me the benefit of the doubt and try what I am offering, I think they would be pleasantly surprised. One doesn't have to take an alcoholic drink, there are many alternatives.'

'Keep plugging away Mavis, men do tend to think they own the world,' put in Ethel. 'I had to tell Christie to stop giving instructions from the sidelines to young Aubrey when he was out batting on the cricket field. Christie, I said, let the children find their own way; the world went on well before you were born and will do so once you are dead, so just let them discover these things for themselves.

'They're funny creatures, all right,' said Dot. 'You know, I think that some men would be too lousy to take their wives out for a bite to eat and some happy company. They don't mind how much money they spend on the booze for themselves but are loathe to spend a penny on their wives.'

'Yes, there's good men and bad men just like there's good women and bad ones,' suggested Olive. 'You are doing your bit to change the balance somewhat, Mavis. Good luck to you. Now let's stop for a breather and have one of your scones and a cup of tea.'

They put down their needles and threads and sat down to a cup of tea and Mavis' scones with jam and clotted cream that had been harvested that morning from Betty the cow and then scalded in the double pot on Ethel's hob.

'They say you need to have a gentle touch to make the scones rise up like this. What's your secret, Mavis?' asked Ethel.

'My secret is that I get Nora Somerville, my cook, to make them for me!'

CHAPTER 38

'It's heart breaking. When I think of the money I spent on those bushes,' Ethel lamented. 'I brought them back last time I was down with Mother, and I thought I had nursed the poor dears through their babyhood. Then just one day of horrid old Mr North Wind and they are ruined.'

The two women were standing near the northwest corner of the block, sadly surveying the burnt, brown, azalea bushes after a particularly hot and windy twenty-four hours. It was a never-ending battle to protect her precious plants that were so young and exposed to the elements. 'They are just like me and my hay fever that all these Gippsland grasses seem to whip up. This climate is so harsh and unforgiving to foreign people and plants. Will we ever get used to it?' Ethel delicately touched her nose with her handkerchief and wiped her teary eyes.

'The only thing you can do,' advised Annie, 'is to drought-proof the garden.'

'What exactly do you mean when you say drought-proof, Annie?' Ethel asked.

'I've learnt from experience, Ethel. In Australia, we need to be very careful what we grow, choosing things that are suitable for our conditions. Just because it grows well in England doesn't mean that it will do well here. Sunny, dry Australia is quite different from wet old England. My best advice to you is to start local by taking a good look at other gardens around Trafalgar and noting the plants that are doing well. Then plant them. Later on, when the garden is established and has bones, you can try exotics. And as for your hay-fever, you poor dear, I'm afraid that our northern hemisphere noses were simply not made for the antipodes.'

'It is very trying to find dead plants in the garden. You plant them in anticipation and hope for the future, but when they fail, a little bit of me dies with them, too.'

'That's very melodramatic, Ethel,' laughed Annie. 'I just plant them and hope for the best. We've had fire and floods and had to start again, so I'm philosophical about gardening. I do it because I enjoy it and am always pleasantly surprised when it comes up trumps.'

'I suppose I want more control than that. I want it to be how I want it to be, and I get upset when things go wrong.' Ethel crushed the dry, brown leaves of the burnt bushes between her fingers. 'Do you think they will recover if I cut them right back?'

'Nope. Pull them out and start again. They are as dead as door nails.' The ever-practical Annie began to yank them one by one out of the ground and pile them in a heap. Resistance was minimal because the roots had ceased clinging to the soil.

'I'm afraid I do get too involved emotionally,' Ethel watched, thinking that perhaps Annie was a little brutal in her handling of her precious plants. 'Gardening is a bit like bringing up children really. I am in charge of their wellbeing

267

from the time I put them in the ground, and water and nurture them, and try to keep the pests away, until they are ready to be picked. So if they die, then it's my fault entirely.'

'Well, be glad that those poor souls aren't your children!' said Annie.

They both laughed as they looked at the poor miserable excuse for plants lying prone on the ground, with not a single spark of life in them.

'You are hard on yourself, Etty,' Annie consoled. 'In the end, we are all servants of nature. You know what they say?'

'And what is that then, Annie?' enquired her friend.

'They say we plant apple trees for our children to play in, and olive trees for our grandchildren. What I am trying to say, my dear Ethel, is to accept that, no matter what you do, some plants take a long time to grow and others simply will not survive in these conditions.'

'I hear what you are saying, Annie. Mother always says that Australia is upside down land. She says Christmas in Australia is never quite the same as it was at her home in Surrey. The house is so hot after Christmas dinner has been cooked that nobody really enjoys the meal. We're eating winter food in summer. It's crazy. She says we should either move the celebration to July or take a picnic down to the river and have our Christmas there. Now would that be adapting to our environment.'

'You're absolutely right, Etty. As it so happens, I'm going to fiddle with Christmas a little, this year. I'm going to cook a chicken and a ham the day before, and just have cold meat and salads on the day. Tom will not have a bar of getting rid of the Christmas pudding and he loves his spuds, so they will be boiling away on the hob. However, if the day is really hot, I will light the copper and boil it all up in that. That way, I'll keep the kitchen cool. So you could say I'm drought-proofing Christmas. We'll see how it goes. Who knows? It could become a regular thing!'

'Well, I'm off down the street to get some chops for tea tonight. Do you ever think, Annie dear, that we Australians will sit down to a simple feed of chops, spuds, peas and pumpkin for dinner on Christmas day?'

'I can't see that happening because I don't think the men would allow it,' Annie answered. 'They love Christmas because they can stay in from the paddocks and eat and eat, and in the end they have to have a nap so the food can digest. It's us women who do all the work!'

'Isn't that just the way of the world?' Ethel laughed as she gathered her hat and purse and bade Annie farewell. They parted ways, she to buy the meat for tea and Annie and her brood to head home to milk the cows.

The warm north winds from the dry centre of the country stirred the air, making it seem that the dogs barked louder and more often than before, and the children coming home from the school were noisier and more boisterous. Perhaps this was also because lessons were winding down for the year and they were excited about the lead up to and actual celebration of Christmas.

CHAPTER 39

'I've broken my front tooth on a piece of toffee apple that I bought at the Christmas Bazaar.' Jimmy came in to the printer's shop looking miserable and clutching his jaw.

'What are you doing eating toffee apples? They're for kids,' Chris opined.

'I know, I know, I'm as mad as hell at myself, but it's your middle son's fault. I had young Mervyn with me, so I bought one for him and then thought I'd have a treat myself. Bit into the bloody thing and it took my other tooth with it. Now I have both front teeth missing and I look like a clown.'

'Troody is in town today, isn't he? I think December the thirteenth is his last visit before Christmas. Go down to the Coffee Palace to see if you can catch him,' advised Chris. 'He might be able to give you a plate to fill the hole. He keeps a few spares, probably dead men's, but that won't worry you, Jim. We need you looking good for Christmas. They tell me that you are forsaking your family and having dinner with the lovely Miss Stewart.'

'Where did you hear that?' asked Jimmy, blushing just a little. 'That's not exactly true. I am helping out in the kitchen for the midday feast and then we are off home to the folks for tea. Mavis was finding it hard to get help because everyone wants to be home with the family for Christmas. I have none, so I put up my hand and offered.'

'Oh, you old fox, it is getting serious then,' remarked Chris. 'Christmas with Mavis, I hope you have bought her a nice gift.'

'Not yet! Anthony Bernicke has a shop full of special treats and chocolates and the like, and Nick Lawson is positively splitting at the seams with toys and pretty things. The town is beginning to look a lot like Christmas. I'll find something; I'll have to ask Mrs J for her advice. Have you got anything for her yet, Chris?'

'As a matter of fact I have,' Chris replied, very pleased with himself. 'You know how I prefer a Bay to any other horse, and my favourite number is three? Well, when I was in town for the Melbourne Cup I put ten quid as a side bet on number three, a Bay called Victory, and blow me if it didn't win, at pretty good odds, as well. I didn't want to come home too cashed up, because Ethel hates me having a punt, so I spent a good whack of it on a gold pendant. I've had a miniature of Ethel and the boys put into it. It's quite beautiful, round with eight little knobs around the sides. I can't wait to give it to her because I know she'll love it and it will look beautiful on my sweet lassie.'

'Eight little knobs around the sides, I bet the jeweller didn't describe it like that?' laughed Jimmy. 'But, being serious with you, Chris, you are what I call a good husband,' he congratulated his colleague. 'You are a true blue couple and if I ever get married, I won't be settling for less. Your Etty definitely deserves the best that money can buy. She has been a real gem the way she's hopped in and helped in this place. We really couldn't get by without her. Plus, she keeps your boys happy and healthy and she's always coming over with food and a cuppa when we work late. Her blood is worth bottling, so I'm glad you've got her something nice.'

Jimmy became aware that he was waxing lyrical so changed tack. 'So if you don't mind, I'll just duck down and get these teeth seen to – last chance before Christmas.'

'Before you go, Jim, what do you think about dropping the paper scheduled for December the thirtieth? I don't think our readers will mind, and that will give us ten whole days off! From a few days before Christmas until January the second. Ethel, the boys and I are heading down to Mentone to be with her folks as soon as the last paper for the year comes out, but we want to be back by Boxing Day for the sports, so we shall probably return on the morning train. Does that suit you?'

'Sounds good to me! A holiday! What's a bloody holiday? Never had one of them on the farm. Those damned cows kept wanting to be milked every day, morning and night, they knew nothing about Christmas and New Year. Yep, sounds good to me! I can do a bit of fishing and perhaps shoot a few roos. Yes sir, that's what I'll do; I'll take a holiday!'

Buoyed by that thought he went off chuckling to himself with a spring in his step to find Mr Trood, so he could get his teeth sorted out before Mavis saw him in such a state.

Jimmy had been gone only a few minutes when Ethel popped her head in. She was on the way back from the butcher's and had some lamb chops for tea in her bag. The excitement of Christmas was starting to catch up with her and she had lingered at the shops enjoying the new window displays and the air of festivity that they cast upon the townsfolk who stopped to examine the wares and ponder about their gifts for Christmas. The season had been good for the farmers so they had money in their pockets.

'The town is buzzing and the shops look wonderful, Christie.' She greeted him with a smile and a kiss. 'Everyone has their decorations up and there are some interesting things in the shop windows. Did you know that Nurse's butchery has changed hands?' she enquired. 'I walked in to there expecting to see Mr Nurse only to be greeted by Jack Kenny all dressed up and looking like a butcher. Apparently, the Kenny brothers are selling meat direct from their own farm, cutting out the middle man altogether. Jack says they can do it at reasonable prices, bringing the meat straight from paddock to counter. I ordered the Christmas ham because, even though we shall be at mother's, we will enjoy it when we come back here. We have the sports day and it will be hot so I shan't want to be lighting the stove and cooking up meat. Is Jack Kenny Jimmy's cousin?' she wondered. 'You'll have to ask him when he comes back with his new teeth,' cracked Chris, laughing and telling her about Jimmy and the toffee apple. School was finishing for the year that afternoon, and the boys would be soon home for dinner, so Ethel hurried to have it on the table for them. School break up was a great day for the kids because the whole of the summer holidays spread out before them and once Christmas was over they would be free to do as they liked for the whole month of January. She could hear them coming as they walked or rode down the side path for the final time that year.

"No more pencils, no more books, no more teacher's dirty looks," the cry went up. Some of the older children said goodbye to their classmates, having completed their lessons for life and now moving on to help out on the farms, finding a local job, or heading for Melbourne to work in the big smoke. George Brown took on two of the young ones as apprentices to teach them the smithing trade that was transforming itself every day. Iron and steel was taking over where wood was leaving off. He needed the help as he was flat out and finding it difficult to keep up with orders. Chris was to take on young Gavin McKenzie as his first ever apprentice, initially to learn the printing trade, but it was envisaged that he would eventually learn to do all tasks associated with the production of a newspaper. He came to them with the assurances of the headmaster, Mr Palmer, that he was an excellent student and had a talent for the written word. Chris and Jimmy immediately liked him for his ginger hair, his cheeky grin and his ability to listen and learn, and so were looking forward to him starting as this would take some of the pressure off them all.

CHAPTER 40

Maggie whispered to Ethel that the bicycles she had ordered for the two older boys for Christmas were ready and George had asked her to find out if she wanted them delivered to the house, or would she prefer that the boys took delivery themselves at his shop.

'I shall have to talk to Christie about it,' Ethel replied thoughtfully, 'but my first thought is that, as we will be away for Christmas Day itself, it might be good for the boys to have them earlier so that they can enjoy them for a few days before we go to Mother's place. Leave it with me. I will pop in and tell you tomorrow.'

Chris agreed on this course of action and so, on Wednesday morning when the newspaper for the week was safely on the street he, Mervyn and Aubrey were waiting excitedly for George to open the front door for business. The boys knew something was up, but they had no idea of the wonder in store for them. They jumped and hopped and wrestled in their excitement, while Chris patiently puffed on his pipe and enjoyed the activity around him as the business centre of town slowly yawned and opened for business.

'Sorry, lads! I'm tardy this morning,' George apologised as he opened the front door and ushered them in. 'Maggie is feeling sick so I was making sure that she didn't have housework to attend to. I've tidied the breakfast things and now it's your turn.'

'Hello, Mr Brown.' The boys spoke in unison.

'Maggie's all right, I hope?' queried Chris.

'She's fine, just women's problems. She'll be good by lunch time.' George smiled broadly, rubbing his hands together. 'First customers for the day, that's good luck in the Chinese lexicon', he joked. 'And how are my favourite young lads in all of Gippsland, today? Come in and let me see what I have for you.'

He winked at Chris, for although he knew their mission, he was about to have a little fun at their expense. 'Now young Mervyn, Maggie tells me that you want a job with me and I am happy to take you on. The hours will be eight in the morning until six at night and your job will be to hold the horses still while I shoe them. Can you do that lad? I can let you off at midday on Saturday if you wish to play cricket.'

'What about school?' Mervyn asked horrified. 'I like school and I want to work in the paper with Pa when I grow up. I'll come and help you Mr Brown, but I don't think I could possibly work for you, could I Pa?'

He appealed to his father, as he had no wish to work for a living just yet, but he didn't want to offend his friend by telling him so.

'Perhaps it's a bit risky,' laughed George, 'we don't want to spoil a good friendship by bringing money into it, do we?'

Coming in on the gag, Chris added, 'Besides George, you can't be poaching my best staff, the lad has told you he is going to work for me.'

'In that case, what else can I do for you, then? Is it the Christmas gift you have come about? We shall have to go out the back for that.'

'Yes, yes,' cried the boys in unison, 'we've come for the presents.'

'This way then,' answered George and he led them past the brightly burning forge, which took over almost one whole corner of the establishment, and then by the coal hopper and the bellows. Above the bench was a wooden panel that held the tools of trade, each in its correct place, as George was a methodical and precise craftsman. Anvils of different sizes and shapes were on the side near the quenching trough that contained water for cooling. A vice and some measuring tools were on the bench. Metal coating and painting equipment gave the shop a modern touch. For the boys, this was familiar territory as Maggie often brought them home with her to spend an hour or two. They walked through the shop and past all manner of metal and wooden implements piled in a little annex by the back door and out into the courtyard where George often worked if the weather was good.

Against a spreading gum tree was an awesomely menacing looking metal object, that caused Chris to exclaim, 'My golly gosh! What on earth is that thing? It looks as if it could rip my arms off.'

'Beauty, Chris, is in the eye of the beholder. If you were a farmer, that ugly contraption would be a thing of beauty. In no time you would consider it more beautiful than your very own wife.'

'I'll tell Etty you said that!' Chris laughed as he walked over to examine the contraption.

'It's a variation of the stump-jump plough that the Smith brothers came up with in South Australia. It does the same thing, but this one has been adapted for the tussocks out on the Swamp. We are having a field day out on Somerville's farm after Christmas so you can come and see it in action then. Bill has offered me his land to show the world what this little wonder machine does and, in return, I will grub some of the tussocks from his paddocks. It absolutely eats them up. You have my permission to tell the world about it in the "Times" and make me a wealthy man.'

'Write down the date for me and I shall send George or Jim out.' Chris was now distracted by work and had almost forgotten the boys, who were becoming impatient with this conversation. They had spotted, leaning against the veranda post, two brown-paper parcels that were shaped for all the world like bicycles.

The men and the boys moved towards them as one. 'Now let's see. These here bicycles are marked "Johnstone Lads, Trafalgar." Would that be you then?' George asked.

The boys gasped in awe as the paper wrapping protecting them was taken off to reveal first, a blue and then, a red bicycle. Their excited ooh's and ah's and thank you's could be heard across the line at the dairy. They were thrilled and couldn't quite believe that they were to be the owners of these remarkable machines.

'So, what do you think of the new bikes, boys?' George asked as Chris wrote a cheque in payment.

'Mr Brown, I love mine! Thank you! It is so beautiful. I'm going to love it until I die,' replied Merv, tenderly rubbing the saddle. 'It is so good, I just love it,' he purred, 'it is the best ever present! And,' he added, baiting his brother, 'red is the best colour.'

'I think blue is the best,' said Aubrey, 'it is really beautiful because it is the colour of the sky and the sea.'

'Red is the colour of Santa Claus and cherries,' Merv piped in, for he found it hard to match the sea and the sky. 'You are the best dad in all of Australia, and you're good too, Mr Brown,' he added graciously, aware that George was standing there and may have had something to do with it all. 'All the other boys will be real jealous and I am going the win the novice's race at the Boxing Day Sports,' Aubrey announced, convinced in his own mind that he could do it.

'Well, to do that, you have to learn to balance and ride it first,' smiled Chris, winking at George. 'I can give you an hour away from the shop but then you are on your own. Merry Christmas, George! I'll see you at our place for Christmas drinks,' he called as they led the two new sparkly bikes out of the shop. 'Thanks for organising them for us. Now it's time to train up for the Boxing Day races.'

'Come back after Christmas when things slow down a bit, boys, and I shall show you how to change a tyre and keep those machines in perfect racing order. Ride down and give Maggie a dink when you get your balance,' he laughed, adding 'have a merry one.'

He waved goodbye and turned his attention to his next customer, surprised to discover that it was Claude Lawrence. 'Hoppy!' said George, 'how can I help you? Something wrong with one of your wagons?'

'No, no,' said Hoppy, leaning on the counter, his face creased with pain. 'Something else. Can we talk out the back?'

'Sure, sure,' said George, waving him through. Grimacing, Hoppy hobbled towards the rear of the building, with a puzzled George in tow.

Meanwhile, Chris, Jimmy and Macca, the new apprentice, were giving bicycle riding lessons. For the next hour they encouraged, cajoled and soothed the learning process as the boys sat on their bicycles and gingerly at first, but gradually gathering confidence, obtained the equilibrium needed to ride a bike. Once learned it is never forgotten.

'Take it easy. Don't ride too fast, watch out for horses and make sure you wear the new saddle in before you ride a long way,' counselled Chris. 'Otherwise you'll have seriously sore bottoms and that won't be good.' The boys grimaced at that thought.

Chris settled Merv on his bike and gave an almighty push. Merv wobbled, teetered, floundered and then, ever so slowly toppled over into the gutter on the side of the road. There was only one puddle on the Main Street and that was where the wagons had cut up the road near the entrance to the station forecourt. Each time he traversed that way, Mervyn took one look at it and slid into it, covering himself with mud and embarrassment. He extricated himself from the still spinning wheels and stood up, his tear ducts about to spill over. But Chris would have none of it and wasn't about to allow him to stop there. However, he was impatient to get back to work.

'Back on the horse,' instructed Jimmy from the side of his mouth that didn't have the cigarette hanging from it. Witnessing Chris' frustration at young Merv's failure to learn to ride as fast as his older brother, he stepped in and took over the lessons. 'No one ever learns to ride a cycle without having fallen off twenty six times. Here lad, let's go again!

This time I'll hold onto the back of you until you get the hang of it.'

And that is what he did. Time after time, as soon as he released his grip, Mervyn would become aware that he was flying solo and falter. However, the interval between each realisation lengthened and in a couple of hours the young fellow could ride almost to Bernicke's store before falling off. His efforts provided much mirth for the older men who had gathered to talk cricket in the station forecourt, as well as the other townsfolk, as they went about their business. Mervyn wasn't one to give up and he was willing to practise until he had mastered the art and although a little battered and bruised, he was very pleased with himself when he reported back to his mother at dinnertime, asking her to come and watch. Little did he know that she had been enjoying the spectacle on and off all morning from the veranda.

Aubrey, on the blue bicycle, was having less difficulty. His legs were long enough to straddle the saddle and touch the ground and that gave him the security to know that he could stop at any time. Longer legs were certainly an advantage and, his mentor, the young Macca, was back at work long before Jimmy returned to the office, hot and exhausted from helping Mervyn. There was still one more newspaper to put to bed before the holiday and they were all keen to finish it with as little drama as possible.

All that day, and the next, Aubrey and Mervyn were on their newly delivered bicycles honing their riding skills while Ethel was at home preparing for the Staff Christmas Party, the first of many such parties in their family home.

CHAPTER 41

As it was mainly a party for those who worked on the paper, the invitation list was short. Just the five members of staff, plus Jimmy's friend Mavis Stewart, the business' benefactors, Mr Alexander and Mrs Sophia Matheson, Annie and Tom and the Donovan family, Maggie and George Brown, and of course Chris' best mate Danny Baillee.

Annie had kindly volunteered to make her famous sausage rolls and Mavis had got 'cook' to bake some sweet pastries. She also loaned the hotel punch bowl and assorted crockery and cutlery. Aubrey decked the sitting room in red and green bunting and he and Merv blew up balloons in the same colours. In the corner stood a bush Christmas tree, a branch Jimmy Kenny had cut from a lemon scented tea tree that was growing out in the scrub near the school. It was decorated in paper chains that the boys had made over a series of evenings from the waste newsprint at the office. Sitting on top was a magnificent star made of cardboard that Ethel had covered with sequins and pearl buttons from her sewing box. The sitting room furniture was pushed back against the walls so that there was room for guests. Ethel and the boys weaved a welcoming laurel out of wattle branches for the front door.

Ethel had prepared a variety of dainty sandwiches, and had speared last season's pickled onions on toothpicks and shaped them into a hedgehog by arranging them around an orange. She had also wrapped steamed asparagus in fresh white bread, baked two sponge cakes and made some patty cakes that she had jammed and creamed. A Christmas cake, iced and decorated with a representation of a jolly old Santa and wrapped with Christmas edging, took pride of place in the middle of the table and the red and green jellies glistened on a beautifully constructed trifle. Mince pies were purchased from McCrory's Bakery because Ethel simply ran out of time to bake them herself. It all looked too good to eat!

When the room was ready and the table set, they all stepped back to admire their handiwork. It all looked sumptuous and they felt pretty pleased with their efforts. Chris's task was to arrange the beer and stout for the men. There would be lemonade for the women and children, and perhaps a sweet sherry shandy for the more adventurous.

At the appointed time the guests duly arrived, dressed in Sunday best and bearing gifts of homemade treats from the kitchen, or flowers from the garden. Annie had made a muslin pouch into which she had popped the dried seeds from last season's marigolds, ready for planting for an autumn display, and Eileen had decorated a home-made box filled with cannas and tiger lily bulbs for planting before winter.

Maggie had meticulously copied the music and lyrics to several new songs, including "The Glow Worm," plus George Evans' "Good Old Summer Time", and Ethel's favourite at that moment, "Bill Bailey, Won't You Please Come Home?". These were joyfully accepted and stored in the piano stool. Ethel optimistically anticipated the elation she would experience when she had mastered them on her new instrument.

Sophia Matheson had potted up a variety of salvias from her garden, all purple and white. As she handed them to Ethel she said, 'These are ready for planting and if you put them in the garden now you will have a pretty autumn display. After they have flowered, cut them back and you can make cuttings with the trimmings to pass them on to your friends. And this,' she added motioning Alex to come forward with a larger potted plant, 'is an Australian Christmas tree, the jacaranda.'

'I didn't know we had our own Christmas tree,' said Ethel accepting the gift.

'Well, we don't exactly,' Sophia replied smiling. 'It comes from South America, but it flowers exactly at Christmas and has the most magnificent purple-blue blooms that drop a pretty carpet underneath. It is probably one of the most stunning trees you can have in the garden when it is in flower, and its feathery leaves make it an asset to the landscape all year round. They come straight out of a fairytale.'

'What a lovely gift! Is there anything special I need to know when I am positioning it in the garden?'

'It doesn't like frosts or wind, so plant it where its showy flowers can be seen easily and where falling litter will not be a problem. Put it in a protected position facing north for the sun, as it likes hot conditions. I grew this from one of the large seed pods.'

The fact that her guests had gone to the trouble of physically making their gifts embarrassed Ethel somewhat because her offerings had been bought from the Hall Committee's Christmas Bazaar a couple of days before. With all that had gone on in her life this year, she just didn't seem to have the time.

The party was a huge success. After the guests had gone and the boys were in bed, Chris and Ethel sat compatibly on the veranda talking about the evening in hushed tones while the rest of Trafalgar slept.

'That was a lovely evening, Etty my dear,' complimented Christie sucking on his pipe. 'What a busy few months it has been for us all, and how well it has turned out. I do believe that we have been lucky to make a very nice group of friends. They are refined but they all enjoy a good time. I couldn't believe it when Maggie said that she would like a shandy and then Annie put up her hand to have one as well. Poor Mrs Matheson's eyes nearly popped out of her head. I don't think she approved.'

'I thought she coped with it with grace,' Ethel defended her matriarchal friend. 'You must remember that she is a good bit older than we are and she finds some modern ways a little confronting. She is used to Victorian ways. We younger women are a bit more forward. But hasn't she got a beautiful voice and didn't she harmonise well with our Maggie? I was really pleased with my piano playing. It's been worth all the lessons and practice to sharpen my skills. I believe I can learn to play anything now and with the sheet music that Maggie gave me I shall have quite a repertoire. Dan was great accompanying me on the spoons. I didn't realise that they could be used as an instrument. That man can play anything!'

'The music was as good as any you would hear in any music hall in the city,' Chris agreed.

'Your Alex is a man of the world as well,' Ethel commented mischievously. 'I hadn't seen that side of him. I only see him when he is conducting the Bible studies on a Sunday and he is always so sombre. He surprised me by letting his hair down. He even danced the Highland Fling.'

'What do you mean my Alex? He's your Alex, Etty,' teased her husband. 'You go to church with him.'

'I will claim him if you won't,' Ethel defended her pastor. 'I think he is a true gentleman.'

'Aye, that he is!' agreed Chris, reverting to the language of his childhood. 'We certainly wouldn't be sitting on this veranda enjoying our comfortable life without the indulgence of your friend and mine, Alexander. I agree, the man is a gentleman and a scholar.'

'Old Tom Donovan certainly came ready for a party with that fiddle under his elbow, didn't he? I laughed when Dan went and found that large bucket and began drumming away on it. It went well with the fiddle. And the dancing was fun. We all got into it. Jimmy and Mavis make a handsome couple. Do you think anything will come of it?' quizzed Ethel.

'They certainly look happy in each other's company, that much I'll say,' answered Chris. 'It would be lovely if it did, but it's only early days yet. Her parents are coming for Christmas so perhaps they will look the old Jimmy boy over and give her their blessings. They haven't known each other twelve months yet. Keep off his case and just let it happen.'

'That would be good, and I am only commenting,' retorted Ethel, indignant that Chris would suppose that she would interfere. 'It would be a perfect match, even though she is a good bit older than he is. He needs a competent woman to look after him.'

'Time will tell,' Chris replied, poking his pipe and knocking it on the arm of the rattan chair. 'It was a pity Troody couldn't come up with something to fill the gaping hole in his front teeth to tide him over Christmas.'

'Yes, I guess he will get them sorted out eventually. But the person I really worry about is dear Maggie. She is so pale lately and I don't think she is well. She so wants a baby and it is just not happening! She and George are a grand couple and would make fantastic parents and now that the business is going so well …' Her voice trailed off. Seeing Chris' mind wander off at the talk of women's things, she pulled herself together and got up. 'Now, let's finish the clean up and get to bed before the sun comes out. It was a wonderful party.'

The few days that followed were busy ones, as the family prepared for the trip to Melbourne for Christmas. Presents for family in Mentone had to be bought and packed, the final newspaper for the year put to bed, and the house tidied and left spick and span. Packing had to be done and the precious pot plants put in the shade so they wouldn't die. Dondi and Betty were walked out to Annie's farm where they would spend the holiday.

While Chris and Ethel were seeing to all of this, Aubrey and Mervyn were riding their new bicycles hard and fast everywhere. Once the first feeling of balance had been achieved, progress proved rapid and after a couple of days they were even dinking their mates on the cross bar. It was all a matter of confidence.

By the time Ethel, looking tired but fashionable in her new coffee straw hat trimmed with black, and with a bunch of fresh red geraniums from the garden at the back of her hair, and Chris in his three piece suit with a new fob watch hanging daintily from the waistcoat pocket, arrived at the station to await the train to Melbourne on the following Wednesday, both were exhausted.

The two older boys were reluctant to leave their new toys at home. Their plan was to take part in the bicycle race for novices at the sports day. Christmas in Melbourne would be fun but it was Boxing Day, the day of the Sports Meeting, to which they most looked forward.

CHAPTER 42

When they reached Mentone that day, a horse and carriage was waiting to transport them to the family home where Mrs Gilbee had cooked several roast joints - lamb, beef and pork - with all the trimmings. Ethel's whole extended family, nineteen people in all, had gathered at the boarding house to celebrate the return of the little clan. It was a grand reunion. In the days that followed Ethel and her mother never stopped for breath, catching up on all the happenings of the past months while Chris endeavoured to show his boys some of the highlights of the big city. They journeyed out to the zoo at Parkville, inspected exhibits at the Museum, watched a cricket game at the Junction Oval in St Kilda and saw a pantomime at the Regent Theatre. They spent a pleasant afternoon sailing small boats at Beaumaris Beach while Ethel, her sisters and her mother enjoyed Devonshire teas in the Rickett's Point Tea Rooms. The bay sparkled in the sun as lovers, picnickers and families enjoyed the day on her shores, parasols protecting the ladies' delicate northern hemisphere skin from damage.

One hot day Ethel, her mother, her sisters and the cousins packed a picnic in a large wicker basket and ate early tea on the Mentone beach, sheltering from the hot sun under a bathing tent. The boys happily splashed in the water and played in the sand and, as their hot sunburnt bodies lay in bed at night they could still feel the waves gently rocking them to sleep.

In the evenings they joined the other fashionable holidaymakers promenading on the Mentone pier and taking tea at the magnificent Italianate Mentone Hotel. The boys liked the thought that this grandiose building, with its spacious lounges, stairways, balconies and a tower for visitors to view the bay, was a vampire's castle.

'It is all so different here than it is in Trafalgar,' Ethel confided to her mother. 'The one thing I really miss is that, in the country the women are so busy just surviving and helping their husbands to make enough money to feed the family, that they have no time for fashion and frivolity. We all make a jolly good attempt at trying to recreate the social niceties and we do have some wonderful events and celebrations, but we lack the grandeur of places like this, where city people can come to see and be seen. Everything we do in Trafalgar has one purpose or another and people don't really care if you wear last season's fashions.'

'Are you homesick, Etty? Are you unhappy in Trafalgar?' her mother asked anxiously.

'Unhappy? Oh, I could never be unhappy with Christie and the boys at my side! What I mean is that sometimes it seems a little foolish to get all dressed up in my best finery just to walk one hundred yards up the road to the Mechanics Institute. And when I get there I often feel over dressed because the other women either can't afford to buy, or don't seem to desire the latest fashions. It just seems pointless. Perhaps I am still a frivolous city slicker at heart.'

'You have only been away from the city for nine months, darling girl. Be grateful that you don't have ridiculous standards to keep up,' counselled her mother. 'You are a lady Ethel, and you will always be that, whether you wear last season's gown or not. Sometimes it is a privilege not to have to break through the mask of fashion. In Trafalgar, what you see is what you get. Are you able to make nice friends there, Ethel?'

'Oh yes, mother. Already I have met other like-minded ladies that I think perhaps will be my friends for a long time. People who, maybe, I would never have associated with in the city, but who seem to fit in well with me and make my life more interesting.'

Ethel then spent the next hour or so telling her mother about Annie, Maggie and Jimmy's Mavis and the other women of Trafalgar.

'There is also a lovely lady, Sophia Matheson. She is about the same age as you, Mother, and she has taken me under her wing. She grows cuttings for me from her garden and shares her recipes and tells me the best way to get stains and things out of the boys' clothes. The Mathesons have Bible Readings at their place each week on a Sunday afternoon and a Tuesday. It is a respite for me in the hurley-burley of family life. I always go on a Sunday because Christie is happy to deliver the boys to Sunday School. He is friendly with the Presbyterian Minister but I don't think he spends too much time in the church. He waits outside for them and smokes his pipe. I don't get there very often on Tuesdays, because you know what it's like, that is the night that the paper comes out and it's all shoulders to the wheel, the boys and me are there folding and packing, and often we don't get away from the office until eight or eight thirty. Sophie is a dear sweet woman and in some ways makes it easier for me being away from you. I do miss you so much.'

Her mother patted Ethel's hand and sipped her tea thoughtfully. 'It sounds to me like you are surrounding yourself with good, strong and remarkable women, Etty. Treasure them, as they will get you through the hard times and make the good times even better. We all need true women friends to share our paths. They hold a mirror to our own lives and help to keep our hopes and troubles in perspective. With good friends you never need to travel life's way alone.'

'I miss you and my sisters, Mother. So much! Friends can never replace the intimate relationships I share with you. But I do agree with you, my female friends are very important to me. True friends are like gold, precious and rare, false friends are like autumn leaves, found everywhere,' she said, quoting an old saying that her Aunty Emily had written in her autograph book years before.

'That is so true, my darling daughter. How quickly our fair weathered friends dropped their dealings with us when your father lost his wealth in the bank crash of the Nineties. And, do you know something? I never missed them! Our good friends gathered round me and still call, even though your father has passed.'

This conversation was interrupted when the boys returned from their adventures; Chris walking sheepishly at the rear with a dripping wet Vernon in his arms. Apparently all had gone well with the boating until they were returning their hired boat to its mooring. Young Vernon insisted on throwing the rope to the boatman and in his enthusiastic endeavours had thrown himself as well, landing in the water. The older boys thought it extremely funny and couldn't wait to relate the tale in detail, right down to the horrified look on Vern's face and the gargling noises he made when rescued. 'All's well that ends well,' Chris interrupted his sons. Too much had been said already. 'Time to go home for dinner!' Then, seemingly, almost in a minute, Christmas Eve was upon them.

Little Vernon was more than a trifle worried that, as they were not at home at Trafalgar, Santa Claus might not know where he was, and asked his mother many times did she think that it would be all right. She reassured him that she had written a letter to the old fellow explaining the logistics and that he knew exactly where they were staying.

The boys hung their stockings from the mantelpiece in the parlour of their grandmother's boarding house and went off to bed, excited about the day to come. Ethel, Chris and Mrs Gilbee sat on the veranda catching the sea breeze, for it was a hot night. They waited for the children to settle, and then quietly went about loading the stockings with fruit, sweets, comic books and a pair of steel and timber roller skates for each boy. Chris had acquired these last items from "The Argus" when he had gone into the city to meet up with old colleagues. A crate of what had been voted "Toy of the Year" had been sent to the newspaper in the hope that the staff might give positive publicity. Chris was invited to choose three pairs to take home.

Ethel knew that the boys would be thrilled with them, although where they were going to find a smooth surface to roll on them in Trafalgar was anybody's guess. As it turned out, the printing office's long wooden floors proved perfect for the skill and Chris was to live to regret his decision to indulge his youngsters with the new toy!

Christmas dawned and with the sunrise, three very excited boys were out of bed and delving into their stockings, eating things edible and then strapping on their new roller skates and rolling round and round the big veranda that surrounded the guest house. There was no sleeping late that morning. After the large turkey had been basted and put in the oven, the family, dressed in their Sunday best, walked the few blocks to the Mary Forrest Davies Memorial Church to pray. 'Mary was a great friend of mine,' explained Mrs Gilbee to Chris as they walked. 'It was a real tragedy when she died unexpectedly young, and because there was no Presbyterian Church, her funeral had to be held in the Mentone Hall. Her husband, Matthew, and his friends built and dedicated this church to her a little more than ten years ago. I always remember her, especially when I come here to pray.'

'I remember her and Mr Davies,' reflected Ethel. 'He was extremely generous with all the money he made from the land boom, and he was a great friend of Father's. It was a shame that they both had to lose everything in the bust.'

'Yes, everything collapsed so quickly, one minute things were booming and the next the bottom fell right out of everything. It killed your father, and it jolly nearly killed Mr Davies. Matthew nearly died at sea, you know. He got wind of the impending bust and, as fast as he could, took a steamer to London to refinance his loans. And would you believe it? The ship he was aboard floundered in wild weather on the Irish Sea, within cooee of his goal. He was a strong man and managed to swim ashore, climb a cliff and make it to London, but he was a day late and so it was to no avail. Unbelievable! He lost everything, just like your father did. It is all gone. He is reduced to living in a small cottage in Mentone Parade. He had it all, and it disappeared,' lamented her mother, sighing deeply and thinking of her departed husband and other things that had passed. 'But he is better off than your father. At least he is alive.' Christmas was always bitter sweet for her since her dear husband had died. What followed was a frantic round of cooking, eating, and celebrating with family and friends. In the afternoon the whole party promenaded under parasols along the beachfront, stopping off on the front lawns of the Mentone Hotel for afternoon tea. At the allotment across the road, on the lawns of Riviera House, the carnival sang out its music as happy holiday crowds tried their luck on the Knock 'em Downs, the Shooting Galleries and the Lucky Balloons. The boys loved this.

They returned to the boarding house for tea of cold collations left over from lunch and a lively game of charades. After everyone had gone home and the boys were in bed, Ethel and Chris prepared for an early start the following morning. They had to be home for the big Sports Day and its accompanying celebrations. There would be time enough for rest when that was over.

CHAPTER 43

'It's a public holiday, mate, and the country trains don't run,' the man at the Caulfield ticket box informed them. 'Next one to Gippsland will be eight o'clock tomorrow morning. Sorry.'

'But we caught the train from Mentone to here. That train was running,' protested Chris. 'We're all dressed up with nowhere to go.'

'The trains to Caulfield are running because the races are on. Only the main suburban lines are operational today. Mate, your best bet is to check into the hotel across the road, spend a day at the races at the track just over there, and then leave from here tomorrow morning.'

Chris' eyes lit up in anticipation. He loved the horses!

'What do you say, Etty dear?' he asked his wife. 'If we troop back to Mentone now, we will have to spend another night there and then get up and do the same thing again tomorrow. Your mother will think I'm a fool for mixing things up and putting everyone out like this. Or we can book into that lovely white hotel over there and spend a day at the races. You always say you want a little more social life, well, here's your big chance. The boys can come and look at the horses and we will have a day out.'

Ethel did not want to have to return to Mentone. She had already said her goodbyes, and that had not been easy. She didn't want to have to repeat the process tomorrow morning. Besides, the family had stayed with her mother for over a week and the poor dear was probably relaxing on the chaise lounge on the veranda restoring her energy stocks. It had been a busy time and it was her one chance for a break before the boarders all returned the next day or the day after. 'Yes,' she said, slipping her arm into Chris', 'let's do that. The boys will miss out on their iron horse races at the Sports Day at home, but will catch up on the original kind. Yes, let's book into the hotel and have a day to ourselves.'

They booked into the Caulfield Hotel where Ethel changed from her travelling clothes, putting on a new white blouse that ruffled at the neck under a navy blue suit featuring a slim fitting jacket that she had purchased on a shopping expedition into town, and which had an amazing matching boater hat decorated with fine plumed feathers that she had bought at the Mentone Haberdashery. The older boys were clean and ready to go in their white shirts and grey trousers and young Vernon looked very cute in his sailor's suit. Taking his wife's arm, Chris, looking dapper in a morning suit with a three-quarter length jacket and bowler hat, walked his family across the road to the races. The expense was not an issue, the newspaper was doing well and once he was back home, Chris rationalised, he would not have much time for fun. He bet a wad of money on Caledonian to win the main race of the day, but unfortunately it was not this horse's year, and he lost more than he dared admit to Ethel. Fortunately she never asked. She was happy because she had selected a young filly for the maiden handicap named Etty Mae, and it had won. She had no money on it because she didn't gamble, but unbeknown to her, Chris had slapped a tenner in the bookie's hand at good odds and nearly recouped his losses.

After they had gotten over their initial disappointment at missing the sports day, the boys enjoyed the carnival atmosphere and all were in agreement that they had all had a marvellous day. They strolled across the park and back to the hotel for dinner and good conversation afterwards with fellow racegoers.

The next morning they boarded the Gippsland train to return home to Trafalgar where the town was abuzz with people and horses and carts that had stayed over the night before. The sports day had been a huge success and having two balls in town on the one evening, which had been the source of such acrimonious dispute, had merely added to the merriment. There were more than enough patrons for both events.

This homecoming felt like the real thing for the family because this was home and life was good. They opened the gate and walked up the garden path to their own front door. 'As soon as I have unpacked, I am going to spend an hour or two in the garden,' Ethel thought as she looked around, taking note of how scraggly it had become in the ten days they had spent away. She observed that it must have rained for there were puddles in the Main Street and she was grateful that the plants she had placed under the tank stand had survived, although she was sure they would all enjoy a good drink. The roses were on their last and a gentle prune would ensure they would flower in autumn. The daisies needed a good cut back but the red geraniums were in flower as were the petunias that formed a carpet of colour. Thankfully, the palm tree had survived her absence.

In her bag she carried numerous brown paper bags of seeds from her sisters' and her mother's gardens. When she had a minute she would plant them into some sand to germinate, as they would provide colour for her spring garden.

The vegetable patch amazed her with the number of tomatoes that had ripened in the time they had been away and the parsley was prospering. Some of the lettuces had gone to seed, the carrots were ready to be pulled and she needed to wrap newspaper around the celery to bleach it ready for the table.

'We have enough silver beet to feed all the neighbours,' she remarked to Vernon who was doing the rounds with her, 'and there's a couple of apricots and plums on the trees.' She was happy to be back.

Chris had other things on his mind and vowed that, as soon as he was able, he would stroll down to the Eagle's, meet up with whoever was there, have a cooling ale, and find out all the town's news. He had been on his very best behaviour whilst staying with his mother in law and longed for a pint of the thirst quenching nectar. The boys couldn't wait to visit their mates.

Left alone, Ethel and Vern made the journey out to Annie's farm to retrieve their beloved pets and caught up on all the news from the Donovan household. Although Jack Donovan had ridden a good race in the road trial, he had failed to feature in the final sprint.

'I'm in training for next year's race, Mrs Johnstone,' he told Ethel. 'Instead of taking the horse down to round up the cows I am riding my bicycle to do the job now. I reckon all I need is a bit of practice. You'll see! I'll be up there with the big boys next year.'

Things were changing on the farm now that he had left school and was helping his father seven days a week. Annie's load had lightened considerably and although she still helped with the morning milking, she was relieved of afternoon duties, thus freeing her to see to the children and cook the evening meal.

'I can't believe it,' she boasted to Ethel. 'I'm up at five and the milking is done by seven thirty. Now, once the kiddies are off to school and the breakfast things are tidied up, the rest of the day will be mine. Mind you, with seven people in the household there is still plenty to do, but I know that once I have cleaned myself up after the morning milking, I'm clean for the day. I don't have to go down there to the shed again at night and suffer the cows and all their bodily fluids. I have time to get out into the garden and to do some sewing for the girls. I never thought the day would come. Thank God for my Jack is what I say.'

'Good for you!' Ethel was really happy for her. 'I am looking forward to seeing my friend in town a little more. You can come and visit in the afternoons when I am tied to the Printing Office. That will be good.'

CHAPTER 44

Annie's stone fruit trees were laden and Ethel headed home with a hessian bag full of plums and apricots.

'I'm so happy you can take them,' Annie commented as they picked the remaining fruit from the trees and gathered the fallen ones. 'I cannot bear to see it rotting on the ground. I have filled the pantry with jams and preserves and have no bottles left, so it's your turn to sweat over a hot stove.'

'For jam, weigh the fruit, bring it to the boil and then add equal weight in sugar. Keep it on the simmer until it sets,' instructed Annie, showing her how to place a teaspoon of jam on a saucer. 'Let it cool, and if it jells then the jam will set and that is the time to remove it from the stove.'

Ethel had preserved fruit many times with her mother so she knew how that worked. All she needed to do was to invest in a preserving kit that she could buy at Bernicke's. It was a one-off expense and hopefully would last for years. She spent the next few days preparing and processing the fruit and when she was done she lined the shelves of her new

301

pantry with jams and preserves that she had made, thinking that this made her house more of a home.

She proudly showed Chris her work. 'Is this all from the fruit trees we brought from the bloke from Shepparton last winter?' asked Chris in amazement.

'No, silly! I had to nip most of the fruit off them as soon as they budded. That gives them a good start. It helps the roots to embed themselves and get established. You can't let the trees fruit the first year, but they will start to produce in a year or two. Most of this fruit was given to us.'

'By whom?' Chris asked.

'Well, the tomatoes are ours,' replied Ethel, 'and we have a really good crop because I have been getting the boys to collect Dondi's manure and using it to build up the soil. Annie gave me apricots and peaches and your David brought in three boxes of produce. Maggie has that huge fig tree at the back of the shop and the boys stripped it for her so she shared some with me. And I am going to have a go at making wine with some grapes that Mrs Plozza - she's Annie's Italian neighbour out on the Swamp - gave me. Lots of people have given me offerings. They are so kind and generous and of course, everyone hates to see any fruit go to waste.'

'Does making this wine require me to take my boots and socks off?' chuckled Chris, adding, 'it certainly looks like we shall have enough fruit and jam to last us through the winter. What a good little ant you are,' he said, giving her a hug.

'Annie says that her pear tree is a beauty and is laden with fruit this year but they won't be ready for picking until late February so that will give me some respite from the bottling. I have a box of tomatoes to make sauce as well.'

'I know how hard you work, Etty. And I do appreciate it even if I don't always say so. We are both doing our best for the boys and I reckon we're a great team. "Never Unprepared!" That is the great Johnstone motto, straight from the coat of arms in the old country.'

'"Never unprepared!" That's a double negative, don't you mean "never prepared" or "always unprepared"? Now that I would believe of the Johnstones!' she laughed.

'Perhaps English wasn't their forte,' Chris laughed along with her. 'They were too busy getting prepared! Talking of preparations, can you make up a moveable feast for us all? On Wednesday, we are going to the banks of the mighty Latrobe with anybody who is anybody in this wee town and we are going to have a magnificent mid-summer's picnic. '

Ethel smiled and, summoning her best interpretation of the Scots accent, confirmed she was set to go. 'Aye, r-r-r-ready,' she said with a laugh. 'That sounds more positive than being never unprepared.'

CHAPTER 45

They packed a little cart for Dondi to pull containing the picnic basket full of goodies, plus some rugs and a couple of kitchen chairs, and headed for the banks of the Latrobe River where they would spend the day eating, relaxing and fishing. Ethel had ordered some bottles of the new aerated waters that Mrs Donahue was supplying for parties and social events such as these, which the children thought delicious, and the adults thought pretty good as well. Perhaps this outing was not as sophisticated as the ones in Melbourne but the people were genuine and the ambience was far more peaceful.

The ladies talked of Lorna Bushby's recent wedding in Morwell to Tom McLaughlin. Many Traf people had travelled down to join in the celebrations and because Lexie Kenny was the bridesmaid and Nick Lawless was the best man, there was much local interest. When their honeymoon train to Sorrento passed through Trafalgar, the young couple were showered with rice and shredded paper. Everyone loves a wedding and while the women were talking of gowns, presents and all the paraphernalia that goes with such a celebration, the men were discussing the logistics of the holy institution itself.

'Ah marriage! For a man it's like being a horse in harness,' lamented Cyril Hunt, the Senior Teacher who was on school holidays and therefore had time to think about these things. 'A man devotes ten hours a day to earning the money and it is up to his wife to support him emotionally and to manage the house so that she creates a happy home for him.'

'Ten hours a day?' joked Tom McGrath. 'You're on six weeks holiday at the moment and I bet you have never worked ten hours a day in your life!'

Cyril lit a cigarette he had been rolling and took the insult on board because he was used to such banter from people who thought, because they had been to school at one time and had sat there doing nothing, that teaching a room full of wriggly children was easy. He inhaled, and not to be put off, expounded further.

'But,' he added, ignoring Tom, 'she fails if she manages everything else, but neglects to manage her man.'

'That would be the day,' rejoined Mick Quinn. 'No woman will manage me. I'll not be ruled by petticoat government.'

'Ha, ha, that is my point exactly,' returned Cyril. 'Mick, my lad, you are being managed by your lovely Irene. It's just that you are so stupid you haven't woken up to it yet.'

'That's rubbish, absolute rubbish. I run my own show. I'm the boss at my house.'

'Just goes to show what a good manager Irene is,' Cyril chided. 'She lets you think you run the show. In reality she has you on a chocolate covered leash. She allows you to have your own selfish ends while all the time she is steering you towards behaviour for the common good.'

'That's dog shite!' Mick was getting a little hot under the collar.

'Mick, my boy, I have taught school for over thirty years now and I have yet to see a harmonious family that does not have a prudent wife and mother at the helm directing operations, and mostly putting everyone else's needs before her own. And, mark my words, she does run the show and it would collapse without her.'

'Well, I'm yet to be convinced,' put in Jimmy Kenny looking up from the fishing line that he was baiting for Vernon. 'I've seen some good marriages in my time, but, by golly I have seen some bad ones, and I tend to agree with you, Cyril. Some women manage to castrate their men while others build them up. If I knew which was which I wouldn't be so nervous about the whole thing.'

At this point, Chris, who had been on the sidelines seemingly asleep in the sun, sat up and chuckled to himself.

'Jimmy, my fine friend, you may not realise it, but you have one foot up the aisle and the other on a banana peel. You're all but there, mate. Before you know whether you're Arthur or Martha, Miss Mavis will wriggle that cute little nose of hers, and you will be under her spell.'

'Is that what you think?' Jimmy asked. 'I'm beginning to think that I am too much under her spell and she is not under mine. Not that I don't understand her not being completely enamoured with a long, lanky fellow with a couple of teeth missing.'

'I thought you two had Christmas together?' asked Chris, adding, 'Methinks that that may be an indication that she likes you more than a little and that she's not entirely disinterested.'

'That's what I thought,' Jimmy lamented. 'But since her parents have come visiting, she seems to have gone a bit cold on me. She has been really hard to pin down lately, always seems to be busy and distracted. Seems to me that she is avoiding me. I invited her here today but she declined to come.'

'Now, that is interesting,' Chris thought. To soften the blow, he said, 'Perhaps she's just busy, Jim. It is the festive season and her parents are still here staying with her, aren't they?'

'Yes, unfortunately.' Jimmy was clearly uncomfortable with this conversation. 'They may be the problem. They totally disregard me, treat me like a servant. "Jim, can you do this; Jim can you do that." All that sort of thing. They never treat me as an equal, or Mavis, either, for that matter. She is always on edge when they are around. If you ask me, they think they are better than everyone else around here.'

'That so, that so?' Chris puffed on his pipe in the silence that ensued until Dan Baillee came to the rescue, steering the conversation away from the topic of Mavis.

'I hear that the widow Adamson has remarried,' he said. 'Now there is a brave woman, she's married that old bachelor Toby Smith who has the farm next to hers. He's a very religious man, only takes a bath twice a year, at Christmas and at Easter. Uses holy water!'

They all chuckled.

'She's brave for more than that,' added Henry Haines joining in the joke. 'A woman who marries the second time runs two risks. One, that she will never replicate the first husband who was everything a man should be and two, and this is the big risk, that she regrets the time she wasted on him in the first place.'

This was the cause of great mirth!

People were in holiday mode. Next week they would be back to business, busy on the farms or in the town but for now, it was time to relax with their neighbours and friends.

'Ern Cook has just got the contract to build a Parsonage for the new Methodist Minister on the block down the road from us,' Chris related after they had returned home. 'It's going to have six rooms, plus an inside bathroom and a pantry. Pretty flash!'

'And I heard that Nick Lawless has asked for tenders to build a new general store in opposition to Bernicke's,' said Ethel. 'I wonder whether there will be enough business to go around?'

'The town is growing so fast that there should be plenty for the two of them,' said Chris. 'All these extra people coming in have to get their provisions somewhere.'

Ethel finished washing up the picnic things and sat down. She broke the companionable silence. 'There is also going to be so many dentists in town that our teeth will be like shiny pearls. Do you think there is enough teeth to go around?'

'Poor Jim won't be able to help there. He has one less this year than last,' replied Chris, placing newspaper on the table and taking the Nugget from the shoe box in preparation for the task of cleaning his and the boys shoes for the morning. 'Why, what is it you heard?'

'There's a new dentist, a Mr Jack O'Neill, who will be working out of Lawless' Coffee Palace and, as well as that, there is another new man named Mr Allan French. They say he gives his patients a whiff of laughing gas so that they thoroughly enjoy the ordeal. The Trood brothers will have to take time out from their magic tricks if they want to keep their patients.'

'Well, I suppose the Troods had the right idea all along. They make us laugh but not with gas, and not when we are having a tooth pulled!'

'Speaking of which', Ethel cut in, 'fun and laughter, I mean, we simply can't miss the New Year's Day Yarragon Bazaar. Can we make a family outing of it please, Christie? The boys are old enough to behave themselves at things like that now.'

'I hear it's the biggest event of the holidays,' Chris replied. 'We will make it our last big hoorah. Let's put on our finery and go. It's back to work for me the next day.'

CHAPTER 46

Very soon the holidays became but a memory as the day-to-day stresses piled up. 'Take a look at this,' Chris ranted, angrily opening opposition newspapers from surrounding towns and jabbing a finger at a similar advertisement in each of them. 'The Inaugural Meeting of the new Racing Club is coming up and three other local papers got the paid advertisement. But poor muggins here, who has done a lot of the work setting the whole thing up, doesn't get a look in. They give it to that tat rag up the road, plus the Warragul and the Moe papers, and yet their own "Trafalgar & Yarragon Times" is left out in the cold. They don't deserve to have a paper in town. I'm ropeable!'

'I agree with you, Christie my pet, but it is useless telling me about it,' Ethel cajoled. 'Speak to the secretary of the Racing Club. After all, this is the first general meeting that the "Times" has been around for, so perhaps they just did what they usually do, and neglected considering you.'

'It's the first ever meeting, period! There is no precedent, so that blows that argument. And not only that, they have sent the printing out of town to Donahue's brother-in-law in Warragul. How do they expect me to make a living if the local organizations don't support me? I'm as mad as can be.' Chris had turned a vibrant shade of cherry. 'I'll talk to John Gibson and see what he has to say; after all, he is acting president.'

'Keep calm and speak to John,' said Ethel. 'Explain our position and give them something to think about. I'm sure it was an oversight; they wouldn't do it deliberately. I saw Hope Gibson down the street this morning and she was happy and chatty, nothing to suggest that she might have a vendetta out against the Johnstones, so keep your hat on and work it out with the powers that be.'

Eventually it was deemed that there had been a mix up between the two roles played by the one man, namely Christopher McCallum Johnstone. On one hand, he was Chris, the member of the steering committee for the newly formed Horse Racing Club. On the other hand, he was Chris, the Editor and owner of the local paper. His two roles had muddied the waters. Because he was the former, some of the other members of the team considered that he should give publicity in his paper for nothing.

Race day dawned and this beautiful part of the world was dressed in its Sunday best for the occasion. Bert Amor ran a Cobb & Co coach out to the course that looked as pretty as a picture amongst crops, which were flourishing as far as the eye could see. In the distance, the Baw Baw range, with the sun dazzling on its eight summits, stood sentry over the hustle and bustle below. The whole of Trafalgar was there. Ladies in their finest attire and gentlemen in their three-piece suits and bowler hats promenaded the mounting area, checking their race books and examining the horses as they were paraded around the circle before each race. Little girls

dressed in white lace and frills with matching bonnets
adorned with ribbons and bows, and little boys tidily attired
in freshly pressed shirts, polished boots and Sunday best
trousers, ran and skipped in and out amongst the crowd.
Bookies had made the trip from Melbourne to set up their
large umbrellas and shout their odds, their pencillers sitting
to the side, nursing Gladstone bags stacked with cash.
A clown in an oversized orange and purple spotted suit, large
green shoes and funny hat, who looked amazingly like
Arthur Adcock in an oversized orange and purple spotted
suit, large green shoes and funny hat, told the kids riddles,
made farting noises, flirted with the ladies and generally
made everyone laugh. With him was a skinny fellow,
instantly recognisable as Terry Trood, who could make
wonderful things happen with a few brightly coloured scarfs.
There were toffee apples, fairy floss, fizzy drinks and a tiny
merry-go-round for four people driven by the leg power of
Bert Richards, who was in training for the Victorian Cycling
Championships. Between the main events, children
competed in underage flat, sack and three legged races. The
crowd was so well behaved that Sergeant Bretherson and
Constables Ryan and Thompson had an easy time and
enjoyed the day along with everyone else.
The day's racing began on time with jockey Willy Walker
taking out the first two races, the first on Pilgrimage, and the
second on a little known horse named Forward. Punters
were more than a little upset about the unsatisfactory start in
the third, where three horses were left at the post. In the
fourth, there was a hung result when the owner of
Mendleson, a six foot six giant of a man, protested that his
horse was interfered with in the straight. The opposing
owner put in a counter claim, so the bookies put off paying a

dividend until the Victorian Racing Committee heard the case later that week.

An unfortunate accident in the main event of the day put a damper on proceedings. Young George Hough's horse, Victoria, dashed into a post about a furlong from home, unseating the lad and knocking out a number of his teeth. He lay on the ground with blood pouring from his mouth. The poor lad was a sore and sorry with reduced smiling capacity for life, but fortunately home was just across the paddock so he limped off to recover.

Young Mervyn got aboard Dondi for the Novelty Pony Race for horses under fourteen hands. The problem was that nobody had asked Dondi and he didn't want to run. Poor Merv could do nothing to move him along.

'What you need, young Merv,' counselled Jimmy who was feeling very pleased with himself after a couple of ales. 'What you need, son, is a long stick with a carrot on the end, and then you could sit on your little mate here and hold it out to him.' He laughed at his own joke. 'Then watch him move forward, there'd be no stopping him!' Mervyn filed that little bit of advice aside for next race meet. He would just have to find a long stick!

'Taking Dondi was a waste of time and energy,' remarked Chris to Ethel as they walked to the Ball later that evening. He was a little out of sorts because although he had backed the horses under Willy Walker, he had lost money overall. 'We could have saved ourselves the effort and left the nag home in the paddock. It took me half an hour to walk him down to the course this morning and he wasn't at all interested in making a race of it. Silly pony thought he was the guest of honour, just there to meet the crowds.'

'That really made me laugh,' chuckled Ethel, 'poor little fellow had no idea that he was supposed to run as fast as he could and Mervyn was doing his level best but he just wanted to meet his friends in the crowd with the hope of getting a carrot or an apple. Poor Dondi certainly isn't a racehorse. But didn't Mervyn enjoy it? He saw the funny side, and you must admit that Dondi is a very important personality in the town. It was an amusing sidelight for everyone.'

There was a slight chill in the air and they could smell the smoke from the wood fired stoves that were now beginning to burn later into the evening. It was a perfect early autumn night after a still sunny day. The sky was clear and open and the stars twinkled over the town, which lay awake well past its bedtime as the crowd danced the night away.

About half way through the program of twenty dances it was announced that Miss Felicity Brown was the Belle of the Ball and Miss Emily McCrory was her princess. For the judging, couples waltzed to Tchaikovsky's "Waltz of the Flowers", the more proficient men dancers gracefully bending this way and pirouetting that way, while others shuffled around in an embarrassed fashion, pushing their partners before them like ploughs.

'Thank the good Lord that I didn't have to make that decision tonight,' Ethel whispered in Christie's ear when they met briefly in the Barn Dance where everyone changed partners between each set, and neighbours and friends caught up. All eyes were on the new, handsome young Moe stationmaster who was making his first public appearance that night. The young ladies certainly liked what they saw, the bolder amongst them setting out to impress.

'I think Mr Bourke is just adorable,' gushed the young Miss Coghlan. 'With those long legs, he moves around the floor like he is a black swan gliding into land. I do so hope he asks me to dance with him.' He did and they made a very handsome couple.

'Mark my words, that young man won't stay single for long,' Maggie remarked to Ethel as they worked together in the kitchen preparing the supper, putting out the teacups and making the tea. The women of the town had done the usual and the supper room bench was heavy with delicious homemade sandwiches, savouries and cakes of all kinds. Closer to supper time the older ladies and gents, Annie and Tom amongst them, who were playing Euchre in the meeting room, would emerge to help them set out the feast on the trestle tables that had been lined with plain newsprint donated by the printing office. Having done everything they could for the moment, the two women were contentedly watching the dancing while chatting.

'He doesn't know it yet,' Maggie said, nodding towards the young railwayman as he swung around the dance floor, 'but he has just slipped into a spider's web. If Catherine doesn't get him, what's the betting that some other girl will have him walking down the aisle before the year is out. That young man is far too good looking for his own good. I reckon that there will be a great increase in the young ladies of this town travelling by train to Moe to do their shopping.'

'You may be right, he looks a good catch,' replied Ethel. 'Lucky man! The Trafalgar girls must be the most beautiful in all the land. It is good for the population to mix and mingle and to go outside of the community to make alliances. It prevents inbreeding. Having said that, though, I hope one of my boys marries a Trafalgar girl and lives happily ever after. That would make me a very happy woman.'

'That's just because you want to keep your grandchildren close by,' laughed Maggie. 'I'm a wake up to you, Ethel Johnstone.'

'There may be a little bit of that in my thinking,' admitted Ethel. She could see the sadness in Maggie's eyes and she understood just how much she would love to have a baby in her arms so that one day he or she might grow up to give her grandchildren. Ethel was of the opinion that children gave one hope for the future.

'Now, tell me, who is that woman with the Lawrences? The one in the black lace standing next to Hoppy? I haven't seen her before,' Ethel asked.

'Is Hoppy here?' Maggie was surprised because she had never before seen him in town on any day except a Friday for market, and he certainly wasn't the dancing type, especially with his prosthesis which was never quite right and caused him much pain. 'Last time I saw that poor man he had a dead child in his arms, and he could hardly walk. So sad and so tragic!' Ethel lamented.

'Perhaps that might be Agnes, his wife. He talks about her but I have never seen her before. She is always working out on the farm.'

'Do you know him well then?' asked Ethel, but the answer was not forthcoming because they were interrupted when Chris, who having finished his duties manning the door, entered the supper room to ask Ethel for the next dance on the program, the Evening Three Step. He had deliberately left himself plenty of time to sample Eileen Keeley's cream puffs that were as light as fairy dust and filled with rich vanilla cream.

'Ah, that John is a lucky man,' he mumbled with his mouth full, savouring the delicacy. 'Imagine coming in from the paddock each night to one of these. Etty, my lovely, you either have to learn to cook like Eileen or save me another one for when we come back.'

Ethel took his hand and laughed as they moved away. 'It will have to be the latter because I will never be as good a cook as Eily.'

Maggie watched them go out on the dance floor, happy in each other's company. She had to accept that she would not be able to follow because George didn't like to dance. He was a typical countryman who was comfortable standing down the back of the hall, talking to the other men, and occasionally sneaking outside for a spot of liquor.

'I'm not the dancing sort, Maggie,' he would say when she would suggest that it would be lovely to trip the light fantastic together. 'You just have to learn to live with that. Besides, blacksmiths don't dance. Look at my rough hands and my clumsy feet. I'd walk all over you, dear Maggie, and you'd be a mess by the end of the first three bars. By all means, dance with anyone who asks you, but please don't make me do it.'

What could she say? Perhaps it was her fate to watch life from the sidelines.

Her reverie was interrupted when, in the brief moment of silence before the band was about to start, she felt a tap on her shoulder. She looked around to see that it was her George with a sheepish look on his face. 'Would you please afford me the pleasure of this next dance, Maggie Brown,' he asked, bowing at the waist.

Flabbergasted, she replied, 'But George, you always said that you would never, ever dance. Never! I certainly won't say no. But what has brought this on?'

'Oh well,' he said, nodding towards the centre of attention, 'I figured that if Hoppy can do it, so can I.'

'Is Hoppy dancing?' Maggie was incredulous because she had spoken to him enough times at the blacksmith's shop to know that his leg stump was always uncomfortable. The music started and they moved off and were just getting into the swing of things when Hoppy and his partner stood in front of them with a smile as broad as the valley in which the town sat and his hand proffered, ready to shake. 'George, I want you to meet Agnes, the better half. We both want to thank you. You're a genius mate, a miracle worker.' Before George could respond, Agnes interjected. 'Mr Brown,' she said, her bottom lip quivering with emotion, 'we are indebted to you forever. I cannot explain what a good thing you have done for us. May God bless you and hold you in his hands.' Suddenly overcome by embarrassment, they moved away, leaving Maggie mystified.

She looked at her man. 'Miracles? Indebted? Blessings? George Brown, what on earth have you been up to?'

'Well, I don't know about miracles, my darling. But I may have helped poor old Claude out. Fiddled with his prosthesis, made it more comfortable for him.'

'You mean …' she said, nodding towards the couple and touching her left knee.

'Yep. He came to me in agony, had heard what we were doing with farm machinery and thought I might be able to do something about it. The prosthesis was Army issue and was ill-fitting, rubbing against him, making him limp and causing him immense pain. There was no way he could do a whole day's work, so Agnes was doing the lot. They have two small children at home and they lost the other little one. Their life was a mess'

'Did you fix it?' Maggie had no doubts that her husband could solve any problem.

'Well, I did a bit of research, got a few manuals sent down from Melbourne, and then gave the prosthesis bit of a lift here, a twiggle there, took a bit of pressure off over there. But the thing that made all the difference was the spring-heeled steel insert and the lambs-wool protectors. It saves his stump and he can do most things a bloke with two legs can do. Look at him now. He's dancing! Hoppy is now happy.'

'Oh, George,' said Maggie. 'You never cease to amaze me. What a wonderful, clever, giving man you are.' They held each other and danced.

It had been a grand day out at Hough's paddock. The town had turned out in force and people from the surrounding districts had taken a day off from their haymaking and harvesting to have some fun. Now, at the Grand Ball, Chris was dancing with Etty, George was dancing with Maggie, and Claude Lawrence was dancing with a newfound belief in life.

CHAPTER 47

'Traf will never beat the Yagpies this year. We just won't be in the hunt. It shouldn't be allowed to happen.' Jimmy shook his head.

'What on earth are you talking about?' asked Chris. 'Who or what is the Yagpies?'

'They,' espoused Jimmy, more than a little perplexed at Chris' lack of knowledge of such a vital topic, 'are the best football team we have ever seen in this area. Yarragon has amalgamated with the Magpies to form the Yagpies, and the result is frightening. They played their first practice match at Willow Grove and they were awesomely good. They will whip our collective arses, if you will excuse my French. Just mark my word.'

'Early days yet, Jimmy. The season hasn't started, so don't panic,' Chris consoled. 'Perhaps by that time you and your mates will be as fit as Mallee bulls. I reckon we have the players to challenge them. There's a meeting next week to consider our options. We will put the best team possible onto the field this year. You just see, they will be scared of the mighty Bloods.'

Chris held up a letter he had received in the mail that day. 'What do you make of this?' he asked. 'It seems that I am not a very nice bloke.'

Jimmy cast his eye over the contents, reading some of the major points aloud. 'Mean, contemptible, dirty. That sounds like something that I should know about. What did you do Chris?' he jokingly quizzed.

'I'd like to know myself,' replied Chris, 'I can't imagine what I have been up to, but I thought I wouldn't have had the time to be mean and contemptible. I've been far too busy to indulge myself in such fun. I have asked around and no one seems to know who wrote it or what it means, so I am unable to ascertain just how bad I am.'

'Well, that's one of the downsides of running a newspaper, Chris. You expose yourself to the public and you never know who is going to have a go at you. Put it aside and if I hear anything I'll let you know, you miserable mongrel! In fact, I'm feeling pretty mean and miserable myself.'

'Why's that? I don't think you have a mean bone in your body, Jim. What's eating you?'

'Nothing really, but I just heard on the grapevine that Mavis is leaving town and Henry Hansen has been engaged to sell her whole stock of furniture. I only know because I saw Henry down at the Station and he mentioned it. Mavis hasn't breathed a word of it to me. It seems that she has left me completely out in the dark. Didn't I tell you that she'd gone quiet and seemed to be brooding over something? I feel like a complete and utter fool; I've been played for an idiot. Mavis is leaving town and has told me zilch. I've bloody had it with women. Never again! I'm angry and I'm bloody disappointed!'

'That's bad, Jimmy. Do you mean to tell me she has never said a word, and that she is about to scamper off like a rat up a sewer pipe, after leading you on like that? That's bloody terrible. Has she mentioned anything, anything at all?'

'Not a thing! I knew she was finding it difficult. She has said a few times that it is pretty hard for a woman to run a business in this town and complained that the only business a woman is allowed to run is a dressmaker's shop or a boarding house, and that she had to do things a hundred times better than the men. The truth is that a lot of the local blokes did not like going into an establishment run by a woman and some of the other women thought she was a sinner for running a pub. I thought she was overcoming all of that prejudice and I certainly didn't know she was thinking of leaving. I had no idea!'

'That's terrible! Perhaps you're better off without her, Jim. You've had your doubts, you said so yourself at the picnic, but I honestly thought she had you all tied up, with the noose around your neck. Think of it as a lucky escape.'

'Yes, you're probably right,' Jim replied, largely unconvinced and failing to hide his hurt. 'I would have thought she would have talked it over with me, that's all. I thought I was important to her.'

'I can see you are upset, Jim. You just have to front up and ask her. You have a right to an honest answer, because when it is all done and dusted, you have looked like a couple, sounded like a couple and walked arm in arm like a couple, so she owes you an explanation.'

'Yes, you're probably right, Chris.'

Jimmy was clearly uncomfortable with the topic, so he changed the subject.

'I just came by the Creamery to get the story about the upcoming Annual General Meeting and was inside with

Archie McKean, when all hell broke loose. We could hear pandemonium, and looked out to see horses and people going everywhere. You know George Irwin, don't you? Lives a few miles out, but is always in town on market day. He's a young bloke, works on his father's farm.'

'Yes, I've seen him around. What about him?'

'Well, he was the cause of it all. He was driving his load of milk down the incline at the factory when the horse's bit broke and it bolted right through the gates and into the yard. Paul Bouchier was delivering horse feed and oats. And everything went every which way, the cart one way, the hay the other, and George flew into the air. That big red bay of his was a bit shaken up. There would have been a dozen other carts with horses attached milling around, waiting to deliver or pick up and I don't know how he missed them all, but he somehow managed to avoid disaster. I breathed a sigh of relief because I thought it was all over, but bugger me, then the wagon went completely over with him underneath it. He must have been saying his prayers, because he came out of it all unscathed. He's lucky to be alive. And the horse was all right as well! The wagon only lost a wheel in all that shemozzle! I'm bloody amazed that no one was killed really! Poor old Alex Gunn, he must be one hundred and seven, was down there, don't ask me why, but it gave the poor old bugger a fright and I must admit, it shook me up as well.'

Chris wasn't fooled about the change of subject. Jimmy was known to say the odd 'bloody' or 'bugger' but only after a few beers in the pub. He rarely incorporated these words into everyday conversation.

'I bet it scared the daylights out of young Irving as well,' commented Chris. 'And we have an eye witness account! That's what we, at this newspaper, love. Write the story

James my friend, and we'll put it in. Did you get the low down on the Annual General Meeting?'

'Yes, I'd got it all before this Irwin thing happened. McKean reckons it's time to expand, build a bigger factory and with all the farmers doing so well this season that it is time to move forward. He is going to propose that at the AGM. Reckons with a modern touch a new expanded factory could handle as much milk as the farmers can produce for the next ten years or more, and that it is better to do these things in times of prosperity than to wait. He expects a bit of lively debate from the soothsayers who say if it ain't broke, why fix it? But on the other hand there are plenty of forward thinking farmers who can see our town as the centre of the milk and cream industry for South Gippsland. The town is thriving. He reckons it's all happening here.'

'Ah, that's what I love about you, Jimmy. You are a man who goes out to get one story and comes back with two. What a champ! Perfect, lets see if we can get all that written for Tuesday and when it is done we have the Cricket Club Presentation Dinner. Are you coming?'

'No, tonight I am presiding over the Bachelor Ball Meeting at Long's Hotel. We reckon that we need to give the dance scene around here a good shake up. We already have some modern music lined up and we reckon we can drum up three hundred likely souls to dance the night away, so that's what I'll be doing. Mavis was going to help, but I reckon that won't happen now,' he added, regret in his voice.

When the day was over, the two men went their separate ways.

CHAPTER 48

The smoke from Chris' weed danced with delight as it curled its way towards the ceiling and hung like a cloud amongst the red Chinese lanterns. After a toast to His Majesty and a hearty rendition of "God Save the King", the Master of Ceremonies noted that the day was not only Saint George's Day but also Shakespeare's birthday, so there was double the reason to celebrate. He acknowledged the unwavering support of Club President George Hough and stated that Trafalgar was very proud of its team, congratulating them for winning the Nurse Trophy and for the sporting way they played "that most gentlemanly of games, cricket".

'We have loved watching you boys, so light up and puff away to your heart's content,' he said.

All of the talk was of the cricket season past and the football season to come. Any other topic always came back to these two things. When there was discussion regarding the influx of Mallee farmers and their stock, somebody commented, 'We've put in all the hard work, building schools, constructing halls, establishing banks, making roads and footpaths and setting up the water supply. They'll get things in a mess and leave us to clean it up. These interlopers should know about the sacrifices we locals have made, and have it made clear to them that they must take their fair share of civic responsibilities.'

Chris, the voice of reason, encouraged them to think more broadly. 'But lads, think of the prospective football players we may have available to play for us. I hear those blokes who were raised in the Mallee don't kick footballs. They practice on bags of wheat! As tough as old nails, they are. I reckon if we are smart, we could get them on side and sign them up before those Yagpies get hold of them.'

This almost immediately convinced the group. 'You may be right,' a committeeman said. 'A lot of those blokes are of German descent, big blokes, big as giants. Some of them have a few brains as well. Yep, we should get them on side as soon as we can. Invite them to the Bachelor's Ball that is being organised. Introduce them to our lovely girls, perhaps they'll make a few alliances and they'll play for us.' The mention of football and the coming season was enough to dismiss the threat posed by the newcomers from all minds. Wally Davies noticed a young lad of his acquaintance and called him over to the group. 'By the way, what are you doing here young Andrews? I thought you and Stan Currie had forsaken the mighty Bloods and gone off to Western Australia. We had a big night in the pub for you only a fortnight ago. Don't tell me you've made your fortune already?'

'Lost our fortune, more like it. That's what we are doing here. We are home to work and make some more money.' David Andrews looked slightly embarrassed about being amongst them that evening, when there had been such a fuss made about his leaving just two weeks before.

'Pray tell, what happened?' Chris asked.

'Well, we woke after the night at the pub with the thickest of heads, but nevertheless we made it to Melbourne and booked into digs. Our plan was to take a cargo ship to Perth, working our passage. We had it all teed up with Stan's cousin who works on the wharfs and we were staying in Richmond with him for a couple of days. Anyway, we saw the ship's captain and were walking up Spring Street about eight o'clock in the evening. It wasn't late and only twilight. This mob of ruffians jumped on us and took all our money. Over eleven pounds! I suppose we looked a bit bush wacky. There was absolutely nothing we could do about it, us two against half a dozen of them. We're bloody lucky to be alive, but we couldn't go anywhere without money. So we're back to make a bit more and then we'll go again. Next time we won't be carrying any on us.'

'Did you call the constabulary?' asked Chris.

'Yes, we made a report. They said they'd look into it but there was probably nothing they could do, the money would have been whacked up and spent.'

'You poor buggers! I really feel badly for you,' said Dan Baillee. 'That was an awful thing to happen, but as you say, thank the good lord that they didn't kill you. Men have been murdered for less.' Everyone mumbled in agreement.

Chris broke the silence, 'Drink up everyone, every cloud has a silver lining. The two boys are both good footballers, so we may not need those Germans of yours, Benny.'

'Maybe so, but we could do with their services to help put the finishing touches to the town tennis court. A couple of big burly Germans would be good for that. They can supply the muscle and the know-how,' Benny replied.

'What's this about tennis courts?' Dan asked.

'Tennis is the big thing in the big smoke at the moment,' said Chris. 'So we thought little old Trafalgar should have some courts of our own. It's very social, both men and women play, so it could be good for the town.'

'Slow down a bit,' Dan warned, thinking on his feet. 'Let's just consider this. If there are young lasses involved, where do you think all the young lads will go? To the tennis, of course! And they play tennis all year round, right? So what do we do in winter for a footy team if all the young men are off playing tennis with the ladies?'

'Hmm,' said Chris, staring into his glass. 'That is a point worth considering.'

It seemed that no matter which path the conversation took it always returned to the football.

As usual Ethel had waited up, and as she was about to extinguish the lamps, Chris remembered Jimmy's news. The alcohol he had imbibed had tempered his usual loathing for gossip and he was chatty. He related the conversation he had had with Jim that morning. Ethel shared Jim's hurt.

'Mavis? Selling up and leaving?' Ethel commented in disbelief. 'Going back to Ballarat to live with her parents again? I can't believe it! And I thought she was doing such a good job. Poor Jimmy, he really likes Mavis and I am sure he has had thoughts of marriage. I wonder what made this happen? There must be something else behind it all. It just doesn't make sense,' Ethel mused intuitively.

'I don't know, Etty, and neither does Jim. But I dare say we will find out after he broaches the subject with her. My advice to him was to talk to her about it and bring it out into the open. At this stage he has nothing to loose. Nothing ventured, nothing gained, so to speak. In the meantime Mavis is selling up on May the fifth and moving on. I believe that all the furniture is almost new, only nine months old. What a waste.'

'Poor Jimmy. Love has let him down yet once again. Do you think he will go with her?' asked Etty.

'God, I hope not!' Chris was taken aback because that had not occurred to him. 'I hadn't thought of that possibility. That would be disastrous; I need Jim like I need my right hand. I just couldn't get by without him. We do it together.'

'Then pay him more, or offer to bring him in on the business,' replied Ethel, forever the businesswoman. Jimmy's romantic life could well be their downfall and they both knew it.

CHAPTER 49

Anthony Bernicke was having a clean out, with everything going cheap and for fourteen days only. Annie was in town for the Monster Clearing Sale. Afterwards, she had stopped by to see Ethel, show her the bargains and wait for the children to come out of school.

'I've had a lovely time. Everything is on sale,' she laughed happily, pleased with her purchases. 'My poor Tom will have to turn those cows upside down to get every last drop of milk out of them. I have had a big buy-up; shoes for everyone, fabric for a new skirt and jacket for me, as well as a pinafore for Eily.' Annie was particularly excited about the new blue and white china teapot that she had coveted for months but had never thought she would be able to afford. The day was sunny so they walked around the garden, inspecting the vegetable patch which was full to overflowing with tomatoes, cucumbers, lettuce, beans, peas, onions and cooking herbs.

'How ever do you manage to grow such delicious looking vegies?' asked Annie as Ethel collected beans and peas for her to take home. 'My legumes have hardly done a thing this year, so disappointing.'

'There's no secret really,' Ethel informed her, 'it's all a tribute to Dondi and Betty's magnificent constitutions. Of course, they are being grown on virgin ground and that may play a part as well.'

'I may have to look into that,' Annie mused. 'After all, I have grown my vegies in the one spot for three years in a row. Perhaps it's time to make new beds.'

'From what I've read,' Ethel continued, 'the soil is best served if you rotate the crops.'

'What? Turn them around? How would that help?' asked the bemused Annie.

'Not rotate them that way, silly!' Ethel laughed. 'What I mean is to plant different crops in different places each year. Apparently, peas and beans put nitrogen into the soil but they take out other nutrients, so next year shift them around and plant things that love nitrogen. From what I can gather changing crops also keeps diseases down. I will get a book from the library that tells the story better than I do,' she offered, 'then we can both learn more about it. Now come and see my autumnal blooms.'

'You should enter that dahlia into the Yarragon Autumn Show,' Annie advised, cupping the bloom in her hand and inspecting it closely. 'It is almost perfect and the colour is quite unusual. What would you call it? Purple or black blue? I think it may win a prize. There are more blooms coming on, so if you can keep the insects away you should have a good one to enter. It's only a couple of weeks away. The only thing is, you will need to know its name. Who gave you the tuber, or did you buy it?'

Ethel felt gratified that her dahlia was being admired, but had no intention of exhibiting it this year.

'One of Mother's neighbours gave it to me when I was down with the boys. She collects them and wasn't quite sure which tuber was which because the dog had got into the shed and spilt the box. She gave me a few, and said that when they flowered to press them for her, and next time I am down there she will name them for me. I suppose I could post one to her for naming. I am overjoyed at the display though. Aren't they beautiful?'

The compost heap where Ethel threw her scraps and peelings had sprung some very healthy looking pumpkin plants that were meandering their way along and over the fence and into the side paddock.

'In another three weeks one of those pumpkins may be big enough to enter in for the largest pumpkin,' Ethel remarked, lifting a leaf to look underneath, 'not that I will. Have you anything you want to enter, Annie?'

'I always enter our potatoes. Each year I have a friendly contest with Spud Murphy from the Darnum side of Yarragon, it's either him or me because the professional growers don't bother. We have a bit of fun with it. I might put a jar or two of my jams and pickles in as well. The mustard pickle came up a treat this year and the cherries have bottled up to look quite beautiful. I used longer, slimmer jars that I got in Brunswick; they are the very latest thing in the city. But I'm like you Etty, I just like to go for the day out and to see what other people are growing.'

'Now, where do you suggest we plant this pear tree?' asked Ethel, carrying a specimen wrapped in hessian. She had taken the trip to Warragul especially to buy it now that the autumn colour was apparent, and she looked forward to a spectacular seasonal display in years to come.

'I want my garden to announce the seasons,' she had told the nurseryman. 'In spring I want blossoms, in summer I want shade, in autumn, colour and in winter, the whole thing can hibernate, so that I can take a rest.'

'This is the tree for you then,' he announced, pointing to a flame red specimen. 'It will announce the spring with snow white pearls, shade half your garden in summer with foliage while it produces sweet fruit and shed rubies in autumn. In the winter it will let the sun warm the bulbs below it. Keep it away from the house so that its roots can reach out,' he advised.

'You choose a place, Etty,' said Annie, 'I am simply here to help you dig. After all, it is your garden.'

And so the pear tree was planted in the back eastern corner, away from the house where it would provide shade from the hot summer sun. As they stood back to admire their handiwork, Ethel closed her eyes and visualised her future grandchildren playing on the swing attached to its ample branches.

'I am going to love this tree,' she thought, ' there is nothing like trees to keep the air fresh and healthy.'

'You know,' she said turning to Annie, 'every night when my work is done for the day and when I am asleep, my pear tree will be busy taking the carbon dioxide out of the air and pumping back clear clean oxygen for my family to breathe. Trees are indeed wonderful things.'

'Is that what they do?' wondered Annie, for she had never heard of photosynthesis. 'I love trees because they allow you to take time to sit under them and to idle a little.'

'End of that thought,' she announced as the school bell rang out for the completion of lessons. 'Here come the villains that prevent my idleness. No rest for the wicked.'

The two women walked through the delicate and feathery salvias that swayed in the gentle breeze underneath the roses, which were looking tired and in need of a good haircut.

Ethel knew that, tempting as it might be to tidy them up, she would have to wait until late June or early July.

'Here comes Harry the Fishy,' Ethel pointed out as they watched a horse and cart round the bend from Contingent Street. 'I shall have to stop him and get some fish for tomorrow.'

'Is that Harry Davis from up Thorpdale Road?' asked Annie. 'Does he sell fish now?'

'And rabbits as well! He comes by every Thursday, with his rabbits and fish. I like to buy from him because he catches them himself and I know they are fresh. Christie is always promising me that he will wet a line in the Latrobe River and catch me a feed, but he never gets around to it. He is always too busy and I don't like to send the boys out, as they are too young yet. They might drown.'

'Another couple of years and Aubrey will keep you in fish,' Annie consoled. 'I never have to buy any because our Jack goes over to the creek every Thursday evening to get me fish for Fridays. He never disappoints me. He loves fishing and seems to always come back home with enough to feast upon. I love fresh fish. I could eat it every day.'

'I'm not that keen on it, but I believe a variety in the diet keeps everyone healthy so I like to serve it once a week, always on a Friday, just like you Catholics.'

The Donovan children skipped towards them, looking nothing like as fresh and clean as they were this morning when they set out for the day.

'I'm off then,' announced Annie. 'Tom and Jack have been busy laying down brick paving in the cowshed. They had to do it because Parliament has passed a Health Act saying so. It's just another expense that we farmers have to endure. Jack Mackey is up in arms about it and I don't blame him. I'll have to help with the milking tonight because we'll have to get it done in the out yard.'

Taking Eileen and James by the hand she turned the perambulator towards home and waved, 'See you next time I am in town.'

CHAPTER 50

As Annie and her brood disappeared into the dust that swirled around the children and the horses and ponies on their way home from school, Harry's cart appeared and pulled to a stop. 'G'day to you, Mrs Johnstone,' he said, doffing his cap. 'And what would you like today, a couple of fresh baby rabbits or some of these beautiful black bream, still kicking, some of them.'

'Kicking? The rabbits or the fish?' Ethel laughed. 'I'll have the bream please, Mr Davis, four good sized ones should do us.'

Ethel turned to see the boys running down the path towards her. 'Mother, mother,' Aub called out, unable to wait to get closer, 'there is going to be a road race out to Willowgrove and I want to go in it. Can I please?'

'Don't you think you are a bit young yet? Say hello to Mr Davis, Aubrey. Can you ride that far? You'll have to ask your father.'

'Hello Mr Davis,' Aub puffed. 'Please Ma, please,' he begged. 'Pop will say 'yes' if you say so. Please! Eddy Mills and Evan

Rees are going to enter and they are not much older than me. And Arthur Richards and Michael Schmidt will be riding, but they are much better than I am, so I won't win it, but I do want to try. Please!'

'As I said, you'll have to ask your father, but I'll put in a good word for you if you take these bream and fillet them for me. Make sure you trim as close to the bone as you can, so we are not throwing out good flesh.'

Harry handed the fish to the lad, who was quickly off to the washhouse to carry out his side of the bargain.

'It is good to see such enthusiasm in a lad, Mrs Johnstone. He knows he can't win but that doesn't stop him from trying. That's a great trait in a boy.' Harry climbed onto his trap and with a tilt of the cap, a flick of the rein, and a "Good day to you", he was off to the Presbyterian Manse to sell more fish.

Smiling inwardly at the compliment regarding her son, Ethel took Vernon's hand and with Mervyn trailing behind she went inside to make the children a snack of bread, butter and newly-made plum jam. She was secretly pleased that her lad had enough gumption to put himself up against the older boys. She would do as promised and have a word to Christie when he returned from James Buckland's funeral in Moe. Everyone in town had been shocked when the fifty-six year old founder of Buckland Brothers General Merchants had died unexpectedly from complications of peritonitis. After twenty-five years in business in the district he was well known and had earned massive goodwill and respect. After the funeral Chris would go onto Donohue's Coffee Palace where many of the men were enjoying the hospitality of Mr Mackcy of the National Citizens Reform League as a way of saying "thank you" for electing him, so Aubrey's request would have to wait until the morning.

'Boys,' said Etty, 'Father won't be home until late tonight so we shall eat early. Get your chores done and I will cook up potato pancakes and bacon.'

The boys set to because they were hungry and this was their favourite tea. Vernon took the bucket, filled it with wheat and went off to chase the chickens in from the side paddock and settle them into their roost for the night. Aubrey went down to the wood-heap to chop enough wood to fill the wood-box and to gather kindling to light the morning fire, while Mervyn took two buckets to transfer water from the tank to the house.

They quite liked it when their father was not home for tea because things were more relaxed, and after she had cleaned up, their mother would sit with them and play a board game. If their father was at home, she would mostly talk to him. This night she lit a fire in the grate in the sitting room because the equinox was almost upon them and the nights were getting chilly.

'Don't stand too close to the fire,' she warned, 'Annie was telling me that last week, out on the Swamp, a little girl was playing in front of the open fire when her clothes caught alight and she got so badly burnt that she died.'

She knew that this was a harsh way of warning them of the danger but it was true, and she wanted to impress upon her lads the importance of care in this matter.

'The good news is that, next Friday you all get a holiday for the Yarragon Show.' Cheers all round. 'And this year I am going to take you all. We were too busy last year but this year we shall take a picnic and go on the train. Annie, Eily, James and Dolly are coming with us. Jack and Tom are entering some of their best cattle in various divisions, so they will take the cart. And you know what? James is going to enter that big black chook he loves so much in the Best Hen Section.

He has to give her a bath and make her all clean and shiny. He's going to bring Chooky, I think that's what he calls her, on the train in a big basket, so that will be fun, won't it?' 'Can I take one of my chooks?' asked Vernon, 'I could take Chinny-Chin -Chin.'

'Who on earth is Chinny-Chin-Chin?' Ethel asked with a smile in her voice. They had ten chooks and they all looked alike. It was news to her that one had a name.

'You know, Ma,' Vernon replied, 'the red headed one with the wobbly chins.' Ethel couldn't for the life of her visualise which chicken had these defining features and as it was already dark outside she would have to wait for morning to be introduced.

'Perhaps next year, Vernon darling! You can watch what James does this time, and then you will know exactly what to do. Besides, I think it is hard work getting livestock prepared for the Show, and I wouldn't want you to wear yourself out. Next year will be good.'

Vern nodded, agreeing with his mother. He knew that the red headed chicken wasn't exactly prize material. Besides, he would have to spend the next twelve months learning how to catch her!

Ethel and the boys spent a happy couple of hours playing drafts and catching up on all the news. She learnt about the narrow escape they had had the previous market day when they were kicking the football on the road out the front, and a mob of cattle came up behind them. One rogue cow took a disliking to young Raymond Mann and charged at him. Ray took off through the fence. The beast then turned its attention to Aubrey who climbed up a gum tree. By this time it was furious and turned around and went for Harry Blake who was a bit slow to see the danger. The drover in charge saw the situation and came by, whisking Harry up onto his saddle while calming the steer. The boys thought it was a huge adventure.

When it was time for bed, Etty oversaw prayers and goodnight cuddles, extinguished their lamps, then sat down to read her book in front of the fire and wait for her husband to come home.

When he did, he was excited by what he had heard that night. 'Mackey will be good for the district', he told her. 'He seems right on top of it and let us know all about this new reform Bill that is presently with the King awaiting his approval. It will fix up a lot of things.'

'How is that?' asked Ethel, sipping the hot milk and honey she had made for them both.

'Well, at present only the rich can apply for a seat in parliament and only the rich can vote. The new Bill will reduce the rateable value of property for a person to be eligible to vote and it will cut down the requirement for a person to be earning two thousand five hundred pounds a year before he can occupy a seat. That's a lot of money and the ordinary Joe Blow earns nowhere near that amount. In future it will only be fifty pounds per annum.'

'That's a big step forward. What else?' queried Ethel.

'Well, they are changing the constitution of the Upper House and that will save a good bit of money. And the most important thing is that the big knobs in the Upper House won't be able to reject legislation that the Lower House deems important for the welfare of the state. If it does, then both houses must go to an election. Once the King signs off on the Bill, there will be a new election within six months.'

'And what about the vote for the other half of the population, us women?' Ethel asked.

'I'm afraid it's not on the agenda just yet, Etty. They are a bit afraid of you dames. It would change the fabric of the parliament. The way they look at it is this – if women get the vote, then women would be over represented.'

'What a lot of rot! How would that happen? One vote is one vote and all people should have equal say.'

'Calm down, Etty! Let me explain. There are something like seventy five thousand more women in towns than there are men, so if women vote it will shift the power from the country to the cities and women will have more say.'

'What towns? There are far more men in Trafalgar than there are women! That's just nonsense.' Ethel was getting cross at the thought.

'I mean the bigger towns like Geelong, Bendigo, Ballarat and Melbourne, the more urbanised towns. It's as simple as this Etty, if women are given the vote in Victoria, the members representing the towns will predominate, making the country districts, the rural areas like ours, subordinate to the towns. We all agree that shouldn't happen, we don't want those city slickers telling us how to live our lives. So it's best to watch it work at Federal level before we try it here.'

'It makes me so angry,' Ethel expounded, 'everyone in the country knows that, without the women working by their sides, the men would make a very poor fist of it. Look at Annie, she works with Tom clearing that land and tending it; she has done as much as he has on that farm. All the women on the land do, plus they cook and clean and have the children. Many a farm goes broke when the woman has died from overwork or childbirth. It's a man's world, Christie, so I'm glad that I had boys, as they won't grow up to be second-rate citizens.'

'Hush, woman! Most of your fellow females don't want the vote. They are happy letting the men run the country.'

'Not this one,' said Ethel in a weary voice, 'not this one! I can see that I'm on my own with this argument.'

'I can see both sides to the story,' Chris consoled.

'Yes, you would, because you are a man,' Etty shot back, impatient with him.

'Etty darling,' said Chris in a conciliatory manner, changing the subject. 'Did I tell you I have appointed a general manager for the new Moe office? His name is George Buckleton and he can start on April the twenty-eighth, so that should take some of the pressure off. Plus, I have engaged young Vere, Dave's youngest to work with him. He doesn't want to go to the west with the family, wants to stay here in the district, so Dave asked me to take him on. I think there may be a young lady who has caught his attention, or something like that. Do you think we could set up a bed for him on the back veranda? We could close it in and Dave said he would give me a hand.'

He must have seen the expression on Ethel's face so he quickly added, 'After all, he is my nephew, and we do need extra help.'

Ethel nodded her assent and Chris continued before she changed her mind.

'We're going to do a generic edition and then add separate Moe and Thorpdale pages. We'll call it the "Moe & Thorpdale Times" and I am going to put the price up to tuppence. What do you think about that?'

'That's very good, Christie. I just hope you aren't biting off more than you can chew.'

'Not at all, my darling, not at all! I might need you to man the counter a bit more, though, as I shall have to spend time over at the Moe office at first, but you won't mind that, will you? We have settled in now and you seem to enjoy being at the counter organising things for us.'

'Enjoy it? Christie, sometimes I am so pushed for time I don't know whether I am Arthur or Martha.'

'Etty, you cope because you are a coper! You are a clever woman. The devil finds work for idle hands, Ethel. Besides, you have a wonderful time at the office. You always seem to be laughing or chatting with one person or the other.'

'That's called good business, Christie, building customer relations, providing service and all of that. I am glad the business is doing well. You are doing a good job too, Christie. Come on, let's go to bed.'

CHAPTER 51

The bar at the Eagle's was a full, the regulars all seated or standing in their usual spots, sipping the cooling ale and catching up on all the gossip before heading home. The farmers were feeling good after a very successful Market Day where the stock had gone for high prices, but the conversation soon turned to another topic.

'Did you see that pair of dappled greys that were in town yesterday?' asked Dan Baillee. 'In fact the whole outfit, horses and trap, was well worth a look. Best I've ever seen in the district. A bloke named Hamilton from St Kilda was driving it.

'I believe that a lady named Mrs Nelson was on board. Her husband is the bloke who has bought the Criterion from Miss Stewart. She was dressed to the nines, a real fashionable missus. All the ladies in Trafalgar will want her off-casts.'

'She stopped overnight at the Criterion,' Paddy O'Sullivan added.

Chris' ears pricked up. He was interested on account of Jim Kenny; and Paddy was a trustworthy witness because he was always in the centre of comings and goings in the town.

'Nelson is not going to run the place,' continued Paddy. 'He just owns it as an investment and as somewhere to keep his art and antiques. He's a city businessman, I hear, and from what I gather, a fellow by the name of Alexander Arthur Hicks will be the landlord. He comes to us with the highest credentials.'

'Oh yes, and what are those then?' asked an interested Dan. 'I believe that he was an associate with John Connell and Son, the wine and spirits merchants from town. He should know his liquor.' Paddy released his information slowly, enjoying being the centre of attention and the font of all knowledge.

'We'll be all drinking over at the Criterion soon,' continued Paddy. 'Apparently they are going to tart the whole place up. Nelson has plans to rebuild and will be furnishing it with all new furniture and fittings and apparently the lighting has to be seen to be believed. No expense has been spared.'

'So we can look forward the Criterion being the best hotel in all of Gippsland then?' Dan quipped.

'You'd have to give some credit to Miss Stewart,' Chris added on Jim's behalf. 'She has done all the hard work in cleaning the place up. It was a cesspit of ill-repute when she took over twelve months ago. She has managed to refine the establishment.'

'I don't know about that, Chris,' Paddy replied, 'but I do know that she has been amply rewarded for her efforts. In fact three thousand pounds amply.'

'That's huge! Wow-wee!' whistled Dan. 'No wonder she took the money. That amount would set you up for life.'

Silence ensued as they contemplated a sum they could only dream about. 'I wonder if Jim knows this,' thought Chris to himself. It was the first time he had heard any of it and it was certainly big news in the town. After a fair bit of discussion as to what could be done with three thousand quid, the group began to break up and the men started to make a move in order to get home before dark.

The Eagle called in his best town crier's voice to all and sundry, 'Arthur Ashby was in and asked me to remind you fellows about the Traf versus Drouin footy match next Wednesday. Jimmy Kellas has been elected captain for the season and the match has been moved to Ashby's paddock because the recreation reserve is a mud heap at the moment. Arthur said that perhaps it's time for a working bee to get the drainage sorted out.

'And on that note, gentlemen, thank you and goodnight.'

CHAPTER 52

Jimmy was feeling more positive about his situation. 'You'll be pleased to know, Chris, that I took your advice and had a heart-to-heart with Mavis last night. I told her I was sick of being kept in the dark like the village idiot and that she owed me an explanation. I asked her to come clean with me.'

'Good for you, young Jimmy. I'm glad you stood up for yourself. You're bloody right. She does owe you an explanation. It's the talk of the town. Paddy Sullivan was down at the pub last night shooting his mouth off about Mavis' business. What has she told you Jimmy?' Chris asked, putting down his pen and sitting back in his chair.

'Yep, she told me she had indeed sold up and was leaving town. She was surprised when I looked hurt. Can you believe that? Surprised! She had the cheek to say that she didn't think it would make any difference to me at all. She assumed I was only worried about my board and keep and said she had negotiated a deal with the buyer and that he had promised to keep her boarders and that he would also keep Mrs Somerville on, she's the lady she has doing

347

housekeeping and the laundry. She reckoned that she was being fair to us all.'

'How did she explain not speaking to you about it?' asked Chris, hurting for his friend.

'I asked her that and she said that she considered that it was really none of my business. That we are good friends and that we would remain so, even if she lived one hundred miles away. She seems to have no idea that I might consider her more than a friend.'

'And I hope you set her right, that you told her about your feelings for her?' asked Chris.

'Not yet, but I will. I will.' Jimmy answered sheepishly, putting his hand to his face where his missing teeth used to be. 'I just have to wait for the right moment.'

'Well, you'd better hurry up,' prompted Chris. 'Jim, make your feelings known. She's not a mind reader. It can't do your cause any harm and it might even do some good. But, take my advice, you'd better be quick and catch the damsel before she is out of your orbit, Jim. Faint heart never won the fair lady.' Chris was beginning to panic for his friend.

'I will do it Chris, in my own good time, I will do it,' Jimmy defended himself. 'You know how I said that I didn't think her folks approved of me? Well, that was not the case at all. They thought I was one of the staff. Makes you laugh, doesn't it? It just bloody well goes to show you how much bloody unpaid work I do around the place. When they were here, the whole family was preoccupied with their own problems and didn't pay me any attention at all. The story is that her old man is a gambler. And not a good one at that! He lost a lot of money on the nags at the spring races and stood to lose the hotel and his whole livelihood in Ballarat. Because he had loaned Mavis the money to buy the Criterion and refurbish it he wanted it back pronto, and pretty well ordered her to sell up, repay the money and to go back to Ballarat and work in his establishment.'

'That's a bit rough,' Chris interjected. He was beginning to feel sorry for Mavis now.

'As it turned out, Mr Nelson had come along at that precise moment and, off the bat, offered her three thousand pounds for the building and the business. How could she refuse? It was two thousand pounds more than she had paid for it twelve months ago, so she took the deal, repaid the old man and pocketed a tidy sum herself. Anyway, this Nelson bloke is a big art collector and society fellow from Melbourne. He is not going to manage it himself but has a bloke by the name of Hicks, a wine and spirits expert from the city, coming to manage the place.'

'So is dear Mavis going back to Mama and Papa in Ballarat?' Chris asked with a sarcastic tone in his voice.

'She's not sure yet,' Jimmy replied. 'She doesn't want to, but she feels obliged so probably will go there until she gets herself sorted out. She told me she plans to purchase another run down establishment somewhere and build it up like she did at the Criterion.'

'When is Mavis leaving town?' asked Chris gently. 'Do you think she would like a send off party? I could get Ethel to organize one at home. After all, she has been very good to Ethel and the boys, and she is a special friend of yours.'

'She's staying next door at Lawless' from next Monday, as she said that she would stay on a week or two, or however long it takes, to finalize things and to give Nelson a hand in the changeover. I think she will be gone by the end of the month.'

'Well, we have to mark the first birthday of our newspaper so what if we organize a joint celebration? After all, Ethel met Mavis on Day One and she has been advertising with us from the first issue. Yes, that's what we'll do. We'll have a party. In the meantime I will need you to run the show for me this Friday. Can you do that?'

'Of course Chris, what's the occasion?'

'I have to walk my little sister down the aisle. Next weekend Elizabeth is going to marry Richard James Moser.'

CHAPTER 53

Chris came into the office on the Monday morning feeling refreshed and happy. It had been a wonderful family weekend. As well having the privilege of giving the bride away, it had been his honour to be best man and partner to his other sister, Polly McKendry, who was the maid of honour. The three little McKendry children completed the wedding party.

'And how did the celebrations go?' Jimmy asked his colleague.

'It was great. Unfortunately Mother and Father are too frail to make the journey down from the hills these days and that is why I gave Elizabeth away. But everyone else was there. The Yinnar church was decked with flowers and Etty had baked the wedding cake and decorated it with Easter daisies and white roses from our garden. The Country Women's Guild catered for the wedding breakfast, speeches were made, and everyone had a wonderful time.'

'And where did the happy couple go on their honeymoon?' Jimmy asked, half listening.

'Inverloch, I think. It's a little seaside village down past Leongatha. Thanks for filling in for me Jim. Now let's see, what we have here?'

'Everything here went well, no disasters, so that's good,' Jim reported. Chris leaned over a page proof, pencil in mouth and examined the roughs of the next week's advertisements. 'It certainly looks healthy, Jimmy my boy. We seem to have turned the corner and have advertisements coming out of our ears.'

'Yes, any more and we'd have to add another two pages,' replied Jimmy, looking over Chris' shoulder. 'We seem to have a spate of new ones, lots of new businesses in town, all wanting to advertise. The only one that has dropped out is that of my cousins who went into the butcher business. They closed the shop.'

'They didn't last long! What happened?' asked Chris.

'I reckon they didn't know what they were getting into,' replied Jim. 'They thought that because they were good farmers and could fatten cattle, that they also had innate butchering skills. But they didn't! They butchered the bloody meat, all right. All the cuts looked the bloody same and people were turned off. They sold the business to a fellow named Kyle, and I reckon they were lucky to get a buyer. Apparently he is a master butcher from town and knows his business. That's his new ad there,' Jim said, pointing to it.

Ethel walked in, interrupting the conversation and flourishing a piece of paper. 'Hold the press, there's one more ad to go in, seeking last minute entries for the wood chopping contest at Yarragon.'

'Not much point going in that,' Jimmy noted forlornly. 'No one will ever beat Jas Strain. He is a great axeman, virtually unbeatable. Many have tried but nobody has succeeded in toppling him so far.'

'You should have a go, Jimmy,' teased Chris, 'you're a big strong bloke. I've seen you swing the axe for Miss Mavis.' Jimmy blushed, ignoring the reference to his lady friend. 'There's far better than me around with the axe. You should see the O'Toole family from Thorpdale. The whole family eats logs for breakfast. They have a couple of sons and even the old girl has a go at it.'

'You're not bad at all, Jim,' continued Chris. 'I reckon you'd give them a run for their money. You've managed to chop up enough logs to keep the fires burning at the Criterion for the last nine months and that's been no mean feat.'

'Talking of the Criterion,' Ethel put in, 'I just heard down the street that Mr Hicks, the man who is going to manage it, is ill. Apparently he can't get out of bed. Has some sort of mosquito-borne disease he picked up in Swan Hill. They say it can be very debilitating. He is in Melbourne in hospital because they couldn't treat him down here. Wouldn't it be nice if Mavis had to take the business back, Jim?'

'How could she repossess it?' Jimmy wondered, interested in what Ethel might tell him. 'She sold all the furnishings at the auction. The place is empty. I know, because muggings here spent the whole day carting the stuff in and out for Henry Hansen.'

'Now that was a fun day, even though it poured rain,' remembered Ethel. 'We bargain hunters didn't care. Henry certainly knows how to work the crowd at an auction. Wasn't he funny? He spent the entire day making us laugh, softening us up so we would splash out and buy. We did, but I think everyone still went home happy and satisfied.'

'He was pretty successful,' Jimmy added. 'Mavis told me later that, even after all the expenses were taken out, she had more money in her pocket than she paid for the furnishings. She had bought them as a job lot from a boarding house in

Ballarat that was closing down. The publican unearthed a huge gold nugget and was taking his loot back to the mother country. He was happy to sell and go and didn't care that his prices were dirt cheap.'

'Mavis will be badly missed,' praised Ethel, mainly for Jim's benefit. 'Even though she's only been in the town for ten months, she has made many friends and she certainly turned the old Criterion around.'

She stopped, but when there was no comment in support from Jimmy, curiosity got the better of her and she could not help herself.

'What exactly was the reason Mavis decided to leave so suddenly?' she quizzed, leaving her normal good manners to the side. She figured that up until this point Jimmy had been speaking fairly freely about the situation for the first time, so she should not miss the chance to find out more.

'Perhaps the most influential reason was that her parents wanted her back at home with them,' Jim replied. 'They had a bit of a hold over her as she owed them money.'

'Oh, but what about you, Jimmy?' asked Ethel. 'Did she take you into her equation?'

'Not really! At that stage, when she made this decision, I hadn't told her of my intentions; she had no idea that I might have plans for the both of us. I just hadn't told her,' Jim lamented. 'I was too slow on the uptake. It's really my fault but we are still friends, so there's a little bit of hope. She's a bit older than I am, but it makes no difference to me. She looks young, she acts young and she is a fine woman, so I say it doesn't matter.'

'Women think more of those things,' observed Ethel, 'so it would be good for you if Mavis had to resume ownership, wouldn't it? It would give the two of you more time. No harm meant to Mr Hicks, of course.'

Chris had been standing by, quietly listening to all of this and added his bit.

'Don't give Jimmy false hope Etty. Nelson has done a lot of planning for that place already, and he has plans before council for the new building. An architect bloke from Melbourne is designing it. No expense spared. Apparently the bricks alone will cost one thousand nine hundred pounds. He has spent a packet already. Even now, he has lots of his own paintings on the walls. For lovers of fine art it is a real treat to go in there. Everything will be top quality and very elegant, a place where anyone can feel comfortable.'

'Thanks to Mavis,' said Jimmy defensively. 'She's already cleaned up the clientele and made it a desirable place to eat. It was a pretty rough establishment before she took it over, that's why she got it for a good price. You know,' he added, 'you can have a trolley load of money, but it counts for nothing if you don't have good health. That is exactly what our Mr Hicks is finding out.'

'Well Jimmy, you just may get your Mavis back, and if you do, put a ring on her finger and stake your claim. Perhaps you should do that anyway, Jim?' advised Ethel.

'We shall wait and see. I can't see myself leaving Trafalgar. Besides, I wouldn't want to be living on her parents' patch and have them looking over my shoulder at me every day.'

'And I'd hate to see you go, Jim,' said Chris, quick to reaffirm his colleague. 'We need you here. You know what they say – if you love it let it go and then, if it is truly yours, it will come back to you.'

'Perhaps Jimmy,' Ethel gently advised, 'the very first thing to do is to lay your cards on the table and tell Mavis exactly how you feel about her. She is not a mind reader, you know.'

Chris knew he simply could not do without Jimmy, so remembering Ethel's advice, he put in his own offer. 'Now that the advertisements are rolling in, I think it's time to renegotiate a new agreement. You deserve a raise, Jim, and you shall jolly well have it.'

Chris was not going to part with Jim easily, Ethel noticed. She thought Jim should follow his heart, but, of course, she would never say that out loud.

CHAPTER 54

'It is going to be greatest ecclesiastical ceremony ever held in Gippsland,' Maggie had excitedly informed Ethel regarding the opening of the new church in Morwell 'Why don't you come with me Etty? It will be a gala event, and Annie is coming, she told me so. It will be such a good day.'

'Oh, I couldn't,' Ethel squirmed inwardly. 'It is just for you Catholics. They wouldn't like me there, nosing around. I know that Christie will have to go to report it, so he can tell me all about it. Thanks for thinking of me Maggie, but I would feel too uncomfortable.'

That is how Ethel missed out on the most elaborate event in that year's social calendar.

'I thought I was in Buckingham Palace with the King,' Chris said that evening as he took off his boots and stretched his tired feet. 'Ah, it has been such a day. You know, Etty, I have never been in a Catholic Church before, and certainly not one like the new building at Morwell. Even the train trip was amazing, standing room only, chock-a-block with women in hats, men in suits, children galore in their Sunday best. The air was bursting with anticipation and excitement. Some of the more devout recited the rosary non-stop all the way there, and others were reading aloud from their missals.'

'I hope you took along your Bible, Christopher Johnstone,' teased Ethel.

'No, I escaped that because I was lucky enough to be with Maggie and George and Annie and Tom, so there was plenty of laughter in our group. They took me under their wings and showed me the ropes. Maggie told me, "When we get there, just follow me and do what I do." Otherwise I would have had no idea. So there I was, splashing holy water over my forehead from the font at the front of the church, bobbing up and down in the aisle, and kneeling and shuffling when Maggie said to do so. I'm sure she added a few bobs and scrapes just to keep me moving and for her own entertainment. All the time I was scribbling away into my notebook, getting it all down. There was so much happening. I have to admit that I was overawed by it all. The church itself is beautiful, the most imposing building we have in the area by far, and the furnishings are elaborate.'

'Where did they get all the money for all of that?' enquired Ethel. 'Did someone die and leave all their money to the church?'

'That may have happened,' replied Chris, 'but I think the congregation undertook a lot of debt.'

'However will they ever repay it?' wondered Ethel, thinking of the simple services conducted at Alexander Matheson's place. The people who came to pray there had barely sufficient funds to keep themselves and their families going, let alone to build an elaborate church.

'You know what some people are like,' Chris replied. 'They think they can buy a place in heaven, and believe me, I have seen some Catholics let their children go without just so that they can give money to the church. This I do know, though, Father Coleman is very popular and if anyone can persuade his congregation to get behind him and clear the debt, he can. The people seem to love him and I think he is indeed an honourable man of the cloth.'

'He covers a lot of territory for one man,' Ethel added. 'He ministers to people up into the hills and all down the line.'

Chris became sidetracked in his thoughts. 'It's interesting though, that Catholic churches seem to be the most well placed and the biggest in any town. They must have very committed congregations.' He then continued his story. 'You would have loved the gardens, Ethel, the whole place looked wonderful. Some nuns came over from Traralgon to decorate the altar with flowers. Etty, you would have enjoyed it, if only for the glorious blooms; I don't know what they were, but I did see red and white roses amongst them. Somebody said that they had pruned them precisely after the spring flowering so that they would be at their optimum for this event.'

'I'd love to meet that person,' Ethel interjected, her mind wandering to her garden, 'just so he could tell me exactly what to do with my roses.'

'I reckon that all the Catholics from this part of Gippsland must have been there,' Chris continued. 'There were several priests and a bishop and reams of altar boys. Do you remember Father Coyne? We met him at the Yarragon fete. He was there in a wonderful set of vestments, for the entire world like Joseph's amazing technicolour coat in the Bible. I shook hands with him and he told me that they had been made the previous winter by a group of travelling nuns.'

'Can you imagine that? Travelling nuns!' Ethel voiced her surprise at the concept.

"Yes, strange, isn't it? Apparently they move about the countryside working where they are needed, sometimes with the sick, perhaps stepping in and caring for a family when a mother takes ill. Anyway, they came through his parish at Leongatha exhausted, because they had spent the previous six months down on the coast teaching the children of fishermen to read and write. There had been a great tragedy at sea where eighteen breadwinners had perished, so they stepped in and helped the mothers and families to cope. Anyway, they stayed in Leongatha for three weeks and for that whole time, just sat inside sewing and praying. They never went anywhere. In the end they produced this wonderful garment, absolutely beautiful, presented it to Father Coyne, said their goodbyes and then disappeared to do good deeds further down the track.'

'What an amazing story! Only God would know what good those wonderful women do. Where would Australia be without women? So simple and so humble, just doing their good deeds, quietly and with humility. Good luck to them! Go on now, tell me more.'

'Well, there was Bishop Maloney in full regalia, big purple hat all trimmed with gold, white and purple embroidered garments, a huge crook. Looked very important and I think he felt that way as well. Afterwards men and women alike bowed down before him and kissed this amazingly huge ring he had on his finger, almost like he was a god. He was surrounded by as many priests as he could muster who led the way for him, pumping out incense, not a woman in sight.'

'No, I suppose they were all quietly ministering to the poor,' Ethel put in wryly.

'He'd come up from Sale for the day,' Chris continued. 'And there were singers from Melbourne. Annie was excited because the choirmaster was a fellow named Edward Comber. She knew him from Saint Ambrose's in Brunswick, where her mother and aunts attend Mass.'

'Oh well, that would have been a good catch up for her and Tom,' Ethel remarked.

'Yes, but I haven't told you the best, Etty. About halfway through the ceremony, Maggie excused herself and left us. I thought this was strange, but maybe she was not feeling well, as it was such a long ceremony. Then at the end, when the entourage was heading down the aisle to go outside, this voice of an angel filled the whole body of the church, singing "Ave Maria". It was sung with such pathos and sweetness that it made my whole body tingle. And do you know who that voice belonged to?'

'No, tell me,' begged Ethel.

'It belonged to our Maggie! Etty, I knew she could sing, but given the correct acoustics and the proper time and place, her voice was heavenly. I was so proud of her.'

'Oh, I wish you hadn't told me that,' Ethel stated her disappointment. 'Perhaps that is why Maggie wanted me to go, but she didn't say she was singing, and I declined. I am so sorry I missed it.'

'I don't wish to be unkind telling you this, Etty, but after the feast that the ladies of the Guild put on in the hall, we all went back to the church for Vespers and there was more sweet and amazing music. Some of the performers were from here – Emily Steven, Ethel Bergin, Nora Foley and Celia Massing sang and Ada Pierce played the violin. That was all very lovely, but when Maggie performed Rossini's "Inflammatus" with full choir you could have heard a pin drop. I thought I had died and gone to Heaven. I have had the most beautiful day. When this job is good, it is very, very good.'

'You may not have wished to be unkind, Christie my dear husband, but by telling me that, you have been. Now I feel deprived and you shall have to make it up to me.'
'I shall, my lovely, I shall. Next time we are in Melbourne I am going to take you to a recital at the cathedral. I promise. But until then I will have to do the singing myself. Will you accompany me on the piano, dear lady while I do my rendition of the Battle Hymn of the American Republic?'
She played the notes while he gave it his all, singing with gusto.

CHAPTER 55

'Maggie why did you not tell me that you were singing at the consecration of the church? I would not have missed it for the world had I known. Christie told me that it was the most unexpected and beautiful thing he had ever heard. I am so disappointed that I missed it,' Ethel scolded Maggie on the following Monday washday.

Maggie was dismissive. 'Well, I did ask you to come, Etty, and I didn't like to press it because you were uncomfortable with the idea. But to be perfectly honest with you, I was so nervous because I felt way out of my depth. Father Coleman is a family friend; George's parents and he come from the same county in the old country, and he especially asked me to do it. I reluctantly said yes but I wasn't sure how it would go. Dear Miss Smallacombe went through the music with me note by note, so I knew my part inside out, but I didn't have any idea how it would all cling together. But, in the end, I loved it. It was the best thing I have ever done. I just lost myself in the music and enjoyed every minute. I did it, Etty, because I think I owe God, and I am so glad I did.'

'What do you owe God?' laughed Ethel, 'All you ever do is bring laughter and joy wherever you go, Maggie. God should owe you for making the world a better place.'

'Be careful not to blaspheme, Etty, I don't want bad luck to come my way.' It was usually Ethel who was warning Maggie to mind her tongue. How the tables had turned! 'If I tell you a secret, Ethel, do you promise not to tell?'

'I'd love to hear your secret Maggie. Please tell me and I will share a secret I have of my own.'

'Oh, how exciting! Two secrets. What's yours?'

'I'm not telling just yet. Let's finish up this washing, get it on the line and then we shall sit on the veranda. I shall make a pot of tea, raid the biscuit barrel of the shortbread I made on Friday and we shall compare secrets,' suggested Ethel. She knew that it was best to take advantage of the sunshine and the breeze to get the washing on the line and dry. Besides, she was unsure whether her secret would be well received by Maggie, so she was a little nervous. The two women worked on, both holding their secrets close to their bosom and it was only when the clean clothes flapped happily in the autumn breeze that they sat down together.

'Now, you tell me yours and I'll tell you mine,' Maggie opened the conversation.

'No, you first, you are the youngest. Fire away.' Ethel poured the tea, added milk and offered a cup to Maggie.

'All right then, here goes,' smiled Maggie, putting down the cup and folding her arms across her chest.

'Ethel, I am sorry but I going to have to give you notice. After the first of July, I won't be able to help you with the boys and the washing any more. You will have to find somebody else.'

'Oh Maggie, are you leaving us? Are you and George moving on? Please stay! The boys and I have grown to love you. I will miss you so much. Tell me your plans.'

It was evident that Ethel was deflated and Maggie was secretly pleased to note that she was genuinely loved and needed.

'Etty darling, I will have to leave your employ, but I will still be around to see you and my boys, because,' she paused for effect, barely able to contain her excitement. 'I'm having a baby in the spring time.'

Ethel jumped up delightedly, spilling her tea in the process. 'Maggie, Maggie, Maggie, I am so, so happy for you. I will gladly let you go, you can stop work any time you like. I am so happy. A little baby for the Brown's! A little Brown baby! That is wonderful news.'

The two women hugged each other in absolute delight.

'I have wanted to tell you for ages now,' laughed Maggie loosening the embrace, 'but I was too afraid to in case something bad happened and I lost the baby again. So I have waited and waited and I have now gone five months! Doc Phelps says that everything should be fine, and that at last I can talk about it. You have no idea how hard it has been. My George can hardly keep the smile off his face. We are so happy and the business is going so well and this new stump jump scarifier that George has developed has been tested out on the Swamp and will do all it is supposed to do. The future looks so bright.'

'What is a stump jump scarifier?' asked Ethel, a little perplexed.

'It's this thing that is really good for removing the tussocks out on the Swamp. They had a field day out at Somerville's to test it out on a paddock. It made ripping those blessed tussocks out look easy. The contraption has four wheels and teeth and George has constructed it so that if it strikes a stump the whole lot lifts from the ground and doesn't get stuck or damaged.'

'Sounds terrifying to me,' laughed Ethel. 'They should call it a stump jump terrifier! I love your wonderful secret, Maggie. You and George will make wonderful parents. Now do you want to hear my secret?'

'Of course I do. Oh, how selfish of me! Anyone would think that I am the only one who has a secret.'

'I have exactly the same secret as you!'

'You mean ..?'

'Yes, we will have babies the same age, Maggie! I am in confinement as well. A new little baby should come to our house early in November.'

Maggie rushed to her friend and they embraced again. 'Etty, I couldn't be happier. That is wonderful, our children will grow up together. Next summer we can sit here together and suckle our babies. I can't wait; my arms ache to hold my little piccaninny. That is such good news.'

'Yes, a new baby each!'

'A baby to make my home happier and my hands busier.'

'Yes, and the nights longer and the days shorter,' added Ethel, with a slight groan.

'Ah, but it will make love stronger, and patience greater.'

'Don't forget our purses lighter and our clothes shabbier.'

'Hush, Ethel, what about the future brighter? I have in my belly a little stranger with a free pass to my heart.'

They laughed, happy and light headed, and again the women embraced, this time with a little jig.

'Keep it quiet, Maggie, nobody else knows yet. I only told Christie for sure last night and I haven't let the boys in on the secret. They don't need to know at the moment, perhaps next month.'

'What did Chris think?'

'Of course he is delighted but being the wordsmith he is, he couldn't resist teasing me with the rhyme, "morning caller, noonday crawler, midnight bawler". Of course, he would prefer a girl this time. I told him that he will have exactly what is given to him and he will love it like he does our boys. I'd like a girl as well, but I'm not putting too many hopes on it because I think I only make boys. We'll see. You tell the boys your news when they get back from school and we will let them enjoy that first.'

'All right, I'll put my feet up and wait for them and they can share the joy. In the meantime, tell me, Ethel, have you got a name for the child?'

'I have always loved Maurice for a boy, perhaps Maurice Christopher, after Christie, but I have absolutely no idea about girl's names. I quite like Estelle, what do you think of that?'

'It's pretty. Is it French or something? You don't hear that name very often.'

'I think it is French, but what I like about it is that it is pleasing on the ear and it means something like shining star. For our wedding gift, Mother gave me a recipe book which I use every day. It's called "The New Practical Housekeeping" and every time I see the author's name, Estelle Woods Wilcox, I think that that is a name I would choose for a daughter. I love it.'

'Yes I've seen that book on the sideboard in the kitchen, but haven't thought much about the name before. But now that you mention it, it is pretty, and I love the meaning. Imagine if you have a girl after three boys, Ethel? She will be a shining star.'

'Have you thought of names, Maggie?'

'It's almost decided for me,' Maggie replied practically. 'If the baby is a boy it will be George junior, and if it is a girl I would like to name her after my dear mother. She would be so thrilled.'

'And what is her name then?' Ethel asked.

'Everyone calls her Kate, her baptised name is Caitlin Mary, but I am inclined to lean towards our Australian spelling of Kathleen and we can shorten it to Kate, Kath or Kathy. Yes, Kathy is sweet. I like that.'

CHAPTER 56

'My dear sweet Etty, you do realize that the second of May marks the end of the first twelve months of trading and exactly one year of successful enterprise?'

Chris and Ethel were together in the sitting room after the boys had gone to bed and it seemed an appropriate time to bring up topic of the party he was planning to celebrate the first year of "The Trafalgar & Yarragon Times".

'Honestly, Christie, I've been so busy with the business and the boys and feeling so squeamish in the mornings, that the occasion would have escaped me, had not you brought it to my attention. It's been a very busy and fast moving twelve months indeed.'

'It has been that. How quickly the time has gone, but I am so happy we were brave enough to make the move down here. We all love it and it seems that we have a business for life. Everything is going so well. So, I was thinking, Ethel …'

Chris paused, approaching the subject with caution.

'When you think, Christie darling, it usually means more work. What exactly are you thinking?' Ethel quizzed her husband.

'What do you think about holding a small celebration for our first birthday?' he asked tentatively. He waited a moment, realizing that he was walking on shaky ground. But encouraged by the slow nodding of his wife's curls, he moved the conversation forward.

'We could invite the businessmen who advertise with us and we could use it as a fishing expedition for potential advertisers who are yet to see the benefits. If we mix the two groups together, then the former may persuade the latter to come on board and year two will be even better than the first.'

'I think that's an excellent idea, Christie, let's do it. A party will be fun. Now where do you plan to have it?'

'I hadn't really thought of that,' he replied, immediately on the back foot because he had assumed that the party would be at their home and that Ethel would do the catering.

'What about at the Printing Office?' That way Ethel could still provide the refreshments.

'That's a little too close to home.' Ethel was a move ahead of her husband. 'Because of my pregnancy, Christie dear, I really don't believe I can cater for a large number of people, especially in this first three months. Why, there are some foods I simply cannot bear to look at, let alone prepare. I just don't feel up to it, but I do believe that a party is a fantastic idea,' Ethel ventured, fielding the ball back into Christie's court. 'If you want my opinion, and if you are trying to impress your customers, wouldn't it be better to have the gathering at one of the local coffee houses? They are set up for that sort of thing.'

'That could be considered,' Chris said slowly, weighing up the options. Personally, he preferred to serve alcohol, not only for him but also for some of his more socially oriented advertisers, and the coffee houses didn't do that. He quickly formulated a compromise in his head. 'How about we have it at the Criterion?' he suggested. 'They will do a splendid job in new, salubrious surroundings and the whole town will be vying for invitations so they can peruse the improved premises.'

Ethel was immediately concerned for Jimmy Kenny's emotional well being. Could he cope with having the party at the scene of his heartbreak? 'What about poor Jimmy? Wouldn't that be too morbid for him to have it in a place that reminds him of lost love and opportunity? It's very early days yet since he was disappointed by Mavis.'

'Ethel, he lives on the premises, so he is dealing with it every day. As well, if I tell you something, will you keep it between these four walls and not let it spread all over Trafalgar?'

'That is insulting, Christopher McCallum Johnstone. I'll have you know I do not gossip. I don't care what anyone else does or says, they can do or say what they like, but I never gossip. You should know that!' Ethel was indignant and a little hurt. 'Fancy saying something like that! I'll guarantee that more gossip goes on down at the hotel run by that Eagle chap than ever passes my lips. How dare you say something like that!'

Chris retreated, chastened and wise enough to know that he had said the wrong thing. After a few seconds, he reached across the table and patted his wife's hand. 'I'm sorry. I was out of line. It's just that Jim told me in the strictest confidence the latest on the situation with Mavis and I'd hate to betray that. But, after all, we are husband and wife, so I don't believe that by telling you I will break that promise.'

Ethel was intrigued enough to let go of her hurt and curious enough to ask, 'What is it? Of course a husband can tell a wife. We should have no secrets between us.'

'The bad news is that Mavis has indeed sold up, but the good news is that all is not lost between young Jimmy and his lady love,' Chris confided. 'On my counsel, Jim approached the lady in question and laid down his hand, saying that he loved her and how hurt and confused he was that she had made the decision to move away without talking it through with him first. He asked was it anything that he had said or done.'

'Jim said that she was genuinely confused. She told him that she loved him as a very special friend but had never considered any romantic notions because she believed that she was far too old for him. Plus, he had never, at any time, given any indication that his feelings for her were more than a fond friendship.'

'Exactly how old is she?' asked Ethel, curious, as women never discussed their ages and she had assumed that Mavis was about the same age as she was, and therefore about thirty five years old. 'She can be no more than five years older than our Jim.'

'That's what you would think,' Chris corrected, 'but in fact she is twelve years older. I think Jim is thirty-one, so that makes her forty-three, a whole generational cycle in Chinese calendar years. She could never give him children.'

He now had Ethel's complete attention. 'She certainly doesn't look her age then. Please go on, what happened? You have my unbridled interest. Exactly what occurred then?'

'Apparently Jim told her he did not care a hoot about the age difference and that he hadn't spoken of his feelings because he had only known her ten months, and that he was a shy country boy who had been biding his time until the moment was right, but he was in love with her and wanted to spend the rest of his life with her. And he asked her to marry him.'

'Good on Jim! I knew all he had to do was to make his intentions clear to Mavis.' Ethel was happy for him but began to worry as she cast her mind forward to the likely outcome. 'So he's leaving here then?'

She was happy that affairs of the heart seemed to be working well for Jim, but she was apprehensive because she knew that even though Chris had Vere, George and young Gavin McKenzie helping him, Jim was simply indispensable. His going would leave a huge hole at the paper. Not only that, she and the boys were very fond of him and would miss him terribly.

'No, there's more. The reason she was leaving in the first place was that her father wanted her back home with him. He'd hit bad times and wanted to save money on staff by having Mavis do the work for him. Her mother says he should sell the business and let them enjoy some time away from drink and drunks while they still can. She wants him to retire from public houses.'

'Well, that is sensible! They must be getting older and why should Mavis live her life to please her old man? Oh the poor girl! After all the hard work she did building the place up and making it respectable and she's losing it through no fault of her own. Her father needs a good spanking.'

'Well, the hard work wasn't entirely wasted. After all the dealing's done, she will end up with more than enough to buy another business.

'Good luck to her then. But that doesn't alter the fact that she may take our Jimmy away from here. Did she say yes?'

'Ah, there is the rub. Not immediately! She was taken entirely by surprise at Jim's proposal. She told him that she now has many things to ponder as he had completely taken her unawares regarding his feelings for her, but now he had declared his love that altered the way in which she was looking at the landscape. She promised to consider it carefully and give him her decision before the end of the week.'

'I can understand her predicament. I kept trying to tell Jimmy to stake his claim, but he is so shy. And I guess she will be leaving Trafalgar very soon.'

'But, and here is the sting in the tale. This sudden sickness of Hicks, the man who was going to manage the Criterion for Nelson has changed everything.'

'Tell me, how.' Ethel was engrossed.

'Mavis won't be leaving town just yet, perhaps she won't be leaving for a long time. She told Jim that she has offered to stay on until Hicks gets better or they get someone else, and that is quite open ended. So for now, Jim and Mavis are staying in Trafalgar and Mavis will be paid to manage her own establishment, while the two thousand pounds profit she got out of the sale gathers interest in the bank.'

'Well, thank God for that!' Ethel's heart lifted. 'Perhaps they may stay forever.'

She leaned forward earnestly. 'We must do everything in our power to make sure that they are happy and that Mavis grows to love Jimmy and this place, so that she doesn't want to leave.'

'Ah, but there's more!' Chris went on.

'Last night, Mavis said to Jimmy that she really wanted to marry him and stay on in the town. She just has to check with that her parents will be all right, so she is taking the train to Ballarat this Monday to talk to them and she will be back here on Wednesday. So our Jimmy has a reprieve and will have an answer by then.'

'That is wonderful news,' Ethel stood up and clapped her hands. 'I am so glad for them; I am so happy for Jimmy. He's been mooching around with such a tragic look on his face and now he has almost managed to catch the lady of his dreams. You know, I don't think the age difference will make one squat of difference. Jimmy loves the lady and she will grow to love him now that she knows it is possible. We should have a party. We will have it at the Criterion. I shall just have to check that the date is available and I will book it. They may even announce their engagement on that night.'

'Slow down, slow down Etty,' Chris cautioned. 'Let's just see what the lady and gentleman in question want to do first. They may have other plans. They may wish to celebrate out on the Swamp with the Kenny family or even in Ballarat with her family. It is not our business so let them decide what they do about it. They may not even commit to each other yet.'

'Yes, I am jumping the gun a bit, aren't I? Surely Mavis is smart enough to know a good man when she meets one, even if he is a bit girl shy. Please, please God let her say yes to Jim.' Ethel sat down and considered for a few moments. 'What if,' she suggested, getting back to the original conversation, before it became sidelined with Jim's exciting news. 'What if, we go ahead with our plan for the party, and celebrate the first birthday of the "Times" on Saturday fortnight, that would be the tenth of May.'

'Hah, Etty, I love the way you come to things from the oddest of angles. We have solved the conundrum of the marking of this special occasion by travelling via your nausea that is being caused by our new family member, through Mr Hicks' unfortunate illness, past Jim and Mavis' romance and now we are back to where we began. We are going to have a party to celebrate the first birthday of the "Times". Problem is solved and all is well.'

'It will be such fun. If we have it in the middle of the day for dinner, then the boys can come. Annie and Tom and other farmers can make it as they will have finished morning milking and will be free before the afternoon session. All your business friends can come because Saturday is midday closing for them. But first, we must make a list of invitations.'

'What a wonderful woman you are, my sweet. You make things happen. We shall have it in the Criterion, and shall invite as many as Mavis can cater for. I will see to the invites and can you, my lovely, see to the music?'

Ethel's mind was already busily working out details. 'I will ask Maggie to sing and I am sure that Dan Baillee will enlist the Brass Band to help if we ask him nicely. That should be sufficient for a daytime affair.'

Chris blew out the sitting room lamp and closed the door after Ethel. 'Now, my lovely wifey, it's time to look after this precious bundle of ours and put the little mother to bed.'

CHAPTER 57

Ethel, Maggie and Annie sat in the sunshine on the front veranda, smocking and embroidering baby's nighties for the new little angels. Annie brought a nightie belonging to Dolly from home, so that it could be pulled apart and a pattern cut. That morning, Maggie and Ethel had purchased white muslin and flannelette from young Nick Lawless' new store and now they were all busily occupied with the job at hand. With them was Gwen Fisher who had come around to share with them some of the finer points of smocking. Maggie had gratefully accepted her offer when it was made after her big announcement. 'Thank you, Mrs Fisher, that will be lovely. I left school in Mallacoota before we got around to the smocking lessons in sewing class, so I missed out. I think they did that for the Merit Certificate, so I really would be shooting blind. I can do with all the help and advice you can give.'

'This baby thing is all going to be so much fun, Etty,' Maggie commented as she measured the cloth, approximating one yard as the length between the end of her nose and the tip of her fingers. 'When we have finished sewing we will do some knitting. I have already almost finished a shawl in white three-ply wool. It has five hundred and sixty stitches so I have to work on circular needles. I have the pattern to make the complete layette and now that I can tell everyone the good news, I can be more public about doing it. Up until now I have only been able to work in the privacy of the sitting room, after tea on a dark night.'

'One thing done well at a time,' Gwendolyn counselled wisely, as she gathered her things together and prepared to leave them to it. 'I'll love you and leave the three of you, but if you have any problems just bring it to the sewing circle next week and I'll have a look at it.' They said their goodbyes and she left them to their own devices.

'We will certainly enjoy having babies the same age; I'm enjoying it already!' Ethel said, as she threaded her needle through the dots she had marked to form the folds on which to make the smocking stitches.

'I'm enjoying it, too,' said Maggie.

'Well, I have news for the two of you, smug and all as you are,' smiled Annie. 'I know you probably think I have been getting fat lately, and have been too polite to comment. Well, I have been. And, there is a reason that I haven't been out in the fields so much lately, and I can sit here on the veranda with you two, sewing and chatting. Ethel Johnstone and Maggie Brown, you are not the only clever ones; Annie Donovan is with child. Little Mister or Miss Donovan is coming to live at our house in three months time.'

'Oh Annie, you sly old thing!' Maggie clapped her hands with glee. 'You are going to be holding a baby before I do and much before Ethel. That is such good news. What date are you due for confinement?'

'My due date is July the twentieth, in the middle of winter. I will so enjoy cradling this infant. With Jack helping Tom in the fields, I can take it easier than I have in the past. No more having to strap baby on my back as I hoe the paddock, or lay it down under as tree as I plant potatoes or put it in a crate while I do the milking. This time I am not going anywhere near a cow for at least twelve months. Tom said so himself.'

'That is the best news! Ethel exclaimed. 'The three of us! Can you imagine? Three babies for three friends, I can't think of anything better.

Maggie took Annie by the two hands and did a de-so-doh up and down the veranda. 'But why so late with the news, Annie?'

'It's to do with the luck of the Irish really,' Annie said. 'We just didn't want the banshees to know about it, so that they would leave us alone and let the baby grow in peace. I know it sounds crazy but these old superstitions tend to stick, and although I don't really believe it, I don't want to chance my luck. You never know, it may be true.'

Realising that this may have sounded crazy, she paused, adding, 'If you know what I mean. In any case, it has worked, because I am happy and healthy and the baby is growing inside me. I thought I was getting too old to conceive. When I told mother the news she said that there is a name for a baby coming later in life.'

'And what is that Annie?' asked Ethel. 'Is it a little latecomer?'

'Well, that could be so,' Annie laughed happily, 'but mother calls the baby "a little autumn crocus". You know, like a perennial, a little surprise that pokes his or her beautiful head out of the soil and brings untold joy to whoever is lucky enough to come in contact. So praise be to God and all of the Saints, Annie Donovan is with child. I am very happy, and so is Tom. God has blessed us greatly and we give thanks.'

'Perhaps Mavis and Jim will have a little autumn crocus, too!' Maggie said. 'Wouldn't it be wonderful if a child came their way? It was thrilling enough when they finally announced that they were engaged. George and I are so looking forward to the trip to Ballarat for their wedding. We have never been there.' As an after thought she added, 'In fact we have never been anywhere west of Yarragon!'

'We will travel with you, if you like,' Ethel offered. 'I am so excited and so pleased that our Jim has won his ladylove. It has all turned out so well in the end. Mavis is going to manage her own place, her oldies are happily retired, Jim stays with Christie in the business, and the town wins a lovely couple. It's all so good!'

'And didn't Troody do such a good job on Jim's teeth?' said Maggie. 'They look almost as good as the ones he was born with. I got used to the gap where one had been knocked out, but when the second went, it was not a pretty sight.'

'I'm sure the new teeth would have helped matters immeasurably when he got down on his knee, looked up at Mavis and asked for her hand in marriage,' said Annie. 'But where on earth would he get the money for dental work such as that? I mean, I know Chris is generous, but on Jim's wage ..?'

Maggie and Annie looked across to see that Ethel was staring into the distance.

'Etty? Etty Johnstone? Do you know anything about that?' said Maggie.

'Well …' said Etty, refusing to turn her head.

'Come on, come on! You know something,' Annie cried.

'Well, I did tell Christie that if he didn't give Jim a decent bonus for all the wonderful work he had done, he would probably lose him, and …'

'And?' the two chorused.

'And he wouldn't get bacon, eggs and sausages for breakfast until he did.'

The three friends roared with laughter.

'Oh, Etty, you may be the perfect city lady, but you have learnt the bush rules of how to play it tough.'

'I guess I had to!' she laughed.

'Well, I think I speak for all of us when I say am thrilled for the pair of them,' said Annie, rubbing her stomach absentmindedly as she felt her baby move. 'Moira says it is an answer to her prayers and she can die a happy woman now that Jim is finally settling down. Mavis was out at their farm last weekend and the ring on her finger practically blinded the cows. She fits into their family like a glove.'

'That's such a lovely thing to hear,' said Etty.

'I just knew she would,' said Maggie.

'Unfortunately,' continued Annie, 'we can't go to the wedding. I am too far along in my confinement and those dashed cows still need milking, but I will cook them a special meal when they come home and we can have a bit of a sing song around the piano.'

As the autumn leaves swirled around the garden, the three women sat on the veranda in the late afternoon sunshine, hands unconsciously on tummies embracing the child within, contemplating that after the winter would come the spring and with it, new life. They were happy, because they were together at this one time and in this one place in the little hamlet of Trafalgar, their home.

THE END

AUTHOR'S NOTE

Ma's Garden is a fictional story about life in a small town over one year in the early 20th Century. The novel is set in 1902 in Trafalgar, Gippsland, in the State of Victoria, Australia. It is based upon fact, a main source being the 1902/03 files of the *Trafalgar & Yarragon Times*, but I have taken considerable literary and chronological licence, allowing the story to unfold without being constrained.

Historical perspective

On May 2nd 1902, the first edition of the *Trafalgar & Yarragon Times* hit the streets. The Proprietor and Editor was Christopher Johnstone, a young man of 26 years old. His parents, Robert and Mary Jane (McCullens) Johnstone had come to Yinnar, some 20 miles southeast of Trafalgar, to farm the land with their large family of 11 children when he was 14 years old. Christopher's fiancé, Ethel Gilbee, was 21 and they married the following year.

The period

The 1902 Census states that there were 1,201,341 people in Australia at the time, there being 6424 more males than females. The figures show that 53% of the people lived in the cities and major towns. Most lived in four-roomed houses, while 30,000 lived in two-roomed houses, 9447 in one-roomed houses and 3423 in tents. Fewer than 14% of the homes had a bathtub. The average life expectancy was 47, the five leading causes of death being pneumonia, tuberculosis, diarrhoea, heart disease and stroke.

The issues

Issues then were very similar to those that worry us today. Australia was in the middle of the worst drought since European settlement. It lasted from 1895 and 1906 and although Gippsland was green, Queensland, New South Wales and all areas to the north of Melbourne were a dust bowl. Many farmers simply walked away from their properties, unable to pay their debts because the dry topsoil had blown away and their animals had died. A plague of rabbits, economic depression and crippling labour strikes all added to the serious effects of the drought.

Like today, Australia was enjoying a minerals boom and people were moving to Western Australia in droves where it was said the gold paved the streets of Kalgoorlie and Coolgardie. There was prospecting in the hills around Trafalgar.

The Public Service had swollen to excessive dimensions and there was a struggle between the city and country because rural people believed that the needs of the towns were being given priority over their own.

A shearers strike and a railways strike had crippled the country while proposed retrenchment and factory reform legislation frightened employers who predicted that wages would escalate. Federal Parliament had granted women the vote but the States were reluctant to follow suit until they saw how it all went. The Victorian Government tagged a referendum on Women's Suffrage to a piece of unpopular legislation, knowing that neither would pass the vote.

Queen Victoria had died, ending the Victorian era and heralding a general questioning of the social limitations and restrictions imposed upon the populace by church and state. There was general optimism for the future and anticipation and excitement about the coronation of the new King, Edward VII. The financial devastation caused by the collapse of the banks and the financial systems in the late 1880s and early 1890s was becoming but a memory.

By mid year, the Boer War in South Africa ended and the *Trafalgar & Yarragon Times* commented on June 7th 1902 that "the war would have cast a shade over the Empire's rejoicing on Coronation Day, but now that peace reigns there will be nothing to mar the great glee and jubilation."

The characters

The Johnstone family home and adjacent printing shop were located on a large block of land on Main Street (Princes Highway), on the opposite side to the station, next to the Post Office. The Bendigo Bank and other shops are located there at present.

Christopher Johnstone opened the doors of the *Trafalgar & Yarragon Times* on May 2nd 1902. It proved to be a very successful country newspaper and operated continuously until 1957 when it and two sister papers serving Morwell and Yallourn merged with a publishing group that included the *Moe Advocate*. The *Latrobe Valley Advocate* followed in its footsteps, eventually leading to the launch of the *Latrobe*

Valley Express, which is still in operation today. Chris was something of a media visionary, being the foundation chairman of radio station 3TR and establishing the local cinema, which the family ran until the 1950s.

Ethel Johnstone (nee Gilbee) lived a quiet unassuming life, always supporting her husband in his many business and civic enterprises. She ran the household, and was renowned for her beautiful garden that consisted of a wide variety of trees, flowers and bushes. For many years before her death she provided the flowers for the four main churches in Trafalgar for Sunday services, weddings and funerals. The palm tree she planted as a young woman was a local landmark until new shops were built on the block in the early 21st century. Ethel died in 1961 and Christopher died not long after in 1962. They are buried in Trafalgar Cemetery.

The ages in the novel of the Johnstone boys – Aubrey, Mervyn and Vernon – have been altered to suit the story. They were, in fact, born between 1904 and 1910, after the founding of the newspaper. However, of those three, two of them grew up to work on the *Times*.
Aubrey worked with his father on the paper, and played District Cricket for South Melbourne. He never married and died at the relatively young age of 40. He is buried in the same grave as his parents at the Trafalgar Cemetery.
Mervyn married Kathleen Donovan from Trafalgar and they had two sons, Peter and Graeme. Kathleen worked alongside Mervyn on the *Times* and then later on the *Gippsland Standard* in Yarram, which they purchased as the *Times* was being sold, and owned and operated until 1971. Kathleen is buried in the Trafalgar cemetery and Mervyn is remembered at

Ricketts Point on Port Phillip Bay in Beaumaris where he and Kate retired.

Rather than the newspaper, Vernon made a career of banking. He married Marion Hart from Rochester and they had one son, Rodney. They settled in Merbein, Vernon passing away in 1984 and Marion in 1998.

The fourth son, Maurice - the baby Ethel is expecting in the final chapter of the book - was actually born in 1916 but also worked on the *Times* until he enlisted in the Army in World War 2, joining a regiment that trained in Queensland and fought in New Guinea. He re-joined the paper on his return but suffered greatly from wartime experiences and eventually died from war-related illness in 1976. He is buried at Springvale. He married Beryl (Fishley) from Melbourne and they had two daughters, Christine and Julie. Beryl has passed on, but her eldest daughter, Elaine Boyles, still lives in Trafalgar.

The family historian, Hiryll Johnstone, has stated that all Johnstones living in the state of Victoria are probably related.

Annie (Hannah Maria Donovan) was married to Thomas Donovan and they were amongst the original settlers on the Moe Swamp. They owned a dairy farm on the Seven Mile Road and had seven children. The children mentioned in the novel are Jack and Eileen who were close in age, then a gap to James ("Drove") and Margaret Mary ("Dolly"). Later, they had three more children - Kathleen, who married Mervyn Johnstone, Leo, and Annie Veronica who married and then divorced Andy Plozza.

Tom Donovan died suddenly in 1939, leaving Annie to run the farm, which she did successfully until her death me than a decade later. She was collecting eggs when she suffered a life-threatening blow to the head, and later died in hospital. Her demise was described on her death certificate as an accident. Some members of the family believed that she was the victim of foul play. Most of the Donovans are buried at the Trafalgar cemetery.

Jimmy Kenny is based on a real life Jimmy Kenny, although I have changed his time-frame and age. He was a great friend of the Johnstone family, who helped on the newspapers and lived for many years in a small converted bedroom at the rear of Johnstone house. He never married.

Sophie and Alexander Matheson are based upon real life mentors for many local business people, Archibald Matheson and his wife. They were Christadelphians, a religion that takes the Bible as its source, and is strongly against war and conscription. They conducted Bible readings and scripture sessions at their home for other like-minded souls. Ethel followed this creed and when Australia was at war received a white feather in the mail for her beliefs.

George Brown was a forward-thinking blacksmith who opened his Trafalgar business in 1902 and, because he moved with the times and incorporated new inventions and developments, his business flourished. He advertised widely on the pages of the *Times*. He and his wife Maggie are fictional characters in the novel.

The Moe Swamp is mentioned throughout the novel. It is the land lying north of the railway line between Yarragon, Trafalgar and Moe. The draining of its 13,000 acres to open the area up for farming in 1889, was considered a significant engineering achievement. But by 1902, the settlers were greatly concerned because it was continually flooding, ruining crops and creating havoc.

Mr Carlo Catani was the Government Surveyor/Engineer who was responsible for solving the problem of the incessant flooding of the Moe Swamp. You can see a monument honouring him and the settlers on the Seven Mile Road.

Dondi, the hotel pony, was an actual fixture at Gordon's Criterion Hotel and was offered for sale with the goods and chattels in a clearing sale. In the book, I have created a second, fictional hotel.

Businesses & Services in Trafalgar in 1902

Businesses and services that advertised or were mentioned in the newspaper included:

Hotel
Gordon's Criterion Hotel, S. Gordon, Proprietor.
This business changed hands thrice in 1902: A. Fallon, Proprietor, late of Queensland; Miss Allen, Proprietor, late of Melbourne; A. A. Hicks, Proprietor, late of Melbourne. 'Best wines and spirits always on hand. Splendid accommodation. Stables.'

Coffee Houses
Federal Coffee Palace, run by Mrs Lawless. 'Meals at all hours.'
Trafalgar Coffee Palace, run by Mrs Donohue. 'The public can rely upon every attention and civility.'
Mrs Jolly's Boarding House, Moe Swamp. 'Accommodation for boarders at reasonable prices.'

Shopkeepers

A. Bernicke's, General Store. 'Don't cough. It's quite unnecessary. Curakof relieves when all others fail.'

M. M. Perriman, Green Grocer. 'Requisites of all descriptions kept in stock.'

Mr H. Davis, Fish Monger. 'Rabbits will also be supplied.'

N. Lawless, Hairdresser and Tobacconist. 'Civility and Attention guaranteed. No matter how small the purchase, you may rest assured, that it will be my constant aim to sell you the best goods that can be obtained.'

Mr Bouchier. 'Supplier of horse and cattle food.'

Butchers

Terry Nurse, taken over by Mr J. Kenny, Cash Butcher.

Mr Magnussen; Mr McLaughlin; Haines, Green & Harris.

Kyle & Hulley. 'Orders delivered everywhere. Give us a call.'

Bakers

McCrory, Baker, 'trusts that by keeping a good article and paying strict attention to his business, to merit a fair share of Public Patronage.'

W. M. Smith, took over from McCrory. 'Give the local baker a trial.'

W. Glare.

Blacksmiths and Wheelwrights

J. M. Dusting, Saddler. 'Repairs executed with neatness, cheapness and dispatch.'

J. W. Wall, Blacksmith and Implement Maker. 'Horses clipped, teeth filed and legs fired. Moderate prices. Can now obtain horses and vehicles at short notice.'

Mr Hampe, Coach Builder. Became a partner of George Brown.

George Brown, Blacksmith and Wheelwright. 'No slipshod work turned out.'

Farm Machinery

George Brown, Trafalgar. 'All kinds of agricultural instruments made on premises.'

John T. Lloyd, Agent for British Cream Separators.

C. Johnstone, Agent for Ruddick's Medicines for Horses, Sheep, Cattle, Dogs; Agent for Alfa Laval Separators.

A. Murray, Agent for British Cream Separators. 'Easy to clean and a perfect skimmer.'

Trafalgar Butter Factory

Mr McKenzie (Manager); Mr Giblet (Dairy Inspector); Thomas A. F. Inglis (Secretary); Committee: W. Murray (Chair), James Inglis (Secretary), Hollier, Evans, Branningan, Matheson, Keogh, Steele, McGregor.

Stock Agents/Auctioneers

R. Stevenson, Trafalgar Agent for Mathieson & Davies.

J. Mitchell, Trafalgar, Local Agent for Jennings & McInnis.

H. Elliott, Local Agent for Henry Hansen of Warragul.

A. O'Neill; Mr A. French; Frank Boileau; Edward Witton; J. W. Borlind.

Financiers

H. Elliott, Agent for Henry Hansen, Warragul. 'Trust Moneys to Lend on Mortgages up to 20,000 Pounds.'

Mathieson & Davies. 'Up to 20,000 Pounds in sums to suit borrowers. Interest at 4%. Freehold security.'

Insurance Agents
R. Aitken, London & Lancashire Insurance Co.
C. Johnstone, City Mutual Life Assurance Society Limited.
W. W. Brandt, Australian Mutual Live Stock Insurance Society.

Solicitors
M. Davine, BA, LLB. 'Visits Trafalgar on Sale days, attends all District Courts.'
Frank Geach, LLB. 'Visits Trafalgar on Sale days of Jennings & McInnes.'
Mr Hubert Kelly. 'Income Tax Returns compiled, loans negotiated and other agency work effected.'

Plumber
Mr W. F. Williamson, Plumber, Tinsmith, Tankmaker. 'All class of work of the above branches executed.'

Builders/Bricklayers
J. Betts. 'Practical Bricklayer in all its branches.'
J. Pheeney, Contractor & Builder. 'Plans and estimates presented on all work.'
Cook Brothers.

Boot Repairers
T. J. McLaughlan.
A. G. Stewart, Saddler.

Transport
E. Jordon, Licensed Carrier. 'Now prepared to convey parcels, passengers or general merchandise between Trafalgar and Thorpdale.'
Mr Bert Amor, Cobb & Co Coaches.

Saw Mills
Collins Brothers, Longwarry and Trafalgar.
Walter Richards, Allambee.
R. Aitkins, Timber Merchant and Undertaker. 'Funerals conducted on the shortest notice, with or without Hearse, on reasonable terms.'

Dressmaker
Marian Coleman. 'Fit and style in latest fashion guaranteed.'

Jockeys
Douglas Gordon; Willy Walker.

Station Master
P. Sullivan.

Post Office
Willie Ellis.

Sanitary Engineer
I. Betts.

Church Ministers
Reverend Hamby, Methodist.
Reverend Fielding, Methodist.
Mr Gilbert, Wesleyan.
Reverend A. Atchison, MA, Presbyterian.
Mr A. Matheson, Lay Preacher and Philosopher.
Mr W. Edney, Anglican.
Mr R. G. Hope, Anglican.
Reverend T. J. Winsor, Anglican.
Father Coyne, Leongatha, Catholic.
Father Coleman, Morwell, Catholic.

Doctors

Dr Phelps. 'May be consulted in Trafalgar on Tuesday and Saturday afternoons.'

Dr Trumphy.

Dr Hayes.

Dr George Federick Thomas. 'Specialist in diseases of the nervous system.'

Dentists

Trood, A. J. & C.B. 'Every set of teeth guaranteed.'

Mr A. French, Surgeon Dentist. 'Painless extractions, laughing gas.'

J. A. O'Neill, Surgeon Dentist. 'May be consulted free at Lawless' Coffee Palace.'

Nurse and Midwife

Miss Theresa Smith. 'Charges moderate.'

Police

Sergeant Bretherton; Constable Ryan, Constable Thompson, Constable Wellwood.

School Teachers

Mr Allan, Moe Swamp School.

Mr Palmer, Trafalgar School.

Mr Blacklock & Mrs McDonald, Tanjil South School.

Mrs T. Fisher, Teacher of Music and Fancywork. 'Pointlace, Mount Mellick, Drawn Thread, etc.'

Miss Young. 'Will teach pattern cutting on Saturday mornings in the Mechanics Hall.'

Miss A. A. Townsend, ALCM, Music Teacher. 'Pupils may enter at any stage.'

Clubs in Trafalgar in 1902

Trafalgar was a busy, self-contained town, with a variety of sporting and social clubs and associations.

Cricket Club

Cricket is mentioned regularly in the files. It is known that Christopher was a cricket tragic who loved the game. Some of the cricketers named in the files include: Tom Nurse, Noel Moore, Ned Parratt, James Finlay, T. Finlay, J. Mitchell, E. Moore, Cooper, Walsh, Wilson, Williams, Mann, Hill, Taylor, Dumparessy, Pavitt, Bromfield, Clayton, Aitkin, Munro, Gray.

Football Club

Trafalgar's Australian Rules Football team was supported by the whole town in 1902. The success of The Bloods was a source of great civic pride and inter-town rivalry. Footballers mentioned in the pages of the *Times* include: J. Kellas, C. and J. Allen, Mitchell, Day, Gooding, Goode, Munroe, Clayton, Hammond, Pettit, Day, Rice, Gooding, McCrory, Laing, Tatterson, Ransom, Raey, Deitrich, Finlay.

Race Committee

A. Bernicke (President); P. L. Donohue & J. W. Wall (Joint Secretaries).

Cycling Club

J. Brown (Secretary); Jim Kellas, Geo Hamilton, John O'Connell, James McCrory, Ron Wall, Janet O'Connell, Gaylene Hamilton.

Rifle Club

G. Murray (Secretary).

Boxing Day Sports Committee
J. V. Keogh (President); A. Wall (Vice President); N. Lawless (Secretary); P. Donohue (Assistant Secretary); E. Lynch (Treasurer).

Narracan Sports Day Program
James Gannon (Secretary).

Horticultural Society
Mrs W. Murray (President); Mrs T. J. Winsor (Secretary). Champions 1902 - Cookery: Mrs Colin Murray, Miss Sampson; Vegetables: Miss Evans; Bloom: Mrs W. Murray; Best Dressed Doll: Dorothy Burkett; Fancy Work: Myrtle Murray; Drawing: Hope Waycott.

Sunday School Picnic
Mrs Coghlan (Secretary).

Catholic Bazaar/ Ball Committee
Mr Wain, Miss A Mulvenna, Mr Flannigan, Lawless, Walsh, Day, Conley, Payne, Kennedy, Kenny, Lynch.

Cemetery Trust
Chas Murray (Secretary).

Mechanics Hall Trust
John Dusting (Secretary & Librarian); M. J. Murray & M. M. Perryman, Bazaar Committee; E. J. McDonough (Committee); J. Miller (Trustee); J. Findlay (Secretary).

National Citizens Reform League
Mr Jas Whitton (President); Mr Inglis (Secretary).

Australian Natives Association (ANA)
Mr Bernicke (President); D. Cameron (Vice President); J. Dusting (Secretary).

Moe Swamp Committee
Mr J. V. Keogh.

Starving Stock Fund
Thomas A. Inglis (Secretary); Mr Gibblett.

Local Council
Councillor Lloyd (Shire President); Councillor Crisp, Councillor Davies, Councillor Evans.

Parliamentary Representatives
Mr W. Murray, MLA for Gippsland West, defeated Mr Arthur Nichols.
Mr Frank Geach, resigned, MLA for Gippsland West for previous 13 years.
Mr Livingstone, MP for Gippsland South.
Mr F. C. Mason was defeated, having held the seat of Gippsland South for 30 years.

- Elsie Johnstone, Melbourne, 2012.

ABOUT THE AUTHOR

Elsie Johnstone was a primary school teacher and special education specialist for 30 years. In 2001 she left teaching to join her husband Graeme in their own business, The Wordsmith's Shop, a unique establishment that boasted 'anything you want written we will write' for a wide range of both corporate and private clients.

It was there that she developed her writing skills. Her first book, *Our Little Town* (2009), is a snapshot of life in the Victorian fishing village of Lakes Entrance across four generations as told by one family.

She and Graeme then lived in Ireland, joining forces to write *Lover, Husband, Father, Monster* (2010), a chilling tale of a well-meaning marriage that goes wrong. It tells the story in two voices, his and hers.

When they returned to their home in Melbourne, she began work on *Ma's Garden*.

Elsie also has had success as a short story writer, winning awards for her snapshots of life, turning real incidents and events into engaging stories with a twist.

ELSIE JOHNSTONE

Other books written by Elsie Johnstone

Our Little Town

Lover, Husband, Father, Monster
(with Graeme Johnstone)

Angel Baby Names

can be obtained through
www.smashwords.com
www.loverhusbandfathermonster.com
www.bookpal.com
www.amazon.com
or through online and traditional book retailers.

Made in the USA
Charleston, SC
28 July 2012